MARVEL

A NOVEL OF THE MARVEL UNIVERSE

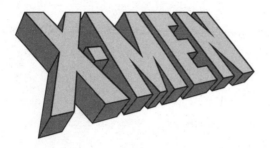

THE DARK PHOENIX SAGA

A NOVEL OF THE MARVEL UNIVERSE

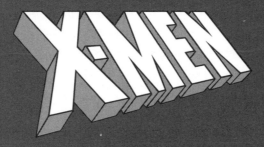

THE DARK PHOENIX SAGA

Adapted from the Graphic Novel
by Chris Claremont, Dave Cockrum, and John Byrne

STUART MOORE

TITAN BOOKS

MARVEL

MARVEL'S X-MEN: THE DARK PHOENIX SAGA
Print edition ISBN: 9781789090628
E-book edition ISBN: 9781789090635

Published by Titan Books
A division of Titan Publishing Group Ltd
144 Southwark Street, London SE1 0UP
www.titanbooks.com

First edition: May 2019
10 9 8 7 6 5 4 3 2 1

FOR MARVEL PUBLISHING
Jeff Youngquist, VP Production Special Projects
Caitlin O'Connell, Assistant Editor, Special Projects
Sven Larsen, Director, Licensed Publishing
David Gabriel, SVP Sales & Marketing, Publishing
C.B. Cebulski, Editor in Chief
Joe Quesada, Chief Creative Officer
Dan Buckley, President, Marvel Entertainment
Alan Fine, Executive Producer

X-Men created by Stan Lee and Jack Kirby

Visit our website:
www.titanbooks.com

A CIP catalogue record for this title is available from the British Library.
Printed and bound in the United States.

For John Byrne, Dave Cockrum, and especially Chris,
who's always reached for the stars.

EPILOGUE

THE SHUTTLE screamed down through the upper atmosphere, gaining speed with each passing second. Heat shields buckled and snapped, splintering off into the air, vanishing into the largest solar flare the Earth had seen in more than a century.

In the pilot's seat, a tall red-haired woman gripped the armrests tight, trying to ignore the relentless voice in her mind:

Welcome to the last minutes of your life.

Jean Grey shook her head, forced herself to concentrate. She ran her eyes across the console, studying each of the ten screens. Nothing but static. The flare had fried the shuttle's electronics, leaving the little ship blind and deaf, its sensors useless. Only one screen was still up and running—it showed an external view of the flare's energy, roiling red-orange-yellow, strobing up and down the spectrum. A hypnotic sight, like the primal energies of the universe.

The screen flickered and went black.

Jean toggled a few controls, tugged briefly on the stick.

I don't know what I'm doing, she thought. *This ship is tearing apart around me, and I can't even see where we're going!*

Leaning back, she closed her eyes. Her thoughts strayed to the people in the shielded life-cell, back in the shuttle's aft compartment. Her teammates, the friends she cared about most in the world. Her mind reached out, unbidden, and touched their thoughts, one by one. Nightcrawler, Storm. Wolverine, his mind filled with grim regret. Dr. Peter Corbeau, the brilliant entrepreneur who had built the shuttle. Professor Charles Xavier, the X-Men's founder.

Cyclops. Scott Summers.

The man she loved.

As the shuttle groaned and shook, Jean wrenched her mind away from his. She couldn't deal with Scott's pain, his dread, right now. A memory came to her: Scott's hand in hers, firm and strong, as they walked together under the trees of upstate New York. The leaves changing, falling all around, dark grass covered in a bright panoply of yellow, russet, and auburn.

The last minutes of your life.

A loud crack snapped her out of her reverie. The shuttle lurched, throwing her back in her seat. She leaned forward, using another mutant ability—telekinesis—to partially counteract the g-force. The attitude gauge was redlining. One of the screens had switched over to LAN mode and bore the block-letters warning:

NOSE WHEEL ALIGNMENT – FAULTY

Panic washed over her. *I'm no pilot*, she thought. *I can't fly this thing!*

Then she remembered…

Yes, you are. Thanks to Dr. Corbeau.

Jean reached into a file of memories, thoughts that were not her own. She scanned and searched until she found the information she needed. Hand trembling, she reached out for the bob switch, making sure to apply just the right degree of force.

Thanks, Doc, she thought…

One hour earlier

"THE FIRE'S almost reached the hypergolic fuel cells, Dr. Corbeau. We haven't much time."

"On the contrary, Cyclops," Corbeau replied. "We have all the time in the world."

Jean watched the two men closely. Scott Summers—Cyclops—stood leaning over the pilot's seat, hands clenched tight on the backrest. His blue-and-yellow uniform was torn and smudged from the recent conflict. Energy pulsed behind the ruby-quartz lenses that covered his eyes, holding back the deadly energies within.

Corbeau swiveled the seat around, tilting his head up to cast a grim smile at Summers. Possessed of a brilliant mind and a flamboyant personality, Corbeau had built a private space-travel empire by leveraging both traits. Even now, with death closing in on the shuttle's occupants, he affected a cool demeanor. His only sign of stress was the hand running obsessively through his thick, meticulously groomed hair.

"We're not going anywhere," Corbeau explained, gesturing at the shuttle's consoles. "The flight-control computer got slagged during our scrap with the Sentinels. Without it, this bird is grounded."

Cyclops grimaced and turned to Nightcrawler. "Any word from Logan and Storm?"

The slender, blue-furred mutant held up a short-range comm device, his pointed tail whipping around with anxiety. "They've found the Professor," he said in a thick German accent. "They are on their way."

Cyclops nodded. His eyes met Jean's for a brief moment, and he smiled a tight smile. Then he turned away again.

They barely notice me, she thought. *Any of them. Even Scott assumes I'll just follow his lead, whatever he decides.*

And why shouldn't he? I always have.

She fidgeted, feeling uneasy. The Sentinel robots had

abducted her from an elegant dance. She still wore the tattered remains of a very expensive black dress.

Cyclops had planted himself in the copilot's seat. "What about a manual reentry?" he asked.

Corbeau's smile became a rictus grin.

"So in case you haven't noticed," he said, "the space station around us is being consumed by fire. What's more, we have no pressure suits—but believe it or not, those are the *least* of our problems."

Nightcrawler let out a hissing noise. "The flare," he said.

"The *solar* flare!" Corbeau spread his arms in a theatrical gesture. "Worst eruption since 1859, and it's just about to reach Earth. The computer was supposed to guide us through it while we sat, safe and sound, in the shuttle's shielded life-cell."

Cyclops glared at the instrument panel. "But we have no computer."

"Right." Corbeau ran his fingers through his hair again, faster this time. "I can pilot a reentry with one hand tied behind my back. Probably invent a new company while I'm doing it." A look crossed his face. "Hmm… maybe it's finally time to get that solar-monitoring station off the ground, so to speak. I bet I could line up some sweet venture-capital funding for—"

"*Doc!*"

"Right, yes." Corbeau looked past Cyclops at Nightcrawler, as if seeing him for the first time. "I was saying, I can pilot the ship with my eyes closed—but I'd never survive the flare, sitting in this unshielded compartment. One of you might, with your mutant abilities. Wolverine, perhaps—"

A wrenching noise came from outside the shuttle, followed by a loud *thud*. The air was growing hotter, too. The station had only minutes left before it cracked apart, exposing all compartments to the cold vacuum of space.

"Actually," Corbeau continued, "high levels of charged particles could, theoretically, cause mutations in the DNA. It might have been something like this flare that triggered the rise of your own *Homo superior*…" He saw the looks he was getting. "Ah, sorry. Not relevant. The point is that none of you know how to pilot the shuttle. We need someone who can survive the radiation *and* steer this baby safely, and there's no one who can do that."

"I can," Jean said.

All heads turned toward her. Corbeau frowned. Cyclops's mouth was set, grim. As always, his eyes were hidden behind his protective visor.

"*Fräulein,*" Nightcrawler said, "you are my trusted friend and valued teammate, but since when are you a trained astronaut?"

"Since now."

She stepped forward, lifting a hand. Corbeau flinched slightly, but made no move to rise from his chair.

"I'm a telepath, Doctor," she explained. "I can access everything you know about flying this space shuttle. I won't exactly be John Glenn, but I can pilot us safely down to Earth."

Corbeau looked up at her. A hint of fear flickered in his normally steady gaze. Then he nodded, almost imperceptibly.

When she touched his forehead, a welter of thoughts washed over her. Recent memories of the X-Men—Cyclops and Nightcrawler—coming to Corbeau's office in Houston, imploring him to help them rescue their captured teammates. The shuttle flight up to this station, an abandoned S.H.I.E.L.D. espionage installation where Jean, Storm, Wolverine, and Professor X were being held captive. The battle against the Sentinels, the escape through smoke-clogged corridors to the shuttle.

More, rising up from the depths of Corbeau's mind. Childhood images of a loving mother, a father who was never satisfied. The thrill of founding his first company, a telecom startup that revolutionized satellite communication. The failure of two, then three marriages, brushed aside by Corbeau's triumphs in the field of private rocketry.

Once, Jean would have found this flood of impressions too much to bear. But over the years, Professor X had tutored her, taught her techniques of strict mental focus. Techniques that only Xavier— himself an incredibly powerful telepath—could have perfected.

Corbeau, she realized, was a particular sort of person—charming, arrogant, accustomed to getting his way. Not the kind of man she tended to associate with. She felt a brief twinge of discomfort at their sudden, uncomfortable intimacy, then cast those thoughts aside and began sifting through his memories. When she found the specific knowledge she needed, she copied it to a mental clipboard and swiftly withdrew.

She shook her head and smiled. "All done."

Corbeau didn't smile back. There was definitely fear in his eyes now.

"I didn't know," he said, and faltered. "I don't know what you are."

The arrogance was gone from him. Somehow that rattled Jean, even more than the touch of his mind. She shivered, turned away—

—and almost collided with Cyclops. His lean, muscular form blocked her way, his arms held rigidly at his sides. His mouth was a downturned line, and his eyes pulsed an angry red behind those lenses.

"You are *not* doing this," he said.

Now

YOU CAN'T *do this!*

Cyclops's thought, clear as a beacon, pierced the wall of the life-cell, stabbing into her mind. All at once she felt his panic, his grief, his anger. She shook her head, banished him from her thoughts. There was no time for that now. Only one thing mattered: piloting the shuttle safely down to the ground.

The forward screens still flickered with static, but a small LCD monitor above her head glowed steadily, displaying a series of equations. Accessing Corbeau's memories, she identified the numbers as altitude and pressure readouts. Unfortunately, the external sensors were still inoperative. The readouts blinked on and off, their information incomplete and unreliable.

However…

Corbeau, she knew, had once managed to reboot a faulty sensor module by sending an electrical pulse through the system. She stared up at the ceiling, studying the manual switches next to the LCD screen.

Grimacing, she pulled down a module and began to reset the switches to an overload setting. Her fingers plucked and manipulated wires, withdrawing every time an electrical spark flared up. The work was slow, almost automatic, as if someone else were manipulating her hands.

A part of her mind began to wander again. Back to that day among the autumn trees, her sandaled feet crunching on the cold, brittle leaves.

"*I love the fall,*" she'd said, reaching out for Scott. He had turned to her, a strange expression on his face. Eyes hidden behind the crimson sunglasses that substituted for his combat visor. He'd said something in return, something that disturbed her.

She couldn't remember what it was.

The shuttle veered sideways, slamming her against the side wall. Her hand caught on the ceiling, yanking loose the lowered panel. Metal scraped against her arm, leaving a bloody gash. She swore and cried out, reaching for the wound.

A distant *crack*—probably another heat shield breaking off— and still the shuttle was blind and deaf.

Sweat covered her forehead. *It must be over ninety degrees in here.* But it wasn't just the heat, she realized. The solar flare held the shuttle in its grip, bathing the ship in immeasurable levels of radiation. Her telekinetic shield screened out some of it, but not all. Her skin was crawling, her stomach churned. Her heart seemed ready to burst from her chest.

What had Corbeau said, back on the space station? "*High levels of charged particles might, theoretically, cause mutations in the DNA.*" Was the storm affecting her on some primal level, rewriting her genetic template? She stared at the blood, pooling dark on her arm. Watched as a drop detached, seemingly in slow motion, and drifted down to the deck plates.

The last minutes of your life.

That voice again. She'd thought it was just her own panic speaking, but now it seemed like someone else. Some*thing* else. Something… other. Was this just the storm? Or was something happening to her? Something deeper, more drastic?

You're going to die.

No, she thought. *No, I'm going to live. I'm going to save them.*

You're going to die.

She tore off a scrap of her black dress, pressed it to the wound.

It will be glorious.

Before she could reply, her telepathy seemed to surge, reaching out in all directions. She saw inside the ship, its hundreds of thousands of circuits and electrical connections, damaged and battered by the solar flare. Outside, raging auroras surged up and down the ultraviolet spectrum.

Far below, on the surface of the Earth, people tossed aside useless phones and radios, staring and pointing up at a sky filled with a once-in-a-lifetime blaze of color. None of them could see the tiny shuttle lost within that massive halo of stellar energy. They seemed so small, those people of Earth. So insignificant. So helpless in the face of the cosmic energies descending upon them.

A thrill ran through her. *So much power… so many beautiful currents.* The primal forces, calling to her like a song. The superstrings, chords of time that linked all things together. Life and death, and all the pain and joy and sorrow that lay between.

The stars. So vast the stars!

Her blood shifted, mutating. Like the blood, the cells, the waters of ancient Earth—

Jean! Please!

Scott!

She shook her head, blinked. Forced herself to withdraw from his mind, confining her consciousness to the interior of the cockpit. She focused on the damaged control stick, the flickering readouts, and the static-filled screens.

Jean, don't do this!

She cut the connection with Scott's mind. She could feel the others back in the life-cell, too: Logan, Storm, Nightcrawler, Corbeau, and the unconscious Professor. But the one mind she couldn't deal with right now was Scott's. If she made contact with him again—if she allowed his grief and his fear and, yes, his love to distract her—she knew she would break down and lose control.

You're going to die.

This time she didn't argue. This time she knew.

Yes, she thought, *I am. But I won't let* him *die, too.*

Sweating, skin crawling, she reached up to the open ceiling plate and resumed her work.

One hour earlier

"YOU ARE *not* doing this."

Cyclops's words hung in the air. Jean stood very still, avoiding his gaze. Corbeau and Nightcrawler moved away, trying to give them some privacy in the cramped cockpit.

She felt more comfortable with Scott than with anyone she'd ever known. In a world of tormented minds—of stray thoughts, intrusions, mental noise she'd had to endure all her life—his mind was an oasis of calm. The easiest one to slip in and out of, a source of constant comfort and support.

Until now.

To her shock, he reached out and grabbed her by the shoulders. "Do you really think you can survive a *record-level* solar flare?"

Anger, then, inside of her. Sudden, unexpected. When she spoke, her voice was cold.

"My telekinesis will keep me safe."

"For how long?" He gestured past her. "You heard what Corbeau said about the radiation."

Dr. Corbeau stared at his own hand. "I'm not even a mutant, and

I think I can feel it working." He shrugged. "Might just be hubris."

Jean ignored him, looking up at Cyclops with steel in her eyes. He stared back for a moment, then released her.

"Look," he said, "it's just too dangerous. We'll come up with something else. I need you to back my play here."

"I've *always* backed your play."

A clatter from outside of the shuttle's cockpit. Cyclops whirled to look, crimson sparks dancing on the surface of his visor. Nightcrawler leaped into position, facing the door, while Jean moved to cover Dr. Corbeau.

"Don't shoot, bub. It's us."

Wolverine lumbered in through the hatch, the unconscious Professor X slung over his shoulder. Storm followed Logan inside, floating on the warm air currents that flooded in from the space station.

"The fire is almost here," she said.

With surprising gentleness, Logan set the Professor down on a small table. Cyclops and Nightcrawler moved to examine him, almost shoving each other out of the way.

"He is not moving," Nightcrawler said.

Cyclops turned to Wolverine. "Is he all right?"

"I ain't no doctor, Summers." Logan shrugged. "Sentinels clipped him pretty good."

Jean reached out mentally. The Professor's brainwaves were dormant, but the electrical activity was constant.

"He'll recover," she said.

"The Sentinels?" Cyclops asked.

"Defeated." Storm spread her dark arms, lightning flashing in her eyes. "They experienced an *electrical* failure."

"But that fire's still out of control," Wolverine said. "So can we get this bus out of the station before we all fry to death?"

Corbeau stared at Jean. "We were just… discussing that."

"Logan," Cyclops said, "take the Professor back to the life-cell. Secure him… better use restraints."

16 "I warned you before we came up here, Summers." Wolverine

paused, his hands twitching. "I don't like takin' orders."

"Logan." Cyclops's visor flared. "Not now."

Logan smiled, feinting forward as if ready for a fight. Then he stopped. His eyes narrowed, as if his acute senses had picked up some deadly scent on the wind. He shrugged, placed Xavier over his shoulder again, and stalked off.

Cyclops turned to Storm. "Ororo, give him a hand?"

Storm frowned. She adjusted her headband, then crossed her arms over her chest.

"Jean," she said. "What are you planning?"

Jean forced herself to smile. "Go on," she said. "Make sure Logan doesn't accidentally skewer the Professor with his claws."

"Or un-accidentally," Cyclops added.

Sorry, Ororo, Jean thought. *You're a good friend, but we'll have to discuss this later. If there* is *a later, for me.*

When Storm was gone, Nightcrawler eyed Jean and Cyclops for a moment. Then he leaped over to the copilot's seat and began a low, intense discussion with Corbeau. Cyclops moved closer to Jean and let out a long, low sigh.

"I'm sorry."

She nodded, not looking at him.

He touched her cheek and smiled. That smile had always melted her heart, made her believe that anything was possible.

"Can we just figure out a plan?" he asked.

"This is the plan."

The telepathic bolt shot out from her, into Scott's brain. He slumped toward her, instantly unconscious.

So easy, she thought. *He's always trusted me. He let me into his mind without hesitation, without putting up any defense.*

She hoped he would forgive her.

Nightcrawler materialized in a puff of brimstone, his bright yellow eyes wide. Before he could speak, she pressed Scott's limp form into his arms.

"Take him aft," she said. "Secure yourself and the others, and prepare for takeoff."

Nightcrawler hesitated. "You are certain you can survive this?"

"I'll get us down."

The blue mutant grimaced, wrapped his arms tightly around his leader's body. Then he teleported away, taking Cyclops with him.

"You too, Doc." Jean started toward the pilot's seat. "Make sure that life-cell's locked up tight. This might get bumpy."

Corbeau opened his mouth as if to protest. Then that fear crept into his eyes again, and he rose from the chair. He edged around her and scurried, catlike, toward the aft compartment.

Jean was alone. Alone with a deadly mission, a deep feeling of dread... and something else, too. A sense of control, of power that she'd never known before. An inner strength, bubbling up from deep inside. Whatever it was...

...it had made itself known, she realized, the moment she'd rendered Scott unconscious.

Trembling, she lowered herself into the pilot's seat and toggled the engines to life.

Now

THE SHUTTLE swooped downward, its nose dipping toward the ground. Jean swore as she lurched forward in her seat. She reached out to activate the restraints—and screamed as a wave of radiation blasted through her.

Curling up in a ball, she willed her telekinetic shields to full strength. The agony receded as her mutant power filtered the radiation, but some of the blast had made it through. She could feel it roiling inside her, burrowing in, slithering around her DNA.

Stupid! She'd lost concentration, allowed her shielding to weaken. One more lapse like that and she'd be...

...well, she'd be dead a little bit sooner. Maybe before she could finish her mission.

Jean.

She jumped. *Scott?*

No. This "voice" was sharper, clearer. The deep, cultured tones of a telepath.

Professor, she replied.

I'm so sorry, my child. His thoughts were so clear, he might have been sitting beside her instead of locked up in the life-cell. *It should have been me. I should have been the one to—*

To sacrifice yourself?

Well…

Professor, I'm flying blind here. I've tried to reboot the sensors, but it's no use. I don't know if I can do this!

Jean, listen to me. You are the most powerful telepath on Earth.

Ha! Next to you.

The. Most. Powerful. He paused. *You have all the information you need.*

She closed her eyes, turned her mind again to everything she'd absorbed. There was so much of it! Corbeau's memories were a mass of information, a sea of data. There was no time—

Jean, listen! Do you remember the meditation exercises I taught you?

She nodded instinctively.

Use them now.

Professor, it's so hot in here. My face is on fire. My stomach feels like a pretzel—

JEAN.

His thoughts were louder now, and cold, like those of a disappointed teacher. He'd only taken that tone with her a few times before, when—as a young pupil, overwhelmed by the thoughts of those around her—she'd allowed self-pity to interfere with her studies.

You must do this. There is no one else. If there were…

She stared at the screens, at a cloud of static.

I understand, she said.

Grab hold of the control stick, the Professor instructed. *The time is coming.* She reached out with both hands and grasped the stick like a lifeline—which, she realized, was exactly what it was.

Now, he continued. *Breathe.*

She stared straight ahead, willing her consciousness to remain within this confined space. That was a lesson he'd taught her. For a telepath, control is essential. Containment is everything.

I've taught you everything I can, the Professor sent. *Now it's up to you.*

She caught a flash of pain. *His injuries*, she realized. *They must be worse than he let on.*

It's nothing, he said. And then, again: *I truly am sorry.*

Xavier broke the connection. The entire exchange had passed in a matter of seconds.

Fighting back the sense of being alone again, Jean willed herself to breathe regularly. In, out. In, out. She focused on the control stick, firm and unyielding in her hands. Forced herself to ignore the raging energies all around.

For a third time, she saw herself under the trees, Scott's hand warm in hers. "*I love the fall*," she said again.

Scott turned to her, nodding, smiling a tight smile. This time, when he spoke, she remembered his words.

"*It's when things start to die.*"

At the time, she'd laughed. So dour, her boyfriend. So serious! Scott was a sensitive soul, a gentle man who probably would have been happier living a quiet life. Yet he'd agreed to lead the X-Men because someone had to, and because he was the best choice for the job. And since that day, every decision—every sacrifice—had taken a toll on him. Every loss was a blow to his heart.

He was about to receive another blow.

A strange tingling sensation manifested on her skin. She looked down at her hands, still locked around the stick, and gasped.

Her flesh was… unraveling. Cracking, splitting, peeling away before her eyes. The skin was turning odd colors: mold green, neon blue, deep red. She could feel the radiation seeping past her shields, spreading throughout her body. Muscles straining and stretching, cellular walls distending and breaking down. Bones straining to break free.

One of the cracks on her palm grew wider. A little flame rose up, crimson red, spreading outward like avian wings. When she leaned down to stare at it, it vanished.

What was happening to her?

She remembered the Professor's words. *The time is coming.*

There was nothing to do but wait.

One hour earlier

JEAN RAN through the prelaunch procedures, eyes darting from one screen to the next. Cabin pressure: nominal. Landing gear: operative. Surface actuators: online. The engines thrummed in her ears—a bit uneven, but growing louder. In a few minutes, they'd be ready for launch.

The remote manipulating arms were shot, but that didn't matter. She stood up and moved to the side bulkhead, running a quick test on the exterior cameras. The aft cam had an off-center view of the hangar bay's door. She could see the leading edge of the fire that was consuming the station, flames licking at the doorway.

"What you doin', Jeannie?"

She whirled around. Wolverine crouched there, as if ready for battle. His eyes were hidden behind the white lenses of his mask.

"You startled me," she said.

"First time ever," he replied. "Ain't easy to get past your defenses."

She grimaced. Innuendo aside, Logan was right. Telepaths were notoriously difficult to surprise.

"I was distracted." She sighed. "I told Corbeau to lock the life-cell."

"I got lockpicks." He grinned, held up his fist, and unsheathed one of his six deadly claws with an audible *snikt*. "Built in."

"What do you want, Logan?"

"I want you to get back in the life-cell and let me take the wheel."

She said nothing. Her eyes flicked to one of the screens. Fuel supply at two-thirds…

"I ain't kiddin', Jean. You know about my healing power… I can bounce back from just about anything. That flare ain't gonna unravel *my* genes."

"Logan, we don't have time for this."

"And what about your boyfriend?" He jerked a thumb back toward the aft compartment. "Cyke's about to start bawling, and I can't take a whole hour of that."

Despite herself, despite the impending tragedy of the situation, she laughed. Wolverine was one of the newer X-Men—she hadn't known him very long. He was crude, rough, and prone to disregard orders. She knew very little of his background, other than a few vague references to the Canadian special service. His claws resembled some sort of cybernetic implants, as opposed to a natural mutation.

What she *did* know was that he'd been nursing a serious crush on her for months. She'd resisted allowing any such feelings in return. What a cliché—the woman with the dependable boyfriend, attracted to the bad boy! But she couldn't deny the strange rapport they seemed to share.

"My power will protect me," she said. But her voice sounded weak, even to herself.

"Jean, you got a lot of years ahead of you." He took a step forward—blocking her way to the pilot's seat. "Me, I've lived long enough."

"I feel like I've been alive forever," she whispered.

He frowned.

"Logan, I can fly the shuttle—you can't. That's all that matters." She smiled, trying to keep the tears out of her eyes. "This is our only shot."

The engines hummed louder. Two beeps from the flight console indicated that the prelaunch was almost complete.

"This isn't you, kid." Wolverine balled up his fists. "You ain't made for this."

Again she felt a burst of anger. *Just like Scott*, she thought.

They don't understand. They'll never understand.

She took a step forward, challenging Logan directly. He snarled, looked into her eyes—and stopped in his tracks.

"Huh," he said.

"You're right," she said, keeping her voice even. "It's not me. But if I'm *me*—if I follow orders, if I hang back and let someone else drive—then we're all dead."

He stared at her. His eyes shifted to the flight console, pausing on the aft-camera viewscreen. The fire had reached the hangar deck, blazing across banks of computers and monitor screens. It would reach the shuttle within seconds.

His head swiveled back. "I could stop you," he hissed.

She just stared back.

A sharp chime went off. She turned to see the same text displayed on all ten of the screens:

LAUNCH ENABLED

When she turned back, Logan was gone.

Trembling, she seated herself in the pilot's chair. Logan was a loose cannon, probably the most dangerous mutant the X-Men had ever recruited. And he hadn't been bluffing. Jean's power was formidable, but if he'd decided to move her by force, she wouldn't have been able to stop him. Logan was a killer, but she'd stood her ground—shown him determination that matched his own. She'd forced him to make a choice, and he'd chosen to back down.

She sat alone for a moment, thinking of a good man whom she loved very much, sitting in agony in the life-cell. And another man who loved her exactly as she was—whose touch she'd never know, but who'd just made the agonizing decision to let her die.

Scott would survive. He'd be devastated, and it might take years for him to recover from the loss. But eventually he would put her memory aside and move on.

Logan, though…

Somehow she knew: *This will cost him.*

An alarm rang out: the fire had reached the outer hull. Jean Grey hissed in a deep breath. Then she shook her head, reached for the controls, and fired off the engines.

Now

ALL AT once the flare passed. The shuttle's engines coughed; instruments began to click and reboot; screens flickered brighter. The comms system blared to life with a hundred overlapping messages.

"—ust coming back up now—"

"—Tower One, do you read—"

"—ergency broadcast system, back online—"

Jean shook her head, struggling to clear her thoughts. The fires dancing across her skin had receded, the air felt cooler. But the radiation still boiled within her body.

"—flare has receded—"

"—ease keep all channels clear—"

Telekinetically she toggled the comms system off. Her hands were still wrapped around the control stick. She tested it, tugging slightly, and a message appeared on the nearest screen.

ENGINE CONTROLS REBOOTING

The Professor's words echoed in her mind: *The time is coming*.

The center screen flickered to life. A haze of red and yellow began to resolve, to take shape. Autumn leaves—hanging from a grove of trees, hundreds of them. Directly below, in the shuttle's path.

And another voice, from the depths of her memory: *When things start to die*.

A beep from the flight console. New text appeared on the smaller screen.

ENGINES ONLINE

She pulled back hard on the stick. The shuttle lurched, g-force pressing her back in her chair. She grunted, pulled again, and gasped as the forward-screen image swung upward with dizzying speed. Bright sky, blue and clear, filled the display.

She let out a cry of joy.

Accessing Corbeau's memories, she reached out with her mind and called up a GPS map. The tree-lined area below, she saw, was called Rockaway Community Park. It jutted out along Jamaica Bay, on the south side of Long Island—New York City, on the edge of Brooklyn and Queens. And just across the bay…

The small screen turned red.

DANGER
ENGINE FAILURE

The shuttle sputtered, went quiet, and began to drop. Jean's stomach seemed to flip upside down. She leaned forward, pulling at the stick. No response.

The voice returned. An ancient presence that was her, and yet not her.

Time to die, it said.

Jean dove into Corbeau's memories, racing through the options one by one. Main engines: offline. Emergency bailout: no time, and Scott and the others would still be trapped in the life-cell. Landing gear: at this speed, it would be crushed on impact.

It's all right, the voice said.

Shut up, she told it. *Shut up shut up SHUT UP!*

There was one chance: the elevons. Corbeau had designed the shuttle to function in glide mode, without the engines. Probably just to show off, she realized. Now his ego might save all their lives.

Quickly, expertly, she extended the wings to their full span. The shuttle bucked and slowed as air pounded against the wings. Jean shook in her seat. They were still dropping fast, but she'd managed to achieve a measure of control over their course.

Now all I need is someplace to land!

Straining, forcing the elevons down and over, she steered the plunging bird toward JFK Airport. Buildings slid by, low and dark, leading to a thick control tower studded with lights. Beyond, a thin green-gray landing strip stretched out like a finger, ending at the blue glimmering bay.

She flipped the comms system back on.

"—maintain holding pattern—"

"—hailing unidentified—"

"Mayday!" she called. "JFK flight control, I'm coming in hot. Clear all traffic, please!"

A flurry of crosstalk.

"Unidentified bird, this is control tower. You are *too low*. Repeat..."

She checked the altitude: 210 meters. The controller was right. At this rate of descent, she'd never clear the buildings.

Jean reached out telekinetically, forcing her power to surround the entire shuttle. She seized hold, struggling to keep its plummeting bulk in check. Then she gritted her teeth and *lifted*.

The shuttle swooped upward, barely clearing the main tower, and lurched down toward the tarmac. Jean felt a brief moment of triumph—

—before the impact shattered her spine.

The shuttle gouged a scar in the runway, then bounced sideways toward the adjoining grass. Sparks rose from its underbelly as it veered back, slamming down hard again. Momentum drove it forward, plowing a hot furrow through the tarmac.

Jean was conscious of a burning sensation, a fire spreading through her broken body. The minds of her friends, her lover, her teacher—all of them cried out from their confinement in the back of the shuttle. She had no strength left to shut them out.

This is the end, she thought.

No, the voice that was not her replied. *It's the beginning*.

As the shuttle screamed forward, Jean's consciousness exploded. Images flooded her mind. Flames dancing on skin; worlds exploding, dying in paroxysms of fire. A cruel woman in leather and boots, with hair like ice.

She saw Cyclops shackled, his face covered in crimson metal. Mouth open in a silent scream.

The shuttle bounced once more, the fuselage cracking in half. Two severed pieces dangled in midair, then plunged into the bay. Engines coughed briefly to life and sputtered out again. Jean Grey made no move toward the controls, no mental effort to prevent the vessel from sinking.

She was already dead.

CYCLOPS BROKE the surface, spitting filthy salt water. He gasped as a wave washed over him, then flexed powerful arms, thrusting upward to keep his head above water.

He looked around as best he could, surveying the scene through the crimson lenses of his visor. Over on the airport tarmac, emergency lights flashed. The edge of the runway hung jagged, crumbling off into the bay. The shuttle had done considerable damage on its way down.

Some of the other X-Men bobbed and floated, dazed, just a few feet away. Logan, Storm, and Nightcrawler were the closest. Just past them, Dr. Corbeau used a lifeguard's shoulder-hold to keep the dazed Professor X above the water. Surprisingly, the Professor seemed to be regaining consciousness.

That was everyone. Almost.

All but one.

"Storm, Kurt," he called. "Get Corbeau and the Professor to safety."

Storm started to answer, then coughed. "One moment, Scott."

"*Ja,*" Nightcrawler said.

"No hurry." Corbeau shook water out of his thick hair. "I trained for the Olympic swim team, back in college."

The dull whir of a helicopter echoed from above. NYPD no doubt, responding to the crash. Hopefully the Professor would recover soon—for his own sake, of course, but his mental powers could also prevent the rescue teams from noticing a pack of costumed mutants floating in the bay.

I can't worry about that now, Cyclops thought. He cast his eyes down toward the water, where the shuttle had sunk beneath the murk. Then he thrust his head upward and began gulping as much air as he could.

The water began to churn. He looked over to see Wolverine chopping toward him, teeth gritted.

"I'm going down for her, Logan," Cyclops said. "Try to stop me, I swear I'll kill you."

"I ain't stoppin' you, Cyke. I'm coming with."

No, Cyclops thought. *She's my love—my responsibility. I have to save her!*

Yet there was no denying Wolverine's stamina. Of the two of them, Logan probably had a better chance of rescuing Jean. Cyclops nodded reluctantly.

They raised their arms, prepared to dive—and Wolverine froze. His eyes went wide as he sniffed the air. Cyclops shot him a look, then realized the water was bubbling all around them. Even through his insulated uniform, he could feel the temperature rising.

All at once the surface seemed to explode, flaring upward in a glow of iridescent fire. Cyclops tumbled one way, catching a face-full of bay water, as Logan was tossed in the other direction. Between them, a gleaming, shining blur of a figure shot up into the sky.

Wiping the water off his visor, Cyclops gasped.

Jean Grey hung suspended in the air, eyes closed, her arms raised toward the sky. Slowly she opened her eyes and turned to look down, like a monarch surveying her subjects. When she spoke, her voice seemed to fill the air.

"HEAR ME, X-MEN," she said. "NO LONGER AM I THE WOMAN YOU KNEW."

Cyclops's brow furrowed. Somehow Jean was wearing a new costume. It gleamed green and gold, its long sash whipping in the wind.

"I AM FIRE," she continued, "AND LIFE INCARNATE."

It was her, and yet it wasn't. Everything about her had changed.

Where did that come from? Jean's never exhibited that level of telekinetic ability before…

"NOW AND FOREVER: I AM PHOENIX!"

"Jean!" he called.

At the sound of his voice she looked down. She seemed to struggle to focus, and then her expression softened. A look of fear crossed her face; she grabbed her temples and *screamed*.

"*Jean!*"

For a long moment she flared bright. Fiery wings seemed to flash outward from her body, blocking out the sun. The police helicopter halted in its approach and circled back, keeping its distance.

Then the energy died.

Jean gasped, went dark, and dropped from the sky.

When she struck the water, Cyclops was the first to reach her. He waved Logan away and hoisted her up, keeping her head above the surface.

"Jean?" he said. "Jean!"

No response.

"She's breathin'," Wolverine said.

Cyclops rested his head on her chest and heaved a sigh of relief. Her heartbeat was strong.

He floated in the water, holding her, waiting for the helicopter to return. Then he realized that the Professor had recovered enough to reach out and alter the perceptions of the rescue teams. When their way was clear, Xavier sent a mental signal. Cyclops hesitated, casting a final look down into the depths of the bay.

"Scott?" Storm called.

He turned to follow the others, paddling slowly toward shore. Keeping a tight grip on Jean Grey, the woman he loved. The woman he would *always* love, he knew with fierce determination—every moment of every day, for the rest of his life.

ACT ONE

SIGNS OF LIFE

CHAPTER ONE

One year later

KITTY PRYDE was *bored*. She'd just sat through a junior-level calculus lecture that was so obvious she could practically mouth the words along with the teacher. All around her, kids two years older than her frowned and took notes, struggling to keep up.

She was getting one of those headaches again, too.

When the bell rang, she texted her friend Robin.

NEED SOME AIR!

Robin was already up on the roof, so Kitty bounded up the steps two at a time and thrust open the door. She was wearing jeans and a short-sleeved shirt, and the fall air made her shiver.

Robin stood leaning against a railing, over past the horticulture club's outdoor roof garden. She was taller than Kitty, but gawky, and her eyes were glued to her phone.

"Hey, Kats," she said without looking up.

"Yo, Birds," Kitty replied. She started over toward her friend, then winced. The headache was growing stronger. It seemed to come from way inside, as if someone had installed an electric motor at the base of her skull.

Robin didn't even notice. "Dad, man!" she said, running a finger down her phone screen. "Enough with the texts. Tell me I'm not alone, Kats. Do your parents insist on turning Christmas into a logistical nightmare, months ahead of time?"

"Chanukah. Remember?"

"Chanukah, right." Still staring at her phone, she added, "Oh great, another assignment in Dumbass Illinois History. I thought high school would be awesome, Kats. Remember how we couldn't wait to get out of Deerfield Middle?"

"Yeah."

"But this place sucks. It sucks 24–7. Nobody here even plays *Dragon Quest* except you."

Kitty staggered, bracing herself against a lawn chair left behind by the horticulture kids. The doctors hadn't been able to identify the source of her headaches, but the pain was getting worse—and more frequent, too. She had an MRI scheduled for next week. Maybe that would show something…

"Dad, come on! Take a pill!" Robin didn't look up from her phone. "Ever since he and Mom broke up, he just won't leave me— hey, what's up with *your* parents? Are they really splitting up, or is that just some *Real Housewives*-type drama?"

"B-birds…"

The pain seemed to pulsate through Kitty's head. She leaned forward and grabbed her temples.

Please, God, she thought. *I'm only thirteen and a half. I can't be dying!*

"Oh, dude, that's the bell." Robin's voice seemed very far away. "We're gonna be late. Ah, I don't even care anymore. Suspend me, lock me up, shoot me at dawn. Anything's better than Deerfield High."

Then something new happened. The pain seemed to dissolve, melting into a strange tingling sensation. It tingled from her head down through her torso, and out into her arms and legs. She felt limp, helpless.

"Kats?"

Almost in slow motion, Kitty saw her friend approaching. Then Robin's eyes went wide. She stopped short, her expression turning to shock.

I'm falling, Kitty realized. The roof grew closer, closer… She held out her arms to protect her face from the impact.

The impact didn't come.

She just kept falling.

Kitty was vaguely aware of wooden beams, fiberglass insulation, and… a dead rat? And then she was in a large room, with screens and diagrams and the periodic table on the walls. Kids were running around, wearing lab smocks and visors, holding up beakers and instruments. Ms. Gennaro, the biology teacher, whirled to look up in surprise.

The bio lab? But that's…

Kitty flailed around. Her hand struck a glass jar, knocking it off a counter. It shattered on the floor, spilling formaldehyde-preserved cockroaches.

Again she fell. Again she winced, and again she kept moving. The tingling sensation spread through her body, phasing her through the floor…

…to the media lab. Her classmate Ahmed jumped to his feet, mouthing her name, as she plummeted down in front of him. She passed right through his display in a shower of sparks. The screen turned to static, ruining the CGI model spaceship he'd been building. She didn't even have time to apologize…

…before she found herself plunging down through the rafters of the gymnasium. *No,* she thought. *This has to stop. Whatever it is, STOP!*

All at once, the sensation faded. The pain, the tingling—all of it vanished. Kitty dropped like a rock, landing on a couple of girls, knocking them off their feet. The basketball they'd been passing dropped to the floor and bounced away.

She looked up, dazed. A dozen tall girls stood surrounding her, all dressed in shorts and loose shirts.

Great.

Seniors.

"Hey, guys." She grimaced. "Go Deerfield?"

They stared. A couple shook their heads.

"What the hell…" Mr. Dido, the gym teacher, pushed his way through the mob of seniors. When he caught sight of Kitty, his unibrow furrowed. "Pryde? You're out of uniform!"

A tall black girl turned to him. "*That's* your problem here?"

"She just fell, like, thirty feet!" another girl said.

Kitty looked up at the ceiling. There was no hole, no debris—no sign of her passage. Which meant only one thing could have happened.

One impossible thing.

Before Mr. Dido could reassert his precarious authority, an ancient speaker on the wall crackled to life.

"kkkTENTION… WILL kkkKATHERINE PRYDE PLEASE REPORrrrrkkkk PRINCIPAL'S OFFICE IMMEDIATELY…"

Wow. Kitty was almost impressed. *This day actually managed to get worse!*

The girls were still staring at her. Some of them seemed amused, others looked curious. Mr. Dido stepped forward, glaring.

"You heard the announcement." He gestured at the wall speaker. "Saves me the trouble."

Kitty turned and trudged away. Whispers and muffled laughter followed her through the door. She pulled out her phone, called up the chat app, and texted Robin.

BIRDS. YOU WON'T BELIEVE WHERE I'M HEADED.

The reply was quick and devastating.

STAY AWAY FROM ME, KATHERINE.

Kitty went numb. She recalled the expression on Robin's face, the last glimpse she'd had of her friend on the roof. That look… it wasn't just shock and surprise. There'd been… disgust, too.

A trio of emojis popped up on the phone. Godzilla, a two-headed man, and a radiation symbol. Kitty didn't need a translation program to know what that meant.

Mutant.

Trudging down the empty hallway, she was barely aware of her surroundings. She'd had one real friend in this school, and now she had zero. The aide waved her into the principal's office. Kitty pushed open the door, swallowing nervously.

An elegant woman in a business suit stepped up to meet her. "Hi, Kitten."

"Mom?" Kitty looked around the small office, instinctively seeking an exit. "Dad? What are you doing here?"

Mr. Chiang, the principal, stood up and walked around his desk. He moved like a bomb-disposal cop approaching an unidentified package. He didn't seem angry, but he was definitely on edge.

"Kitty," he said. "I asked your parents to come in."

"What?" Her head was whirling. *They can't know what I just… what just happened. I don't think anybody really saw it— except Birds. Did… did she report me?*

"Kitten, it's okay." Her father tried one of his lame smiles on her. "Principal Chiang thought we should discuss your educational situation."

"My what?" she said. "Listen, I know my grades have slipped, but it's really just… I'm bored, that's all."

"Bored." Her father looked away, shaking his head. "She's bored."

"We know you're smart, darling." Her mother shot a glare at her father. "That's why you're having trouble."

"Smart, yes, smart!" Kitty said quickly. "And I'm… *rebellious*, that's the problem. I'm, you know, still getting used to high school. Studies have shown that the early teens are a point where acclimatization to a new environment requires—"

"Kitty! Calm down. You're not in trouble here." Mr. Chiang gestured toward a far door, behind his desk. "We just want you to meet someone."

The door swung open, revealing a striking woman with pale skin and severely cut platinum-blond hair. She wore a spotless white business suit with a slit in the long skirt, and thick-rimmed glasses that seemed to magnify her hard, staring eyes.

"This is Ms. Frost," Mr. Chiang said. "She represents a very exclusive, private academy."

Kitty's eyes strayed to the woman's boots. They were white, like the rest of her clothing, with heels just a little too high for business wear.

"Hello, Katherine." Ms. Frost stepped around the desk, a smirk teasing at the corners of her lips. "It's good to meet you." She held out a perfectly manicured hand.

Kitty stared at it, studying the frosted nail polish. When she glanced up, the expression on Ms. Frost's face made her shiver. The way she was looking at Kitty…

Like I'm something good to eat.

"Kitten?" her father said. "This could be important to your future."

"Don't be rude," her mother added.

Ms. Frost moved in very close and smiled—a smile with a hint of a threat behind it. In her white clothes and pale makeup, she seemed to be made of ice.

"I'm sure we're going to be great friends," Ms. Frost said.

Kitty reached out to take her hand, bracing for the woman's cold grip. To her surprise, the handshake was firm and very, very warm.

Somehow, that was even more disturbing.

CHAPTER TWO

THE POLICE sergeant was pushing seventy. He limped over to his desk, dropped himself into his chair as if it were the last place on Earth he wanted to be, and let out a string of rapid-fire questions, all in Greek.

"Sorry," the young woman said. "English?"

The sergeant glared at her.

She looked away, brushed a few wet strands of matted red hair out of her eyes. They were alone in the cramped station room. Four desks, one piled high with paper, CRT-screen computers on the other three. A blue-and-white Greek flag hanging loose on the wall, not quite covering a crack in the plaster.

"Name?" the sergeant asked.

"Jean Grey."

He started typing on the ancient keyboard, speaking out the letters. "G–R–A–"

"E."

He threw up his hands and turned to her.

"Just tell me what happened, Ms. Grey."

"I already told the constable. Twice."

"And now you are going to tell me." He gave her a hostile smile. "Three times, if necessary."

She clenched her fists tightly at her sides. *I could read your mind,* she thought. *I could change your mind. Make you help me, make you do anything I want.* But no. She no longer dared use her powers… not even for simple matters, like moving objects remotely. Not after what had happened.

"I was on the beach, after my ship arrived. I climbed up on a rock to get a better look around. A group of boys sneaked up on me, grabbed my purse, and pushed me into the water."

The sergeant frowned. He tapped a pencil on the desk, as if he were solving a mystery of great importance.

"You didn't see these boys coming?"

"I was distracted."

"By our beautiful beaches?"

"I was… staring at the water."

A flash of images came to her. A crashing impact on tarmac, pain slamming up through her spine. Water rushing in all around, filling her punctured lungs. A strange transformation.

The sergeant was talking.

"I'm sorry," she said. "What?"

"I said, did you get a look at the boys?"

She looked up as another officer walked in. This one had to be in his eighties. Her gaze strayed past the officer to a handsome, well-built civilian in a suit, tie, and expensive-looking overcoat. He had thick dark hair and a neatly trimmed beard.

"Anything at all?" the sergeant prodded. "Hair or eye color, clothing?"

"I-I caught a glimpse of the one that shoved me. He had dark hair and a… I think it was a scar, on his cheek."

The sergeant resumed the laborious task of typing. The well-dressed man turned to stare at Jean. She smiled back, embarrassed.

"Mr. Wyngarde?" the second officer called. The man shrugged and followed him to another desk.

40   "I do not know that we can help you, Ms. Grey."

"What?" Again, the anger. "Half this island is over sixty years old. How many kids are there, anyway?"

He shrugged, gave a lazy smile. "It is not so easy."

"They took my suitcase—my clothes. Cards, my passport, even my phone. I have no money!"

"The constable can help you with your passport. It takes a few days."

She sighed.

Across the room, the octogenarian officer was speaking in low, halting tones. The handsome man—Wyngarde, that was his name—appeared to be exercising patience. A little strained smile flashed on and off his face.

I could read their minds, Jean thought again. But no, that wasn't an option. It might never be again.

"Look." She turned toward the sergeant, pasting a smile onto her face, and wrung a few drops of water out of the hem of her sundress. "My clothes are soaked. I have no money, and I can't even leave until the passport is replaced. Where will I stay?"

"As I say, the beach is beautiful this time of year." He shrugged, turned away. "We are done, yes?"

She stared at his back. Something seemed to rise inside her, a violent spirit. Something that had always been with her, and yet seemed as new as the life she was trying to build in this remote, alien place.

It terrified her.

She rose without a word and stalked out of the room.

OUT ON the steps, she sat trembling in the bright autumn sunlight. In the distance, past the low white city buildings, ancient stone ruins rose up from barren soil. Yet another retirement-age officer shuffled past, shooting her a hostile look.

Don't cry, she told herself. *Don't do it. Don't give them the satisfaction.*

"Excuse me."

She whirled around and shot to her feet. On the step above, the man from inside—Wyngarde—smiled down at her. He stood at a jaunty angle, one leg slightly raised, as if posing for an old-style publicity photo.

"I couldn't help overhearing." His voice was deep, rumbling, yet very inviting, with an accent that was vaguely British, probably upper class. "I believe we may have a similar problem."

She cocked her head. Something about this man inspired trust. She felt strangely at ease with him.

"Is that your usual line?"

"Is it working?"

Despite herself, she laughed.

"My expectations," he continued, "are limited to lunch. At present." He held out a hand. "May I?"

She hesitated. Then she spread her arms, indicating her wet dress.

"Under the circumstances," she said, "how can I refuse?"

THE MATRONLY hostess's face lit up when they entered the restaurant. A dreamy expression crossed her face as she led them to a corner table on the second-floor deck, overlooking the sunlit beach. Before Jean knew it, a glass of wine sat in front of her on the table.

"I take it you come here often," she said, leaning across the checkered tablecloth.

Wyngarde smiled. His first name, he'd told her, was Jason. He seemed the sort of man who could walk into any room in the world and feel at home. There was something very old-world about him… a gentlemanly quality that seemed out of place in modern times.

"I love the Cyclades," he said. "I've sampled all the islands across the Aegean Sea. Kirinos holds a special place in my heart."

"Really?" she said, then lowered her voice as the hostess

returned with a basket of bread. "I thought it would be… I mean, an old professor of mine spoke highly of the place. But most of the population seem to be retired."

"There are a lot of pensioners," he allowed, "but this place… it's like stepping into a time warp. In many ways, nothing has changed here since the days when Jason and his Argonauts sought the fabled Golden Fleece."

She took a long drink of wine. It felt good going down.

"My work is… demanding," he continued. "Sometimes I just need to leave the modern world behind. To seek out a simpler, slower way of life."

"That's why I came here, too. I guess." She grimaced. "Looks like it's working out better for you."

"Well, at least you've managed to give up your phone."

She laughed.

"Are you drying out yet?" he asked.

"Some."

"You won't get your things back," he said, abruptly turning serious. "That urchin who robbed you… his father is mayor of the island. The police are helpless in this matter."

"Ah." She favored him with a crooked smile as the alcohol began to hit. "I take it you've had run-ins with the same little brat?"

"I was at the police station complaining about him."

She frowned. "If the police can't help, why bother?"

"Where else am I going to meet a beautiful young woman on an island of pensioners?"

She looked down, embarrassed.

The touch of his hand on hers startled her. She looked up to see his intense dark eyes staring into hers.

"There is a sadness in you," he said, "that I cannot attribute to a robbery. Or a damp sundress."

She blinked, nodded.

"Is there someone?" he asked. "Or… was there?"

"There was," she said. "He died."

Wyngarde nodded, clasped his hand tightly around hers.

"They all died," she whispered. *Scott...* She could feel the wine hitting her, psychic walls crumbling. *No*, she thought, *don't do it. Do not let your mind touch his.*

"Jean Grey." He spoke her name slowly, meticulously. It sounded alien, unfamiliar, as if it belonged to someone else. "I cannot take away your pain. But I *can* offer you a fresh set of clothes."

She snorted. "I bet you can."

"It's about to turn cold. I presume your sweaters were lost with your luggage."

"Yes." She sighed. "I used to love the fall."

"I love it as well." He cocked his head, keeping his eyes locked on hers. "It's a time of promise."

She looked up, startled.

"Of new beginnings," he added. A waiter arrived and stood at attention. Wyngarde gestured magnanimously toward Jean. "The lady will have...?"

A wide smile stole across her face. She raised her glass to Jason.

"A fresh set of clothes," she said.

WYNGARDE'S RENTED house lay just outside the city, on the edge of the ruins. A crumbled stone archway to nowhere, several meters high, cast a long shadow across the simple cottage.

"It's not much," he said, ushering her into a sparsely furnished bedroom, "but you should be able to find something in your size. Closet's over there."

"This 'something,'" she replied. "It belongs to a lady friend? Do you *have* a lady friend?"

"Had. Will again, someday. I hope." He smiled, a mischievous grin. "Take your time." Wyngarde left and closed the door.

Jean stood for a moment, breathing hard. Entirely alone, she realized, for the first time since her arrival on Kirinos. She sat on the bed and stared at the white walls, at the hotel-style painting of flowers hung over the headboard. Then she stood, crossed to the closet, pulled open the door—and stopped, surprised. The space inside was quite large. She fumbled for a light switch, then grabbed the chain hanging from a bare bulb...

...and gasped.

The racks were hung, as promised, with a variety of women's clothes. But not the sort of clothes she'd imagined. Everything here was vintage, even antique. Cotton petticoats, Victorian-era shifts, bustle bloomers, a hooped underskirt. A rainbow of wide, poofy dresses, all in a row. Camisole with a bow at the neck.

She stepped farther inside. The lighting seemed to grow darker, more sinister. And so did the clothing.

A shoe tree hung with garters. A shelf of stockings, all neatly rolled... some in fishnet, some black with seams. Corsets in a variety of colors—some of them patterned with flowers, others in plain white or black—all hung to show off their thin, waspy waists. Along the floor, a row of lace-up boots ranging from ankle-height to full thigh-length. All with heels—not crazy platform heels, but provocatively high nonetheless.

She frowned, let out a hiss of disgust.

So much for new beginnings. Guess I'm sleeping on the beach tonight.

She turned around to leave, strode back out into the room— and froze. The room had changed, grown darker. Thick ashy drapes hung against paisley-patterned wallpaper. Twin gas lamps protruded from the wall, flanking a canopied, four-poster bed hung with sinister black curtains.

She moved to the bed, knelt on the edge, and thrust aside the curtains. On the wall above the headboard, where the innocuous painting of flowers had hung, there was now a posed portrait of... Jason Wyngarde? The face closely resembled him, down to the carefully cultivated beard, but this man wore a top hat and tight jacket, a riding crop clutched firmly in one gloved hand. His eyes leered down from the wall, burning into Jean's brain.

Instinctively she scurried back, almost falling. Backed up toward the closet and stopped again, just inside the door.

A polished black corset hung on a rack. Next to it was a

cape, dark as midnight, with a scarlet lining. They were the only two items along this wall. Jean reached out, feeling a mix of revulsion and curiosity, and touched the corset. It was hard, but warm to the touch. She ran a finger down the firm stays, the thick black laces, stopping only when her finger reached the narrow waist.

A single word rose, unbidden, to her mind.

Mine.

Ice ran through her. *The voice,* she thought. It hadn't spoken to her since the shuttle crash. Not since she'd become... what? What *had* she become?

"Find something?"

She whirled around. Wyngarde stood in the closet doorway, a questioning look on his face. An ordinary beach bag was slung over his shoulder.

"Jason." She pulled her hand away from the corset. "What is this?"

He took a step back. "I'm sorry?"

She blinked, shook her head. Behind him, the room had reverted to its previous appearance—white walls, a low uncurtained bed. The painting on the wall was once more an innocuous still life, not some portrait of a depraved ancestor.

"I..."

She stumbled forward. He reached out to catch her, shifting the bag easily to his back. His arms felt strong, solid. Warm.

What's wrong with me? she thought. *My psychic power... is it playing tricks on me? That voice, the hallucinations... is this just my grief, punishing me in ways I don't even understand?*

Am I going mad?

"Easy." Wyngarde's voice was as comforting, as mellifluous as always. "Oh, your dress is still wet. Here... how about this?"

He wrapped a comforting arm around her shoulders and ushered her back inside the closet, gesturing toward the wall that had held the black corset. In its place, now, a simple one-piece swimsuit hung on a plastic hanger.

She scanned the other racks. Slacks, jeans, T-shirts, sneakers.

A shelf of sloppily folded yoga pants. Jean hefted the swimsuit, raised an eyebrow.

"It's a bit low-cut."

When she turned to look, Wyngarde was smiling. He reached into the beach bag and held up two diving masks.

"Perfect for scuba diving," he said.

HE TOOK her down below, to a sea bed lined with dark, barely visible coral. A hard, jagged surface, with caverns that looked as if they led to the center of the Earth. Jean had some experience diving, yet she'd never been this deep before.

Well, once. But she couldn't remember that very well.

The sea writhed and darted with life. Small striped fish, swarming as thick as a storm cloud. A manta ray, wings stretched wide. A creature shaped like a starfish, but with a pulsing, bulbous body. Something that looked like a sheet of inky paper, warping and fluttering in the ocean current.

Wyngarde touched her arm once. She turned to see him pointing at a large log. As she watched, its closest end twisted upward toward them. It opened silver-dollar eyes and a mouth twice as long as a man's body.

Jean reared back, momentarily panicked.

When she turned to Wyngarde, the look in his eyes was strange—almost hungry. As if he were enjoying her discomfort.

She turned away, pointed upward, and kicked toward the surface.

"I'M SORRY if I disturbed you."

She sat on one of the stone ruins overlooking the island, staring at the ocean dimly visible in the distance. Torches lit up the night, signaling some sort of celebration in the town below.

"I just… I love diving," Wyngarde continued. "So many fascinating things at the bottom of the sea."

"You have no idea," she murmured.

Hugging her legs, she pulled herself up on the stone bench. The borrowed swimsuit seemed suddenly inadequate. As if in response, Wyngarde stole up behind her and draped a wrap around her shoulders.

"I can keep myself warm," she protested. But she pulled the wrap tighter.

"They're celebrating the Festival of Aphrodite." He planted himself next to her on the bench, his warm body beside hers, and pointed down at the torchlights. "A night consecrated to love, when all cares and woes are cast aside."

She looked away again. "It should be so easy."

"Jean."

His finger was soft on her chin, as if he were leading her somewhere. Unhurried, at her own pace. She turned to look into his piercing eyes.

"What happened to you?"

She felt walls crumbling inside. The truth coming out, in defiance of all common sense.

"I died," she said, with a little laugh.

His eyes went wide.

"I mean, I *almost* died." She stood up, felt the walls rising again. "It's complicated." A small burst of power rose up from her palm. Twin flames, forming the shape of a raging bird of prey. She blinked, willed it away, and whirled around.

Wyngarde was staring at her, that hungry expression in his eyes again. For a moment she panicked.

Did he see?

He turned away and jumped up onto a stone landing. An ancient staircase led into the ruins, twisting around a half-fallen temple. He pointed up along the path.

"Come with me," he said.

"I think I should be alone."

He gestured, arms wide, taking in the island and the revelers below. "Do you want to disappoint Aphrodite?"

THE STAIRCASE ended at a sheer drop, atop the highest hill on the island. Wyngarde stood behind her, his hands resting on her shoulders. She felt disoriented, confused. Something about all this was very wrong—but it also felt very, very right.

"Look down," he said. "Can you imagine how it was for the gods of old? Living high above the mortal world, atop Olympus, gazing down at humanity? Knowing they—*we*—existed, continued to live, only at their sufferance?"

At this height, his house was lost in the gloom. The torches were mere dots, tiny smudges of flame winding in a line from the town all the way out along the beach.

"Gods," he repeated, "living only for the moment. Careless of the consequences of their actions, a law forever unto themselves. Can you imagine such power?"

"I can."

He took hold of her arm and whirled her around. Before she realized what was happening, he grasped the back of her neck and kissed her hard. He smelled of night breeze and musky, old-world cologne. For a moment, she felt intoxicated, lost.

Then she pulled away, mumbling apologies. She stepped to the edge, staring up at the clear, sharp stars.

"You said there was someone," he prodded. "And that he died." She nodded.

"Was this when you had your... when *you* nearly died?"

"No. More recently—much more." She felt tears rising. "Fifteen days ago, he died."

"This man... I think possibly he loved you. Probably very much, as any man would."

"I don't know about... yes. Yes, he did."

"But perhaps he never truly understood you."

Again, she felt something rise inside her. Something dark, something terrifying.

"May I ask the circumstances of his death?"

When she turned, there was fire in her eyes. "Have you ever heard of Magneto?"

Wyngarde stood his ground. Returned her gaze without flinching.

"I have."

"He killed..." *Scott,* she thought, but she couldn't bring herself to say his name. *Scott. Oh, Scott.*

"He killed them all," she finished.

Wyngarde stared at her. "Magneto."

"Yes." Her voice caught. "He trapped us in a volcano deep beneath the Antarctic shelf, and then he killed them."

All the sadness, all the grief she'd pushed down these past two weeks, washed over her. She thought of Storm, with her gentle manner and lightning-flash eyes. Of Nightcrawler, blue-furred and demon-tailed, with his quick smile and easy words of comfort. Colossus, the Russian farm boy whose metal skin concealed an enormous, gentle heart. Logan, whose fierce love she'd never been able to return.

Scott Summers. With his bright, beautiful, deadly eyes.

Again Jason stepped up behind her, placed gentle hands on her shoulders. "Stay with me, Jean. This is important."

The grief welled up within her, threatening to burst free. She cupped her face in her hands, not caring anymore whether she cried in front of this stranger. But to her surprise, no tears came.

"When Magneto... murdered your friends. Your lover." He squeezed his hands, holding her firmly in place. "What did you do?"

All at once, the grief became something else. Like raw iron transmuted, by some alchemical process, into sharp, piercing steel.

"I killed him," she whispered.

Her head whipped up, eyes burning. With the slightest of motions, she flexed and broke free of Wyngarde's grip. She rose up into the air, spread her arms wide, and glowed bright.

Wyngarde stared up at her, a cold hunger in his eyes.

"Such power." He paused, then repeated, "A law unto themselves, looking down on mortal men."

Her own power swelled inside—the power she'd repressed, the power she feared more than anything in the world. Feared both because of what it could do, and because it had failed her when she needed it most. But there was no stopping it now. When she spoke, the voice within seemed to be talking directly through her.

"Foolish man," she said. "This power you speak of, I already possess."

Wyngarde watched, nodding.

"The gift of creation is mine," she continued. "Through me, the circle remains unbroken. From me comes the end that is a new beginning."

For the first time, his expression wavered. He took a step back, away from the edge.

"Mine is the fire that consumes, yet from its ashes brings forth new life." She raised her head, overwhelmed by sensation. "For I am the PHOENIX!" The power rose, built to a crescendo. She felt it course through her, like hot needles piercing every cell in her body. The stars seemed to beckon, calling her back to some home beyond human memory.

And then, just as it had before, the power faded. The wave passed, the fury receded. Jean wavered in midair, then dropped down to hover a few feet above Wyngarde. She shook her head, struggling to process the fierce, chaotic impulses coursing through her.

"Just like before," she whispered.

"Before." His eyes were wide now, studying her. "With Magneto?"

"Yes." She nodded. "All this power. The power of… of the gods…"

She turned away, eyes flashing.

"…and *I couldn't save them!*"

Once more the power surged. Fire blazed in all directions, blackening the ancient walls, setting small shrubs ablaze. A stone column toppled and fell, tumbling down the hill.

As Jean rose, she caught a last glimpse of Wyngarde. He'd retreated, picking his way down the long stone staircase. He turned once, shielding his eyes from her godlike luminance. Yet she swore she saw that same animal-like hunger in his eyes, the excitement of a wild tiger closing in on its prey.

Jean Grey—the Phoenix—whirled in midair and glanced down at the island of Kirinos. The townspeople stood clustered along the dark beach now, pointing their fire-sticks up at the light show in the sky. Some of the torches had already gone out.

She turned away and shot out over the sea. She flared bright—one more flickering torch of the gods—and vanished into the autumn night.

LOUKAS LEAPT up the stone steps two at a time, nimble fingers grabbing for handholds in the worn rock. It was still dark, a few hours before daylight, but he knew every inch of these ruins. Loukas was the best climber on Kirinos.

Up ahead, at the top of the staircase, a low campfire burned, smoke rising up into the air. Loukas bounded up to the top, then stopped.

A man sat on the landing, staring into the fire—but it wasn't the man Loukas had expected. This man was gaunt, slumped, his face lined with age and acne scars. Scattered gray hair, like a used mop, lay across his misshapen head. Cold beady eyes reflected the sparse firelight.

Loukas stepped back, his foot crunching on a pebble. The man whirled around and jumped to his feet. Loukas shifted his backpack and looked down, considering whether to run. He scratched the scar on his face—a nervous habit. When he looked back up—

Jason Wyngarde stood where the gaunt man had been. Tall, imperious. An impatient frown on his handsome, bearded face.

"You're late," Wyngarde said in Greek.

"Had to wait for my father to pass out." Loukas gestured down at the beach. Only a few torches still flickered in the night.

"You have it?" Wyngarde asked.

"You got my money?"

"Don't test me, boy." A dangerous light flared in Wyngarde's eyes.

Loukas nodded quickly. He swung the backpack around, opened it, and handed a flowered purse to the man above.

"It's all in there," the boy said. "Money, credit cards, passport. Even her phone." He grinned. "I made a few overseas calls."

Wyngarde's eyes widened as he ran his fingers through the purse. "Jean Grey," he murmured.

"She was an easy mark." Loukas laughed. "Stupid American." Wyngarde looked up then, anger in his eyes. Loukas backed down a step, suddenly afraid. Calming, Wyngarde reached into his fancy coat and pulled out a wad of euros.

"She is a Queen," he hissed, shoving the money in the boy's face. "My Queen."

"S-sure," Loukas said, reaching out to grab the euros. Wyngarde handed them over and turned his back, raising a hand to dismiss the boy. Then the Englishman strode over to the fire, stared down at it for a moment, and tossed the purse into the flames. As the smell of burning plastic rose up, Loukas turned away.

Crazy, he thought. *Tourists—they're all crazy.* But this one, at least, seemed to have plenty of money. Loukas leafed through the bills, thinking of all the candy and games he could buy. *Have to hide it from Dad, though. He'll just drink it away.*

He looked back, just once, before making his way down the steps. Wyngarde sat before the fire again, staring at the papers and cards as they curled and burned to ash. Loukas wasn't sure, but he thought he heard the man's whisper carried on the night air:

"My Black Queen."

CHAPTER THREE

The Massachusetts Academy
A Place Where Special Flowers Grow
Since 1825

KITTY PRYDE ran her fingers over the embossed folder. Beneath the elegant script was an old etching, like the ones she'd seen in her dad's *Wall Street Journal*. It showed an old Gothic tower with a high window, and a single rose curled across the image.

It was clearly meant to suggest a long heritage of learning. Generations of scholarship, monks toiling away at illuminated manuscripts, late nights spent in contemplation and conversation with sharp minds. Learned people doing lofty things.

It made Kitty think of dungeons.

"Kitten? Don't you want to say goodbye to Ms. Frost?"

"I'm good, Dad."

She didn't look up from the kitchen table. Ms. Frost was creepy, just like her school. Kitty imagined herself locked up in that tower, like some fairy-tale princess.

"I don't know what's got into our girl, Ms. Frost." Mom's voice came from the front door, across the foyer. "I apologize for her behavior."

"Normally you can't shut her up," Dad said.

"Carmen!"

"It's fine, Ms. Pryde." Emma Frost's voice was like butter. "Kitty's at that awkward age. I deal with girls like her all the time."

Kitty frowned at the folder. *Special flowers? Is that supposed to be me?*

"You have my brochures," Frost continued. "I'll be in touch." The front door opened, then closed.

Mom walked back into the kitchen and threw herself down into a chair. "What is the matter with you?" she demanded. "And don't try using those headaches as an excuse."

Kitty waved the brochure at her. "Excuse me for not wanting to go to Creepy Evil Hogwarts."

Dad walked over next to his wife, shifting his feet awkwardly. "I thought Ms. Frost was quite, um…"

"I bet you did," Mom muttered.

"Look," Kitty said. "I know what this is really about." Mom and Dad exchanged awkward glances. "If you're serious about sending me away to school, then I guess you're really splitting up."

Mom looked down, started fidgeting with her fingers. Dad crossed to the cabinet, eyed a bottle of scotch for a moment, then poured himself a glass of water instead.

"It's not as simple as that," he began.

"It sounds *exactly* as simple as that."

"Maybe you'll like the representatives from the next school better."

"The *next* school?"

A chime came from the front door.

"Saved by the—"

"Don't even." Kitty jumped up, furious, and stalked to the door.

"Kitten…"

Kitty ignored them. "Welcome to the Muggle residence," she snapped, wrenching open the door. "I'm your poor, misunderstood wizard—I mean *flower*—"

She stopped.

Blinked once, twice.

A tall, regal woman stood at the door, head cocked in a quizzical expression. Her dark skin and bright blue eyes formed a striking contrast with her snow-white hair, which was swept back under an angular, African-patterned tiara. She wore a long dress with an elegant vest-jacket that showed off muscular arms.

"Muggle?" The woman frowned, and checked her phone. "Perhaps we have the wrong address."

A hairy man in a leather jacket lumbered up behind her, twirling a ring of car keys. His hair was pulled up in twin spikes, and thick muttonchop sideburns framed his sneering face.

"Perhaps," he growled, "we got a smartass, 'Roro."

Kitty started to reply, then noticed the third visitor. He was tall and very large, with thick muscles bulging against his tight shirt and a kind look in his eyes. He couldn't have been much older than Kitty herself. Well, maybe a little older…

"Hey," she said.

"*Dobroye utro*," he replied. Then, with a sheepish smile: "That means good morning."

Kitty blushed. "Cute accent."

The woman stepped forward, clearing her throat. "We are from the Xavier Institute for Higher Learning. My name is Ororo Munroe… might you be Katherine Pryde?"

"I might."

"Kid," the hairy man snarled, "are you or aren't you?"

"That depends," Kitty said. Behind her there was the sound of raised voices, and she turned. In the kitchen, half-visible around the bend of the hallway, Mom and Dad were gesturing angrily at each other.

"On, um…" The tall boy gave her another charming, crooked smile. "On what does it depend?"

Kitty waved them back and stepped outside the door. The three strangers gathered around her.

"Can you get me out of here for a while?"

"MOM AND Dad are driving me off a cliff with this private-school stuff. They didn't even tell me about you guys." Kitty sipped at her drink, let out a sigh as the tiny chunks of ice slid down her throat. "Thanks for the 'cino, Ms. Munroe. It's the only thing that helps with my headaches."

The odd group sat at a small table in the local coffee shop. The crowd was sparse on a weekday morning.

"Why did they not prepare you?" the large boy asked. His name, she'd learned, was Peter.

"They knew I'd bail," she replied. "Same with that creepy lady this morning."

"The woman in white," Ororo replied. "We saw her leaving your house."

"Nice-looking gal," the hairy man—Logan—said. "Weird scent, though."

Kitty raised an eyebrow. "Scent?"

Logan shrugged.

"Logan," Ororo said, "perhaps you and Peter would care to peruse the establishment's beverage selection."

"They got no beer," Logan said. "What's the point?"

The woman gave him what looked like a good-natured glare. Kitty had the feeling they'd been through this routine before.

"Awright, awright." Logan uncurled from his chair like a cat climbing to its feet. "C'mon, Petey. Let's go look at the six-dollar sodas." Peter smiled warmly at Kitty, then followed Logan to the counter.

Kitty leaned over the table. "That guy's a little intense."

"Logan?" Ororo nodded. "He is. It is his strength, and his curse, as well."

Kitty studied her for a moment. There was something about Ororo—about all of them—that she trusted. It didn't hurt that the big guy had great muscles *and* a terrific smile.

"Are you a model?" she asked. "It's just—ah, I'm sorry. I've never seen anyone with dark skin and blue eyes and white hair. It's beautiful—*you're* beautiful, I mean. I'm talking too much. I do that."

"It's all right." Ororo smiled. "So far as I know, Kitty, I am one of a kind… and so are you."

"Because I'm smart?" she replied. "I know, I know my grades have gone down—"

"No. Not that." Ororo hesitated. "Kitty, our school has recently suffered a series of setbacks. In fact, we were forced to close down for a time."

"But you're opening again?"

"Yes." She looked up with those clear blue eyes. "Have you ever heard of Magneto?"

"Sure," Kitty said. "He's a terrorist, attacked the space center at—" She stopped.

Whirled around to look at the counter, at the coiled, hairy man staring in disgust at some brightly colored fruit drink. At Peter, leaning against a display case, munching on a Danish.

"You're the X-Men," she whispered.

"Yes," Ororo replied. "We agreed it was all right to tell you."

"You're mutants." Kitty paused. "Some of my friends think… think mutants are dangerous."

"What do you think?"

"I think your school probably isn't a dungeon."

Ororo frowned, looking puzzled.

"Tell me about Magneto," Kitty said.

ORORO TOLD her. About the day, mere weeks ago, when Magneto—their greatest enemy—had captured them, every member of the core X-Men team, as easily as flipping a light switch. He'd imprisoned them in an escape-proof sanctuary in the heart of a live volcano, deep beneath the frozen wastelands of Antarctica.

They escaped, of course. When Magneto responded to

the base's alarms, they ambushed him in a tightly coordinated formation. Jean Grey linked their minds in a telepathic network, allowing them to work together at the speed of thought.

In the end, they managed to nullify Magneto's abilities—but in a supreme irony, the X-Men discovered that only his power had been holding back the raging fury of the volcano. With their enemy defeated, deadly magma poured in through cracks in the ceiling, flooding the base. A river of molten rock, hot enough to incinerate human flesh, separated the X-Men from Jean and Magneto. They saw the magma wash over Jean—heard her scream—

—and then they ran for their lives.

Wolverine's enhanced senses located a hidden escape route. Nightcrawler teleported ahead, guiding the others to a secret tunnel leading to a hidden Antarctic refuge. They returned to the volcano site as quickly as possible in their modified SR-71 Blackbird jet, equipped with state-of-the-art seismic equipment, but all readings showed the same thing. The volcano had collapsed, magma flooding through every inch of the underground caverns. There was no refuge, no hiding place, and no sign of life.

Normally, they would have breathed a sigh of relief. Magneto, their most powerful foe and a constant threat to world peace, was dead at last.

But so was Jean Grey.

ORORO WENT quiet for a moment. Kitty sipped her drink and frowned, trying to figure out what to say.

"I'm sorry about your friend."

"Jean was the most…" Ororo paused, wiped a tear from her eye. "The most *alive* person I have ever known. She died once before, and—I believe—literally forced herself back to life. We all believed she would be with us forever."

"She sounds like… like somebody you'd want to know."

"She was the best of us. But she is gone." Ororo turned her

intense gaze on Kitty. "And now we seek new recruits."

"Recruits…" A thrill ran through her, half excitement and half alarm. "You mean new *X-Men?*"

"Students, to begin with. Mutants who seek training, instruction in the use of their abilities. Eventually, perhaps, X-Men as well."

"You… you're Storm, aren't you? And that's Wolverine, with the lousy attitude."

Ororo nodded.

"I don't recognize the big guy," Kitty said.

"He is Colossus." Ororo smiled. "But I think he'd prefer you to call him Peter."

Again, Kitty blushed.

"Peter is young," Storm continued. "He is not accustomed to losing teammates, and has taken Jean's death hard."

Over by the counter, a young clerk was asking Logan about the juice bottle in his hand. As Peter watched, grimacing, a single claw shot out of Logan's hand, making a *snikt* sound, and pierced the plastic bottle. He held the bottle up to his mouth, drinking through the newly created claw-hole.

The clerk backed off, eyes wide.

"But the one I worry about is Logan—Wolverine," Storm said. "At the best of times, his temper threatens to consume him. Now he seems to be inviting violence at every opportunity."

"Hang on a minute." Kitty held up a hand. "Before… you said you were looking for mutants."

"Yes. Like ourselves."

"So you think *I'm* a…?"

"Are you?"

Kitty looked away.

"We have methods of detecting the emergence of mutants, Kitty. A machine called Cerebro, which alerts us when a young person's powers begin to manifest. Your actions recently triggered such an alarm."

Kitty swallowed nervously. She remembered the odd sensation

of falling through wood and plaster, one floor after another, through the walls and ceilings of Deerfield High.

"However," Storm continued, "Cerebro was constructed by our founder, Professor Xavier. He is currently off-world—"

"Off-*world*?"

"It is a long story." Storm smiled. "The point is, only the Professor's mind is capable of linking fully with Cerebro. The rest of us… well, the process can lead to errors." She leaned forward, took Kitty's hand in hers. "So I ask you again. Do you believe you are a mutant?"

Kitty's mind raced. The X-Men were heroes who'd saved the world a dozen times, but people still distrusted them—hated and feared them because they were different. No, not just because they were different. Because they *embraced* that difference.

And why shouldn't they? Mutants could do amazing things. Fly, read minds, lift buildings. If Kitty really was one of them— if her abilities could help people in need, contribute to the advancement of humanity—why on Earth would she want to hide that? To pretend to be less than she was?

Even as she framed the questions, she knew the answers. Because of people like Robin. She and Kitty had been best friends for years. They'd gone to dance classes together, built homebrew computers from kits, stayed up all night gaming more times than Kitty could count. There was no one in the world who knew her better. But it had only taken one display to erase that friendship forever.

"Storm…" Kitty began, not knowing what she was going to say next. She felt a sudden urge to disappear, to run away and forget she'd ever heard the word *mutant*.

The back wall exploded.

CHAPTER FOUR

KITTY LEAPT to her feet, shielding her eyes from a fusillade of glass and metal. Before she knew what was happening, Storm's arm had slammed across her chest, pushing her back from the table.

Three huge men stood in a giant hole that led to the back parking lot. At least, she *assumed* they were men—they might have been robots. Their bodies were entirely covered in thick red metallic armor. Each of them held an identical high-tech weapon, like a cross between a dueling staff and a laser gun.

The coffee-shop patrons took one look at them and fled, almost trampling each other on their way out the front door. The hipster clerk just stared. A china mug slipped from his grip and shattered on the floor.

One of the armored men stepped forward. "Targets acquired," he said in a heavily filtered voice. "We've found the X-Men."

Logan moved toward them. He held up both fists and unsheathed his claws.

"Sure have," he said.

"Kitty," Ororo said, motioning her away. "Leave this to us."

She looked from Storm to the armored men. One of them raised his weapon, aiming it at the table.

"*Go!*" Storm said.

Kitty broke and ran. She skirted a round table, heading for the side of the shop. When she reached the wall, she stopped, turned to look back—

—and gasped.

Peter, the young X-Man, had positioned his body between his teammates and the attackers. As Kitty watched, his entire form swelled, growing even more massive. His skin shimmered and glistened as every inch of it turned to solid, gleaming metal.

Fire erupted from the armored man's staff. Kitty's breath caught in her throat, but the X-Man's steel body blocked the flame, shielding Storm and Wolverine from its searing heat.

They really are mutants, Kitty realized. *They're used to this— using their powers in combat, facing incredibly powerful enemies. Risking their lives.*

They're used to it.

I'm not.

Concentrating, she turned and ran—straight through the side wall. Phasing through solid objects had become easier these past few days. Her head barely throbbed at all. She found herself in a narrow storeroom piled high with T-shirts and canvas bags filled with coffee beans.

I'm not running away, she told herself. *I'm not. I'm just going to get help!*

On impulse, she turned and charged toward the back of the store. She phased through the wall, emerging into the parking lot right next to the gaping hole the attackers had blasted into the building. Pieces of wood and plaster lay strewn across the pavement, littering an unoccupied loading zone. A clash of alarms blared out from the nearby stores.

A strange black vehicle the size of a minibus floated just off the ground a few feet away. It looked like a cross between a hovercraft and a manta ray, and it bore a stylized "H" logo with a pitchfork design. Armed men—more of them—poured out of the vehicle. They wore Kevlar body armor, with eerie blank-faced masks bisected down the middle. They drew hand lasers and ran toward the now-exposed coffee shop.

Before the men could spot her, Kitty ducked back through the wall into the storeroom. From there she could hear the sound of laser blasts and tables crashing in the adjacent room.

What am I doing? she thought. *I'm not an X-Man—but I can't just abandon them, either!*

She crept up to the side wall, allowing her power to build slowly inside her. Then she crouched down and pushed her head through the wall, back into the main seating area of the coffee shop. The first thing she saw was the man with the flamethrower. He'd backed Peter—Colossus—up against the wall, pushing the flaming tip of his weapon closer and closer to Peter's face. The X-Man's steel skin remained untouched, but the expression on his face showed he wasn't invulnerable to pain.

A flash of steel caught Kitty's eye—Wolverine's claws. He was slashing, leaping, running faster than she'd ever seen a person move. Sweeping a single deadly claw through the air, he forced another of the red-armored men to back away.

"Don't know who you fellas are," Wolverine said, "and frankly, I don't care. Right now I just feel like killin' something." He unsheathed the rest of his claws and jabbed forward, straight toward the man's chest. The gleaming metal blades seemed to slow and stop, skittering off some invisible barrier in a shower of sparks.

"Logan!" Storm called. "He is protected by some sort of force field."

The man lunged forward, his staff catching Wolverine hard on the chin. The hairy X-Man grunted and fell to the ground, then scrambled back to his feet.

Across the room, Storm faced off against the third attacker, keeping a table between them. As he took a step forward, she raised a hand; a gale-force blast of wind appeared from nowhere, flipping the table into the air and slamming it into the armored man's chest. He grunted, lurched back, and swept aside the table with a swipe of his gauntlet.

Kitty watched in a state of shock. She'd seen super hero battles on the news, read accounts of these fierce, rapid-fire exchanges of power—but she'd never witnessed one in person. The X-Men really were more than human.

Am I like that? she thought. *Will I have to fight for my life, too?*

Storm turned toward the hole in the wall, her eyes strobing from yellow to white. Outside, the sky turned dark. Lightning flashed.

"Ororo!" Wolverine yelled.

Storm ignored him, reaching out to summon the lightning. A jagged bolt lanced down, arcing through the hole in the wall to engulf her attacker in a burst of light. The armored man stood perfectly still as the electrical corona around him glowed bright, then faded. He shook his head, brushed a hand against his shoulder—then he continued forward, unharmed.

"Listen up," Wolverine said. "Each of these clowns seems equipped to counter our specific powers."

"So I see," Storm said, eyeing the man moving toward her. "Your recommendation?"

Logan leaped up, grabbed hold of a hanging light fixture, and swung toward Storm's opponent.

"Let's switch," he said.

Storm glanced at Colossus, who still stood backed up against the wall by the third armored man. She caught Peter's eye for a moment, then spread her arms and flew—*flew!*—toward him, knocking the armored man off his feet with a savage blast of wind. The man's weapon pinwheeled through the air, trailing a gout of flame. She gestured, creating a sudden, localized rainfall to douse the fire.

Wolverine had landed on the back of Storm's first opponent. The attacker lurched and swung his arms, but Logan held on tight, raising a fist and slashing his claws deep into the man's armor. The man cried out and dropped to the floor.

66   A pool of blood spread slowly from the man's unmoving body. Kitty stared at it in shock. *I'm gonna be sick…*

Across the room, Colossus's steel fist slammed down on the last opponent's head. The armored man's force field stopped the blow short of his helmet, but the impact was heavy enough to knock him out. He struck the floor with a metallic *CLANG.*

"Sweet dreams, *tovarisch*," Peter said.

All at once, it was over. The three attackers lay unmoving in the remains of the coffee shop. Tables were overturned; coffee stained the floor, pooling in dark brown puddles. Storm moved toward Wolverine, who waved her off.

"I'm good," he said. "Barely worked up a sweat."

"I sweated a bit," Colossus said, gesturing toward the smoking flamethrower on the floor. His face was gleaming metal, his eyes blank.

Kitty blinked. None of them had noticed her yet, in her hiding place half-inside the side wall of the coffee shop.

If I show myself again, she thought, *I'll probably wind up going with them. But if I run—if I just bail, right now—*

Suddenly there was pain. Something like a whining noise, just below the audible spectrum, seemed to stab into her skull. Colossus cried out, grabbing his temples. Storm fell back; Wolverine doubled forward. Before Kitty realized what was happening, the three X-Men had fallen to the floor.

"They're unconscious."

Kitty gasped. She knew that voice. She forced herself to focus, to concentrate on staying intangible within the wall. Not daring to move.

A woman strode into the coffee shop, through the hole in the back wall. She was clad entirely in white: thigh-high boots, tight shorts, an ivory corset stitched tight in back, and a swirling cape fastened at the neck with a ruby pendant.

Kitty recognized her right away, despite the bizarre clothing. *It's Ms. Frost!*

The blank-faced men poured into the coffee shop. Two of them took up position at Wolverine's arms and legs, lifting him with some effort. Another pair hoisted Storm off the floor.

"Load them in the speeder," Ms. Frost said. "No, wait—strip them first. Search their uniforms and their persons; remove anything that might be a weapon or signaling device. Take special care with Storm. We know about the lockpicks in her headdress—make sure she hasn't got any other surprises."

"What about the Pryde kid?" one man asked.

Ms. Frost looked around. Kitty ducked behind a bookcase, staying out of sight.

"The X-Men were our primary target," Frost said. "I can find the girl whenever I like. Where's she going to hide? Math class?"

The sound of sirens filled the air. "That's enough," she snapped. "Pawns! Come on. Let's move."

The teams assigned to Logan and Storm hefted their bodies, carrying them toward the waiting hovercraft. Colossus—Peter—had reverted to his human form, but even so, the two men assigned to him struggled to lift his large body. Ms. Frost snapped her fingers, summoning reinforcements.

A blank-masked figure gestured toward one of his heavily armored comrades, lying limp on the floor. "What about the knights?"

Ms. Frost smiled. A terrible, cruel smile.

Yup, Kitty thought. *She'd lock me up in a tower, all right.*

Frost glared at the fallen man. "The *knights,*" she sneered. "They had all the power they needed to defeat the X-Men, yet they performed like amateurs." She lowered her head and furrowed her brow. Kitty felt a slight echo of the pain, the subsonic whine that had rendered the X-Men unconscious.

Ms. Frost, Kitty thought. *She's a mutant too!*

Kitty jumped as a trio of small explosions went off inside the fallen men's armor. Their bodies spasmed, arched, and went still.

Two of the Kevlar-clad men exchanged glances. One of them gasped.

"Compose yourself," Frost snapped. "The Hellfire Club pays good wages, and we expect our money's worth."

The Hellfire Club?

Step by step, keeping pace with Frost, Kitty edged her way along the side wall. *Peter,* she thought. She barely knew him, but the sight of him so helpless made her…

…well, it made her furious.

She phased through the back wall, emerging into the open air and ducking out of sight. The Kevlar-clad men were loading Logan and Storm into the strange manta-shaped hovercraft, with Peter close behind. They still hadn't noticed her.

Ms. Frost paused in the doorway of the hovercraft. She took one last look at the devastated coffee shop and smiled. In her ivory cape and boots, she seemed like an evil fantasy queen, somehow transported into the modern world.

Kitty hesitated. Wondered, again, just what the hell she'd gotten herself into. One last time, she considered bolting and leaving the X-Men to their fate.

Oh, screw it.

As the vehicle rose into the air, she sprinted toward it, willed her body to become intangible, and leaped inside.

CHAPTER FIVE

AT THE northernmost tip of Scotland—above the Highlands, past the Orkneys, beyond even the Shetland archipelago—lies an island that appears on no maps, no satellite surveys. An aircraft flying overhead would see nothing but a barren rock battered by waves, its craggy surface unmarred by the slightest trace of plant or animal life.

But if that aircraft were to swoop down closer, the rock would begin to blur and shimmer. A complex of domes and towers would appear, protected by a highly sophisticated stealth shield. This remote speck of rock is Muir Island, home of the world's foremost Mutant Research Center.

Inside the central dome, Jean Grey hovered in midair, wearing her green-and-gold Phoenix costume. Energy blazed forth from her outstretched arms, spreading high and wide to fill the four-story testing chamber. Collectors and sensors, studding the walls and the domed ceiling, hummed and cycled, monitoring and analyzing the fiery display.

The energies of the Phoenix coursed through her. *It feels… rapturous,* she thought. *Glorious… otherworldly…*

"You're holding back."

Jean looked down. Dr. Moira MacTaggert—lean and fiftyish, founder and owner of the research center—sat at a console, her eyes darting from a large monitor screen to a smaller laptop computer.

"What?" Jean felt a flash of anger. "Moira, I can see those readings from here. They're off the scale."

Moira pulled down a visor to shield her eyes from the blinding energy. "Nevertheless, you're holding back," she repeated.

Jean sighed, looked up toward the rounded ceiling, and closed her eyes. She reached deep inside, willing the power within her— the Phoenix Force—to emerge in all its glory, to spread its wings and take flight. Yet some part of her resisted the effort.

All her power, all the strength of the reborn Phoenix, hadn't been enough to save Scott and the X-Men. And when she'd tried to heal her pain, sought sanctuary on the island of Kirinos, that same power had ruined a promising relationship with a handsome man.

No, she told herself, *that's avoiding the truth.* Yes, her power had failed her at crucial times. Yes, she felt guilt over the loss of her friends, sorrow over the death of Scott Summers, and fear that the power would fail her again, would ebb and die when she needed it most. But her worst fear was that the power *wouldn't* fail. That it would emerge full blown into a force beyond her control, beyond all comprehension.

"Power down, dear," Moira said, rising to her feet.

The hum of the sensors dropped suddenly, cycling down to silence. Jean lowered her arms, allowing the cascading energies to fade, and dropped silently to the floor of the chamber. Moira walked over to join her, tapping on a tablet.

Jean forced a smile. "So I'm a disappointment?"

"More like an enigma." Moira frowned at the screen. "Your cells are in a state of constant mutation."

"Into what?"

"I don't know. But it looks like it's been going on for some time."

"Since the shuttle crash." Jean hissed in a breath. "When I died."

"Possibly." Moira looked up, concerned. "I wish you'd come to me sooner."

"The Professor was monitoring me… until he left."

"Charles!" MacTaggert scoffed. "He was never much of a diagnostician—not the sort you need. Come on, let's try something else." She tapped at the screen three times. Jean turned in surprise as an elaborate chair rose up from the metal floor. Its arms and back were studded with sensors, and it was equipped with wrist, ankle, and throat restraints.

"This is a more tightly calibrated measuring device than the large testing chamber." Moira gestured for Jean to sit. "I've found it particularly useful for gathering data on telepaths and telekinetics."

Jean settled herself into the chair and touched one of the wrist shackles. It felt tough enough to hold a gorilla. She turned to Moira and raised an eyebrow.

"Adamantium alloy," Moira said. "I've, ah, had some fairly dangerous mutants in here."

"Am I a dangerous mutant?"

Moira looked her in the eye.

"You're a very powerful young lass," she replied. "Who may or may not be in full control of that power."

Jean grimaced and nodded. Moira fastened the shackles over her wrists.

"Can we skip the collar, at least?"

"Aye, I think this will suffice." Moira stepped back, nodded, and turned away.

"Wait." Jean felt a stab of panic. "Where are you going?"

"Nothing to worry about, dear." She walked out past the monitoring console to the outer edge of the room, and tapped the screen again.

Jean watched as a clear plastic barrier, reinforced with metal threads, dropped down from the ceiling. It touched the floor with a dull thud, sealing Jean inside the chamber. Her panic grew stronger. She tested the restraints, rattled them slightly. The Phoenix seemed to roil and surge within her, like a caged beast.

"Can you hear me, Jean?" Moira's voice crackled through the chamber's speakers.

"Yes." Jean tried to force herself to be calm. "What do you want me to do?"

"Just be yourself."

"Not sure I know who that is."

Beyond the barrier, a look of worry crossed Moira's face. She flashed a quick smile and turned back to her tablet.

Jean drew in a deep breath, leaned back, and concentrated. She reached inside, struggling to grab hold of the Phoenix Force. As always it was elusive, resistant to her control. A part of her, yet outside of her as well. Ancient, alien, terrifying.

"Don't rush things," Moira said. "We've got time." She paced back and forth. "Why don't you catch me up on things? Tell me about Antarctica."

"Antarctica," Jean echoed. "What do you want to know?"

"Did you actually kill Magneto? The most powerful mutant on Earth?"

That's not an idle question, she realized.

"I—I'm not sure." She leaned back. Felt a rush of unpleasant sensations, dark memories she'd tried hard to forget. "The molten rock... it separated me from Scott and the others. I was alone with him, with the—the man who'd captured and humiliated me, who'd subjected my friends to days of torture.

"He gave me that look," she continued. "The one I'd seen on him a dozen times before. The glare that said, *You're nothing. All of you, humans and mutants alike. I would kill you all to save myself.* I wanted to punch him, break him in half, make him feel the pain I'd felt at his hands.

"And then I heard Scott cry out. I'd never heard a sound like that before, and I couldn't hear him in my mind. But I knew it was him. Magneto... he pulled a length of metallic ore out of the volcano's walls and sort of swatted it at me. As if I was a fly, some sort of insect that had wandered into his house.

"And I felt this whole new level of rage. Not human rage—something else."

74   "The Phoenix," Moira said.

"Yes." Jean squeezed her eyes shut. "I reached out with my mind, with my power—it was like nothing I'd ever felt before. I barely had to form the thought when it seized hold of him, lifted him off the ground. I felt his ribs snap, heard him scream in agony. And I...

"Moira, I *liked* it. I wanted more.

"So I squeezed harder. I-I think I felt his heart burst. I'm not sure. Then the magma... it flowed over us. I felt a searing, scorching heat, so I lashed out, forcing it away. And then, all at once, my power crested and began to fade. I remember thinking, *No! Not now!* But it was no use. I was spent, exhausted, my reserves depleted. I felt myself losing consciousness, watched helplessly while molten fire consumed the rocky cavern."

She opened her eyes. The Phoenix Force had flared up all around her again, forming the familiar shape of a bird of prey. The chair held her tight, tiny circuits humming with activity.

"You're doing great," Moira said. "Keep going. How did you survive?"

"I woke up days later, on the surface. Lying in the snow, my costume in tatters. I don't know whether someone rescued me and left me there, or..."

"No injuries?"

"There wasn't a mark on me."

"Mmmm."

Jean knew what the older woman was thinking. *The Phoenix. It took control, guided me through to the surface, and kept me alive while my body regenerated. All without any conscious thought on my part.*

"Moira," she said. "I can't move."

"Won't be much longer." Moira paused, peered in through the barrier. "What happened after that?"

"There was a U.N. base just a couple miles away. I managed to make it on foot." She shivered at the memory. "The scientists there... they were so kind. They checked all radio reports, air traffic. There was no sign of the X-Men or Magneto, no one flying in or out.

"That's when I knew they were dead.

"My power... it seemed to have retreated, receded deep inside me. I couldn't fly, could barely keep the air warm around me. I had to get out of there, but the thought of returning to the school... to Xavier's... it was too much. I wasn't ready.

"I boarded the first ship leaving Antarctica... it was headed for Italy. But we ran into some mechanical trouble, had to change course. The nearest island was Kirinos, a small Greek port. A coincidence... I remembered Professor Xavier talking about Kirinos, about his visits there. He said he'd spent some of the happiest times of his life on that island. It seemed like fate, so I decided, well, to stop over. Kind of an impulse, but it felt right." She laughed. "Does that sound stupid?"

"You're a powerful telepath. Your 'impulses' might hold hidden depths."

"I... I suppose."

She felt strangely warm. Energy flowed from her body, radiating outward—but the chair seemed to hold it in, to channel it in waves. The air glowed crimson all around. Moira had passed out of sight, beyond the thick plastic barrier, but Jean could still hear her.

"What did you find on Kirinos?" the scientist asked.

"What?" Jean replied. "Nothing... nothing really."

Just a man, she thought, *who made me feel... strange. Like the life I'm living might not be the life I'm supposed to lead.* But she wasn't ready to talk about that yet—and even if she were, Moira wouldn't understand.

"I lost my passport," she continued. "I was going to wait for a replacement, but then I, uh, decided not to bother. I flew out over the ocean until my power faded again, then caught a ride with a passing ship."

"You wee hitchhiker, you."

"Ha! Yeah, I suppose so. Anyway, at that point I figured I'd better get an expert opinion on my, let's say, *erratic* powers. You're the second greatest authority on genetic mutation, so—"

"Jean…"

She looked down, startled. The restraints were *melting*, slipping off of her wrists. Flowing like the magma beneath Magneto's volcano, leaving her gloves and the skin beneath unharmed.

"Enough," Moira said. "Enough! Shut it down, please."

Jean clenched her fists, willing the Phoenix to withdraw. The glow around her faded away, slowly but steadily. As the plastic shield began to rise up toward the ceiling, Moira ducked under it and hurried inside.

"Well," she said, examining a melted wrist shackle. "That's a first, aye?"

Jean shifted back and forth. She felt like a high school student who'd just embarrassed herself in front of the teacher.

"What's the verdict?" she asked.

Moira turned, cocked her head.

"First of all," she said, "I'll thank you to know I'm the *greatest* authority on human mutation. And if that follicly challenged patriarch were t'roll 'is way in here right now, I'd tell him the same thing."

Jean laughed.

"Second…" Moira smiled. "How about some tea?"

JEAN TIPPED her wooden chair back, letting the warm tea slide down her throat. She'd changed into jeans and a loose shirt, using her telekinetic powers to transform the molecules of her costume. The Jean Grey of a year ago could never have performed that feat, but the Phoenix pulled it off with barely a thought.

Moira stood at the counter, pulling a jar of cookies out of an old wooden cabinet. A wood-burning stove burned in the corner, filling the room with heat. Jean cast her eyes across the plain oak table, the simple toaster and wooden cutting board.

"This is very… rustic," she said.

"Not like the rest of the complex, aye?" Moira crossed over

to the table, carrying a tray. "I bought this place from an old… hermit, they used to call 'em. He built a home here with his bare hands. It was beyond repair—I tore most of it down, but I kept this room. Had the center constructed around it."

"It's soothing," Jean said.

"My little retreat from force rays, Juggernauts, and Multiple Men." Moira gestured toward the cookies. "Go ahead."

Jean picked one up, bit into it. It melted on her tongue, sweet and delicious. "Fo what'ff the verdict?" she asked, covering her mouth.

"Jean, is there anything else you can tell me?" Moira leaned across the table. "You say your powers have been coming and going ever since the shuttle crash. Any recent, I dunno, anomalies? Spikes in energy, unusual displays?"

Jean turned away, remembering. *Kirinos,* she thought. Her power had surged, burning bright, and that strange voice— the Phoenix—had spoken through her. *"Mine is the fire that consumes."* Had she really said that? Where had they come from— those ominous words, and the power behind them? She didn't know, but she knew what had triggered them.

Jason Wyngarde. His strange manner, his eerie house, and the rough kiss she could still feel on her lips. Wyngarde was an enigma—he'd barely flinched when she mentioned Magneto, or when her power lit up the sky. If anything, he seemed enticed by her fury, by her tales of tragedy and death. What sort of man was he?

"Jean?" Moira was staring at her.

"Things have been… off," she said. "With Scott."

She paused, startled at herself. She hadn't meant to say that. Hadn't even realized it was true until the words came out of her mouth.

"I love him," she continued. "Loved him, I mean, and I know he loved me. But after the shuttle crash, things were different. *I* was different. I felt myself withdrawing, pulling back from him… from all of them." She felt tears rising to her eyes. "I think he was afraid of me, Moira."

She looked up at the older woman, seeking comfort, but the look in Moira's eyes made her heart sink. Moira turned away, fussing with the teapot.

You're afraid of me, too, Jean realized.

"You've been poking at me for days," Jean said. "You must have *some* answers."

"Dear, I'm just barely figuring out the questions." Moira sighed. "I've compared your readings with the data Charles sent me last year. The wavelengths are different, the power levels are orders of magnitude higher. Whatever happened to you on that shuttle, your psi powers have taken a quantum leap."

"And you're worried I can't handle it," Jean said. "Well, I'm worried, too." She stood up, paced over to the wooden stove. Raised her hands to warm them, and felt an echoing flame inside.

"Maybe I should have stayed dead," she whispered.

"What?"

"Nothing."

She took a moment to compose herself, then turned back to Moira. "I should check in with my parents. I emailed them when I left Antarctica, but they haven't heard from me since." She rummaged in her pockets, then let out an embarrassed laugh. "You know, I haven't even got myself a new phone yet."

Moira reached into a drawer, pulled out a small phone, and tossed it to Jean. "Punch in your number."

Jean tapped at the screen, then frowned. "It says 'no service.'"

"Ah, hang on a tick," Moira said. "This is a rock in the ocean— no cell towers. I've also got security concerns." She crossed to the counter and reached behind the toaster. At the touch of a hidden button, a panel opened on the wall, revealing a touchscreen.

Jean smiled. "So much for rustic."

Moira tapped in a security code. "Try it now. You should have satellite access."

Jean held up the phone—and froze. Text messages filled the screen, buzzing one by one as they popped up.

JEANNIE – YOU ALIVE, DARLIN?

IT'S KURT. TRYING YOU AGAIN.

JUST ARRIVED BACK IN WESTCHESTER.

IF THERE'S ANY CHANCE YOU'RE OUT THERE...

"Oh my god," she breathed.

Moira crossed over, alarmed, and peered over her shoulder. "Oh!" She squeezed Jean's shoulders, smiled briefly, and withdrew.

Jean stood alone for a moment. The phone buzzed again and again, texts scrolling down behind the cold glass. She swiped the messages away, clicked over to the dial pad, and tapped in a number she knew better than her own. Then, trembling, she slumped against the counter and waited for the answering click.

"Scott?" she whispered.

CHAPTER SIX

"LANDSCAPERS ARE clearing the grounds now," Nightcrawler said. "Skyship's ready to go, the Blackbird is being serviced. The dorm rooms are a little dusty… there's evidence of a rodent infestation upstairs."

"Of mice and mutants," Cyclops mused, striding with purpose down the hallway. He was dressed in khakis and a sports jacket. "Let's get the exterminators in first, then the cleaning service."

"Right." Nightcrawler wore his X-Men uniform; he kept pace with Cyclops, capering and leaping along the dusty halls of the mansion. "Oh, and a pipe burst in the library during our time away. It's been repaired, but we're going to have to replace some of the multicultural studies books."

"They could probably use some updating anyway."

Nightcrawler continued his litany of tasks that needed to be done. Security systems, fiber-optic upgrades, new computers for the science labs. A set of high-capacity washing machines to handle an increased number of students.

Cyclops barely heard a word. One phrase, two simple words, kept echoing in his mind: *She's alive.*

"Don't ask about the Danger Room," Nightcrawler said.

"I wasn't asking."

"Good." Nightcrawler sighed. "I'm working on it." He leapt forward, planted both feet on the wall, and stuck his body out horizontally to block Cyclops's path. Then he grinned. "Have you spoken with her?"

Cyclops smiled.

"Few minutes ago," he replied. "Her plane just arrived at the airport… she's planning to fly the rest of the way under her own power."

"It's a miracle," Nightcrawler murmured. "Jean Grey, alive. Again."

"She's hard to kill, all right."

Three workmen squeezed past them, carrying a pile of lumber. "Leave it by the elevators," Nightcrawler said. "*Danke*." Then he turned somber. "Scott, I…"

Cyclops held up a hand, cutting him off. He'd never been comfortable with displays of emotion, and he wasn't ready to let his feelings out yet.

She's alive.

"Is the website ready?" he asked. "We'll have to be ready to handle a flood of applications." He paused, then added, "I hope."

"Soon." Nightcrawler dropped to the floor, shook his head. "There is so much to do. Reopening the school is one thing… expanding it like this is a major initiative."

"Blame Storm. She argued—persuasively—that despite our losses, we still have a duty to help as many young mutants as we can. To not just carry on the Professor's dream, but to build on it."

Nightcrawler cocked his head. "I had a feeling she also wanted to distract you from your loss."

"That's possible." Hesitantly, Cyclops gave another smile. "Not an issue now, I guess."

"Jean's return is indeed the best possible news." Nightcrawler reached out a hand to touch his friend's shoulder. "Perhaps this will be a new beginning for all of us."

Cyclops frowned. A strange sense of unease came over him—he couldn't identify the source. "Any word from Storm?" he asked. "She sounded pretty optimistic about signing up our first new student."

"Still nothing. She is overdue to check in." Nightcrawler pulled out his phone, frowned at it. "I will give her a call. As soon as I…" He paused, shivered dramatically. "…inspect the Danger Room."

Cyclops let out a small laugh.

"Find me when Jean arrives," Nightcrawler said. He whirled around and vanished in a puff of sulfuric smoke.

Then Cyclops was alone. Alone in a hallway that smelled of fresh wood, disinfectant, and brand-new electronics. All mixed with just a hint of crisp fall air… and brimstone.

He continued down the hall, through the foyer, and into the sitting room with its leather chairs and fireplace. He'd spent more than half his life in this house, learning to control his deadly abilities. It was a school and a training center, but it was also a refuge. A home.

This is where I met Jean.

When he'd heard her voice on the phone yesterday—when he'd learned she was alive—he thought his heart would burst. All his life, Scott Summers had trained himself to hold things inside. His power, his emotions. Jean was the only person he'd ever opened up to, the one who made him laugh and cry without reserve. His partner, both in life and in the X-Men.

When she'd died fighting Magneto, his emotions had shut down. He couldn't allow himself to feel anything at all. He'd believed, deep inside, that if he allowed himself to grieve—to feel that loss in his heart—he would crumble.

Now she was back. In a short time, they'd be reunited. What had Nightcrawler called it? *A new beginning.*

Scott Summers—Cyclops—burst into tears. He slumped against a door and sank to the floor, great sobs wracking his body. He held a hand up to his eyes, pressing his ruby-quartz sunglasses firmly into place. Even now, overcome with emotion, he could never forget the damage his optic beams could do.

He was about to see Jean again. That knowledge made his stomach jump… in anticipation, yes. But also…

She's been different. Ever since the shuttle crash, Jean had been distant. Sometimes she almost seemed like a higher life-form, as different from him as—

He stopped dead, struck by a disturbing thought.

As a mutant is from a normal person.

He shook his head. It didn't matter. None of it mattered. As long as Jean was back, as long as they were together, the rest would work itself out.

She's alive.

He rose to his feet, dusting off his jacket. Glanced at the door before him, ran his fingers over the nameplate.

PROFESSOR C. XAVIER

For just a moment, he wondered what lay ahead. Then he crossed to the front door, walked out onto the lawn, and began watching the skies.

JEAN GREY soared above the Westchester countryside, scarlet hair trailing behind her like a comet's tail. She projected a mental screen all around, shielding herself from casual observation. All an observer on the ground would see was a shooting star, making a rare but innocuous appearance during the day.

She breathed in the cool air, relieved to be out in the open after the long transatlantic flight. Strange sensations warred within her: guilt, whispering voices, and a nameless dread that seemed to grow with each mile she covered.

The crescent-shaped town of Mount Kisco gave way to a thick blanket of trees. Some were still green, but most had turned to a panoply of fall colors: auburn, russet, and yellow. A few were just gray racks, their bare branches already devoid of leaves.

In a small clearing, a few miles ahead, lay the secluded Xavier Institute. As Jean caught sight of the twin spires that flanked the main entrance, her heart jumped. She felt a surge of nausea, an odd sense of being watched—

—and then she was somewhere else.

BENEATH HER, a powerful black stallion pumped its legs, galloping across the countryside. Four smaller horses, ranging in color from chestnut to roan to dark gray, kept pace, their hooves shaking the Westchester countryside. Up ahead, a pack of savage dogs scurried and barked, leading the pack toward some unseen prey.

She studied the riders. They wore breeches, boots, and top hats, sharp riding crops held firmly in their hands. Jean herself wore tight slacks with a crisp white shirt beneath a long, cinched jacket. Everything was perfectly tailored, cut to fit her and her alone.

I am Lady Jean Grey, she thought. *This is my manor, and these men are my guests.*

She had no time to probe the source of these thoughts. A sixth powerful horse pulled up beside her, whinnying as it drew near. She turned to look, and a warm feeling washed over her.

Astride the horse, Jason Wyngarde favored her with a mischievous grin. This wasn't the Wyngarde she'd met on Kirinos—at least, she didn't think it was. This man, with his top hat, gloved hands, and menacing leer, resembled the portrait she'd seen in his house.

All that passed through her mind in an instant, washed away by a single thought. *My love.* That was who he was, what he meant to her. Sir Jason Wyngarde, consort and true love of Lady Jean Grey. The musk of his cologne filled the air, making her blood race with excitement.

The horse beneath her let out a sharp whinny. Jean looked

ahead to see the dogs clustered on the ground, surrounding some unseen creature.

"Whoa, Satan," she called, jerking sharply on the reins. "Whoa!"

Wyngarde swung his mount around, dismounting in a single graceful motion even before the horse came to a stop.

"I'll deal with the hounds, milady," he said, flashing another grin. He waded into the pack, lashing his riding crop to one side, then the other. "Back, you curs," he said. "Back, I say!"

The dogs whimpered and withdrew.

By the time Jean maneuvered her own mount to a complete stop, Jason stood in the thick grass, feet planted firmly on the ground. His back was to her, but she could see the jagged deer's antler grasped in his hand. It was enormous, longer than Wyngarde's own powerful arm.

"We're fortunate, milady," he said. "The beast still lives."

She smiled. The savage force, the power that had been growing within her these past months, seemed to swell with pride.

"As the first to run it to ground," he continued, "to you falls the honor of administering the *coup de grâce*."

Jean tossed her hair back, swung a leg over, and dropped to the ground. The guests maneuvered their horses around in a semicircle, eyeing their hosts. They seemed eager, hungry for the kill.

Wyngarde held out a long, curved knife. She reached out and grasped the hilt, feeling an odd thrill as her fingers closed around the "H" symbol and pitchfork design carved into the wood.

"The finest sport the Hellfire Club has ever enjoyed, milady," Wyngarde said. "When you selected this particular prey…"

Jean's pulse raced. She raised the knife, feeling a song rise within her.

"…it was a master stroke."

She looked down and gasped.

On the ground lay not a deer, but a man. A hairy man, completely naked, with sharp, curved antlers fixed to his head with tight leather straps. His legs bore the bloody marks of a dozen dog bites; his eyes were glazed, half-closed. His faint moans barely sounded human at all.

Jean stood still for a moment, the knife held high in her hand. Past and future collided in her mind, twin realities warring for dominance. One was dark and savage, a world where Jean Grey, Lady of Wyngarde Manor, hunted human prey for sport. The other…

"Milady?" Wyngarde said.

The world seemed to grow dim. She swooned, her feet falling out from under her. All her power, her fury, seemed to wash away. She struck the ground and rolled onto her back, struggling to stay conscious.

"*Jean!*"

She looked up. Through a blurry haze, Wyngarde stared down at her, his dark eyes narrowed in concern.

"J-Jason?"

She squeezed her eyes shut.

When she looked up again Scott's face was there, his eyes concealed, as always, behind those ruby sunglasses.

"What?" he asked.

She sat up, shaking her head. The familiar grounds of the Xavier Institute surrounded her. In the distance a grounds crew snipped and trimmed hedges; a few women were planting trees over by the entrance.

"Scott," she said. "Oh, Scott."

"You were coming in for a landing. And then you just seemed to… fall out of the sky…"

She looked down. The riding uniform was gone, along with the horses, the dogs, and the… the prey. She was back in her Phoenix uniform, gold boots and gloves over a lime-green bodysuit. Scott knelt before her, his trim muscular arms on her shoulders, his brow furrowed with worry.

He was the most beautiful thing she'd ever seen.

She lunged forward—and then they were together, holding each other close, burying their faces in each other's hair. He smelled warm, familiar, strong. "Never," she gasped, tears running down her cheeks. "Never lose you. Never again."

"Jean." His voice was strangled, hoarse. He held her tight, running his hands through her long red hair. "Oh, Jean."

There was a sudden whiff of brimstone and a distinctive *BAMF* sound. Jean pulled back and turned to see Nightcrawler standing on the lawn, watching them.

"Elf!" she cried.

But one look at Nightcrawler's expression made her scramble to her feet. Scott was already standing.

"It is *very* good to see you, Jean," Nightcrawler said. "But I'm afraid we have a situation."

CHAPTER SEVEN

SHE FELT as if she'd been running forever.

Kitty Pryde sprinted down the long Chicago street. At this hour, South Loop was utterly deserted. Rows of four- and five-story buildings lined the wide avenue, but the few retail establishments at street level were shuttered for the night.

Pausing in the entrance to a long-abandoned hotel, she doubled over to catch her breath. Had she really given her pursuers the slip? Four times since midnight she'd thought she'd lost them. Each time, they'd found her again.

Still. Maybe now—

A pair of blinding headlights lit up the night. She looked up, exhaustion warring with her survival instinct.

No, she thought. *No, not again!*

The limousine shot down the street, straight toward her. It was turbocharged, faster than a vehicle of its size had any right to be. On its hood, between those arc-bright headlights, was emblazoned the stylized "H" and pitchfork.

Got to keep moving!

She turned toward the hotel, concentrated, and phased

through the brick wall. Three minutes and four dusty, roach-filled rooms later, she emerged in the wide alley behind the building. She leaned against the brick wall, breathing hard.

A rat paused in the act of rummaging through an overturned trash can, and whirled to face her. Then it twitched its nose and returned to its task.

That's it—I'm spent. Whoever these guys are... whatever their grudge is with mutants... they can have me.

The limo lurched into the alley with a screech. Its headlights swept across her.

On second thought, no. No they can't!

She ran out into the alley—and tripped. As she started to fall, the limo driver slammed on his brakes. The vehicle swerved—just a moment too late. Its side bumper clipped Kitty's arm, sending her sprawling to the pavement against the wall of the opposite building.

She cried out in pain, then lay still for a moment, her eyes squeezed shut. She touched her arm.

Is it broken?

The car door opened. A man stepped out, heavy boots clomping on the street. He wore Kevlar armor and a blank-faced mask. He took several heavy steps toward Kitty. Then he stopped and looked up, past Kitty, his eyes growing wide.

"What the hell is that?" he asked.

Kitty whirled around—just as the far end of the alley exploded in a burst of flame, rising up to form the shape of some inhuman, mythical bird of prey.

JEAN GREY stood in the mouth of the alley, feeling the power build. The man in the blank-faced mask froze. The teenage girl scurried away, shrinking back against the building wall, her eyes darting from one side to the other.

The masked man scrambled back inside his vehicle and

slammed the door. His partner gunned the engine and the limo shot forward, straight toward Jean.

She smiled and spread her arms.

The Phoenix Force shot forth, striking the car head-on. The hood melted instantly; the engine block exploded. Tires flew off in both directions as the front end of the limo crunched into the pavement, throwing up sparks and thrusting its occupants forward into the windshield.

One of the tires rolled to the side of the alley, nearly striking the terrified girl. In a burst of sulfur, Nightcrawler appeared out of thin air and yanked her out of the way.

"*Guten Abend,*" he said. "Fräulein Pryde, I presume?"

He smiled, displaying pointed teeth. The girl flinched away. He gave her an apologetic look and scooped her up in his arms. As she struggled in his grip, he began climbing the wall, away from the battle scene.

"Do not be frightened, *Liebchen,*" he said. "I'm one of the good guys—we spoke on the phone! Let's be off, shall we?"

Jean stepped forward, examining the wreck of the limousine. Light radiated from her Phoenix form, illuminating the predawn alley in shades of yellow and crimson. One of the masked men writhed and groaned, entangled in the metal remains of the car. The other was trapped, unmoving, beneath the steering wheel.

Jean reached out telepathically and touched his mind. He was alive. Barely.

"Jean!" Cyclops ran up behind her, carrying a bulky handheld machine—the portable Cerebro device they'd used to track the novice mutant. "Are you all right?"

"Never better."

"What have you done? I asked you to stop that car, not reduce it to junk."

A flash of anger within her. A hint of old resentments, of unfinished business.

"You're not a telepath, Scott. You didn't feel the girl's stark terror, or the sadism of the killers chasing her." She gestured at the smoking wreckage. "They got no more than they deserved."

Scott frowned. He shifted his feet and hefted the mini-Cerebro, moved its strap from one shoulder to the other.

He's still afraid of me, Jean realized. *Nothing's changed.*

"Cyclops!"

They looked up. Four stories above, Nightcrawler leaned over the edge of the roof, waving his arms.

"Get up here!" he cried. "Fast!"

Before Scott could reply, Jean reached out and enveloped him in a field of telekinetic force. With barely a thought, she levitated the two of them up through the air, bringing them down softly on the roof. To their surprise, Nightcrawler stood alone.

"Where's the girl?" Cyclops asked.

"Good question," Nightcrawler replied. "She broke away from me when we landed—and dove *through the roof!*"

"Well, she's definitely our mutant." Cyclops frowned, began pressing icons on the machine's screen. "I think I can track her with—"

"I've got this," Jean said.

She spread her arms, circling them through the air in a dancer's motion. When her hands returned to her sides, the Phoenix costume was gone. She wore a T-shirt and casual blazer above a pair of skinny jeans.

Reaching out with her mind, she swung open a trapdoor in the roof and strode toward it, ignoring Cyclops and Nightcrawler. She could feel their doubt, their worry, clouding the air like static. It was unfocused, scattered. Some of it was concern for Kitty Pryde's safety—but they were also worried about her. She swept their thoughts away, forced herself to concentrate.

An attic staircase led down to a disused warehouse space piled high with boxes. Again she allowed her thoughts to fan out, searching for the only other mind in the room.

A mind filled with terror.

"Hey," Jean said.

She gestured at a half-ton box, sliding it aside with a casual display of telekinesis. Kitty Pryde sat revealed, backed up against a corner of the room. She glanced at Jean, then dropped to her knees and started to phase through the wall.

"Wait! Easy, there. Easy."

The girl paused, her hand still inside the wall. Turned wide eyes toward Jean.

"You're among friends, Kitty. I'm Jean Grey—one of the X-Men."

"X-Men?" Kitty echoed.

She's exhausted, Jean realized. "Our friends, Storm and Logan—they came to see you. Remember?"

The girl pulled her hand out of the wall.

"Jean Grey," she repeated. "Storm… she said you were dead."

"Yeah. I got better." Jean reached out, and the Phoenix aura rose up from her hand. "There's nothing to be afraid of. I promise."

Again, Kitty shrank back.

I could make her understand, Jean thought. *I could reach out and fill her mind with images, impressions. Hell, I could change her mind, if I wanted to. But she's not an enemy. She's just a terrified young… mutant.*

"Look," Jean said. "I know how frightening all this can be. I was only fourteen when my power first manifested… fifteen when I came to the institute." She paused, smiling. "They called me Marvel Girl, then. You believe that? Marvel Girl."

A small laugh escaped Kitty's lips.

"There are people who want to hurt us," Jean continued. "They want to use us as weapons, or just wipe us from the face of the Earth. That's a lot to deal with when you're trying to keep from reading the mind of the kid next to you in AP Bio."

Kitty nodded. "Or falling through the wall."

"Or, yeah, the wall thing." Jean smiled. "Point is, you don't have to let it destroy you. You can learn to control your powers, face the world on your own terms. But you can't do it alone."

She took a step forward. This time, the girl didn't flinch.

"Let us help you," Jean said. "Let *me* help you—"

Before the words were out, Kitty rushed to her. The girl wrapped dirty arms around Jean and started to sob, great wracking breaths forced from her small body. Jean dropped to her knees on the warehouse floor and held Kitty tight.

By the time Cyclops and Nightcrawler found them, Kitty was fast asleep. Jean cradled the girl's head, feeling more human than she had for a long, long time.

"SO WE'RE chilling with our frappuccinos when these guys in armor *just break down the wall!* And your friends, Storm and Peter and that hairy dude with the claws, they all throw down, but the armored guys, they've got flamethrowers, you know? Like in that *Call of Duty* game my dad likes."

"Easy, child," Nightcrawler said, moving toward her. "Slow down."

Kitty scurried away from him, planted herself at a console across from the pilot's seat. Her jeans were torn, her arm clotted with blood.

Can't blame her for being anxious, Jean thought. *It took us all a little time to get used to Kurt's demonic appearance.*

They sat in the large command area of the X-Men's skyship, hovering just off the shore of Lake Michigan. Stealth screens protected the ship from prying eyes. Jean didn't trust that tech, so she'd blanketed the area with a psi-probe as an extra precaution. So far, no swimmers or boats had triggered her alarms.

Cyclops walked out of the back area, carrying a first-aid kit. "Kitty, let me have a look at that arm." The girl stuck out her arm and resumed speaking.

"Storm and Peter and Hairy Guy, they mopped the place up with the armored goons, but then that lady came in—the one I told you about before, the one that came to my school and tried to recruit me at my house? She looked… well, she looked different, that's for sure. Major wardrobe change… less preppy, more burlesque."

"Emma Frost," Jean murmured.

"She's supposed to run this school in Massachusetts," Kitty continued. "Like yours, I guess. Well, more like the Dr. Evil version of yours. Anyway, she just kind of... blinked, I guess... and your friends all grabbed their heads like they'd been tasered. I heard it, too, like a dentist's drill in my head, but not like they did. She took 'em out without firing a shot."

Jean looked over at Cyclops. He paused in the act of unspooling a bandage, nodding as their eyes met.

"A telepath," he said.

She nodded. "Powerful one."

"Then a bunch of other guys carried 'em off, into the sci-fi hovercraft. She called 'em pawns—they wore the other kind of armor." Kitty gestured. "That kind."

Jean glanced toward the back of the command room. The two attackers from the alley sat propped up against a storage locker, bound at the wrists and ankles.

"I didn't know what to do, so I tagged along for the ride. Ms. Frost, she took Peter and them to this big industrial park just outside the city. Locked 'em up in cages, said something about experimenting on them, one by one. I freaked out, lost it a little I guess, and Ms. Frost spotted me. I think she actually *heard* the panic in my head.

"I ran, hid inside another one of their hoverthingies while it was taking off. When we got to the city limits, I bolted. I've been running ever since."

Cyclops sealed a large bandage around Kitty's thin arm. She winced.

"You're mostly just scraped up," he said, "but some of these cuts are pretty deep. Keep this on for a day or two, you should be okay."

He stood up, walked over to Jean, and smiled. She'd missed that smile, more than she knew. She reached up and touched his glove with her own.

"I'm through tangling with shadows," he said.

Jean nodded and rose to her feet. Kitty and Nightcrawler

watched, curious, as the two of them crossed to the back of the room. They stood above the prisoners for a moment, studying them. What had Kitty called them?

Pawns.

Cyclops gestured at one of the men. "Can you mind-scan him?" The pawn still wore that blank, bisected mask—but Jean could feel the fear radiating from him.

"As good as done."

She knelt down and reached for the man's head. He tried to wriggle away, but his wrists and ankles were bound. The Phoenix fire rose up, forming a faint halo this time. Jean touched the man's head, allowing her power to reach out. All at once, she was inside the mind of—

—LAST NAME *Quinones—first name Juan to one side of the family, Johnny to the other. Mother from Texas, father from Puerto Rico. Birth certificate? Don't know—nobody knows—*

Rough childhood in Chicago—runt of the family—four older brothers—Johnny/Juan a punching bag—prove myself make 'em proud make 'em pay. Running numbers good money till it's not—damned internet—poor hungry need cash—Mom's damn oxy problem not helping—

Filipe says Frost Enterprises hiring. Stupid mask heavy armor but pay's good pay's real pay's fast. The hell is this place anyway? Call us pawns—some knights, bishops. Rich people, expensive suits. Lady in charge—White Queen—don't ask about her. Last guy did is drooling in a straightjacket. Don't—

Somebody else, too. Even worse. Don't sneak up on him, he don't like that. Looks different, they say, at night or when he's angry. Sometimes smooth and suave, sometimes dirty like a scarecrow. The Mastermind, he calls himself. Master Master MASTERMIND—

THE MAN bucked, his body flopping like a fish. Jean held onto his head, gritted her teeth, and probed deeper. *Mastermind,* she thought. Whoever that was, the name was enough to terrify this pawn.

Frost Enterprises, she thought. *Tell me more.*

Outside city. Map, location, fences all around. Guards at every station—

She concentrated, reading the floor plan in his mind. The guard schedule, the nature and extent of its weaponry and defenses. He didn't know everything…

Who are they? She pushed harder. *Who's behind all this?*

Inner… Inner Circle—

She struck a wall. Jean blinked, surprised. This man had no psychic powers, no innate defenses—yet her probing had triggered some sort of barrier, forcing her back. Oddly, she found herself smiling.

That might have stopped Marvel Girl, she thought. *But not the Phoenix.*

Who? She pressed forward, her power an angry song within her. *Who do you work for?*

The man stiffened, cried out. The wall within him began to buckle.

The—

The Phoenix flared bright, forcing itself inside his mind. It was fierce, terrible. Unstoppable.

The Hellfire Club—

○─────────○

"JEAN!"

Cyclops's hands on her shoulders pulled her back to reality. She loosed her grip on the masked man's head, barely noticing as he slumped to the floor.

Hellfire Club, she thought.

Nightcrawler appeared in a puff of smoke, startling her. The blue-furred mutant pulled off the man's mask, began examining him. His eyes were blank, staring.

"What did you do to him?" Cyclops asked.

Anger flared in her. *Again? Again you question me?*

"I need a moment," she said.

She walked away, toward the pilot's seat. There wasn't space for privacy in the command room, but she had to get a bit of distance. Not just to calm her thoughts, but to process what she'd learned.

The Hellfire Club. She'd heard that phrase before, in the vision she'd experienced just before her arrival at the mansion. Things had happened so quickly since then—a young mutant in trouble, teammates captured, the battle with the armored men. She'd had no time to reflect on the nature of the time slips, no time to process what had been happening to her. The sinister room in Jason Wyngarde's house on Kirinos, the horrific hunt—what did it all mean?

Wyngarde. He was the one who'd mentioned the club, referred to himself as a member. Was it some sort of secret society? Had an ancestor of his belonged to it, decades or centuries ago?

"Jean?"

Cyclops was staring at her again. Not with alarm, but with concern—the concern of a man in love. That look, the expression on his face, made her heart ache.

I've got to tell him, she thought. *All of it, everything that's happening to me. I'll explain that some unknown force—maybe a new manifestation of my mutant power—has been catapulting me back through time. He'll be alarmed, but he'll understand. Together, we can face anything.*

Then she remembered the tingle up her spine when she'd touched the black corset. The thrilling scent of Wyngarde's cologne. The pumping of her blood as she rode to the hounds, knife raised to end the life of a helpless man.

How do I explain all that?

"This man is alive," Nightcrawler said, climbing to his feet, "but he appears to be in some sort of coma."

"It wasn't me," Jean said.

They all turned toward her.

"All I did was trip some sort of… psychic switch in his brain," she explained. "Somebody else must have planted it there. To keep out nosy telepaths."

"Somebody else?" Kitty let out a laugh. "Somebody with a platinum dye job, I bet."

Jean nodded. "The White Queen."

Kitty blinked. "White *what* now?"

"It doesn't matter." Jean straightened herself. "I know where Logan and the others are being held, and I know how to get in."

Scott was staring at her. In his eyes, she saw a terrible flash of doubt. He turned away quickly, but the damage was done. For the first time, she wondered: *Does he actually think I'm lying to him?*

Cyclops crossed over to the pilot's console, avoiding her gaze. "Fire up the engines, Kurt," he said. "Let's go."

CHAPTER EIGHT

FROST ENTERPRISES occupied seven secluded acres to the southwest of Chicago. Groves of thick fir trees surrounded it on all sides, shrouding the complex in darkness.

The limo glided through the night air, decelerating to an almost silent halt as it reached the guard's station. The car's paint job was spotless, its surface as clean and unmarred as if it had just been thoroughly scrubbed. The driver lowered the tinted window and stuck his head out. He wore a pawn's mask and Kevlar armor.

"Juan Quinones," he said, handing over an ID card. "Reporting in."

The guard swiped the card, then smirked at the driver.

"Juan?"

The driver stared at him.

"C'mon, Johnny." The guard waved the card in the air. "Since when do you go by 'Juan,' man?"

The driver shrugged. "Just trying it out."

The guard swept his eyes across the front cabin. In the passenger seat, a second pawn sat huddled under a blanket. Only a masked face was visible.

"What happened to you, Rick?" the guard asked.

"Tangled with the muties," the driver replied. "He needs a little patching up."

The passenger waved a hand, feebly.

The guard gestured toward the back seat, which was hidden from view behind tinted windows. "You bag 'em?"

"Came up empty."

The guard whistled. "Queen's not gonna be pleased."

"Tell me about it." The driver sighed. "Time to take our medicine."

"*Vaya con Dios... Juan.*" The guard reached into his booth, triggered the gate mechanism. "You're gonna need it."

Inside the gate, a narrow paved road wound around the complex. Warehouses and laboratories rose up at uneven intervals, shielded from one another by metal fences and copses of trees. The limo cruised toward an employee parking lot, moving at a steady, unhurried pace.

Cyclops parked the car. He whipped off his pawn mask and his ruby-quartz glasses, slapping his visor into place before his deadly eye-beams could blast forth. The passenger shrugged off the blanket and tore off her own mask.

"Slick job, *Juan*," Kitty Pryde said.

Cyclops raised an eyebrow. "This is your audition for the X-Men? Sassing the leader?"

She shrugged, smirking. Cyclops toggled the privacy barrier down and turned toward the back seat.

"Kurt, you ready?"

Nightcrawler stuck his head through the barrier window. He gave an exaggerated thumbs-up sign.

"Good—you're with me. Kitty, you've been here before, you said you're good with computers... scout around, see if you can hack into the system, but *do not engage these people.* They're armed and extremely dangerous. Got that?" He paused, then added, "If you find the others, free Wolverine first. Then stand back."

Kitty nodded, eyes wide. She gave a little salute, melted

though the car door, and was gone.

"That one," Nightcrawler said, "is quite something."

Cyclops nodded. "She might be just what we need. A fresh start." He clicked open the doors, and they stepped outside into the cold air. A two-story laboratory building stood nearby, its entrance guarded by three men in pawn uniforms. They didn't even glance over at the car. The parking lot was dark, gloomy enough to conceal two costumed figures from view.

"Something feels different," Nightcrawler said, keeping his voice low. "About this mission, I mean."

Cyclops shrugged. "It's Jean's plan."

"Maybe that's it."

"Speaking of which…"

He gestured up at the top of a line of trees. A light was rising there—a distant glow. The pawns noticed it, too. They moved away from the building, pointing upward and talking in low voices.

Nightcrawler grinned. "Follow my lead." He vanished in a puff of smoke, reappearing a few meters closer to the building.

Cyclops took off at a run, ducking low, keeping his eyes on the treeline. High above, the distinctive flame trail of the Phoenix resolved into view, blazing across the sky. The guards ran toward it, barking into their shoulder radios.

Cyclops glanced back as he reached the door. The guards were clustered out in the parking lot, visible in the glow of a light pole, staring upward. Jean was too high, moving too fast, for them to make out her human form within the flame.

Nightcrawler teleported in, startling Cyclops. "You have the keycard?" he asked. Cyclops nodded, pulling out Johnny Quinones's card and running it across the security pad. With a click, the door slid open.

The corridor inside was all metal, lined with heavy doors and clouded windows. They'd pieced together a rough layout of the complex from Kitty's description and Jean's mind-scan of the pawn. If the information was accurate, this building held the testing lab where the other X-Men were imprisoned.

"We appear to be lucky so far," Nightcrawler said, indicating the empty hallway. In the next instant they heard footsteps coming from around the corner, several yards ahead.

"Why did you have to say that?" Cyclops reached for his visor.

"Hold on a moment, *mein Freund*." Nightcrawler touched his arm. "There's something I've been wanting to try."

Cyclops stepped back, frowning. A pawn strode into view, his weapon raised. A second guard joined him, then a third.

"Kurt?" Cyclops said.

The blue-furred mutant vanished, reappearing in midair beside the first pawn. He punched the man in the face and teleported again, reappearing behind the second pawn. He brought both fists down on the man's neck and vanished, just as the third pawn was turning.

He appeared again, slightly higher this time. "Boo," Nightcrawler said, slamming his fist into the man's masked face. The three guards dropped to the floor simultaneously. Another *BAMF* and Nightcrawler reappeared back where he'd started—at Cyclops's side.

He hadn't touched the floor once.

"Very impressive," Cyclops said.

"Thank you, sir!" Nightcrawler gave a theatrical bow.

Scott.

Cyclops jumped, looked around. The voice had been in his mind.

Jean?

No. This was someone else.

Scott Summers? the voice said.

"Kurt, we've been spotted." He whirled toward Nightcrawler. "Go. Find Storm and the others!"

Nightcrawler hesitated. "But—"

"They've got a telepath—she's inside my head. I've been compromised; you need to go on alone. That's an order."

Nightcrawler nodded. "Be careful." Then once again, he vanished.

Cyclops shook his head, tried to clear it. When he looked up,

past the bodies of the fallen guards, he knew what he would see.

"Emma Frost, I presume."

She stood alone, an icy vision in high boots, a tight corset, and a dramatic white cape. Her sharp eyes showed no fear, no hesitation at facing off against one of the most powerful X-Men. Again, her voice sounded in his head.

A pleasure.

He felt tendrils of thought, electrical impulses probing, reaching into his brain.

You've suffered a loss, she observed. *I learned that much from your friends. But your psychic structure… it doesn't match that of a man in mourning.*

Cyclops stepped back, closing his mind as best he could. Forced himself to think of trivial things—celebrity gossip, traffic reports in Westchester, the topiary around the mansion.

Chilly outside. Do I need a haircut?

"Oh!" Emma said aloud. "You've been taught defenses. By someone close to you, perhaps?"

"What's your game?" he asked. "Why are you kidnapping mutants?"

"That?" She made a dismissive gesture in the air. "That was Shaw's idea. You'll meet him soon enough."

He stepped forward, touching the control stud on the side of his visor. She didn't move.

"Do I have to go through you?" he asked.

"That's one option." She smirked, then looked strangely thoughtful. "Yet I think the two of us have a lot in common."

He felt a burst of anger. Behind his visor, his eyes flashed red.

"Now I'm sure of it," she murmured. "Summers, we're both in the business of training mutants to use their gifts. My school is just a bit… stricter than yours."

He shook his head, tried to clear it. She'd withdrawn her probes, respecting his privacy… for some unknown reason. Yet the sight of her, the sound of her words, touched something inside him. Something he couldn't identify.

"Ms. Frost… Emma," he said. "What do you *want*?"

"You know, no one ever asks me that." She gave a little laugh. "I think of myself as a fourth-wave feminist. I seek to advance my status within a very stuffy, male-dominated—but powerful—organization."

"The Hellfire Club."

"Yes!" she said. "And it's not just about me. I'm a sort of warrior, fighting in the cause of all women. That's why I sought to recruit your little Kitten. Remember her? Frizzy-haired nerd with the annoying habit of walking through walls?"

"What have you done with them?" he demanded. "Storm and the others?"

"I've been… tapping their minds. Collecting what they know, gaining valuable bits of, shall we say, intel. I've learned a lot about your school, your team. A lot about you, too."

"Are they alive?"

"I play a rough game, Scott, but they'll recover. So far." She took a step forward. "I have something else in mind for us, though."

He felt rooted to the floor, unable to move. He could smell her perfume now—a sharp, intoxicating scent.

"I'm not attacking you, Scott Summers." She reached out and touched his chest. "I'm giving you a chance. Shaw is… well, our relationship is complicated. You know how that goes."

I do, he realized.

"The point is…" She smiled. "I might prefer a different partner. Someone less steeped in the stifling traditions of the club, less rooted in the past. Someone more my equal." She raised her head toward his, touched his chin. "Imagine," she breathed, "your X-Men, soldiers in the most exciting game of all. A game with rules, rewards… punishments…"

Her lips were inches away now.

"…and you, their White King."

Her words were absurd, insane. And yet, there was something about this woman… He found himself drawn closer, mesmerized on a level he could barely understand.

Jean, he told himself. *Think of Jean! She's just come back from the dead, for the second time. You can't betray her now, can't be taken*

in by some telepathic trickery—

Emma pulled away. She turned, raising an eyebrow.

A deep-red glow appeared from a branching hallway, expanding to fill the corridor. As Cyclops watched, the light resolved into the fiery form of a bird of prey, its flaming head whipping from side to side in silent fury. At the creature's heart stood Jean Grey. Her eyes flashed bright, then darkened to a smoldering, inhuman yellow.

As she turned to face Frost, every inch of her body seemed to pulse with rage.

"The White Queen," she said.

Emma's eyes went wide—the first sign of doubt, of weakness, that Cyclops had seen in her. She studied the Phoenix, watching it for a long moment yet betraying no fear. When Emma turned back to face him, a strange emotion seemed to play across her face.

With a shock, he realized it was pity.

"Oh," she said. "Oh, Scott Summers, I am so sorry."

DIRECTING THE X-Men to the Frost complex had been easy. Navigating the maze inside? That was *hard*. Kitty hadn't exactly memorized the floor plan. On her previous visit, she'd been too busy running for her life.

Midway down a narrow corridor, she heard footsteps and froze. She phased through the wall, into a small supply cabinet, and waited until the heavy tread of boots faded into the distance.

Think, Pryde! Where did Jean Grey say the holding cells were? What did she read in that guy's brain? Kitty paused only momentarily to consider the absurdity of that thought. Then she phased back into the hallway and continued on her way.

She ducked in and out of the corridor, hiding whenever someone approached—doctors in their lab coats, pawns in those creepy masks. She barely managed to phase through the wall before a trio of knights, in their heavy red armor, ran past with guns drawn.

It's getting easier to use my power, she realized. *Is this what it's like to be an X-Man?* Even with all the danger, she had to admit: *It doesn't suck.*

The corridor dead-ended at a massive steel door. Glancing around quickly, she ducked her head down and charged through—then stopped cold, suppressing a gasp.

The room held three cages, all suspended from the high ceiling. Storm occupied the first one, with Wolverine in the second, and Colossus—Peter—in the final cage. Slumped inside the barred enclosures, they all looked drugged. None of them looked up at her arrival.

Kitty started toward Peter—but no, Cyclops's orders had been clear. *"Free Wolverine first,"* he'd said. *"Then stand back."*

She moved toward Wolverine. He knelt on the floor of the cage, almost naked, his hands gripping the bars. He really looked like an animal, a mindless beast. Not even hostile—just helpless.

"W-Wolver..." she said. "Logan?"

He didn't look up. She reached toward him—and felt a wave of dizziness.

The cages, she realized. *They must... do something to your brain!* Backing off, she circled the cage. On the side facing the wall, an LCD touchscreen with a small keyboard jutted out above the cage's central lock. The screen was mounted on a metal arm, far enough from the cage that she could reach it without feeling wonky. Kitty rolled up her sleeves and cracked her knuckles.

"Time to hack this bad boy," she said, then raised a hand to her mouth, terrified that someone might have heard. Holding her breath, she listened.

Nothing.

○————————○

FIVE FRUSTRATING minutes later, she still hadn't found the command to open the cages—but using the touchscreen, she *had* managed to hack into the Hellfire Club's main server. The menu page bore the club's insignia, the stylized "H" and pitchfork that she'd seen on their hovercraft, with animated flames rising up from it. Subliminal images winked on and off, too fast for her to make out.

She browsed the menu. A page with a comedy mask, adorned with a sinister mustache. A message board devoted entirely to whips. An auction site with an alarming selection of leather clothing.

I'm in the Dark Web, she realized. *There are subsites here devoted to slavery, human trafficking. What else are these guys into? How deep does their network go?*

One thing's for sure. This isn't "suitable content" for a thirteen-year-old!

Wolverine let out a groan. Kitty looked up from the screen. Frustrated, she swiped at the lock with the back of her hand. Her power activated instinctively, protecting her from harm. As her hand passed through the mechanism, the lock clicked open.

She backed off, startled. *Huh,* she thought. *Guess I don't know everything about my power. Maybe I need some of Storm's training after all!*

The cage door swung open, and Wolverine rolled out. Kitty held out her hands, caught him—and together they tumbled to the floor. Logan groaned again, and clutched at his head. Then he saw her.

"You're... the kid."

"And you're surprisingly heavy."

"Why's it so... flamin' hard to think?"

"It's the cages—they make you dopey. Come on... you should be okay in a minute." Still eyeing him with alarm, she led him away from the cage. Logan moved like a wounded animal, all sharp motions and low grunts. She knew he was one of the good guys, but he was also the most frightening man she'd ever met.

"Not just the cages," Logan growled, louder and angrier this time. "That ice lady... she did somethin' to my head." He glanced at the cages holding Storm and Colossus, then growled again. "What're you doin' here, kid?"

"I'm rescuing you!"

"All by yourself?"

Before she could reply, a bolt of force slammed into her from behind. Kitty twisted around and tried to phase, but it was too late. Some sort of charge surged through her, sapping her strength. She fell to the floor, unconscious.

"OKAY, MUTIE. Freeze it right there."

Wolverine glared at the two pawns standing in the doorway. Normal humans. No special powers, except for the weapons in their hands.

A wave of dizziness passed over him. He'd felt this way once before, back during the Weapon X project. When he'd been kidnapped and drugged, his skeleton forcibly bonded to a layer of unbreakable Adamantium.

What did that witch do to me?

The dizziness passed. Ignoring the armored men, he crouched down to check on Kitty. Her eyes were closed, but her pulse was steady.

"Let's climb back into that cage, mutant." The pawn's mask distorted his voice, but his gun hand shook slightly. "Nice and slow."

Wolverine turned toward him, holding up both fists. "Chief, you just made the biggest mistake of your life..."

Snikt.

"...and the last."

CHAPTER NINE

JEAN'S POWER was a song inside of her. Loud, pounding, drowning out all thought, all reason. She could barely hear the words of the icy woman standing before her.

"So," Emma Frost said. "Jean Grey, not so dead after all."

Jean glared into the White Queen's eyes. When she spoke, her voice filled the air, echoing inside Emma's mind. Jean barely recognized it herself.

"I understand you consider yourself something of a telepath."

Frost maintained eye contact, but took a step back. "You and I—we're not so different," she said. "Restless, powerful women. Driven by need, and surrounded by men…" Her eyes strayed briefly to Scott Summers, who stood watching. "…who will never, ever understand."

Jean stepped forward, sending mental tendrils out through the air. Frost deflected them, managing to keep her thoughts concealed. But Jean could see the effort written on her face.

"I know you," Jean said. "I know your petty games. Your 'Hellfire Club.'"

Frost laughed.

"You think *this* is the Hellfire Club?" she gestured around. "This hamster cage, this glorified office park? No. Oh no, dear. The Hellfire Club is as old as the trees, as primal as the fires of the human heart." She smiled. "Be careful you don't get burned."

"Tell me, little Queen." Jean gestured toward Cyclops. "Did you offer that warning when you tried to take that which is mine?"

Scott flinched. A flicker of fear crossed his face—or was it guilt?

Frost studied him for a moment. She seemed to be searching for words, struggling to express some unknown concept. When she turned back to Jean, her expression was oddly soft. Almost... kind?

"You're so... bound together," Emma said. "Caring, well-meaning, yet weighed down by your shared history. You're—"

"What?" Jean felt the power, the rage, building inside her. "*Say it.*"

"It's... not my place."

"Tell me. Tell me what you see—what the *White Queen* decrees."

"Jean," Scott said.

Again, the song. Deafening, red hot, filling her mind. Pure wrath, passion beyond imagining. Mind on fire, talons poised to attack. Flaring bright, spreading its wings.

Frost moved closer, almost to the edge of the flame. She looked into Jean's eyes, her gaze wavering only slightly.

"You're doomed," she said.

With an inhuman cry, the Phoenix struck.

THE BLAST lifted Cyclops off his feet, hurling him backward. He cried out, shielding his face from the heat, and struck the wall with a dull thud. Then he slumped, dazed, to the floor.

Looking up, his vision blurred, he saw the two women facing off in the narrow hallway. Jean's power was like a living thing, a writhing talon of fire emanating from her outstretched hand. Emma Frost held both hands to her head.

"I do," Frost said. "I do consider myself a telepath."

The Phoenix claw reached out, trailing fire, and grabbed hold of the White Queen. Frost struggled, but the flame construct held her tight. It lifted her into the air, shook her, and slammed her into the wall. Plaster and metal buckled and fell away, revealing a sterile medical laboratory on the other side.

Jean Grey smiled.

A familiar *BAMF* sound, and a whiff of brimstone. Nightcrawler reached out with a three-fingered hand and lifted Cyclops to his feet.

"What…" The blue-furred mutant turned to stare at Jean and Emma. "What in the world is happening?"

Storm and Wolverine sprinted into view. Colossus followed behind, carrying a limp form in his arms. "Kitty!" Cyclops said. "Is she hurt?"

"She will recover." Colossus lowered the girl to the floor, and she stirred. "She was struck by a force bolt."

"I'm fine," Kitty said, rubbing her head. "Just a little—*what the holy crap is Miss Grey doing?*"

Cyclops whirled to look. Emma Frost had regained her feet, thrusting her head forward to project rapid-fire mental bolts at her adversary, so intense they were visible to the naked eye. Jean stood her ground, fiery psi-waves rippling out from her. She seemed unconcerned, unaffected by her opponent's attack.

She's playing, Cyclops thought. *Toying with her prey.*

Ceiling tiles rained down. Cyclops gestured for the others to retreat—but Wolverine shouldered past him, almost knocking him down.

"Jeannie?" Logan said. "She's *alive*?"

"Oh," Storm whispered.

"Apologies, *mein Freunde*," Nightcrawler said. "I had no time to tell you."

"Cyclops," Storm said, staring past him. "That woman… the one battling with Jean. She is the one who captured us—who probed our minds." There was a quaver in her usually calm voice.

"Quite painfully," Colossus added.

"Two telepaths," Cyclops replied. "We can't even perceive the levels they're fighting on." Frost's words, just moments ago, echoed in his mind. *A game with rules, rewards… punishments.* He shook his head, disturbed by the memory.

A talon of fire forced Frost down, pressing her against the floor. Jean hovered like a wrathful god, arms spread wide. Her expression was frightening, inhuman. Psychic energy filled the air, buzzing in Cyclops's head. He began to "hear" bits of their thoughts, snippets of mind-static coming from the two women.

—little Queen
Draining my…
I could
Powerful more powerful than
I could show you
Hellfire Hellfire Hell…

The sound of footsteps rose above the clamor of combat. He whirled around as three men in heavy red armor approached, each holding a glowing power staff.

"Knights!" Kitty shouted.

Cyclops stepped forward, reaching for his visor. "I've got this," he began—

—but Storm was already airborne. She spread her arms and called down a fierce wind, whipping and swirling in the narrow hallway. The knights flailed, waving their staffs against the driving air currents.

Colossus ran forward, his body transforming to steel, and punched one of the knights on his helmet. The room shook with the vibration of metal on metal. The knight dropped to the floor, senseless.

Logan leapt onto the second man. His claws pierced the knight's armor, drawing blood from the man's stomach and leg. The knight cried out, staggered away, and fled down the corridor, stumbling over a chunk of fallen ceiling.

"Sorry, Cyke." Logan sheathed his claws. "Still not much good at takin' orders."

"I'll let it go," Cyclops replied. "This time."

Only one knight remained, raising his staff to attack. Nightcrawler teleported into the knight's path—holding Kitty in his arms. She reached out, eyes wide, and pressed her fingers *through* the knight's helmet. His limbs stiffened, sparks danced on the joints of his armor. He toppled and fell.

Cyclops turned back toward the battle. The corridor wall was a pile of debris now, opening into the two-story laboratory beyond. Tables and sinks lay overturned; water gushed from exposed pipes. And in the center of the room…

Emma Frost struggled up to a crouch, bracing herself against a desk. Jean hung in midair, the Phoenix Force reaching down to envelop her enemy. As Emma cried out, Cyclops heard their thoughts again:

Killing me
I could
One last
I could show you
Last chance

Logan stared at Jean. "We gotta help her."

"I don't think she's the one that needs help." Cyclops pointed down the corridor. "Get out of here—all of you. This place is about to blow."

Wolverine planted himself between Scott and the lab. "I ain't leavin' Jeannie."

"Logan," Cyclops said, "you're exhausted. Get to safety."

Wolverine didn't move. He unsheathed his claws with a menacing *snikt*.

"Get the *kid* to safety," Cyclops insisted.

Logan snarled aloud. Then he glared past Cyclops at Kitty, who stood with Storm, Colossus, and Nightcrawler.

"C'mon," Logan said, and he started off. Storm took to the air, pausing only to glance back at Jean's flaring energies. Colossus grabbed up Kitty in his arms, and Nightcrawler hesitated only a moment before teleporting off ahead of them.

Inside the lab, Jean had Emma by the neck. With a flaming claw, she lifted the platinum-haired woman up off the floor. Frost's eyes went wide; she tugged at her throat, gasping.

Jean hovered above, a wicked smile on her face. When she leaned down to address her captive, her words filled Cyclops's mind:

I could show you secrets.

He leaned forward. In Jean's eyes he saw… everything. Worlds, stars, galaxies. Ancient truths, fiery energies wielded by giants in times long past. Primal forces exploding in the hearts of suns, power that could rip holes in time. All gone, forgotten, buried beneath the sands of time. Until now.

Would you like that?

"No!" Frost twisted her head away.

"Jean!" Cyclops called.

Would you like to see?

"JEAN!"

Her head whipped around, her eyes struggling to focus. For the first time, she seemed to notice him.

"Don't do it."

Her eyes—those eyes that held stars and atoms—narrowed. *She's going to kill me,* he thought. *With just a fraction of her newfound power, she could reach out a claw and end my life. First me, then Emma, and then…*

Abruptly, Jean looked up toward the heavens, dropping Emma Frost with an almost casual motion. Frost clutched her throat as she fell to the heat-scorched floor. The Phoenix flared bright—

—and blew the roof off the building.

Cyclops's instincts told him to run, but he couldn't leave her. Couldn't abandon the woman he loved, no matter what she might have done—or what she was becoming. He fired an optic beam upward, reducing a ceiling tile to dust just before it could strike his head. Another eye-beam snapped a falling window in half. He snapped his head from side to side, up and down, deflecting and shattering pieces of wall, ceiling, and insulation.

Alarms rang out. In the distance people ran, screamed, shouted orders. A pair of pawns scrambled past, masks hanging loose from their faces. They didn't even pause to look at him.

Dust filled the air. He couldn't make out Jean or Emma, could barely see half a yard in any direction. Coughing, he forced himself to stay alert. One stray piece of falling rubble could take his head off.

Soon the debris stopped falling. The alarms went silent. One wall of the corridor still stood upright, but the roof had been blasted open. The first rays of morning sun slanted in from one side, catching motes of dust as they settled to the pockmarked floor.

Cyclops turned, with mounting dread, toward the lab. An enormous roof-support beam, braced at a diagonal angle, blocked the hole in the blasted-out wall. Beyond that, he could see a shoulder-high pile of ruins—tables, laboratory equipment, splintered ceiling plates, and bits of fallen roof tiles.

Jean!

Unleashing a pinpoint shot from his visor, he sliced the support beam in half. Before the pieces hit the ground he was running into the room. He reached down and began to dig. Lifting a wooden plank, he tossed it aside. Grabbed up an entire severed lab sink, hefted it, and dropped it with a heavy thud.

Jean, he thought, projecting his mind outward. *Are you in here?*

He dug further, unearthing roof tiles and table legs. A desktop computer with a shattered screen. His gloves tore on a row of track lighting that had fallen from the ceiling. The metal cut through skin, but he didn't even notice the blood dripping from his fingers.

Answer me. You can't be dead. You can't!

The pile of debris behind him grew higher than the one in front. Still he continued digging, grabbing hold of… a piece of a gold sash? He held it up, and felt his heart sink.

Whatever you are, whoever you want to be… I don't care. I just want you. Today, tomorrow. Forever.

There was a stirring in the rubble. He leaned forward, scrabbling with his bare hands.

I won't lose you again!

Jean exploded upward, scattering the remains of the debris. As he stumbled back, the Phoenix rose up around her, shrieking at the open sky. She levitated into the air, her mouth open in a silent scream.

Then she fell, collapsing into his arms. He caught her and held her tight, dropping to his knees. He stroked her hair, cherishing the warmth of her strong body, the feel of her arms clutched loosely around his neck. She groaned and twisted in his grasp.

When she looked up at him, the Phoenix flame was gone. She seemed puzzled, disoriented.

Utterly human.

"It's so quiet," she said.

He smiled. "Come on," he said, setting her down and placing an arm around her shoulder. She smiled back, and together they limped their way out of the devastated building.

OUTSIDE, THE early dawn had given way to chaos. Pawns and knights, some in only partial armor, scrambled into jeeps and hovercrafts. Sirens rose and fell in the distance. Flames raged through the lab building, flaring dangerously close to the adjacent trees.

Scott's arm felt good around Jean's shoulders. *I've missed that,* she realized. *I've missed a lot of things.*

Once again the Phoenix had taken control of her. Again it had crested, swelled to a crescendo—and then collapsed, leaving her utterly spent. She'd managed to rein it in, defeating the enemy and saving her friends' lives. But each time, the power burned hotter. The flame rose higher, tempting her to give in to its unearthly hunger.

Where will this end?

As they limped down the walkway away from the building, a black limousine screeched up to meet them. The driver's-side window slid down to reveal Logan at the wheel, with Nightcrawler seated beside him.

"Need a lift?" Logan asked.

The back-seat window rolled down. Storm smiled out at Jean. On the opposite side, Kitty was seated a little too close to Colossus.

"You were so brave in there," Kitty said to him.

Colossus's eyes widened. "I was?"

"Jean." Storm clicked open the door. "It is *very* good to see you."

"We have a lot of catching up to do," Colossus added.

Scott waved Jean toward the car. She hesitated, glanced back briefly at the burning building. Smoke poured out of it, filling the air. She coughed, smelling the dark ashy scent—and something else, too.

A musky cologne.

She froze. Whirled around just in time to see a man on horseback, riding away toward the main gate. A man out of time—in riding breeches, a top hat, gloves, and an impeccably tailored jacket.

Jason?

He turned and flashed her a smile. That wolfish leer that seemed to stir her deepest, most forbidden desires.

No, she thought. *No, not again!*

When she blinked, he was gone.

"Jean?"

Scott held the limo door, staring at her. His face was so close she could make out his pupils through the thick ruby quartz of his visor. Without warning she leaned in and kissed him, hard. He let out a little surprised noise, and his lenses flared red. Then he grabbed her neck and pulled her close.

"Awww!" Kitty said.

"Yeah, it's a beautiful thing," Logan growled. "But can we get this crate movin' before the cops arrive?"

Jean pulled away, shaken by the intensity of the moment. She took a step back and gestured inside the car.

"After you," she said.

Scott paused, a strange look on his face. Then he nodded, smiled, and climbed inside. Jean followed, squeezing Storm's hand as she took her seat.

"My friends," Jean said.

Logan leaned his head through the divider window. He studied her for a moment, then nodded. She smiled, fighting back tears. She could feel Scott's eyes on her, sense the worry in his mind. But right now, that didn't matter.

We're together again. Joy surged through her. *All of us.*

Logan turned and gunned the engine to life. The limo sped away, straight into the rising sun.

CHAPTER TEN

"THIS ONE!" Kitty said, pointing at a white house just slightly larger than the others on the block. She took off at a run, heading for the front door.

A tart wind had begun blowing off Lake Michigan, turning the air chilly. Scott and Jean wore slacks and light jackets. He looked around at the quiet street, the neatly trimmed hedges, and he squeezed her hand.

"This feels nice," he said. "It feels… normal."

Jean smiled as Kitty stuck a key in the door. "That's a great kid."

"Yeah." He glanced at Jean. "Maybe someday…"

The door flew open. "Kitten!" A trim middle-aged woman grabbed the startled girl up in her arms.

Scott grimaced. They'd been afraid of this. Kitty had been missing for nearly thirty-six hours, and her clothes were still dirty and torn. The skyship didn't carry a selection of tween-sized jeans.

"Mom! I'm fine." Kitty struggled in her mother's grip. "Hey, I've figured out which school I want to attend, and which one I *don't*."

As she spoke, a large man appeared in the doorway. "I'll handle this, Theresa," he said.

Scott held out his hand. "Mr. Pryde, I'm Scott Summers. I'm the one who spoke with you regarding—"

"I know who you are," Kitty's father snapped. "What I want to know is *what have you been doing with my daughter?*"

"Dad," Kitty protested, "I'm fine."

"Fine?" Theresa Pryde lifted Kitty's arm. "Look at these bruises!"

"The other people from your school—they said they'd bring her back in an hour. That was *yesterday*."

"And the coffee shop they went to—it was practically leveled! We thought our daughter was dead."

Scott locked eyes briefly with Jean. Something in her expression unnerved him. He turned back quickly to the Prydes.

"It was an unfortunate... coincidence," he said. "Perhaps we could come in and discuss it?"

"I don't think so." Carmen Pryde crossed his arms, glaring. His wife stood beside him in the doorway, clutching Kitty—who looked as if she might die of embarrassment. "In fact, I demand that you stay away from my daughter. I don't want you anywhere near her, ever again."

"Dad!" Kitty said.

"Your father's right." Theresa Pryde's eyes narrowed. She peered at Scott, then Jean. "In fact, I'm going to conduct an investigation of your so-called 'institute.' What are your secrets, Summers? What exactly are you doing with the children you..."

All at once, the air changed. Scott felt a strange tingle, a warm sensation on his skin. Mrs. Pryde stopped and looked down, shaking her head.

"What was I saying?" she asked. "Carmen?"

"I..." Mr. Pryde shook his head. When he looked up again, a smile spread across his face. "Summers," he said, holding out his hand. "Of course. Good to finally meet you."

What the hell? Scott stared at the hand for a moment. Finally, he reached out and gave it a tentative shake.

"My wife and I were very impressed by Ms. Munroe's presentation yesterday," Mr. Pryde continued. "Right, dear?"

"Yes. Oh yes." Mrs. Pryde smiled, as well. "In fact, we've been discussing your school quite a lot since then."

"We were just about to have brunch." Carmen Pryde gestured inside the house. "Won't you join us?"

Scott stared for a moment, then glanced toward Kitty. The girl seemed baffled. She looked from her mother to her father, then over at Scott. Then she shrugged.

Jean, he thought. *She did this.*

He turned toward her, a questioning look on his face. She gave him a strangely self-satisfied smirk, and shrugged.

She used her telepathic abilities, he thought, with growing alarm. *Not against an enemy, but two ordinary people. She modified their memories, changed their perceptions to suit her purposes.* Jean had never done that before. It ran counter to everything she believed in.

Then he remembered the Hellfire pawn—the man in the skyship. *After Jean interrogated him, he collapsed. She blamed that on Emma Frost, but... did Jean go too far with him, as well?*

"We'd love to come in, Mr. Pryde," Jean said. She followed the Prydes inside, not looking back.

Scott stood alone on the steps. He trembled in the cold, remembering Jean's behavior inside the Frost lab. She'd been savage, almost feral. So different from the girl he'd grown up with, the woman with whom he'd fallen in love. More powerful, more decisive. More ruthless.

And yet, in many ways, she hadn't changed at all.

There's something I'm missing, he thought. *Someone is manipulating us—some unseen presence. I've got to find out who or what it is.*

He frowned, remembering the smirk on Jean's face. It was familiar; he'd seen that look on someone else—recently. With a shock, he realized who it was.

Emma Frost. The White Queen.

"Scott?" Jean reappeared in the doorway, smiling pleasantly. "Aren't you coming in?"

He swallowed, nodded, and stepped inside.

INTERLUDE ONE

EMMA FROST seated herself in front of the mirror, grimaced, and grabbed hold of her arm. With a quick, violent motion, she wrenched the shoulder back into its socket.

Pain shot through her, but she was careful not to cry out. Even here, in her private quarters deep beneath the streets of New York, she could not afford to show weakness. The Hellfire Club had eyes and ears everywhere—even in its own Inner Circle.

She held up the arm, tested it. It would be sore for a week—Jean Grey had really done a number on her—but nothing seemed to be broken. She glanced at her face in the mirror, then daubed a bit of concealer on a bruise.

Standing, she crossed over to a partly open door set into the stone wall. A large walk-in closet held a supply of boots and other Hellfire gear. She laced on a fresh corset, wincing at the pressure on a sore rib. Uncomfortable as hell—but that uniform was part of the role she'd chosen to play.

Over by the vanity, an open bureau drawer caught her eye. It was filled with comfortable clothes: white jeans and stretch pants. She stared at it and let out a wistful sigh.

In this world, a woman had to make choices.

"Ms. Frost?" A rugged, middle-aged man stuck his head through the doorway. "We're needed."

"One moment, Shaw."

She glanced down at the bureau, at the comfortable clothing inside. Rolled her eyes, stretched out a high-heeled boot, and kicked the drawer shut.

Not today.

Pulling the ivory cape off a hook, she whipped it around her shoulders—and froze, noticing her neck in the mirror. She raised a hand to her throat, touching the faint red circle left behind by the burning talon of the Phoenix. For just a moment, during the battle, she'd seen something. A deep pain, an infinite hunger, so terrible it could set the universe ablaze.

Jean Grey's words echoed in her brain:

I could show you secrets.

"Ms. Frost?"

"Coming!"

She threw her head back, curling her mouth deliberately into a haughty, regal grimace. Then she fastened the ruby jewel around her neck and stalked off to join her King.

THE CHAMBER of the Inner Circle was large and dim, its darkness broken only by candles, torches, and a few LCD screens. Displays of weapons lined the stone walls, including muskets, axes, and dueling pistols. At one end of the room, up a short flight of stone steps, a row of paintings—portraits of powerful men from earlier centuries—hung above an elevated meeting table, flanking a large wall screen.

Emma entered the room, touching her throat. Shaw was pacing back and forth on the level just below the meeting table. A larger man—Harry Leland—sat at the table, his mouth filled with the remains of a game hen. Bits of meat flecked his unruly red beard.

"...once again successfully employed millisecond trading to enhance our portfolio," Shaw said. "I am pleased to report that the Hellfire Club is now one point eight billion dollars richer than we were yesterday."

"Mmhh!" Leland said.

Emma pushed her way inside, past a pair of latex-clad servant women holding trays of food and cocktails. She cast her gaze across the chamber, past the rows of wooden tables where the Circle held its private feasts. Only one figure sat at those tables now, a man hidden in shadow on the far side of the room. He watched Shaw and Leland in silence.

"The bulk of the increase comes from military-grade weapons manufacturing," Shaw continued. "Speaking of which, Pierce and I have quite an interesting meeting scheduled with the new ruling Saudi prince."

Leland spat out a bone. He tossed aside the picked-over carcass and reached for another game hen. A servant woman rushed up the steps with a tray containing a dozen more.

Shaw eyed Leland. "You disapprove?"

The big man paused, lowered his food. He glared at Shaw.

"Diplomacy," he sneered. "Millisecond trading. This is what we're reduced to?"

"At least I'm *increasing* the club's assets." Shaw gestured at the table. "All you seem to do is consume them."

"That's what we were born to do!" Leland banged his fist on the table and rose to his feet. "In the days of the *original* Hellfire Club, a man controlled his own destiny. By his will, his sword arm, and the divine right of his birth. He took his enjoyment whenever and wherever he wanted to!"

Emma turned away, disgusted. Leland—known as the Bishop—was a boor, the useless son of a rich family. Shaw, her White King, was twice the man Leland would ever be. Yet she could see that the effects of Shaw's lifestyle, his pursuit of hedonism, were taking their toll on him, as well. His waistline wasn't as trim as last year, his eyes were more sunken from drink.

Decadence had its price.

And yet, she reminded herself, *they're both very powerful men. Stepping stones in my own ascent to power.*

Leland continued raving. "Servants should be whipped!" he said. "Commoners should be taught their place. And women…"

Emma spun around, her cape whirling through the air. As Leland paused to look, she planted her most frightening smile on her face.

"Yes, Sir Leland?" she asked. "Women should be…?"

He blinked. A speck of food fell from his mouth. Then he recovered his composure, raised a hen's leg, and bit off a large chunk in one swipe.

"Vessels," he spat.

Emma stepped toward him, marshaling her mental powers. *Enough,* she thought. *Enough insults. Enough of this… man.*

Then she felt a voice in her head—calm yet imperious. Shaw's voice, transmitted through the mental link they shared. *Not worth it, my dear. Let events take their course.*

She bristled. Shaw was her King; in accordance with Hellfire tradition, he commanded her. He believed that he was her master; someday he would learn that she was *his.*

Yet not today. Emma paused for a last glare at Leland, then frowned and turned away. As she did, a sharp laugh echoed from the shadows. The third man, the hidden man. Candles on the wall silhouetted him from behind, revealing a thick head of hair, a carefully sculpted beard.

"Wyngarde?" Shaw said. "You find this amusing?"

Jason Wyngarde stood, his large dark eyes wide. He turned to gesture toward Leland. "This one goes on about destiny, about the divine right of birth. About *women.*" He paused. "What does he know of any of those things?"

"How dare you?" Leland slammed a fist down on the table. "You miserable peasant!"

"That's right," Wyngarde replied. "You were born a rich man, and you've squandered that wealth in the pursuit of pleasure.

128

Food, drink, designer narcotics—and, of course, women. Myself? I was born on the floor of a carnival tent. Everything I have— everything I am—I *made* myself."

"Sir Jason," Shaw said. "As amusing as this exchange might be, I have a more pertinent question for you."

Wyngarde turned, raising an eyebrow.

"You knew of my plans for the X-Men." Shaw's eyes narrowed. "Why did you not inform the Inner Circle that Jean Grey was alive?"

"She is my… pet project." Wyngarde smiled a wolfish smile. "I have been shaping her. Exploring her potential."

"Which in itself compounded the problem." Shaw gestured at Emma. "Ms. Frost was unprepared for the Grey woman's presence, or for her greatly enhanced power levels. Our dear White Queen might have been killed."

Emma didn't enjoy being used as a pawn in their arguments, but she held her head high. Wyngarde stepped around his table, walked up to her, and kissed her gloved hand. His eyes were dark, snakelike.

"Apologies, milady," he said.

She nodded warily.

Wyngarde whirled away. He sprinted to the front of the room and up the steps of the dais. He perched himself on the edge and stared down in distaste at the remains of Leland's meal, spread out on the picnic table below.

"You speak of women, Sir Leland," he said. "I, too, am a slave to beauty. But I seek more than that."

The look in his eyes was strangely unnerving. Emma moved toward the elevated dais, with Shaw following close behind.

"I crave their secrets," Wyngarde continued. "*All* their secrets." He raised his hands, drawing them apart in a magician's flourish. A hazy image of a young woman filled the air, surrounded by a corona of energy. It was an illusion, Emma knew. That was Wyngarde's mutant power: illusion.

He pulled and stretched the image, bringing it into sharper

resolution. A flame-haired teenage girl dressed in jeans and a formal jacket, dragging a ragged suitcase behind her.

"This is Jean Grey," he said, "the day she first joined the X-Men."

Wyngarde's hands flashed in the air. The girl grew taller. Her garb changed to a blue-and-yellow costume with a stylized "X" on the belt.

"This is dear Jean in her original costume… as Marvel Girl…"

Again, his hands swept the air. The girl's face grew longer, her expression more mature. The costume morphed into a striking green minidress with a domino mask.

"…the older, more experienced Marvel Girl…"

The costume changed again—into an emerald bodysuit enhanced with gold boots and gloves. A yellow sash whipped dramatically from its waist.

"…and, finally, as the Phoenix."

Wyngarde stepped directly through the image and marched back down the steps, toward Shaw and Emma. Behind him, the Phoenix illusion flared up, energy flashing around her in the shape of a savage bird of prey.

"My pawn advances rapidly," he continued. "Soon she will reach the final square of the playing field. The very edge of her world."

"A Queen." Leland laughed, spitting food. "You seek a Queen, to rival Lord Shaw! And of course, to rival *you*, milady." He pointed a drumstick at Emma.

She struggled to retain her composure. The Phoenix image shone bright atop the dais, its fiery corona surging and fading in cycles. Emma remembered the heat of that flame on her throat, around her waist.

I could show you secrets…

Shaw was looking at her. She shrugged in his direction, keeping her face stoic.

"Well then," Shaw said, turning back to Wyngarde. "Let the game begin."

The servants passed among them, distributing glasses and pouring wine. Wyngarde smiled and raised his glass.

"To the game."

The three men toasted first. Emma hesitated, then raised her glass to join them.

"To Hellfire," she said.

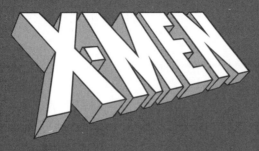

ACT TWO
HELLFIRE AND DAMNATION

CHAPTER ELEVEN

PETER RASPUTIN, the X-Man called Colossus, leaned forward to peer at the tablet computer. It looked tiny in his hands, like a child's toy.

"'Horrid impieties,'" he read. "What does that mean?"

Nightcrawler leaned over his friend's shoulder. "Go back to the search results." As Colossus struggled to hit the "back" button, he added, "Your fingers are enormous. Give that to me."

Storm glided across the large cockpit of the X-Men's Blackbird plane—hovering an inch above the floor, riding on a subtle current of air. "What are you two doing?"

Colossus gave a sheepish grin. "Googling 'Hellfire Club.'"

"Hellfire Club. References." Nightcrawler planted his feet on the side bulkhead, hanging sideways as he read from the tablet held tight in his curled tail. "Eighteenth-century secret society in Britain. Risqué villains on a 1960s television show. Nineteen-eighties sex club, New York City."

"Let me see that last one," Storm said.

Colossus and Nightcrawler watched in surprise as she grabbed the tablet. She held it up at a few different angles, studying the

X-MEN: THE DARK PHOENIX SAGA

screen with a mixture of interest and disdain. Then she handed the tablet back to Nightcrawler, shrugging.

"I like the Mohawks," she said.

"I do not believe any of these organizations are the Hellfire Club we're dealing with," Colossus said, swiping hurriedly to remove an image from the screen.

"No," Nightcrawler replied, "but our mutant-hunting friends may be inspired by their historical counterparts."

Across the cockpit, Cyclops sat in the pilot's seat. Listening to the conversation, he let out a sigh of relief. Storm and Colossus seemed to have recovered from their ordeal at Frost Enterprises. Learning that Jean was alive had raised their spirits, too.

Logan, on the other hand…

On the far side of the cockpit Wolverine sat alone, glaring out of a window. *He got the worst of the torture,* Cyclops thought, *at the Hellfire Club's hands. At Emma Frost's hands. But is that what's bothering him?*

Cyclops checked the altitude, then turned to a screen to study the landscape that lay ahead. Patches of green gave way to bare rock as the Blackbird pushed farther into the New Mexico desert. He toggled the stick to autopilot and unbuckled his seat belt.

Wolverine didn't look up as he approached.

"Enjoying the view?"

He crouched down beside Logan and looked out the window. Outside, under the marine blue sky, Jean Grey soared along under her own power. Her fiery hair seemed to blur into the Phoenix flame, forming a comet's tail in the bright sunlight.

"Guess you are," Cyclops said.

"I'm glad she's breathin'," Logan growled.

"Is that all?"

"Doesn't matter." Logan still didn't turn his head. "She made her choice."

"That's what I'm afraid of."

Logan looked at him, then, with a frown. "Where the hell we goin', Summers? We left Albuquerque behind a few hundred miles ago. We're way off the commercial routes."

"Call it a… sanctuary. Where we can regroup, figure out our next move."

"That makes sense." Logan stared at the red-haired figure flying alongside the Blackbird, above the desert wasteland. "She's different, ain't she? Since the shuttle."

"Yeah."

"I could have stopped her, you know."

Before Cyclops could reply, Wolverine sat up straight. He braced both hands against the window and stared through it.

"What the hell is that?"

Storm, Nightcrawler, and Colossus all rushed to the windows. Below, a network of large buttes jutted up from the ground, flat rocky structures dotting the vast expanse of the desert. A winged figure soared upward, moving toward the approaching Blackbird. Powerful muscles flexed snow-white wings, pistoning up and down to carry the figure higher.

"Is that… a bird?" Colossus asked.

"No," Cyclops said.

Jean broke formation, circling away from the Blackbird. She swooped down to intercept the arriving figure, slowing as she drew near. The winged man swung easily into a vertical position and wafted up on the dry air currents to meet her.

Then they hugged.

"That is Warren Worthington the Third," Cyclops said. "Also known as the Angel."

WARREN WORTHINGTON had been a founding member of the X-Men, a teenage inductee to Professor Xavier's very first graduating class. He was also heir to one of America's larger private fortunes. That wealth had allowed him to purchase Angel's Aerie, a high-tech, state-of-the-art, solar-powered complex located atop a remote butte in the New Mexico desert.

Ever since he'd come of age, Warren's duties to Worthington Industries had kept him extremely busy—busy enough that he'd never even met most of the current X-Men. Cyclops had hesitated to call on him for help, but as usual the winged mutant had laughed away Scott's objections.

"Sorry for the short notice, Warren," Cyclops said, debarking from the Blackbird. The others followed behind him.

"Nonsense! Anything for the old alma mater." Warren smiled, watched as Jean spread her arms and touched down to a graceful landing. "Besides, it's worth it just to see Red here again. You still with this loser, Jean?"

She smiled and slapped him on the shoulder.

Just like old times, Cyclops thought.

One by one, the X-Men walked out onto the exposed butte. A slate patio led to a high-windowed ranch house with solar panels on the roof. The real attraction, however, was the view. Mountains rose up in every direction, dotted with fir trees, scrub brush, and a stunning combination of slate- and rust-colored terrain.

"This is a beautiful home, Angel," Colossus said, staring off into the distance. "Beautiful country."

"Such arid air." Storm spread her arms, summoning a breeze. "It feels lovely."

"*Wunderbar.*" Nightcrawler teleported around the patio in multiple jumps, inspecting every corner. "Do you not agree, Wolverine?"

Logan leaned on a railing and shrugged. "Canadian Rockies," he said. "Now *that's* beautiful country."

"Make yourselves at home," Warren said. "The house is entirely automated—you want anything to eat or drink, just use that pad over by the door." He smiled at Jean. "Jeannie, I've got your favorite: fresh lemonade."

She wrinkled her nose. "I haven't drunk that stuff since I was fifteen."

"Warren," Cyclops said. "A minute?"

Warren caught his eye and nodded. He ushered Scott away

from the others, toward the side of the house. Nightcrawler and Colossus moved over to the house's command pad and began tapping at it. Logan stood behind them, glaring.

"It's spelled b-e-e-r," he growled. "How flamin' hard is that?"

Cyclops could feel Jean's eyes on his back. *Is she monitoring my thoughts?* In the past, he'd always known when Jean established a telepathic link with him, but she'd grown far more powerful recently—and far less hesitant to use her power, too.

"Is there, uh…" Cyclops paused. "Is there somewhere private we can talk?"

Warren grinned. "Privacy you want?"

Before Scott could react, Warren had scooped him up under his arms and hoisted him into the sky.

"Privacy you got."

"Warren!"

Laughing, Warren carried him higher. The house receded, the X-Men shrinking to tiny dots below.

"Warren, is this trip really necessary?"

"Can't get more private than this, Scott." Warren shifted in flight, descending toward another chunk of bare rock. "No one in sight, and no hidden microphones. Even if there's a spy-eye in orbit, nobody's going to bug a butte." Cyclops braced himself as they came in—fast—for the landing, but Warren spread his wings at the last minute, braking expertly.

He's improved, Cyclops thought. *Gained greater control of his wings.*

Warren touched down softly. "Okay! We're alone." He released Cyclops. "What's the story?"

Cyclops opened his mouth—and his mind went blank. Suddenly, the events of the past few days seemed overwhelming, impossible to summarize.

"Someone's after the X-Men," he said finally.

Warren laughed. "Someone's *always* after the X-Men."

"This is different."

As Warren listened, Cyclops recounted the entire story. Of

Jean's supposed death at Magneto's hands, and the decision to reopen the school. Of Storm's recruitment of a new mutant named Kitty Pryde, and the team's capture by a mysterious cabal fronted by a telepath called the White Queen.

"White Queen," Warren repeated. "She got a human name?"

"Emma Frost," Cyclops replied.

"Frost?" Warren looked surprised. "I've heard of Frost Enterprises, but they've always seemed like a legit operation. Do you know what these mutant-hunters want?"

"Jean mind-scanned one of their... pawns, they're called," Cyclops said. "They call themselves the Hellfire Club."

Warren's surprise turned to shock. Cyclops stared at him. "You know them?"

"I'm a member."

Scott blinked.

"So is Candy. My girlfriend," Warren explained. "I inherited the membership along with my business, when my folks passed away."

"What is it? The club, I mean?"

"It's... it's an old, stuffy establishment society, based in New York. Kind of risqué, though. Lots of burlesque photos on the walls, dungeons in the back rooms." He shrugged. "Candy and I visited once, but we didn't like it. Never went back."

Scott nodded, thinking.

"They really caught us off guard, Warren. That's why I brought the team here, instead of back to Westchester. Partly to throw our enemies off-balance and buy us some breathing space—"

"—and partly because you don't think the mansion's safe."

"Yeah." He hesitated. "But that's not all."

"Scotty." Warren grinned. "Spill."

"I'm worried about... well, about Jean."

"Someone mention my name?"

He whirled, startled. Jean rose up from the desert below, wafting up to land, feather-light, on the surface of the butte. She wore her Phoenix costume, but she carried an incongruous blue picnic cooler under her arm.

"Time for a break," she said, spreading a blanket on the ground. "Anyone hungry?"

"I, ah…" Warren eyed the two of them. "I feel like sort of a third wheel here."

Jean grinned at him. "Perceptive lad."

"I'll leave you two alone." Warren spread his wings and rose up into the air, kicking up a cloud of dust and sand. "Scott, we'll finish our talk later?"

Scott nodded.

"Later, Jeannie."

Then they were alone on a flat barren rock, fifteen hundred feet above the desert floor. Jean knelt down on the blanket and began pulling plastic containers out of the cooler. Scott glanced up at the sun, climbing toward its highest point in the huge sky, then looked away. It was too bright, even through his lenses.

"So," he said.

She didn't look up. "So."

"What's up, Jean?"

"I could ask you the same thing."

Her costume began to shift, changing into a pair of casual shorts and a loose top. She didn't move, didn't even blink during the transformation.

"You never used to be able to do that," he said.

"A lot of things are different now," she replied. "We're a long way from the Danger Room."

He swept his arms around, taking in the sky and the open land all around. "It's all a Danger Room." She gave a short, grim nod in response.

"Jean…" He sat down on the blanket, directly in front of her. "I don't understand what's happening to you."

She reached into the cooler, not looking at him. "Don't you?"

He frowned. "What?"

"I heard you two together." She busied herself with the containers: salad, eggs, chips. "I saw the way you looked at her."

His heart sank. *Emma Frost.*

"Jean. That was just—"

"You don't understand. Listen to what I'm saying." She looked up, finally, her eyes filled with pain. "When you met her… when she touched your mind. Didn't you feel something?"

He swallowed.

"Didn't something… stir inside you? Something dark, forbidden? Maybe something you didn't even know was there at all?"

He felt transfixed, held by the pull of her eyes—and she wasn't even using her power. She leaned forward, bringing her lips close to his.

"*That's* what's up with me," she whispered. "That's how I feel, all the time. And it's tearing me apart, because I love you so very, very much."

He hesitated. Not wanting to ask, but knowing he had to.

"Is there someone else?"

She looked away. Rose to her bare feet and crossed to the edge of the butte.

"I met someone," she said. "On Kirinos. When I thought you were dead."

He opened his mouth—and froze. *I'm a fool,* he thought. *I've been so caught up in this Hellfire business—and so relieved to see her alive—I never thought about what* she's *been through. When I thought she was gone, it nearly destroyed me. I never realized…*

…she was grieving for me, *too.*

"This someone," he said. "Is it serious?"

She stood for a moment, her back to him, arms crossed over her chest. Then she turned, strode back to the blanket, and knelt down in front of him. Before he knew what was happening, she reached up and wrenched the visor off his face.

"Jean!" He squeezed his eyes shut.

"It's all right," she said.

"You know what will happen if I open my eyes. Without the ruby-quartz shield to contain my optic blasts—"

"I said it's all right." Gently but firmly, she drew him down to the blanket, rolling to position him up on top of her. "Open your eyes."

"I could kill you!"

"No." Her voice was soft, soothing. "Nothing will happen."

He fluttered one eyelid. *The energy,* he realized. *The pressure I live with, all the time…*

It's gone.

"Open them," she repeated.

Slowly, he did. Her eyes came into view, lovely and sincere, staring up at him. Normally, he viewed her through a red tint. Now, for the first time, he could see all the colors in her face. The striking green of her eyes, the pale gloss on her lips. That lovely hair, flame red, flowing down all around.

"Oh," he said, then found himself at a loss.

"I'm telekinetically keeping your optic blasts in check. I just wanted to see your face." She flashed an embarrassed smile. "You have a good face."

"How can you do that?"

"Like I said, a lot of things are different." She swept her fingers lightly across his cheek. "But a lot of things are the same."

A thousand questions crossed his mind, all at once. For once he forced them out of his mind. He took her in his arms, pressed her gently down to the blanket, and kissed her. She gasped, wrapped her arms around his neck, and returned the kiss with an intense, hungry passion.

They lay there for a long time, entwined, lost in each other. Hot sun beating down on their backs. Their hands strayed and roamed along each other's bodies, touching, testing. Remembering, rebuilding the bond that had linked them together since they'd first met, all those years ago, in Professor Xavier's class.

At last she rose, propped herself on one elbow, and stared at him. "I want to tell you everything," she said.

He nodded eagerly.

"It's not that simple," she said. "You may not like what you see."

He smiled, touched her face. "Looks okay so far."

She grimaced briefly. Then, all at once, she reached out and touched his forehead. He gasped as images flooded through his mind. The feel of Magneto's ribs snapping under her power, the heat of the deadly magma flowing all around. The children on Kirinos, snatching her purse and shoving her into the water. The police station; the first meeting with a handsome, friendly stranger.

The images grew more surreal. A secret closet with a night-black corset. A portrait of the stranger, or his ancestor, hanging on the wall. The thrill of a fierce steed galloping beneath her. An animal that was really a man, facing bloody death at her hands. And a final glimpse of the handsome stranger... just yesterday, outside Frost Enterprises, as the X-Men made their escape.

When Jean removed her hand, Scott blinked. It took him a moment to remember where he was.

"That's a lot to process," he said.

"Uh-huh."

"This... man..."

"Wyngarde."

"In the vision... the one in the past. You were married to him?"

"I'm—I'm not sure."

"But he mentioned the Hellfire Club."

"Yes. Definitely."

He sat up, shaking his head. Reached for his visor, then remembered he wasn't wearing it.

"What are we being drawn into, Jean?"

"I don't know." She knelt up behind him, placed her hands on his shoulders. "But I think I know what we have to do."

He turned, curious.

"I'd like to re-establish our psychic bond," she said. "The one we used to have, before I... before the shuttle accident."

"Of course. Yes."

"Not so fast." She stared into his eyes. "My powers are different now. My telepathy... it's much stronger. This would be a real sharing, Scott. Part of me in your head, part of you in mine."

144   He nodded.

"Total communication," she continued, her voice breaking. "Total intimacy, total trust. I know I'm asking a lot, and I-I would totally understand if you weren't ready… if you didn't want to…"

He touched her cheeks, turned her face gently toward his. Wiped a tear from her beautiful eye.

"I do," he said.

CHAPTER TWELVE

ANGEL'S HOUSE boasted a screened porch, fully automated kitchen, three dens with satellite TV hookups, a four-lane bowling alley, and a lounge equipped with every conceivable gaming platform. Plus two tennis courts indoors and three more out back, fenced off from the edge of the butte.

Logan wanted none of it. He prowled around, up and down flights of stairs, until he came to a basement room with a grimy, graffiti-etched bar. CRT-screen television suspended from the ceiling, next to a framed marlin hanging on the wall. Even a neon sign for Schlitz beer.

Not a single window to let in natural light.

He sniffed the air, hardly daring to believe the evidence of his enhanced senses. Behind the bar, next to a stack of plastic cups, an ancient tap was still filled with some stale, pre-microbrew beer. Logan let out a long, exhausted sigh, poured a cup, and planted himself at the bar. The wooden stool creaked underneath him.

Ten minutes and four plastic cups later, he'd almost managed to forget the things that were eating at him. That telepath witch poking around in his mind. The fact that he'd had to be rescued by a kid who was barely out of diapers. And, most of all, Jean Grey's strange return from the dead—so soon after he'd had to face losing her.

He downed a fifth beer and crushed the cup in his hand. Logan's healing power meant that alcohol moved through his system at an incredible clip. No matter how much he drank, the buzz only lasted a few minutes.

He could never truly forget.

"There you are."

He turned toward the door, unsurprised. He'd heard the newcomer a mile away. Warren Worthington descended the staircase, his wings carefully folded around his body.

"I, uh…" Worthington stepped into the room. "I see you found my little sanctuary."

Logan rose, moved to the tap, and poured another cup.

"It's about my speed," he said.

"Listen…" Worthington's gaze strayed to the pile of discarded cups. Suddenly, Logan hated him—those pretty eyes, those carefully sculpted muscles. A rich kid, born to privilege, and told every second of his life how special he was. Had he ever gotten those lily-white hands dirty?

"I'll pay for the beer," Logan growled.

"No, no, it's not that."

Worthington reached onto the bar, picked up a remote control, and aimed it at the hanging TV. It took a long time to flicker to life. Logan frowned, looked up at the screen. There was no picture—just block letters.

OMNI-WAVE PROTOCOL
CONNECTION REQUESTED
LOGAN PLEASE ACCEPT

He turned to Worthington. "What the hell is an Omni-Wave protocol?"

"I have no idea. But that signal is interfering with every screen in the building."

"So take a message."

"It won't respond to any of us." Worthington looked impatient. "Would you just accept it so we can finish our GTA game? Colossus was winning, and I can't let that kid beat me in my own house."

Logan gestured at the screen. "What if it's the Hellfire Club or something?"

"I doubt they're attacking us with person-to-person phone calls."

Logan shrugged, conceding the point.

"I got it," he said, holding out his hand.

"Thanks." Worthington tossed him the remote. "Oh, and leave some beer for the rest of us, huh? It's tough to get trucks out here."

Logan glared at the door as Worthington left. Then he walked back to the tap and poured himself two fresh cups. Paused, and poured a third. Then he aimed the remote control at the TV and pushed play. No response. He tried input, audio, unmute, and the up and down channel and volume buttons. Nothing. The message remained on the screen.

He planted himself back on the stool, leaned forward, and fixed the TV with his best stare.

"Logan," he said. "Hit me."

There was no wavering of the image, no sense of transition. All at once the message was gone, replaced by the crystal-sharp face of Professor Charles Xavier, founder of the X-Men. He glared out of the screen, eyes intense beneath his bald pate.

Logan almost spat out his beer.

"You certainly took your time," Xavier said.

"Charlie?"

"Logan, I have asked you not to call me that." Xavier's voice was so clear, he might have been standing in the room. "I answer to Professor, Professor Xavier, or if you must, Charles."

"Got it, Chuck."

Xavier shook his head and moved away from the camera. He wore a strange red-and-black tunic, and his usual wheelchair had been replaced by a sleek hover-device of some kind. The walls behind him were featureless metal, broken up by floor-to-ceiling viewports showing a field of stars.

"What's this about?" Logan demanded. "Where the hell are you, anyway?"

"On a world called Imperial Center, very far from Earth. My consort, Lilandra, is about to be crowned Empress Majestrix of the Shi'ar Empire."

Logan nodded. Shortly after the shuttle accident, Xavier had fallen in love with the Princess Lilandra Neramani, heir to the throne of an empire that had ruled an alien galaxy back when terrestrial life was still learning to walk on land. When Lilandra was called back to assume the throne, Xavier had gone with her. None of the X-Men had heard from him since.

"Empress," Logan repeated. "Sounds like you're comin' up in the world, Chuck. Or worlds, I guess." He lifted his cup in a toast.

"It is… difficult, actually. Lilandra's increased responsibilities are taking up more and more of her time."

"Relationships." Logan shook his head. "Didn't know it was so easy for you to call home, Chuck. Kind of makes me feel neglected—on behalf of the team, I mean."

"There's nothing *easy* about it." Xavier's brow furrowed. "I had to bribe a Kree high official just to get ten minutes on this— oh, there's no time to explain. I've received a disquieting packet of data from Moira MacTaggert. She's concerned about a situation that directly affects the X-Men."

Logan felt the effects of the beer fade away. As sobriety returned, so did the worries that had been occupying his mind. "You've missed a *lot*, Chuck. Never thought I'd say this, but I wish you were here."

"As do I," Xavier replied. "In fact, I plan to return to Earth as soon as possible after the coronation."

"We're up against some crazy Ren-fair freaks or something," Logan continued. "They got a telepath—this witch that can get right inside your head. She went after this teenage kid—"

150   "Logan!"

He looked up, startled.

"None of that—nothing else matters." Xavier leaned forward. "This is all about Jean."

Logan lowered his beer. "Keep talking."

"Has she seemed… different to you?"

"You mean less dead than she was?"

Xavier just glared.

"Yeah, she has," Logan admitted. *An' I've been too preoccupied to deal with it,* he thought. *Cryin' in my beer over some witch messing with my head, while Jeannie needs me.*

"I believe a part of you knows what's going on with her," Xavier said. "In fact, you may be the only one who *can* understand."

"It's my fault," Logan replied. "When Jeannie crashed the shuttle last year… I never should've let her do it."

"Muzzle your self-pity, Logan. Had you stopped Jean from piloting the shuttle, all of us would be dead."

Wolverine blinked. "Charlie, that might be the first time you've ever given me a good review."

"I am *not* calling to compliment you."

Logan peered at the screen, eyes sharp. Something in Xavier's tone had awakened the predator in him. *That's what I am,* he thought. *The predator in the group.*

"I need the Wolverine," Xavier continued, "for a mission."

There it is.

Logan downed his beer, slammed the cup on the bar, and turned to face the screen.

"You got him," he said.

CHAPTER THIRTEEN

"SORRY, ORORO," Kitty Pryde said. "No luck with the wicked witch's 'Massachusetts Academy.'"

The girl's voice was tinny over the phone's speaker. Storm shifted the device in her hand so that Colossus, sitting next to her, could see as well. "Oh! Hey, Peter," Kitty said. "Tight suit."

Colossus pulled nervously at his collar. "Hello, Katya."

Storm smiled. *I can see where this is going,* she thought.

They sat in the back of an elegant limousine, parked on the edge of Midtown Manhattan just three blocks west of Avengers Tower. Colossus—Peter—wore a three-piece tuxedo, perfectly fitted to his massive frame. Storm had chosen a long white dress with an African-patterned hem on the sleeves and wrap.

Wolverine and Nightcrawler sat in the opposite seat, both wearing their X-Men uniforms. Nightcrawler leaned forward, listening to Storm's conversation. Wolverine just stared out the tinted window, his mask raised to reveal his scowling eyes. His mood seemed even darker than usual.

"Thank you for trying, Kitty," Storm said. "We should have expected Ms. Frost to have excellent security."

"Security? Nah, 'Roro, I broke through the firewall like *that*."
She snapped her fingers. "Trouble is, all the records are squeaky
clean. Transcripts, teacher evaluations, term-paper assignments.
There's even a photo of a prom."

"A prom?"

"Yeah." Kitty grimaced. "I think they 'shopped it to make it
look more multicultural, but that's the biggest crime I can find."

"No mentions of the Hellfire Club?"

"Or just Hellfire?" Nightcrawler added. "Or Club?"

"Sorry. No mutants in cages, no blank-faced goons."

Well, Storm thought, sweeping her wrap around her shoulders.
That—as they say in this country—is that. "I must go, Kitty," she
said. "Once again, we appreciate your—"

"Wait!" Kitty leaned forward, her face looming almost
comically large on the screen. "Are you gonna infiltrate the whips-
and-chains gang? Can I come along?"

"Not this time, child." Storm smiled sweetly. "But remember,
if you get the slightest hint that they may be after *you* again,
contact me immediately. Personally."

Kitty nodded unhappily.

"We will see you soon," Storm said. She clicked the phone off.

"A girl who can walk through walls *would* be useful on this
mission," Nightcrawler suggested.

"I will not risk Kitty's life again," Storm said firmly. "It was
I who brought her into this, and the Hellfire Club almost killed
her. We are trained for this sort of thing, while she is—*Peter will
you please stop fidgeting?*"

Colossus froze, embarrassed.

"Does your suit not fit right, *mein Herr?*" Nightcrawler asked.

"It is not that." Colossus looked down. "I have never worn
clothes like these… They feel marvelous. Yet it does not feel right
to wear a suit that costs more than my father earns in a year."

"I don't know." Nightcrawler leaned back against the plush
seat, hands folded behind his head. "I'm getting rather accustomed
to traveling in luxury vehicles."

Wolverine let out a snort.

Storm touched Colossus's knee. "You are homesick."

He nodded. "It has been too long."

"Let us get through this crisis, little brother. Then we will see about arranging you a visit to Russia."

He flashed her a small smile.

Storm leaned forward and rapped on the opaque front window. The barrier slid down to reveal Cyclops and Jean, their faces nearly touching in the small window space. They, too, were dressed in evening clothes—Scott in a black jacket and tie, Jean in a long black backless gown.

"We're up to speed, Ororo," Cyclops said. "Jean's been monitoring everything."

Ororo frowned. *Monitoring?* Jean, like Professor X, had linked the X-Men together telepathically in the past. To Storm's knowledge, however, she'd never eavesdropped on their thoughts without explicit permission.

"Kitty struck out, people," Cyclops continued. "That means it's up to us. We're going in."

Storm hesitated. The Hellfire Club was about to celebrate its biggest birthday party since the turn of the millennium. Warren Worthington had managed to obtain four invitations for the X-Men under assumed names. It was the best plan they'd managed to come up with, under the circumstances. And yet...

"Cyclops," Nightcrawler said, "are we certain that you are not simply walking into... well, a trap?" He paused. "A *death*trap, perhaps?"

"It's a risk," Cyclops acknowledged, "but there's no indication that the White Queen and her allies know we're coming. More importantly, I don't see a good alternative. We have no hard evidence connecting Emma Frost with the Hellfire Club, and we can't afford to be wrong about this. We need proof, one way or the other.

"Ororo, Peter: once you're inside, keep a low profile," he continued. "See what you can learn through eavesdropping and casual conversations. If you manage to get close to someone who's clearly Hellfire Club, do *not* engage them. The last thing we need right now is to draw their attention.

"No phones—they're not secure. Jean will link our minds telepathically… we'll be in constant contact."

Wolverine looked up sharply. "That go for me an' the elf, too?"

"Everyone, Logan."

What's the matter, Logan? Jean's voice sounded in all their minds. *Afraid I'll learn all your secrets?*

"I like my privacy, Jeannie."

She blinked, then spoke aloud. "Sorry… just joking. I'll confine my scans to surface thoughts."

Wolverine nodded and reached for the door latch. "Let's get this over with."

"One more thing," Cyclops said. They all turned to face him. Even Colossus stopped picking at his collar.

"The Hellfire Club took three of you hostage. They experimented on you, poked around in your heads." He paused. "I know it was a wrenching experience. If any of you want to back out of this, I completely understand—but it's got to be now. Storm?"

She grimaced, remembering. The White Queen had only performed a brief scan on her before turning her attentions to Wolverine, but Storm could still recall the woman's icy mental fingers in her brain, the chill sensation of thoughts being probed and analyzed.

"I am fine, Scott."

"Colossus?"

The big X-Man gave a hesitant smile. "I cannot waste this suit."

"Logan?" Cyclops twisted his head through the limo's barrier window. "You got the worst of it. You ready for this?"

Wolverine stared at Cyclops for a moment, then turned toward Jean. A dark look crossed his face. It was gone in an instant, but it was enough to make Storm shudder.

"Always," he said.

A STEADY rain fell as Scott Summers approached the ornate wooden door, holding the umbrella above Jean's head. She nuzzled in close to him, her face warm against his shoulder.

You know I could telekinetically repel the raindrops, she said in his mind.

That wouldn't be very "low profile," he replied. *Would it?*

He cocked his head and ran a mental check. Jean had hooked up the X-Men's minds in a sort of extended network, allowing Cyclops to access any of their thoughts, one at a time or in combination, by clicking a series of mental "icons." It was unquestionably the best communication system they'd ever used—on more than one occasion it had saved their lives. But tonight, for some reason, it made him uneasy.

Ororo and Peter are already on-site, Jean said. *Nothing to report yet.*

A costumed attendant wearing a powdered wig and velvet vest swung open the door. Cyclops nodded, handed the man his umbrella, and held out his arm to Jean. Together they stepped inside.

The room was vast, multileveled, filled with men in three-piece suits and women in long elegant gowns. At first glance it resembled any old-line private club, with freestanding bars in the corners, tables piled high with appetizers, framed photos and paintings hung on papered walls. A grand staircase dominated the center of the room, sporting a bright crimson carpet liner. Swing music filled the air, just loud enough to make conversation difficult.

At a closer look, though, the true nature of the establishment became clear. The photos were hundred-year-old shots of women in corsets, posing with whips. A man in an executioner's hood roamed the crowd; the waitresses wore high heels, fishnet stockings, and ultra-short skirts. A huge banner hung above the staircase:

DO WHAT THOU WILT

They crossed the room, passing a table where an octogenarian in a tuxedo sat leering at a waitress in her twenties. *The Hellfire Club*, Scott said. *Is this it?*

Jean raised an eyebrow. *It's about what I expected.*

Find Storm, okay? Scott said. *And make sure Peter's doing all right. I'll check in with Wolverine and Nightcrawler.*

Jean gave him a brief smile and an even briefer kiss. Then she turned toward the staircase and glided away, black dress flowing in her wake. He watched her for a long moment, inhaling the old-world blend of cologne and pipe tobacco pervading the air.

Then he turned to the menu in his mind and tapped a pair of icons. *Kurt?*

The link went active immediately—he could feel Nightcrawler's and Wolverine's minds on the circuit, though neither of them spoke.

Everything good?

Ja, Nightcrawler said. *We are—*

We're in the flamin' sewers. Wolverine's tone was harsh. *Just like you wanted, boss.*

Good, Cyclops replied. *I know it's nasty work, but we need you in position.*

We are, Scott, Nightcrawler responded. *In position, I mean. The rain is still coming down heavily… water is rising down here.* A pause. *And, uh…*

Kurt? What is it?

Scott, there are extra power and communications cables down here. The Hellfire Club appears to be drawing a tremendous amount of electricity… as much as an entire skyscraper.

That's odd.

And, uh… Nightcrawler hesitated again. *Well, Wolverine decided to, er, attack the cables with his claws.*

Elf. Wolverine's smile came through over the circuit. *That was supposed t'be a surprise.*

I told you, Logan, Cyclops said. *We're trying to keep a low profile.*

Relax, Summers. All I did was strip some of the insulation off the power lines. Water's rising down here… when the water hits 'em, they ought to short out. Blow every light in the club, I bet.

Cyclops hesitated. To the left of the central staircase he could see the tall, distinctive figures of Storm and Colossus, surrounded by a crowd of tuxedo-clad businessmen. He spotted the eye-catching red of Jean's hair on the other side of the room, next to one of the small cocktail bars.

He frowned. What was she doing?

Anything goes wrong tonight, Logan continued, *I figured a surprise blackout might come in handy.*

It'll be a surprise to us, too, you know. But, um, fine. Stay in position—Cyclops out. He cut the connection, switched links. *Jean?*

No answer.

Jean!

Still nothing. A hint of panic ran through him.

Scott?

Jean! What are you doing over there? You sound… far away.

I think I saw something.

What kind of something?

I'm not sure. Her "voice" was even quieter now. *B-R-B.*

Jean?

Cyclops? That was Ororo. *Just reporting in.*

One moment, Storm. Jean?

Again, no answer. He scanned the room again, but she was gone.

What is it, Storm?

Peter and I find ourselves… uncomfortably popular. We have already been propositioned multiple times, in assorted combinations.

Under other circumstances, Cyclops might have found that amusing. Instead he frowned, and started moving toward the small bar where he'd last caught sight of Jean.

At the moment, Storm continued, *we are reluctantly engaged in a vigorous discussion of nineteenth-century paddling techniques.*

That's different. How, uh, how is Peter doing?

I believe he regrets leaving the Motherland.

As Cyclops pushed his way toward the back of the room, the crowd grew thicker. Two incredibly drunk men lurched toward him, their arms wrapped around a waitress. The smile on her face looked extremely strained. He dodged out of their way, gritting his teeth.

Chin up, Ororo, he sent, and he knew it was lame. *Just see what you can—*

Scott—

Jean again. Her thoughts were barely audible.

Jean? What's going on?

Scott, I don't think I can fight him.

Fight who? He spun around, searching the crowd. *Jean, where are you?*

He twisted sideways, almost colliding with a wall of laughing businessmen in tuxedos. He grabbed hold of the banister at the foot of the staircase to steady himself.

Can't fight him can't fight it…

Jean, talk to me. Tell me what you're fighting!

It's me. It's inside me.

Again he searched the room, left to right and back again. He couldn't see her, couldn't even see Colossus and Storm anymore. Just drunken partygoers and tired, reluctant women serving up drinks and pained smiles to the men who'd hired them. Then another "voice" cut into the circuit. A man's voice, deep and loud and commanding.

My beautiful flower…

Cyclops whirled, seeking the source, and found himself facing the staircase. When he looked up, his mouth dropped in amazement. Jean was climbing the stairs, just a few steps up, her fiery hair cascading down the pale skin of her back. A man in buccaneer boots, a silk shirt, and a velvet jacket guided her slowly upward, his hand wrapped firmly around her shoulder.

"Jean!" Cyclops cried. "Jean, *wait!*" She stopped a few steps from the top, but she didn't turn around. The man glanced at her, then swiveled his head to look down. His neatly trimmed beard framed a lupine smile.

The man's thought echoed in Cyclops's mind: *…almost in full bloom.*

Wyngarde, he realized. This was Jason Wyngarde, the man she'd met on Kirinos. Cyclops had seen him in Jean's thoughts, back in New Mexico.

Jean? Why is he—hey! Cyclops took off after them—but he stopped short as a gloved hand grabbed his arm. He jerked to a halt, still on the bottom step, and whirled around.

Emma Frost.

She stood in full Hellfire garb, cape swirling around her. A few passing drunks hovered nearby, leering and muttering obscenities, but on the whole she hardly stood out among the costumed multitude. Cyclops wrenched his arm away, and started up the staircase.

Don't, Emma warned in his mind.

Wyngarde and Jean had almost reached the top of the stairs. As Cyclops moved toward them, Emma seemed to glide up past him. She stopped a step above, blocking his way.

"Move," he said.

You won't like what you find.

He hesitated. The look on her face wasn't cruel or even playful. It almost looked like… sympathy.

Your link with her, Emma said. *It's gone.*

With a shock, he realized it was true. He could no longer sense Jean's thoughts—their newfound intimacy, their enhanced mental bond, had vanished. He couldn't sense any of the other X-Men, either. The team was deaf, dumb, and blind.

"What have you done?" he demanded.

Me? she responded. *Nothing.* Emma reached down to touch him on the shoulder. *She's just gone.*

He peered past her. Up above, Wyngarde and Jean turned around a corner, passing out of sight.

Trust me, Emma said. *Sometimes it's better to walk in the shadows than stare at the sun.*

He lifted his glasses and shot a narrow energy blast past her head. The beam struck an ornate carving atop the banister, shattering it into wooden shards. Emma cried out, startled, as a chunk of wood struck her cheek. Losing her balance, she stumbled down the stairs, scattering drunken men in her wake. A couple of them reached out for her. She managed to dodge them, but just barely.

"Get out of my head," Cyclops snarled, sprinting up the stairs. A group of businessmen and women, all in tuxedos and evening wear, stood blocking the landing. He shoved them aside and sprinted down a corridor lined with old wallpaper, dimly lit by hanging bulbs. Muffled laughter and moaning sounds leaked through the walls on either side. He ignored the noises and pressed forward.

Jean!

He ran, seemingly forever, twisting and turning down madly winding hallways. A sense of futility settled over him, as if he'd been running down the same blind alleys, the same dark corridors, fighting the same useless battles all his life. With no Jean, no voice in his mind to guide him or warn him or whisper assurances in his ear.

Up ahead, to the left, a door was just closing. He caught a glimpse of a woman's bare thigh, pale, muscular, rising out of a polished black boot fastened with high laces. He cried out her name—and then he knew. Knew that something was terribly wrong, that he'd misjudged the situation on a critical level.

A mental blast seared through him, pounding into his head, slamming him back against the corridor wall. There was no defense, no time to respond. He screamed in pain and fell to the floor, the world swimming around him. A voice sounded in his mind.

Told you.

Not Jean's voice. Emma's.

He looked up, struggling to focus. Jean stood in the hallway, her hand smoking with power, glaring down at him with a look of utter contempt. She wore a black mirror version of Emma Frost's outfit—boots, tight shorts, and a leather collar studded with sharp spikes. A cape was fastened at the throat with a single red rose.

And that corset. The black corset she'd described to him, the one from the closet on Kirinos. Laced around her waist, binding her body as tightly as the strange grip that Wyngarde seemed to

hold on her mind.

"Jean," he croaked.

Wyngarde stepped up behind her, laid a hand on her caped shoulder. He cast his eyes down at Cyclops's limp form and grinned.

"Magnificent," he said aloud. "Magnificent, my love."

She turned to face Wyngarde. Her eyes flashed with hunger, and she grabbed him by both cheeks. She kissed him hard on the lips, her hands roaming up and down his vest and coat.

Cyclops watched in horror, desperately struggling to remain conscious. But his strength was gone. As the hallway dissolved to black, the last thing he heard was Wyngarde's silky, dominant voice:

"My Black Queen."

CHAPTER FOURTEEN

STORM'S SENSITIVE ears picked up the scream. She whirled around, summoning a mild wind to gently push aside a trio of men in bear costumes. She searched the room, peering over the heads of the drunken revelers.

Cyclops?

Nothing—no response. The telepathic link was broken.

She turned back to Colossus. The young X-Man had been backed into a corner, beneath a wall sconce, by two middle-aged men and a very drunk young woman. One of the men had a hand on his bicep.

"Metal restraints!" the man said. "*Much* stronger than leather."

"Leave him alone!" The young woman giggled, spilling a bit of champagne on Peter's arm. Storm strode over and grabbed his hand.

"We must go."

Colossus disengaged himself gratefully from the group. "Did Cyclops call you?"

"I think he is out of the game. In any event, we've lost telepathic contact."

He looked alarmed. "That means something's happened to—"

"To Jean. Yes."

The middle-aged man grabbed Colossus's arm again. "Have you any experience with metal?" he asked, slurring his words. Colossus paused for a moment. Then a halo of energy surrounded him and he began to grow, to swell up. In an instant, his skin transformed to solid, gleaming steel.

"A bit," he said, pulling free of the startled man's grip.

A crowd was gathering at the base of the staircase, singing a Celtic song in painful, off-key tones. They hadn't noticed Peter's transformation, but the guests nearer to him began pointing in alarm, their drinks spilling over onto the floor.

"Well," Storm said, "I suppose the infiltration stage of this mission is concluded." She took to the air, spreading her arms to raise a wind current. Her dress dropped away, revealing her black-and-ivory X-Men costume beneath. The nearest guests stared at her and retreated, holding up their hands against the wind.

"This way," she said, gliding toward the staircase. Colossus followed at a run, his thundering footsteps shaking the hall. A sea of tuxedos parted for them.

Storm paused at the base of the staircase, noting the shattered wooden carving atop the banister. A tuxedo-clad waiter stood partway up the flight of stairs, sweeping up the pieces. As Storm wafted up toward him, he turned to face her. He dropped his broom, let out a little gasp, and scurried away.

Colossus took the steps three at a time, wooden beams crunching beneath his feet. Storm paced him from above.

"I heard Cyclops cry out," she said. "At least, I believe it was him."

"Perhaps our trap has sprung?" Colossus replied.

"Goddess grant that we can deal with whatever we've snared."

Atop the stairs, the landing gave way to a narrow corridor lined with doors. They rounded a corner—and came face-to-face with a stocky, middle-aged man. He stood blocking the hallway, his hands planted firmly on his hips. He wore tights and the sash of a martial-arts master, with protective boots similar to the X-Men's own. His chest was bare.

"Ororo Munroe," the man said, a sadistic grin breaking out on his face. "And Peter Rasputin. I am Sebastian Shaw."

Storm paused in midair. Behind Shaw, the corridor stretched into the distance. All the doors lining it were closed.

"I advise you to surrender," Shaw said.

"To you?" Colossus pounded forward. "Do not make me laugh." He raised a metal fist.

"Be careful, little brother!" Storm said. "He is only human. Your blow could kill him."

Colossus nodded. His fist lashed out, stopping short as it made contact with Shaw's chest. *Good,* Storm thought. *He pulled the punch just in time. That should be just enough to defeat this hired martial artist without seriously injuring him.*

Shaw didn't flinch, didn't even move. Where Colossus's fist struck him, a small burst of energy seemed to flash, then dissolve into his bare chest. Colossus stepped back, stunned.

"My blow had no effect!" he said.

"Wrong," Shaw said. "Both of you."

Before Storm could react, Shaw clasped his fists tightly together and swung them through the air. The blow slammed into Colossus's midsection and, incredibly, knocked him into the air. Five hundred pounds of metallic mutant crashed into a table at the end of the hallway, shattering the mirror behind it.

"Peter!" Storm cried.

Like a hunter stalking his prey, Shaw took a step toward Colossus. The X-Man looked up from the floor, dazed.

"I am no mere human," Shaw said, leaping into the air. "I am a mutant—as much as you are, my unfortunate friend." Colossus kicked upward, grimacing, and dealt Shaw a powerful blow to the stomach. Shaw let out a strangled gasp—then twisted in midair and landed gracefully. He reached out, grabbed Colossus's outstretched leg, and swung him up off his feet.

Peter didn't hold back that time, Storm thought, watching her teammate struggle in Shaw's grip. *That kick would have smashed a tank.*

"My power," Shaw said, "is to absorb any energy directed against me. Your attacks only make me stronger…"

Colossus struck the wall with a thunderous crash.

"…which makes me the one enemy you can never defeat."

Peter slumped to the floor and was still.

"Now…" Shaw turned to look up at Storm. She drifted backward in the air, almost touching the wall of the cramped hallway, and glanced down at Peter. He was barely moving, but his body hadn't yet reverted to human form. That meant he was still partially conscious.

More important, it meant he was alive.

"Half your team is beaten, Storm." Shaw gave her a hungry grin. "And the battle has barely begun."

I don't want to leave Peter, she thought, *but his armored body is too heavy to carry. And I must warn Nightcrawler and Wolverine!*

"Yield," Shaw continued, "and I will show mercy."

"Never," she said.

She concentrated, amplifying the humidity in the air. A thick fog rose up all at once, with Sebastian Shaw at its center. He stumbled and lashed out with his fists. Storm swooped easily around him and flew back toward the staircase. The last thing she saw, through the thick mist, was Colossus's armored body lying still on the floor.

Forgive me, little brother.

○———————○

WOLVERINE SLASHED upward, his claws digging through layer after layer of soil. When he struck concrete, the resistance almost knocked him off-balance. He inched back, bracing himself against the walls of the vertical tunnel he'd just dug.

"Pay dirt," he called down.

Below, in the sewer, Nightcrawler stood hip-deep in water. He grinned at his teammate and gave a thumbs-up sign.

Grunting, Wolverine pressed one arm against the dirt wall of the tunnel. Then he flexed the other arm and thrust upward. His Adamantium-tipped claws shattered the concrete to rubble.

He climbed up into the third-level subbasement of the Hellfire Club. It was dark, deserted, with water heaters and power generators humming away in the corners. A huge furnace pumped and whirred, linked by pipes to a network of rusty oil tanks. Before he could yell down again, Nightcrawler appeared ahead of him in a cloud of brimstone.

"We're in," Nightcrawler said. "So far, so good."

"Yeah." Logan brushed sewage off his costume. "Too bad you couldn't just 'port us in here from outside."

"Without knowing the layout," Nightcrawler replied, "I might have materialized inside something. And unlike our new recruit, I cannot walk through walls."

"I know, I know." Logan sniffed the air. "Still, this caper's goin' down easy—a little too easy, you ask me."

Nightcrawler shrugged. "Do they not say in this country, 'No news is good news?'"

"Depends on the channel. You hear anything from Cyke or Jeannie?"

"No." Nightcrawler frowned. "In fact, I do not seem to sense them in my mind anym—"

Wolverine caught the scent—just a moment too late. A man darted out of the shadows and grabbed Nightcrawler by the throat, lifting him into the air. The newcomer was tall, with carefully coiffed blond hair, and dressed in period garb—crushed-velvet vest, long coat, breeches. He spun around and held out Nightcrawler in front of him like a shield.

Logan dropped to a crouch and snarled. *Easy enough to take 'im out,* he thought. *But I might tag Kurt by mistake.*

"Elf," he said, "'Port away!"

Nightcrawler gasped. His head whipped back and forth in the man's grip.

"He cannot." The man's voice was cultured, with a trace of a finishing-school accent. "I am projecting an electrical field through his body, preventing him from concentrating."

"Good for you," Logan said, and slashed out. His claws raked straight down the man's arm, cutting through coat and silk. An electrical charge shot through Logan; pain seared through him, from his arm up to his chest.

When he paused to assess the damage, what he saw made him gasp. The man's arm hadn't moved—he still held Nightcrawler's throat in an iron grip. But where Wolverine had sliced into him, the flesh had been torn away to reveal a complex of sparking wires.

"You savage!" the man exclaimed. "Look what you've done!"

Wolverine stared. "You're a freakin' robot."

"I am not!" The man's brows narrowed in rage. "Donald Pierce is a *cyborg*." His other hand swept out, grabbing hold of Wolverine's arm. Before Logan could react, he found himself flying through the air. When he crashed into an oil tank, the impact went straight up his reinforced spine. He shook his head and climbed to his feet, a dangerous smile creeping across his face.

"I know all about cyborgs. I'm sort of one myself." He held out both hands, displaying his claws. "Loosely defined."

Nightcrawler let out a strangled gasp and went limp in Pierce's grip. Wolverine leaped to his feet and sprinted across the basement—but before he could cross the distance a sword slashed out from the side, blocking his way. Logan whirled, snarling, to see a portly man with a red beard. A dull smile covered the man's face as he lunged forward, jabbing at the air.

"The name is Leland," the man said, "Harry Leland, and I'm afraid I can't allow you to attack Sir Pierce again."

Wolverine laughed. "You're welcome to try an' stop me."

"Dear boy." The man's smile grew wider. "Challenge accepted."

Logan stepped toward Leland, raking his claws menacingly against each other. Leland holstered his sword and held out both hands. All at once, a great weight seemed to descend on Logan—his back, his legs, his arms. Each step grew more difficult than the last.

"You X-Men are not the only mutants in the world," Leland said. "My own talent involves mass."

Wolverine dropped to the floor, gasping.

"Simply by concentrating," Leland continued, "I can increase the weight of any object. Or any person."

Must weigh tons, Logan thought. *And I'm gettin' heavier all the time. But I can't give up. Gotta save the elf... warn the others...* He reached out, stabbed a claw into the floor, and used the leverage to wrench himself forward.

Pierce approached, still holding Nightcrawler's limp body. "Impressive." His other arm sparked and sputtered in the air.

"Indeed," Leland said. "So refreshing to test ourselves against mutants, instead of the, uh..."

"The cattle?" Pierce asked.

"The *flowers*," Leland replied.

The two men laughed.

Logan ignored them. He sliced into the floor again, anchoring his claws in the concrete. With a tremendous effort, he pulled himself forward another six inches.

"I could have used your help at the Circle meeting, old chap," Leland said. "Shaw and his little *Queen* were playing their power games again."

"It couldn't be helped." Pierce shrugged. "Business abroad, you know."

"Well, it's good to have you back. Men of breeding are an increasingly rare thing in this world."

"You flatter me," Pierce smiled. "But you speak the truth, of course."

Logan's skull seemed to be made of lead. He was less than a yard away from Leland, but it might as well have been miles. He could feel the pressure on his back, sapping his strength.

"Kill you," he growled.

Leland turned at the voice, as if he'd forgotten Logan entirely. "Perhaps, dear boy." He twisted his hands in midair. "Or else...?"

Once again, the pressure increased sharply. Logan's spine began to creak, bones bending like twigs. Then he felt the floor beneath him buckle and crack open—and he fell. His increased mass propelled him through layers of concrete, dirt, and metal, back down into the subterranean levels beneath the building.

He burst through the ceiling of the sewer, tumbling down to land with a heavy splash. A wall of filthy water assaulted him, the impact knocking him unconscious in an instant, and then he was swept away from the Hellfire Club on an unstoppable tide.

STORM SOARED through the upper levels of the club, startling couples and threesomes as they poked their heads out of secluded rooms. Locating a utility staircase, she glided up to the top floor, where a pair of double doors led to a high-ceilinged library furnished with old leather chairs and wooden desks. Shelves of musty-smelling antique books stretched up the walls.

She touched down and pulled out her phone. Tried to reach Wolverine, then Nightcrawler. No answer. *Enough,* she thought, and raised her arms to summon the lightning. A powerful bolt burst forth, blasting against the bay windows.

Nothing. The lightning dissipated, sparking harmlessly into the air. The windows remained shut.

Some sort of defensive energy field, she realized. *This Hellfire Club… every part of it is built for confinement.* She eyed the door. *Only one route left: back downstairs and out the front door, using the party guests to cover my escape—*

"Surprise."

Shaw lunged out of the shadows. She took to the air, but he was too fast—he grabbed her ankle and held it in an iron grip. She struggled to free herself.

He seems to know all about our powers, she thought. *My only hope is to do the unexpected!* She raised her arms as if to summon a windstorm, but instead kicked out with her free leg, clipping Shaw hard across the chin. He cried out and released her, sending her tumbling through the air. But before she could seize the advantage, he caught hold of her cape and pulled her toward him.

"Have you forgotten, Storm? I absorb kinetic energy." He flipped her upside down, sending her plummeting toward the floor. "Your attacks merely… agitate me." She struck face-first, crying out in pain as blood filled her mouth.

"Why?" she gasped. "Why… us?"

"An accident of genetics." Shaw lifted her up by the hair, turned her to face him. "I have an instinct for money. It's raised me from humble beginnings to become one of the preeminent industrialists of the twenty-first century. If I—if the *Hellfire Club*—can isolate the genetic X factor that creates enhanced-power beings like ourselves, we can exploit it in the marketplace."

She wiped blood from her face. "And you're not about to experiment on yourself."

"Why should I?" He smiled. "When there are so many lovely, fascinating subjects to choose from."

He twisted her around and slammed her head into a bookcase. She caught a quick glimpse of old books falling from the shelves, leather-bound tomes tumbling to the polished wood floor. And then she didn't see anything at all.

SHAW TWISTED Storm's cape around his fist and began dragging her across the floor. Then he paused, turned toward the door, and cocked his head.

Emma? Do you hear me?

No answer.

We have defeated the X-Men, he said, *and with no losses of our own. The Hellfire Club is triumphant.*

Only a slight buzz in his mind betrayed the White Queen's presence.

It's been a long time since I used my mutant ability, he added. *I'd forgotten how good it felt.* He crouched down, hoisting up Ororo as if she weighed nothing. *Are you proud of your King?*

Laughter. Light yet harsh, ringing in his mind over the

telepathic link. She was a cruel one, his White Queen—yet such was the way of the Hellfire Club. Its currency was power, its instrument cruelty. So it had been in times long past, and so it would always be.

He sighed, slung the unconscious mutant over his shoulder, and started down toward the basement headquarters of the Inner Circle.

CHAPTER FIFTEEN

JEAN!

That was Scott Summers's first thought upon waking. Then came pure, claustrophobic terror.

I can't see!

He whipped his head one way, then the other. Metallic restraints clanked, pulling taut against his throat. He lay on a cold stone floor; a thick glove bound his hands tightly together, holding his arms behind his back. A metal collar and hood covered his entire face and neck, so tightly that he couldn't even move his mouth to speak. His captors had placed his visor over his eyes, and the hood pressed it painfully against the bridge of his nose. When he tried to use his glove controls to open the visor, the energy flashed briefly and then died. All he could see was a haze of red.

The hood, he realized. *It's infused with ruby quartz. My power is useless!*

"Ho!" a rumbling voice said. "He's awake, Pierce."

"Watch out for that one, Leland. He's the leader." The second voice was higher, silkier. "These others are still out."

Who? Cyclops wondered. *Who else have they captured?*

He heard a slam, like a door being thrown open. Heavy footsteps approached, growing louder. Then a large object—a body?—thudded onto the floor, just inches away from him.

"That's the last of them." The third voice was deep, commanding. "The Hellfire Club is victorious."

There was a faint moan from the floor. Cyclops recognized the voice: *Storm!*

He forced himself to concentrate. As a teenager, he'd learned to adapt to situations where he couldn't see his surroundings. A necessary skill for a boy who often had to squeeze his eyes shut in order to avoid injuring his fellow students.

The air in the room was cold and dry. Sounds of humming machinery, crackling fires. *This must be the Inner Circle's sanctum… probably somewhere beneath the building itself.*

"How's your arm, Pierce?"

"Just a scratch, Shaw. Easily repaired—I'm fine now."

Shaw. Emma Frost's… what? Lover? Master? Partner in her sick games?

"Scratch—ha!"

The new voice sent chills up Cyclops's spine. He'd only heard it once before—briefly, just before losing consciousness—but he'd *felt* it, experienced its power secondhand, inside Jean's mind. On the butte in New Mexico, when he'd opened himself to her thoughts and memories.

Wyngarde.

"Wolverine cut through your precious bionic arm like a stick of butter," the voice continued.

"Jason, darling."

No. Oh no.

Jean.

"We've just won a splendid victory," she continued. "Why spoil it with harsh words?"

He knew her voice better than anyone's, better even than his own, but he'd never heard it like this before. So oily, so full of guile and deception.

"Your Black Queen speaks true, Wyngarde," Shaw said. "This was a group effort. We all did our part."

"Did we?" Wyngarde paused. "I believe we're missing one X-Man."

"Wolverine is dead," Leland said.

Wyngarde snorted. "I doubt that."

"If he lives, I'll kill him again. With my bare hands." That was Pierce again, his voice charged with anger. "No man draws blood from me and lives. Especially not some *filthy mutant.*"

"Take care, old boy," Leland replied, an edge creeping into his voice. "Remember the company you keep."

"Gentlemen," Shaw said. "*If* Wolverine survived, he'll be far away by now. We'll deal with him in time, just as we have with all the others."

All the others, Cyclops thought. *That means they've got Peter and Kurt, too.*

"Let us celebrate," Shaw continued, "while the sheep upstairs conduct their petty bacchanal. All unaware that we will soon fleece them, along with the rest of the world."

"As you say, Shaw," Wyngarde said. "Just remember that it was *my* Queen, Jean Grey, who provided the key to our victory."

Pierce sniffed. "We would have won in any case."

"You think so? Very well, I'll release my hold on her. We'll see how long you last."

"Enough!" Shaw's voice grew louder as he moved toward the group. "I propose a toast. To the Hellfire Club—and to Jean Grey, our Black Queen."

"Long may she reign," Wyngarde said.

Those two—they're the main players, Cyclops thought. *They're sparring with each other, jockeying for power. Shaw with Emma at his side, and Wyngarde with his... his Black Queen. They're the only two that matter. Leland and Pierce are nothing... surrogates, playing pieces.*

"The manor is secure, Sir Jason." Jean's voice again. "Do you wish to discipline the staff further?"

The manor? Cyclops thought. *The staff?*

A slapping sound. Like a riding crop against leather.

Wyngarde's right, Scott thought. *Jean is the key. Somehow he's enthralled her, drawn out some flaw inside her that's allowed him to take over her mind. Turned her into a twisted reflection of herself.*

"Later, my dear," Wyngarde said. "For now, let us enjoy the fruits of my—of *our* victory."

Wyngarde pulled her close and kissed her. His eyes, his rough beard, the musky scent of him—all of it formed an overwhelming cocktail, flooding her senses. Her blood surged and she responded, pressing herself urgently against him—

Wait. Cyclops jumped, startled. *How did I know all that?*

The link, he realized. Our telepathic bond—it's still active. Jean tried to sever it, to cut herself off from me, but some trace of it remains. What had they pledged, back in New Mexico? Total intimacy. Total trust.

Time to put that to the test.

He cleared his thoughts, remembering the concentration exercises taught to him by Professor X. The red haze before him faded to black. Distantly, he heard Storm groan again, but he ignored the sound, forced it out of his mind. He banished all outside stimuli, focusing his consciousness on one thing and one thing alone: a tiny pinpoint of red, a faint light shining off in the darkness.

Jean, he thought. *Jean, I know you're there. I know you're hurting. Let me in.*

The light grew brighter, hotter.

Remember all we've shared. Let me in!

○———————○

MIND LIKE FIRE *like the heart of a sun*

Pure power pure rage

They don't understand. They'll never you'll never understand. Flames dancing on skin corset laced tight worlds exploding in fire fire fire fire I am fire. Fire and life incarnate

Ice leather burning freezing

Love the love the fall. Trees changing leaves dropping. The circle unbroken

Welcome the voice within without. Ancient unknowable ME. Inscribed on genes, etched in racial memory

Welcome to the last minutes

Shackles fastened whip cracking charged particles might cause mutations in the

Face on fire stomach churning

Me it's me it's inside me

Oh oh Jason oh my love

Naked man with animal horns

Lady Jean

Sky lit up like a star like a furnace the fire that consumes rage rage against the men against the humans they hate mutants hate women hate all that is different hate ME

Love me I could make you love me. Make you do anything anything I wish. You exist you live you continue at my sufferance Lady Jean I am Lady Jean Grey Jason oh my Jason your scent your voice your arms bind me set me free this life

I am Phoenix I am rage am fire

This life may not be the life I'm meant to

I AM LADY JEAN GREY AND THIS IS MY MANOR

CYCLOPS REELED, tumbling back. In his mind's eye, he raised his hands to ward off the blinding light, the chaos assaulting his senses.

Is that really her? he wondered. *The anger, the resentment… the sense of claustrophobia, of being* caged *all her life?*

"*This life may not be the life I'm meant to…*"

A terrible thought came over him. *Have I been holding her back? Preventing Jean from… from becoming her best self? I've shared her thoughts, her fears… loved her, laughed and cried with her. But even with our minds linked together, I never knew… never understood the depth of her…*

He swallowed, blinked back tears behind the hood.

Maybe I never knew her at all, he thought darkly. *Maybe no one can ever truly know another person.*

No! This is Wyngarde… it's all his doing, somehow. Part of his chess game, his gambit to seize control of the Hellfire Club. He's taken over her mind, implanted some fantasy inside of her. If it's the last thing I do, I will stop him.

Marshaling his strength, Cyclops struggled to his feet. The light grew brighter again, threatening to overwhelm him. He forced himself to face it head-on, to open himself to its secrets.

Show me, my darling, he thought. *Let me see the nightmare world you're living in, through your eyes.* But the light seemed to flare, resisting him. Then it softened, relented. There was a sensation of flight, of falling…

…and then he saw.

The room was huge and bright, tall windows framed by ornate curtains. Gas lamps illuminated the large space, darkening the drapes with a coating of ash. A chandelier dominated the high ceiling, thick candles dripping wax down their sockets.

The main hall, he realized. *The gateway to Lady Jean's manor.*

Again her thoughts assaulted him.

Rage burning ice leather—

He forced them away, using the Professor's exercises to build a mental wall. Focused on hearing past the noise, on seeing Jean and her surroundings as she saw them. A scarlet-haired lady, tall and proud, fists planted on the cinched waist of her corset. Club members gathered around her like a pack of competing suitors. He studied them one by one, collecting impressions of the Inner Circle.

Donald Pierce. Tall, effete, his long face cruelly lined.

Harry Leland. Large, heavy, arrogant, casting a casual leer in Jean's direction.

Sebastian Shaw. Rough, thick-bodied, with a brawler's hands

and cold eyes.

Jason Wyngarde, at Jean's side. Rakish, with his neatly trimmed beard and mustache. Smiling as if he owned everything in this room, everything in the world.

"You're far more… receptive than the White Queen, dear." Leland reached out a hand to cup Jean's chin. "I like that." His other hand strayed to her waist. Jean's eyes flashed and she edged away, almost imperceptibly, out of his reach. Then she smiled.

"I like you, too, Squire Leland."

Cyclops felt a flash of anger—and helplessness, too. In this place, here within Jean's mind, he was powerless to act. All he could do was watch.

"Where *is* your dear Queen, Sebastian?" Wyngarde asked. "Shouldn't she be sharing in this celebration?"

"Emma has her duties," Shaw said.

Wyngarde laughed. "You don't know where she is."

Shaw glowered and looked away.

"Boys, boys." Jean looked from one to another. "Aren't I enough for you?" They all smiled.

She's manipulating them, Cyclops thought. *Playing to their basest instincts. Oh, Jean…*

"Speaking of duties." She held up a coiled whip. "Perhaps it's time to administer some discipline."

She turned toward four figures propped up against the wall. One wore the rugged clothes of a farm laborer; another was clad in a dirt-specked white dress. A third, mustachioed figure had the sharp eyes and colorful ascot of a rogue from some past era. All their arms were cuffed behind their backs.

That's us, Cyclops realized. *The X-Men, as Jean sees us. Colossus, Storm, Nightcrawler…*

He stared through Jean's eyes at the fourth figure. The man wore a tricorn hat, dark glasses, and a dour expression. Like the others, he was bound, helpless.

…and me. He blinked. *That's me.*

"A rebellion." Jean paced back and forth, slapping the whip against her hand. "Among my own household staff! The servants I fed, clothed, trusted, raised up from nothing." She paused, reached up to grab Colossus's chin in a rough grip. "It hurts, Peter. Do you understand that?" His eyes went wide, but he made no reply.

"But the worst betrayal," she continued, "the wound that cuts the deepest... is yours, my dear Ororo." She paused, looked at Storm. "Have I not treated you well?"

Storm frowned. "We have always been friends, Jean."

"Friends?"

Jean slapped the whip across Storm's cheek. Ororo cried out. She struggled, but the ropes held her arms tight.

"We are not *friends*," Jean continued. "You are my slave. You were born my family's slave, and as such you will die."

Storm's mouth opened in shock. Slowly, her expression turned to rage.

"Is this what you want, beauty?" Jean held up a large ring laden with metal keys. "The keys that will free you and your companions?"

Storm stared into Jean's cold eyes.

"Who *are* you?" she asked.

Jean laughed—a loud rasping sound.

Cyclops recoiled, looked away. He couldn't stand this—not any longer. Jean's viciousness, her naked racism, her cruelty toward helpless victims—

—abruptly, the room wavered. Drapes turned to stone, windows to video screens. Gas lamps morphed into wall-mounted torches. Cyclops lurched, felt the tug of the bindings against his arms—

—and then, somehow, he could see the room. Not as Jean saw it, but as it really was. A dark stone chamber, lit by candles and torches, state-of-the-art computers juxtaposed with displays of antique weapons. Rows of wooden tables, an elevated meeting area at the far end.

Nightcrawler, Storm, and Colossus stood lined up against the wall, chains and cuffs binding their arms as well. They wore their costumes, and high-tech collars—no doubt equipped with inhibitor technology to negate their mutant powers.

182   Jean looked unchanged. Tall, imperious, clad in the same dark

corset, heels, and cape she'd worn in the illusion. The uniform—the cruel armor—of the Black Queen.

"Jean." Storm's voice carried an uncharacteristic undertone of fury. "In the name of the love we shared, I will endeavor to remember you as you were."

"Whereas I," Jean replied, "will not remember you at all." She smiled and dangled the keys before Storm's eyes.

No, Cyclops realized, *not keys*. The object in Jean's hand was Storm's headdress, which held a selection of tiny, sophisticated lockpicks.

Wyngarde stepped up to join Jean. Leland let out a laugh, and Shaw snorted in approval. Pierce followed, smiling in silence.

They look the same, too, Cyclops thought. *The Inner Circle of the Hellfire Club, in their expensive, foppish cosplay. Their arrogance—the greed and hatred of the elite—is the same in any time period.*

Then the image faded to a deep, featureless red. He found himself back in his own mind, cut off from Jean's thoughts. Once again, he was blind.

"Herr Shaw." That was Nightcrawler. "Pardon my asking, but why are we still alive?"

Shaw's footsteps sounded on the stone floor, growing closer.

"As I explained to Ms. Munroe," he said, "super-powered beings are proliferating throughout the world. If we can custom-build mutants through genetic engineering… well, then the possibilities are limitless."

"And we are to be your guinea pigs," Colossus said.

"Yes." Shaw paused. "Actually… looking at it from your perspective…"

Cyclops gritted his teeth in frustration. He was helpless, caught in a trap designed specifically for him. Lost, quite literally, in the dark.

"…it might have been better if we *had* killed you."

CHAPTER SIXTEEN

THE PAWNS never saw him coming. One minute they were fanned out on the dark patio at the back of the club, searching around dumpsters and stacks of kitchen supplies. Their mission: locate any additional X-Men who might be hiding in the shadows.

The next minute, Wolverine exploded up out of a sewer grate, claws slicing savagely through the air. The pawns scattered, raising high-powered rifles. Logan leaped toward them, grinning. Those blank, bisected masks hid their expressions, but he could smell their fear on the wind.

One of them fired a shot, wild, into the air. "Davey," he yelled, "he's coming for you!"

Been in better brawls, Wolverine thought. *Odds here are only three to one.* He touched down, swiping out with his right hand. His claws sliced into one of the pawns, tearing through Kevlar and drawing blood. The man cried out, grabbed his stomach, and doubled over. His eyes went glassy, his mouth began to foam, and he fell.

Make that two to one. Sorry, Davey.

The remaining pawns pointed, shouted, and aimed their

rifles. Logan didn't stop, didn't even slow down. He leapt up onto a crate of kitchen supplies and launched himself across the patio. His claws jabbed deep into the second pawn's chest, knocking him backward into an old metal trash can. The man moaned and slumped to the ground.

A barrage of rifle fire split the air. Logan dropped, striking his head on the stone patio with a heavy thud. Pain lanced through him. *That's a concussion for sure,* he thought, squeezing his eyes shut. Fortunately, his mutant healing power was already repairing the damage. Shaking off the pain, he rolled, keeping his body low to the ground. He edged around a pile of crates, moving toward a dark fence at the far end of the patio.

He paused in the shadows, gasping. He'd nearly drowned tonight. The floodwaters had washed him almost a mile down the sewer pipe before he'd managed to claw his way up out of the rushing current. Getting back here had been an adventure in itself.

"Don't move," the remaining pawn said.

Wolverine smiled. Retracting his claws, he stepped out of the shadows.

The man stood across the patio, up against the stone wall of the building. His rifle shook in his hands. "Wh-what's that smell?" he asked.

"I ain't had time to shower," Wolverine said. "Listen, bub. I know what you're thinkin'."

"Huh?"

"You're thinking, 'He's hurt. An' he's five meters away from me, an' I got a full clip of ammo in my rifle. So the question is, can I kill Wolverine before he cuts me into airport sushi with those freaky claws of his?'"

The man glanced back toward the door that led to the kitchen. No one was coming to his aid.

"It's a decent question," Logan allowed, "but you gotta consider all the factors. One: Wolverine is nearly unkillable. Two: Wolverine's claws are made of Adamantium, the strongest metal on Earth. Three: five meters ain't really all that far for me. But here's the kicker. Your bosses are holdin' the Wolverine's friends inside that cut-rate kink parlor, and one of those friends is real, real important. Not just to me—maybe to the whole world.

"Point is, you really don't want to get between the Wolverine and his friends." He paused for effect. "Your play, hero. But I gotta warn you: I'm on a mission."

The pawn hesitated. Then he lowered his rifle and let it clatter to the ground. Logan was on the man before he could make a sound. Adamantium-reinforced fingers clamped around the pawn's throat, lifting him up into the air.

"I—*gkk*—I surrender!" the man gasped.

"'S'all good, bub. I ain't gonna kill you."

"What *dgggkk* you want?"

"Thanks for askin'." Logan smiled up at him. "I want to know every detail of the Hellfire Club's layout. Especially the secret hangouts, leather closets, and VIP rooms of the dirtbags that run this place."

The pawn hesitated. Logan squeezed.

The man nodded.

Three minutes later, Logan smashed the pawn's head against a dumpster—not fatally, just hard enough to knock him out.

Must be goin' soft, he thought, *but the man did come correct. Now all I gotta do is find that elevator to the subbasement, which means I gotta get across the main floor quietly. And then…*

Then he'd have to deal with Jean. But he didn't want to think about that—not yet.

He turned toward the building, wrenched open the kitchen door—and froze. A dozen chefs and waitresses stood facing him, all holding up kitchen knives. More pawns provided backup, some holding rifles, others with energy weapons. And behind *them* stood a quartet of large men wearing powdered wigs and Revolutionary-era military coats, brandishing heavy wooden clubs.

Wolverine sighed. *So much for "quietly."*

He loosed his claws and lunged forward to do what he did best.

"CYCLOPS? CAN you hear me?"

He clenched his bound fists in frustration. *Yes, Storm, I can hear you, but I can't* see *you—and I can't speak, either!*

"Something is happening," she said.

He straightened his back against the wall, cocking his head to listen. The Inner Circle members had moved away, but he could still hear them on the far side of the room. He strained to pick up their voices.

"…disturbance upstairs, Shaw."

"Well? What is it?"

"Not sure. Something about an intruder in the kitchen."

"Well, make sure they're confined. Call in extra security."

An intruder, Cyclops thought. He had an idea who it was, but that could wait. For now, the important thing was that Shaw and the others were distracted.

"Mmmmph?" he said.

"What?" Nightcrawler replied.

"*Mmmean.*"

"I do not—oh! Jean?" Nightcrawler paused. "She's just sort of… standing there."

"Perhaps we could try speaking with her again?" Colossus asked.

Cyclops shook his head. He edged away from them, along the wall, his chains clanking across the floor.

"Scott?" Storm asked.

He ignored her. They meant well, but they couldn't help him now. Only he could pull this off. It would require total concentration and every ounce of willpower he had.

And I have to do it fast.

He cast his mind back to New Mexico… to that day on the butte, when he and Jean had lain together on the picnic blanket. Just the two of them, alone under the glaring sun. He remembered leaning in to her, speaking the two words that had unlocked so much:

I do.

She'd gestured, just slightly, like a magician showing off, and then they were somewhere else. A place of eternal mist—no earth, no sky, barely any sense of up or down. Soothing sounds: crickets, birdsong, waves crashing just out of view. And Jean. Smiling, lovely, her arms spread to welcome him. So warm, so human, so utterly different from the cold, venomous Black Queen.

The astral plane, she'd explained. *A telepath's little retreat.*

They had talked, then, about everything. Talked without words, without walls, without holding back. Talked about their lives, their friends, their fears and hopes and dreams. Their first meeting on the steps of Xavier's school, years ago, Jean dragging that ragged suitcase behind her. They talked about love, about loss, about fear and hate and vengeance. About being lost, and coming home again.

Now, held captive in the sanctum of the Inner Circle, Cyclops squeezed his eyes shut and remembered. The sounds of the astral plane, the gentle scent of pine on the breeze. Most of all, he remembered the woman he knew, the woman he loved. Her psychic imprint, the shape of her thoughts.

Her beautiful soul.

All at once he was there. The shackles, the collar, the hood were all gone. He flailed, panicking. Without Jean's presence to anchor him, the astral plane was vast, disorienting. Just that endless mist, shifting and writhing in time to the rhythm of his thoughts.

No, he thought. *Not my thoughts. I'm no telepath—I can't do this alone. If I'm in here, so is she.*

"Jean?"

No answer.

He felt a moment of doubt. *Am I going crazy? I've never tried anything like this before. Maybe this is just my imagination… a hallucination triggered by sensory deprivation?*

"JEAN!"

He looked around, then down—and shook his head in surprise. Once again he wore a tricorn hat, high-cuffed pants, and old-fashioned boots. *This is the outfit from Jean's hallucination,* he realized. But there was something new: a long sword with a plain metal handle, fitted into a scabbard at his waist.

"I know you're here," he said.

A shape began to form in the mist. A block of stone steps, leading upward to an ornate wooden door. The door to the Hellfire Club.

This isn't going to be easy, he realized. *She's making me conform to the eighteenth-century reality of her timeslips. Whatever Wyngarde has done to her, his control runs deep.*

With a creak, the door swung open. A flame-haired figure appeared, black cape fastened around her neck by a familiar rose.

She's dressed as the Black Queen, he thought. *That's not good.*

"Jean," he said. "It's Scott." He couldn't tell whether he was speaking or thinking the words. She pulled her cape close and furrowed her brow.

"Do I know you, sir?" She stepped back, her boot heels clicking. "Your voice is strangely familiar, but your garb marks you as an American rebel. King George's enemy—and mine."

Ohhh-kay.

"Try to remember," he said, striding toward her. "I'm Scott Summers. You and I… we're X-Men, and so much more."

A flicker of doubt crossed her face. He kept talking.

"I don't understand…" He gestured at the façade of the Hellfire Club, half-formed in the mist. "…well, a lot of things. I think you've been hurting, more than I realized. I'm sorry I wasn't there… sorry I didn't see it until now.

"But this isn't freedom, Jean. It's just another cage." He paused, feeling very small. "It's not what you want."

Her eyes flashed red. "How would you know what I want?"

"I don't," he admitted. "I guess that's what I'm saying—I don't know." He held out his hand. "But I'd like to learn."

She stood for a long moment, staring at his hand. Then she looked away sadly. The mist seemed to mesmerize her, showing her something he couldn't see.

"I had a dream," she whispered. "Of a man who was so important to me, I would do anything for him. Follow him, defer to him… deny myself the things I wanted most."

He stepped back, stung. "I-I never meant to—"

"How could I have been so foolish?" When she turned to him, her eyes were hard. "You will want to leave, knave," she said, "before my husband arrives."

My husband.

Then he was there. Behind her, beside her, in the doorway. Jason Wyngarde, his hand clamped possessively around her waist. Tall and fierce in his riding breeches, boots, and the same velvet jacket he wore in the outside world. He held a sword, a long curved blade with a carved, ornate hilt.

"Foolish boy," Wyngarde said. "Neither you nor your X-Men mean anything to my lady wife." Jean leaned in to him. Eyed his sword for a moment, her eyes going wide.

Then she turned to glare at Cyclops. "Begone, sir," she said. "Or my Jason will cut you down where you stand."

Cyclops stared at her. Aside from the three of them, nothing in this place seemed solid. Even the steps, and the doorway framing them, wavered and shimmered in the mist.

Wyngarde stood proud, arrogant, sword raised. *Who is he?* Cyclops wondered. *Why is he here? How has he managed to put Jean in his thrall—to come between us, to intrude on our secret, private place of communion? No — I can't worry about that now. Whoever he is, I have no choice. I've got to fight him on his terms.*

He drew his sword. "En garde, Sir Jason."

Before Cyclops could react, Wyngarde was down the steps. He blocked Cyclops's thrust with a simple flick of his wrist.

"Ha!" Wyngarde exclaimed. "The stripling bares his fangs and imitates the action of the tiger."

Cyclops feinted. He'd studied fencing years ago, but he was rusty—and unaccustomed to combat on the astral plane.

"I've known of your psychic rapport from the moment it was established," Wyngarde continued. "Such a lovely, precious moment on the desert sands. So pure."

Cyclops lunged, angry. Wyngarde stepped aside, dodging the thrust.

"I knew you'd try to contact her here. You've played right into my hands."

"How?" Cyclops slashed the air. "Who *are* you?"

Wyngarde stepped back, raised his sword in an on-guard position. He seemed offended.

"You don't remember?" he asked.

Cyclops stared at him, baffled.

Wyngarde's face, his entire body, began to waver. The handsome, rakish figure seemed to shrink, to melt into a withered shell of a man. Clear skin became pocked; lush, full hair thinned to a smattering of gray strands. Even his eyes contracted, sinking to tiny points set deep within narrow sockets.

"Mastermind," Wyngarde said.

Then Cyclops remembered. Mastermind had been one of Magneto's minions, a carnival trickster with the power to cast illusions. One of the misguided souls Magneto had recruited to his original "brotherhood" of evil mutants. A relatively insignificant player in the struggle, doomed to follow more powerful leaders.

Until now.

A savage smile crept across Mastermind's ravaged face. As he thrust his sword forward, his form grew larger, his back straighter. By the time the tip drew near, he was Wyngarde again. Cyclops barely managed to raise his sword in time.

"You," Cyclops began, "you were never—"

"Never much of a man?" Wyngarde said.

"I wouldn't presume to judge something like that."

"I wasn't," Mastermind snapped. "But things have changed, boy. After I slay you in this duel, Jean Grey's final link with the X-Men—with the life she once led—will be severed."

Cyclops stepped back again, looking toward the doorway. Jean stood at the top of the steps, watching the duel with wide eyes.

Wyngarde lunged forward, slashing back and forth. His sword sliced through the air; he seemed faster, more agile than any swordsman Cyclops had ever seen.

That's not an accident, he realized. *The astral plane is controlled by Jean—it's her power that makes all this possible. And he's controlling her. Which means I'm playing by his rules.*

This match is stacked against me. I can't win.

"Jean Grey will be mine," Wyngarde snarled. "Body and soul—my love, my thrall, my bloody Black Queen. Together we will rule the Hellfire Club and, in time, the world itself."

There was time for one last, desperate gambit. Cyclops shifted sideways, feinted—then tossed his sword from his right hand to his left. If he could manage to throw his opponent off-balance—

Wyngarde lunged. The long blade struck Cyclops's left hand just as he was catching his own weapon. He cried out, recoiled, and dropped the sword, watching as it spun off and vanished in the mist.

Wyngarde grabbed Cyclops's vest and pulled him close. The rogue mutant's scent was musty, charged with sweat. "A chivalrous man," Wyngarde said, "would allow you to surrender."

"You said it yourself," Cyclops spat. "You're not a man at all."

Jean took a step toward them. She seemed entranced, almost mesmerized by the battle.

Wyngarde released Cyclops and stepped back. He grinned, swinging his sword with a flourish. For just a moment, as Wyngarde lunged forward, Cyclops saw him again as he truly was: a second-rate henchman with delusions of world conquest. A sad, withered pretender to greatness.

Then the sword pierced his heart and his world turned to pain. He doubled over, gasped, tried to speak. His hands, bloody and trembling, grasped the blade, and he tumbled down to a surprisingly hard landing.

"CYCLOPS!" Storm cried.

Standing on the elevated dais, Shaw whirled around. He ran down the steps, gesturing for Leland and Pierce to follow. They crossed the room, past the tables—then smiled, one by one, as they spotted Cyclops's body sprawled out on the stone floor.

"He just collapsed!" Colossus said. "What happened?"

Nightcrawler dropped to his knees, struggling against his bonds. He leaned over and lowered his ear to Cyclops's chest.

Wyngarde and Jean were the last to approach. They pushed past the others, staring down at the prone figure. Wyngarde wore a triumphant smirk. Jean's face was hard, angry.

"He met a better man," Wyngarde said.

"Kurt?" Storm asked.

Nightcrawler looked up, his eyes wide with horror.

"He's not breathing."

CHAPTER SEVENTEEN

"ACH, MY mistake." Nightcrawler leaned down again, moving his head close. "He *is* breathing—"

The door burst inward, shattering to splinters. A snarling figure stormed inside, claws bared. Two masked Hellfire pawns clung to his back.

"Finally!" Logan snarled. "The champagne room."

Ignoring the weak blows of the pawns on his head and arms, he surveyed the scene. Along the opposite wall, Nightcrawler watched the battle, along with Storm and Colossus—all bound, helpless. Cyclops lay at their feet, his face covered with an opaque red hood. He wasn't moving, but Logan could hear his heartbeat.

A trio of figures stood in the corner, hidden in shadow. One of them smelled alarmingly familiar—but he couldn't worry about that right now. Leland and Pierce were already advancing on him.

He sheathed one set of claws. Then he reached up, plucked a pawn off his back, and hurled the man through the air. Leland saw the pawn coming and, on reflex, reached out with his power—increasing the pawn's mass.

Logan smiled. *Bad move, dude.*

The pawn slammed into Leland with the force of a guided missile. The two men crashed into a table, splintering it to pieces.

Pierce barely glanced at his fallen comrade. "Good," he said, turning to face Logan directly. "Now I may fulfill my vow—and slay you where you stand." His hands crackled with electricity.

The remaining pawn managed to get in a decent blow to Wolverine's ear. Logan reached up and backhanded him on the head.

"In more civilized times," Pierce continued, "our differences would be settled with pistols at twenty paces. Under the circumstances, however, a more expedient solution is preferable. Good lord, man, you smell like a hog farm—"

Logan rolled his eyes. He reached up, grabbed the dazed pawn off his back, and threw the man into the air. Instinctively, Pierce sent out a bolt of electricity at the approaching pawn. The bolt struck the man in the face; he arched and screamed in pain, reaching forward, his hands scrabbling in the air.

Pierce realized his mistake—too late. "No!" he cried.

The pawn slammed into Pierce, still arching and twitching under the electrical current. His hands reached for Pierce's throat, closing over it by pure instinct. Pierce gasped, unable to catch his breath. He reached up and tried to pry away the pawn's hands, but the man's eyes rolled back in his head. His muscles had convulsed, freezing his grip in place. Pierce staggered backward, and the two men dropped to the floor.

"Score one for the hogs," Logan said.

Pierce and Leland lay still now, along with the various pawns. Logan turned to call out to his teammates. "Need a hand, 'Roro?"

"It would be appreciated, Logan." Storm strained at her bonds.

He kicked off and sprinted toward them. He'd covered about half the distance, dodging shattered tables and broken glass, when a movement caught his eye.

"Logan!" Colossus yelled.

Wolverine whirled around, following Peter's gaze. Across the room, the other three figures still lurked in the shadows. One was short and stocky, the other tall, with an arrogant bearing. The third was almost completely hidden, but he caught a glimpse of boots, pale skin, a cape—

He sniffed the air, his breath catching in his throat.

Jeannie.

Footsteps—pounding outside the door. Three of the big men in powdered wigs burst in, waving clubs in the air.

Logan clenched his fists, sheathed both sets of claws, and leapt to his feet. *Better cool it with the claws,* he thought. *These might be Inner Circle—but they could also be legit employees, caterers, or rent-a-cops. Even Secret Service, given the guest list out there.*

As the first man vaulted over a table, Logan punched him in the gut, sending him flying backward. When he elbowed the second one in the chin, he heard a bone crack.

"Enough," a gravelly voice said from the far end of the room. The third fighter withdrew, holding his club in the air in a casual gesture of surrender. The speaker stepped out of the shadows: a fierce man, about Wolverine's size, with a thick muscular body. He picked his way carefully around the unconscious forms of Leland and Pierce.

"You the head perv around here?" Logan asked.

The man gave a ceremonial bow. "Sebastian Shaw."

Wolverine's eyes darted back and forth. The remaining wig-man stood in the doorway, smirking—but he made no threatening moves.

"No fatalities, Wolverine?" Shaw glanced down at the fallen pawns. "I'm almost disappointed."

"Night's young."

"Logan," Storm said, her eyes wide. "Be careful."

"Okay, *Sebastian.* Here's how this is gonna go." He unsheathed one claw for emphasis. "First, you're gonna release my friends over there."

Shaw grinned. "Doubtful."

Wolverine slid out another claw. "Second, you're all gonna clear out. Every pawn, knight, leather-crafter, and one-percenter in the house. And third…" He paused, unleashing the third and final claw on his left hand. "…I'm gonna have a word with the lady in the back."

In the shadows, a corona of flame rose up. It faded so quickly, Logan wasn't sure whether he'd actually seen it.

"Why wait?"

The tall, arrogant man strode out into the light. His trimmed beard made Logan want to punch him in the face. Shaw seemed to consider the situation for a moment. Then he stepped back, ushering the newcomer forward with an exaggerated gesture. "Wyngarde?"

The bearded man nodded in acknowledgment. He stopped, reached out, and beckoned back into the shadows.

"Come, my dear."

Wolverine watched in shock as Jean Grey stepped into view, nearly unrecognizable in her Black Queen uniform. She walked stiffly, formally, as if the corset restricted her movements. Logan felt a sinking feeling, a roiling in his guts. Jean's scent was right, but the look on her face made his neck hairs stand up.

"Jeannie," he said cautiously. "How you doing, girl?"

"She is splendid," Wyngarde said. "Now that she has escaped her former, confining life."

"You mind, Mustache? I'm talkin' to the lady."

Wyngarde glared briefly. Then he reached out and touched Jean's black-gloved hand. She took his hand, without taking her eyes off Wolverine.

This is bad, Logan thought. *She's like a weapon waiting to be fired. A bullet in the chamber.*

"I was wrong about you, kid." He chose his words carefully. "Back on the shuttle. I said you weren't made for this life."

A rustling behind him—a disturbance in the air. He didn't look around.

"Turns out you're a lot like me," he continued. "You got all this stuff bubblin' up inside you. Fury, resentment. Violence."

Again the air moved. He didn't turn to look, didn't shift his attention. Just raised his claws and gutted the henchman with the wig an instant before the man's club would have made contact with his skull. The man trembled on the end of Logan's claws, blood sputtering out of his mouth. He made a terrible sound, voided himself, and went limp.

Nightcrawler gasped. Storm let out a hiss. Logan grimaced, but didn't turn to acknowledge them. As a rule, he tried not to use deadly force in front of his teammates. This time, it was unavoidable.

"Animal stuff," he continued. "You and me, Jeannie—we understand these things." He gestured at the X-Men, then at Shaw. "They don't."

He shook the dead man loose from his claws, flinging the body into the air. It landed with a thud at Shaw's feet.

Jean was still watching him. There was fire in her eyes—and something else, too. Something he couldn't identify.

"Point is," he continued, "you gotta learn to control that stuff. To tame the animal. Otherwise, you find yourself walkin' down a path where there's no coming back." He paused. "Let me help you?"

Jean took a step forward. Wyngarde followed, smiling at his Queen.

"You think you *know* me," she hissed.

Logan stepped back. He could feel the pressure building—the trigger pulling back, ready to fire.

Jean's eyes swept the room. She studied the freshly killed man at Shaw's feet, then Shaw himself. The unconscious forms of Leland, Pierce, and the pawns. Nightcrawler, Storm, and Colossus, standing helpless above Cyclops's unmoving body. She glanced briefly at Wyngarde with an odd, blank expression.

When she turned back to Logan, her eyes flashed.

"None of you," she whispered. "None of you truly know me."

Wyngarde stepped forward. He smiled at Wolverine, the smile of a man who believed he held all the cards. "My Black Queen," he said. "Take him."

"A pleasure," she said.

Jean raised her arms, a sly smile creeping across her face. Energy sparked from her hands, bright against her dark gloves.

The Phoenix Force rose up to surround her, glowing like a star.

The psychic bolt blasted Logan across the room. It sliced through him, tearing his costume, ripping a thousand little cuts in his skin. He plowed straight through a table, smashing it to pieces, and crashed into the stone wall not far from the door.

He shook his head, struggling to remain conscious. Wyngarde's smug, satisfied laughter reached him, as if from a great distance. When he looked up again, Jean was advancing on him. Her body glowed, the black cape swirling around her like a devil's cloak. Her eyes bored into his.

Looks like this is it, he thought. *No comin' back. No way back from the path, Jeannie.*

For either of us.

He struggled to his feet, bracing himself for the battle. The wounds hurt like hell, but his healing factor was already closing them, little fissures knitting together at an amazing rate. He crossed his claws in front of his face, peering through the latticework at Jean's relentlessly approaching figure.

All his senses rose to full alert. Mapping the room, seeking a way out, an escape from this impossible situation. He noted the location of the helpless X-Men against the wall; the bodies on the floor; the broken tables; the torches guttering on the walls. Jason Wyngarde, standing just out of range with that maddening grin on his face.

And one other thing. A high, faint sound, just a few meters away. *Click.*

CHAPTER EIGHTEEN

CLICK.

All at once, the pressure on Cyclops's throat eased up. *My restraint collar,* he realized. *It's open!*

His arms were still bound behind his back. He shrugged his shoulders, nudging loose the hood covering his head. Then he climbed to his feet, braced himself against the wall, and twisted his head to one side. The hood slid off and fell to the floor.

He scanned the room quickly: stone walls, a large viewscreen, a few shattered tables, and a doorway that looked like a wrecking ball had gone through it. In the center of the room, Jean and Wolverine circled each other, dodging around the broken tables. Shaw and Wyngarde stood at a safe distance, watching the conflict. None of them had noticed Cyclops's escape—yet.

"Scott," Storm whispered. She moved toward him along the wall, followed by Nightcrawler and Colossus. He shook his head, motioning them to silence.

A psychic blast shot from Jean's outstretched hands. Logan leapt into the air, barely dodging it, and lunged toward her. Jean stepped back, heels clicking on the stone floor. As she reached out to blast him in return, a slight smile flickered on her face.

"Jean," Cyclops said, keeping his voice low.. "She did this—freed me with her telekinetic powers, using the fight with Logan as a distraction. She's broken Wyngarde's hold on her."

A wide, joyous smile spread across Storm's face. "She is back."

Wyngarde was staring at Jean, a hungry, triumphant look on his face. *He doesn't know,* Cyclops realized. *He thinks he's still in control of her.*

Cyclops reached out, testing the psychic connection he shared with Jean. He could sense her again, in his mind... but the link was weak. Her thoughts were closed to him.

"Peter," Storm said, "what are you staring at?"

Colossus jerked his head toward the battle. "Wolverine..."

Logan stalked forward, advancing toward Jean with his fists clenched. She rose up and spread her arms, the fiery avatar of the Phoenix spreading out all around her.

"...he is not using his claws," Colossus finished.

Jean wafted backward through the air, moving toward the elevated meeting table atop the dais. Logan leapt off in pursuit, hurdling a row of tables. Shaw and Wyngarde followed, skirting around the rubble.

"He's in on it," Cyclops said. "Logan's figured out that she's playacting. They're working together, distracting the Circle—moving them away from us. Giving us our shot."

Nightcrawler moved in close. "What is our play?"

Cyclops frowned for a moment. Then he edged awkwardly along the wall, his chains dragging on the floor. "Peter," he said. "Hold still." Taking careful aim, he shot a pinpoint eye-beam at Colossus's binding sleeve.

Nothing happened. The device absorbed his beam harmlessly.

"*Unglaublich,*" Nightcrawler exclaimed. "Looks like the Hellfire Club learned from our gambit back in Deerfield."

"We switched combatants then, and managed to defeat them," Storm explained. "They seem to have taken steps to prevent that from happening again."

202

The bright flash of Jean's power caught Cyclops's eye. He turned just in time to see Wolverine hurtling through the air, straight toward the large wall screen above the main meeting table. A thunderous crash shook the room as Logan's Adamantium-reinforced form shattered the glass, passing straight through the screen to gouge a hole in the stone wall.

"*Logan,*" Nightcrawler said.

"Scott," Storm said, "your eye-beams. You must do something."

Cyclops peered up at the elevated dais. Wolverine's body was lodged in the wall. He twitched once, then slid, limp, to the floor.

"Not yet." Cyclops's visor flashed red with barely contained power. "Logan's got a tough skin, and Jean knows what she's doing. Let her play this out."

"Perhaps we should move closer?" Colossus suggested.

Cyclops nodded, gesturing for Storm to lead the way. They edged around the remaining tables, past the unmoving body of a man with a wig. Their progress was slow, hampered by the chains still binding them. Cyclops dropped low and followed, using the others to shield him from view.

If Shaw and Wyngarde don't see me, I might be able to press my advantage. They don't know I can use my optic blasts.

He almost tripped over a body: Donald Pierce, lying still on the floor. When the sound of Cyclops's chains reached his ears, his eyes shot open. Nightcrawler grunted, whipped his partially bound tail through the air, and swatted Pierce in the face. The cyborg jerked to one side and lapsed back into unconsciousness.

"I do not like that man," Nightcrawler said.

"Quiet!" Storm hissed.

Wolverine lay twitching, barely conscious, in a pile of glass beside the meeting table. Wyngarde took Jean's hand, and together they climbed the steps of the dais.

"Now, my Queen," Wyngarde said, staring down at the feral mutant. "Finish him."

Jean rose up off the floor, her black cape swirling in the air.

She turned to gaze down at the X-Men, now revealed on the floor below. A cold smile crossed her face.

Cyclops felt an icy chill of doubt. *What if I'm wrong? What if… Is she still under Wyngarde's control?*

Jean pivoted in midair and stared down at Wyngarde. He seemed small beneath her. The Phoenix flared, larger and angrier than ever before.

Wyngarde's face went pale.

"Poor man," she said. "Poor, foolish man."

Her force bolt struck the floor, gouging a hole in the stone—but Wyngarde was no longer there. Cyclops looked around, first one way, then the other. There had been no flash of energy, no telepathic flare or *BAMF* of smoke. Yet there was no sign of Wyngarde, either—not in the room, in the shadows, or in the doorway. He was gone.

A simple illusion, Cyclops realized. *Mastermind—Wyngarde— managed to enthrall Jean by tapping into her telepathic abilities, but his own power is to create illusions. He caught us all by surprise, kept even Jean from seeing him, just long enough to make his escape.*

FOR NOW, Jean replied.

Her voice was like thunder, a nova exploding in Cyclops's mind. He turned just in time to catch the terrible look of rage, of godlike wrath, on her face. Then she swooped through the air, arrowing down toward the entryway. The Phoenix spread its wings, melting stone, igniting a dozen little fires along the surface of the battered door. She soared through the opening—and then she, too, was gone, vanished into the bowels of the Hellfire Club.

Jean, he thought. *Jean, answer me!*

Nothing. The telepathic link was gone again—as if that fierce, violent sending had burned it out once and for all.

Or else she's cut me off on purpose…

"Cyclops?" Storm called.

He whirled around, chains clanking on stone, to see Leland and Pierce facing the X-Men. Leland's expensive jacket was torn, and a bit of blood had pooled up at the corner of his lip. With a sinking feeling, Cyclops realized they had his team backed up against the wall.

"So," Pierce said. "One lamb seems to have escaped the pen."

Leland laughed and pointed at Cyclops's bound arms. "Not quite escaped," he said.

Shaw stepped up between them. His chest was bare, arms crossed in front of him. "Never say die," he said. "Eh, X-Man?"

"Shaw." Cyclops's visor glowed.

"I already told your teammate." Shaw smiled. "I can absorb all forms of kinetic energy—including your optic blasts."

"Herr Shaw." Nightcrawler jerked his head toward the smoking doorway. "Do you not have other problems to attend to?"

"You mean Wyngarde?" Shaw laughed. "He was a pretender. In his obsessive quest for a Black Queen, he has sown the seeds of his own demise. As I knew he would."

"Jean is no one's *Black Queen*," Cyclops said.

"Precisely." Shaw stepped forward, peering directly into Cyclops's visor. "You and I are the only two Kings here. We inspire loyalty—through strength and, at times, through discipline."

A distant crash, somewhere above the chamber in which they stood. Cyclops jerked at the sound.

"Believe me," Shaw continued, "I do you an incredible honor by placing you in this company. But the nature of Kings is to battle until only one remains." He stepped back, appraising his prisoner. Then he dropped to a crouch, holding his fists up like a boxer.

Leland stepped back, his eyes glinting. Pierce let out a cold laugh.

"Your eye-beams versus my... special skills." Shaw danced forward, jabbing the air. "I look forward to—"

Click.

Click.

Click.

Click click click click.

Cyclops's arm binder went slack, dropped to the ground. He whirled around just as the control collars fell from Storm's and Nightcrawler's necks. Colossus reached up and thrust his collar away, flexing his arms to shatter the remains of his restraints.

For a moment, everyone froze. Then Shaw took a step back, beckoning Leland and Pierce to follow. Storm, Nightcrawler, and Colossus gathered around Cyclops, shaking life into their stiff limbs.

Past the Inner Circle members, the doorway was still wreathed in smoke from Jean's fiery departure. Yet Cyclops could just make out a swirling cape and a slim, wasp-waisted figure.

Storm had seen it, too. "Jean?" she whispered.

"No," Cyclops said.

Emma.

Her laughter, deep and superior, rang out in his skull. It rumbled and rose, coalescing into three mocking words.

Last favor, Summers.

Then she was gone. A phrase she'd spoken, hours earlier, echoed in his mind: *Better to walk in the shadows than stare at the sun.*

Shaw's eyes were still fixed on the X-Men. *He didn't see Emma,* Cyclops realized. *He doesn't know she was here.*

Storm's eyes flashed. She raised her arms, summoning a wind. Colossus took a single, thunderous step forward. Nightcrawler scurried up the wall, preparing to pounce.

Shaw flexed his muscles. He opened his mouth to order the attack—then whirled in surprise as a blue-gloved finger tapped his shoulder.

"Night's not so young anymore," Wolverine said.

Snikt.

CHAPTER NINETEEN

OUTSIDE, THE rain pounded down. Lawyers in suits strode through the deluge, umbrellas held high. Young women ran between awnings, purses balanced over their heads. A pair of tourists paused in front of an old building and pointed, curious, at the stylized "H" and pitchfork on its façade.

A homeless man stirred, shivered. Pulled his wet sleeping bag tight.

Jean Grey felt it all. All their thoughts, their pains, their joys. Her power was a drumbeat inside her, a relentless pounding. It no longer sang, no longer spoke to her in words. It simply *was*—and it would not be denied.

She climbed the back staircase of the Hellfire Club, boots clicking on concrete, cape swirling around her. Her stride was steady, measured. Her back was straight, forced upright by the merciless corset of the Black Queen.

The corset. Its laces dug into her skin, forcing the breath from her body. But she needed it, just a little while longer. Needed to hold everything inside.

Until the end.

As she passed the main floor, chaotic thoughts assaulted her. Old men fantasizing about waitresses, young couples making out beneath tables. A drunken stew of lust, ambition, and despair. She quickened her pace. Soon, she knew, all this would be done. Soon vengeance would be hers.

Despite herself, Jean's thoughts strayed to the X-Men. They were her friends, her teammates… in a very real way, her family. Her mind reached out, back down to the subbasement, and touched…

PETER RASPUTIN.

Colossus stood sparring with Donald Pierce, the cyborg squire of the Hellfire Club's Inner Circle. They danced around like boxers, stepping in and around the wreckage of the tables.

"Get away from me," Pierce snarled. "You freak."

Colossus's thoughts went dark at the insult. *Oh, Peter,* Jean thought. *You were so young, so innocent when you joined the X-Men. I'm so sorry for what's happened to you.*

To all of us.

She surveyed the room. Over by the door, Nightcrawler and Storm were engaged in combat with Sebastian Shaw. Logan sprinted across the stone floor, chasing the frightened Leland. There was no sign of Scott.

Colossus clenched his fists. "You speak as though I am less than human, Pierce."

"Because you *are!*"

Pierce leaped through the air. Colossus transformed his body to solid steel, increasing his mass in an instant. Pierce landed before him, grinned, and reached out to grab Colossus's metal hands. Then, slowly, he forced the young mutant backward.

"On your knees," Pierce hissed. "*Mutant dog.*"

Colossus's eyes went wide as his opponent continued to press him down. Jean could feel his surprise at the man's strength—and something else, too. Shock, disbelief.

"Are you..." Colossus winced. "Are you not a mutant yourself?"

Pierce's mind erupted in outrage. Jean found herself drawn to the source, wrenched away from Peter Rasputin into the chaotic thoughts of...

DONALD PIERCE.

Hate you hate all mutants joined Inner Circle one purpose one goal kill the others take back wealth for real *humans. Shaw Wyngarde Leland all of them all mutants freaks abominations not human slaves animals kill them work from within bide time exterminate kill kill mutants*

Rage erupted in Jean, echoing Pierce's own.

His bigotry, she realized. *It's... familiar. The dehumanization, the hatred so strong it requires utter domination, total erasure of the other person's self.*

It's the way Jason felt about me.

Pierce cried out at the force of Jean's thoughts. Colossus seized the opening, spreading his arms as wide as he could. Before Pierce could break the grip, his left arm came loose in a shower of sparks and wires. He screamed.

Colossus tossed the severed arm aside. Then he lurched forward, grabbed Pierce by the lapels, and dangled him in the air.

"I am proud of who and what I am, little man," Colossus said. "And I have no need to destroy others in order to justify that." Pierce's arm stump flashed harmlessly in the air. Colossus reared back and threw him across the room...

...and Jean's consciousness jumped again. Into the body of...

HARRY LELAND.

He looked up just in time to see the blond-haired missile flying toward him. He scrambled, stumbled, held up his hands—

and then Donald Pierce slammed into him, sending the two of them crashing to the ground in a jumble of limbs. Leland rolled over, groaning in pain.

"Get off me!" Pierce yelled, scrambling to his feet. He looked down at Leland, pure hatred in his eyes. "Mutant bastard!"

"So, *old boy*," Leland growled. "Your true colors shine through at last."

"I'm through with you." Pierce turned and marched away. "Through with all of you *mutant scum*—" Abruptly an Adamantium-reinforced elbow jabbed out to block his path. Pierce's chin made contact, hard, and he dropped again. This time he stayed down.

"Scum and proud," Wolverine snarled.

Jean could feel Leland's momentary amusement at Pierce's misfortune. *He deserved it,* she thought. *The elite—they'll turn on anyone. Even their own.*

"How 'bout you, Harry?" Logan asked, turning to face Leland. "You got something to say about mutants?"

"You misjudge me, dear boy. I *am* a mutant." Leland raised an eyebrow in contempt. "But I have nothing in common with *gutter filth* like you."

"Guess there's all kinds of hate in the world."

Leland's mind was a stew of resentment: *How dare this rabble invade my sanctum? Challenge my power?* As Wolverine drew closer, he recoiled at the odor. "Have you *literally* been in the gutter?"

"Rather be there than here." Logan unsheathed his claws. "Say your prayers, big man."

Leland's hand flashed out, power flaring. Wolverine toppled forward, his mass increasing to the point where his legs could no longer hold him upright. Instinctively, he lunged forward, claws outstretched.

Too late, Leland realized his error.

Wolverine's claws pierced his coat, his vest, his chest. Leland tumbled backward, pulling his attacker on top of him. Logan's increased mass forced his claws all the way through Leland's torso, exit wounds staining the floor with blood. Leland let out a horrible gasping sound.

As he did, Jean leapt away, out of his mind. Into…

LOGAN.

No. No, no, she couldn't bear that—not now. Wolverine knew too much. He understood her too well. She cast about desperately, randomly, for…

KURT WAGNER.

Nightcrawler was jumping up and down in the air, disappearing and reappearing, striking a blow every time he came down and then teleporting back up again. As Jean slipped inside his head, she saw his target: Sebastian Shaw.

"Enjoying yourself, Herr Shaw?" Nightcrawler vanished again, only to reappear two meters above. "I am."

He is, Jean realized. Kurt had led a difficult early life, shunned for his demonic appearance and paid starvation wages by his employers in the circus. But his acrobatic ability, the thrill he felt whenever he executed a difficult maneuver—that had always brought him joy.

Shaw ignored the blows. He crouched down, feeling his way along a line of wide stones set in the wall. His moves were careful, unhurried.

As Nightcrawler lashed out again, Jean realized his mistake. *Shaw absorbs kinetic energy. Kurt's attacks aren't hurting him— they're making him stronger!*

She considered warning Nightcrawler, sending him a direct telepathic message, but decided against it. That might distract him at a crucial point in the battle.

Nightcrawler dropped down, fists swinging. Shaw smiled, reached up, and swatted him out of the air. Kurt cried out and flew across the room, gasping for breath. Jean flailed, disoriented, and flashed out of Nightcrawler's dazed mind…

SEBASTIAN SHAW.

He turned back to the wall, continued testing the stones until he heard a clicking noise. The thrill of triumph, of dominance over his enemies, surged through him. He was the White King, leader of the Hellfire Club's Inner Circle. He already possessed more wealth and power than any monarch in history, and soon he would control the greatest currency in humanity's future: the mutant X-gene.

Jean reeled, stung by the arrogance of his thoughts. *You, too,* she thought. *Anything you see, you must dominate. Anyone who will not bow to you, you would destroy.* Her anger roiled. *You abusive, prideful men. I will bring you down. I will bring you all down.*

The temperature dropped suddenly, shockingly. Wind whipped against Shaw's bare chest, and ice began to form along his skin. He shivered and spun around.

"Storm," he spat.

Ororo hovered a few inches off the floor, holding out both hands to summon the blizzard. Jean had rarely seen her in her true majesty, her mastery of weather on full display. She was wild yet controlled, unimaginably beautiful in the use of her power. The power that was her pride, her heritage, her birthright.

For a split second, Shaw felt panic. Then Jean sensed another presence in his mind, watching from a distance. A telepath like herself, monitoring and manipulating everyone in the room.

Emma Frost.

Shaw moved toward Storm, forcing his way step by step through the maelstrom. Before he could reach her, Jean leaped away. In the end, it wouldn't matter—but she didn't want the

White Queen to learn of her presence here, not yet. Better to leave Shaw to his fate, and move on to…

ORORO MUNROE.

Storm's power was a simple, perfect melody, a chorus of notes rising to a crescendo. Jean recognized the sensation with a profound sadness. Once she had wielded her telepathy with the same ease, the same sense of control. Once she'd been happy.

No more.

Shaw pressed toward Storm, his teeth gritted against the wind. He planted his legs, like tree trunks, on the cold stones—but the assault was weakening him. This time, Storm wasn't attacking him with kinetic energy. Her power was altering the environment of the room, from a distance. Unlike the other X-Men, she could actually hurt him.

Raising her arms, Storm summoned the full fury of the elements. An icy gale gathered and swirled, almost lifting Shaw off his feet. For a moment, his muscular form was lost in the blinding storm.

When the wind died down, he was gone.

Storm dropped to a crouch, waving away the last of the wind with a swift gesture. She reached out to touch the wall—just as a hidden door slid shut.

"Damn," she said. She felt along the wall, searching for the trigger mechanism. But there was no trace, not even a visible seam where the stones had resealed themselves. Shaw had made good his escape.

Storm rose to her feet, turning to survey the room. Wolverine lumbered over to join her, wiping blood off his claws. Nightcrawler picked himself up off the floor, rubbing his head.

Colossus paused above Donald Pierce's unconscious body. He bent down, frowning, to pick up Pierce's severed arm, and stared at the smoking stump with an odd expression. To Jean, watching from a distance, it seemed more like sorrow than rage.

Suddenly she was overcome with emotion.

This is it, she realized. *Time to say goodbye.*

Ororo, she thought. *Of all the new X-Men, you were my closest friend. The sister I never had. I wish you peace, happiness, fulfillment for all your days.*

I wish it for all of you.

And then she was gone.

———o———————o———

JEAN CLIMBED the final step to the top floor of the club. The sounds of revelry, the screams of horror and ecstasy, had faded to dim echoes. She was alone.

All at once, a new sadness came over her. She paused a moment to identify the source. *Shaw,* she realized. *He and Emma are snakes, manipulators. Neither of them truly trusts the other. Their nature is betrayal, their entire lives a game of feint and thrust. The only thing they crave is power, in all its forms.*

And yet, they share a bond. A mindlink. Just like…

She forced the thought away. That part of her life was over; those thoughts could only lead to maudlin, pointless despair.

The corset. So tight, so binding.

Soon, she told herself. *Soon we'll be free.*

She pushed open the door and entered the library. Then, like a predator in the shadows, she settled in to wait.

CHAPTER TWENTY

IN A tunnel deep beneath the Hellfire Club, Emma Frost leaned against the wall, running a well-manicured finger down the screen of her phone. She smiled as a series of security-cam feeds scrolled past. Each of the club's private rooms was equipped with a hidden camera—and those cameras were capturing some very interesting footage.

She lowered the phone and looked down. A trickle of rainwater had seeped into the narrow corridor, pooling and rising up on the stone floor. She lifted her boot, grimacing in distaste as her glove touched the muck.

"Getting your hands dirty?"

Sebastian Shaw emerged from a hidden passageway, entering the tunnel with the grace of a tiger. The large stone slid back into place behind him.

"When I must," she replied. She saw his torn pants, and raised an eyebrow. "You've been down in the mud yourself."

"The weather witch got me," he said, brushing off his shoulder. "But of course, you already know that."

"We've captured some useful video," she said, holding up

her phone. "Should provide months' worth of... *leverage*... over certain Washington luminaries."

"Thank our Latverian business partners for that idea. The bad news is, I'm afraid the X-Men are lost to us." He paused. "At least we can blame the chaos on them. When word gets out that they disrupted our celebration, they'll be branded as international terrorists. 'Worse than Hydra...' That has a ring to it."

"And Wyngarde?"

"His little *toy* is about to explode in his face. I think the 'Mastermind' will have his hands full for a while." He came up behind her, placed a hand around her waist. "But you know that, too." He kissed her neck, tightening his grip.

"Sebastian," she said. "Something is troubling you."

He said nothing. Nuzzled his nose into her neck.

"You know you can't hide things from me," she said.

"No." His voice sounded uncharacteristically vulnerable. "But you hide a great deal from me."

She smiled again. Reached up and stroked his thick hair with a white-gloved hand. "I wish I could *feel* you more," he continued. "Like—"

"Like Scott Summers and Jean Grey?"

He paused, then nodded.

"No you don't," she whispered. "Trust me, you don't wish that at all."

"Trust you," he mused, as if the idea had never occurred to him before.

Such a child, she thought. *A boy playing at men's games—but then, aren't they all?* "Well," she said, starting off down the corridor, "we'd better see what's left of Leland and—"

"Emma," he called.

She turned. He hadn't moved. Shaw stood in the narrow hallway, his shoes nearly submerged in the rising water.

"The X-Men," he continued. "Did you help them escape?"

All at once, the air seemed to change. They faced each other, wary and tense, like the predators they were. Lives, nations, even worlds seemed to hang in the balance, thick and shrouded in the moist air.

Then Emma's expression softened. She moved close to Shaw and touched his chest. Pressed her cheek to his and waited, patiently, until he reached out and pulled her closer.

"Darling," she whispered. "You know I belong only to you."

His hand trembled on her back. He pulled away, nodded, and smiled.

"Come," he said, starting off toward the surface. "There's much to be done."

She smirked, twirled the phone in her hand, and followed.

AS THE hidden elevator slid to a stop, Cyclops hissed in a breath. *I'm about to step out into the main hall in full costume,* he realized. *Might as well paint a target on my back—especially with Wyngarde still on the loose.* Yet there was no time to concoct another plan. His civilian clothes were long gone, and Jean's psychic link with him was broken.

He had to find her fast.

The door slid open and his eyes went wide behind his visor. The main hall looked as if a bomb had struck it. Tables lay overturned, bars had been smashed and plundered for bottles. Lights flickered, painting the scene with a chaotic strobe effect. Drunken women laughed as they picked their way through the broken glass. Men sat on the floor in small groups, crying and muttering over whiskey bottles.

On the far side of the central staircase, thick smoke rose up from behind an improvised fortress of overturned tables. Cyclops moved in that direction, keeping low. A trio of laughing drunks nearly stumbled into him, oblivious to his presence.

Behind the tables, two men and two women sat cross-legged on the floor. The men were shirtless; all four wore matching tribal smears on their faces. They'd lit a fire in a pile of tablecloths and chair legs, and built a makeshift spit out of a centuries-old sword. One of the women was turning the sword-spit, roasting a large pig. Her eyes followed the gray smoke as it wafted up toward the high ceiling.

The lights flickered again. Cyclops shook his head, feeling as if he was in a dream.

"So much for smoke detectors," he murmured.

The woman looked up in response—and screamed. She pointed at him and scrambled backward, dropping the sword. The heavy pig crashed into the fire, throwing up sparks.

"Hey, hey…" Cyclops began.

The two men grabbed the woman protectively. The other woman looked over at Cyclops and started yelling.

"It's all right!" Cyclops said. "I'm just…"

The woman's screams were incomprehensible gibberish. Her companions joined in, pointing fearfully at him. A passing drunk paused, eyes wide, then fled in terror.

What's going on? Cyclops wondered. *Why are they all afraid of me?*

The lights flickered once more, then went dark. Instantly the room dissolved into chaos. He could hear glass breaking, doors crashing open. People ran, screaming, in all directions. The only light came from the smoldering, dying cookfire on the floor.

A thick hand grabbed hold of his shoulder, pulled him into an alcove along the wall. He whirled, eyes flashing—then stopped.

"Cyke," Wolverine said. "We gotta stop meetin' like this."

"Logan." Cyclops pressed himself against the wall. "I don't… I don't understand."

"One word: Mastermind," Logan said. "He made all those people see you blasting the room with your eye-beams. I caught a quick glimpse of him, then he did his cheap disappearing act again. Don't know where he's hiding now."

Cyclops nodded. He looked past Logan at the shadowy guests, visible now as silhouettes running wild in the darkness.

"I saw it, too," Wolverine continued. "Saw you zap that gal, knock her right into the fire. Would have believed it myself, 'cept you didn't smell right."

"Logan." Cyclops paused, gathered his breath. "I don't know if I've ever said this before, but thanks."

Logan turned away.

"What?" Cyclops asked. "What is it?"

"Nothing." Wolverine growled. "Least my little blackout should cover our escape."

"Right, the thing with the sewers. I forgot." Cyclops paused, thinking. "Get the others out of here, okay? I'll find Mastermind. And Jean."

Logan hesitated. Something in his expression sent a chill up Cyclops's spine.

"What?" Cyclops asked. "Have you seen her?"

"No. Not since…" Logan paused. "Listen, there's somethin' I gotta tell you."

"It'll have to wait."

"Yeah, but—"

"Logan! There's no time. Jean's over the edge… she's dangerous. I'm worried about her, but I'm also worried about what she might do."

A chandelier crashed down in the darkness. People scurried away, laughing and screaming. Half their voices still sounded panicked; the other half seemed to have decided it was all some elaborate, drunken game.

"Get Storm and the others, take them to the skyship. I'll call you as soon as I find Jean. I… I know how you feel about her."

"And I know how she feels about you."

There was something odd in his voice, something Cyclops couldn't read. It wasn't just concern, or even unrequited love. This was something deeper, darker.

"What?" Cyclops asked.

Logan shook his head, dismissing the question, and clapped Cyclops on the back. "Go get our girl," he said.

Cyclops frowned, nodded, and ran for the staircase.

JASON WYNGARDE entered the library.

Jean stood motionless, a shadow among shadows, her face supernally calm. The lights had gone out ten minutes before, leaving only the ambient glow from outside. But even in bright daylight, he wouldn't have seen her. Her power, her ever-growing telepathic prowess, concealed her from all eyes.

She was terrified, a fear that reached to her very core. But that would have to wait. All that mattered now was the Phoenix's rage.

You're no telepath, Jason, she thought, keeping her mind carefully shielded. *How did you plant yourself so deeply in my mind?* She tried to push him away, to banish his vile, invading thoughts. But their bond, forged through deceit and illusion, was too strong.

> *Hellfire Club failures losers beneath me*
> *Lost Jean lost my link to her*
> *How? Anticipated every contingency*
> *Must escape retreat regroup*

His surface thoughts were vile enough—petty hatreds, a small man's plans for power and influence. But the rage, the resentment that lay beneath, made her cringe.

> *X-Men hate X-Men make the world hate them*
> *Leland Pierce Shaw hate them too hate them more*
> *Rich born rich they buy women like slaves*

He stood facing the wall, clenching and unclenching his fists, raw contempt and misogyny leaking from his mind. As the psychic flow intensified, she embraced his dark thoughts. Invited them in, allowed them to stoke the fires within her.

> *Kill women love women why don't they love me*
> *All my life all women selfish selfish hate them*
> *Force them make them see make them feel my pain*

I am the master Mastermind Jean Grey
Jean Grey love her hate her bend her to my will
Secrets know her secrets know all their secrets
Master master master I AM THE MASTERMIND

"Jason," she said aloud.

He turned in the dark. "Jean!"

"Surprised, *Mastermind*? You're not the only one who can create illusions." A corona of flame appeared at her mental command, illuminating them both. "Perhaps women *don't love you* because you think of them as less than human." She smiled, took a step toward him. "Did that ever cross your mind?"

He staggered back, toward a bookcase.

"Why are you here?"

His fear pulled her closer. It was intoxicating. She stepped past him, made a show of picking up a book at random. Her eyebrow rose as she noticed the title: *Magick Without Tears*, by Aleister Crowley.

"I knew where you'd go. I know all about you," she answered. "You made a mistake, Jason. On the astral plane." She flipped pages, not looking at him. "You slew the man I loved—truly loved—before my eyes."

He glanced left to right. She didn't need telepathy to read his thoughts.

"Instead of severing the connection to my former life," she continued, "that was like a bucket of ice water in my face. You thought you'd enslave me forever, but instead you shocked me awake."

"No." He shook his head. "I compensated for that reaction. My power, combined with your own telepathy—it should have—"

"Your power is *nothing*."

She reached out, let loose a mental force bolt, and blasted him across the room. He crashed into a mirror, shattering it, and slumped to the ground in a pile of broken glass.

Her flame burned brighter, hotter. It rose up, shimmering and shifting, taking on its customary shape. But the Phoenix was wilder now, more savage. It cried out, wings reaching desperately for the sky. It was changing, growing, just as she herself was. Learning, seeking, evolving.

Mutating.

"Foolish man." She strode toward Wyngarde. "Have you any idea what you've done? The forces you've set in motion?"

He reached up, dazed, from the floor.

"No," he gasped. "No more."

"You came to me at my most vulnerable. How? How did you know where to find me? You're not a telepath—just a cheap illusionist."

"White Queen," he said, holding out a hand to ward her off. "She scouted you out... told me all about you. When you thought... other X-Men had died, in Antarctica... we seized our chance."

"You sabotaged the ship I was on." With the slightest mental effort, she lifted him up off the floor. "*She* knew I'd go to Kirinos... she sent you there to meet me, and my own telepathy did the rest."

He hung in the air, twisting and flailing. He tried to speak, but she held up a black-gloved hand. "You exploited my grief," she continued. "Made me trust you, filled an emotional void inside me—and all the while, you were using me. You implanted your twisted illusions inside me."

"Not—not *all* me." He struggled for breath. "The illusions— the timeslips. They came partly from you."

"Oh, I know."

She turned away, leaving him hanging in midair.

"You tapped into my... my fantasies," she said. "The most private, repressed part of my soul. You gave me something I secretly wanted." She whirled, fire in her eyes. "*But you never really knew me.*"

He stared down at her in terror. No longer a player, a swaggering King of the Hellfire Club's Inner Circle. Just a scared child, huddling for warmth in a carnival tent.

"You trade in women's secrets." She paced around him, eyeing his helpless form. "You ferret them out, using your cheap illusions.

Not so you can *know* these women, be a friend or a partner to them. Just so you can enslave them."

He swallowed loudly.

"I could show you secrets." She stopped before him, smiling. "Would you like that?"

He shook his head.

"Would you like to see?"

Within her, the power surged. Fiery, unstoppable; ancient and new at the same time, all barely contained by her desperate will. Fueled by rage, bound for vengeance, burning with the primal energies of the universe.

With a single stroke, she thrust it into his brain.

Wyngarde stiffened. His consciousness expanded at the speed of thought, racing from one side of reality to the other. A million worlds, a billion stars, a trillion tragic deaths. His mind bent, buckled, and threatened to snap in two.

"'Looking down on mortal men,'" she quoted. "Isn't that what you wanted?"

He screamed, writhed in desperation, his legs pumping in midair. She stayed with him, pouring more and more power into his tiny, human mind. Forcing him to consume the food of the gods—the massive, inescapable truths of existence.

When his mind snapped, he let out a gurgle. Hung loose in the air, eyes slack. He appeared in his true form now, all illusions gone. A gaunt, gray-haired scarecrow of a man, thin rope of drool hanging from his lip. Jean lowered him to the ground and propped him up against the bookcase.

"Goodbye, *Sir Jason*," she said. "You won't be coming back."

His eyes stared at her for a moment. Then his head slumped sideways, his jaw went slack.

I almost envy him, she thought. *Jason Wyngarde is at peace. Phoenix doesn't know the meaning of the word.*

She whirled away and strode out of the room. The corridor was dark, but she sensed the presence right away. *No*, she thought, *not him. Not now!*

"Jean!"

She flinched away, staggering against the wall before Scott could touch her.

"Jean. What's wrong?"

Keep him out, she thought. *Got to keep him out of my head. If he knew... if he had any idea...*

"We've got to go," he said. "Storm just called... the police are on their way, with orders to arrest the X-Men."

She turned to him, barely able to process the concept. *The police? How could that possibly matter, in light of the forces unleashed here today?*

"Jean? Do you understand me?"

She caught a glimpse of his face—and felt a sudden, bottomless sadness. *Such a good man. So true, so faithful. So filled with concern.*

My love.

She turned away, willing herself not to cry. *Not now,* she told herself. *There will be time for tears later. There will be plenty of tears.*

"Kurt's summoning the skyship," he said. "We have to leave *now.*"

She nodded, forced a smile onto her face, and started off down the hallway. She could feel his anxiety, his fear for her, leaking through her defenses. That fear, she knew, was just the beginning.

"This way," she said, leading the way to a hidden staircase.

CHAPTER TWENTY-ONE

THE SKYSHIP rose from the surface of the Hudson River, unnoticed in the driving rain. The surrounding area was completely dark—piers, streets, a row of old warehouses that stood between the water and the majestic Hellfire Club building. The only light came from a line of cars filing slowly out of the area.

"The blackout has spread," Colossus said, staring out the large side window of the ship. "You seem to have caused more damage than intended, my friend."

Wolverine didn't answer. His neck and arm hairs stood on end, and he had to struggle to keep from baring his claws. Every instinct in him cried out *danger*.

And it ain't the weather.

The skyship lurched; Logan grabbed the wall for balance. In the pilot's seat, Nightcrawler sat struggling with the controls. Storm stood just behind him, her arms spread in the air.

"Storm," Nightcrawler said. "Can you tone down the, well, storm? Just a little?"

"Apologies, Kurt." Her brow was furrowed with concentration. "I am gathering its power around the ship, to hide us from prying eyes. At least until you can activate the stealth shield."

Wolverine ignored them. The source of his anxiety was crouched against the opposite wall of the skyship's command area, staring out the window. Jean Grey—still wearing the uniform of the Black Queen. Cyclops knelt down next to her, talking in a low, soothing voice. With his enhanced hearing, Logan managed to make out the words.

"…Wyngarde?" Cyclops asked. "Is he still… you know. In your head?"

"No," Jean replied. She didn't move, didn't turn away from the window. "I dealt with him."

"Oh."

A shimmer of energy flared briefly around her. Cyclops retracted his fingers, as if afraid he'd be burned.

Wolverine recalled Professor Xavier's words: "*Nothing else matters. This is all about Jean.*"

"So tight." Jean touched her stomach, fingered the loops fastening the corset there. "So binding. He said… this was supposed to be freedom. But it's not."

"Jean." Cyclops touched her shoulder. "You've been through a lot, but it's over now."

Wolverine's claws slid free. His instincts were screaming even louder than before. Jean's scent smelled wild, wrong. Her body was coiled, tense, like that of a cornered animal.

"It's not." She laughed, a terrible, cold laugh. "It's not freedom at all."

"We'll figure this out," Scott continued. "I'll contact the Professor. He'll know what to do."

Back off, Summers, Logan thought fiercely. He circled around the back of the room, angling to get a better look at them.

"Please," Cyclops said. "I want to help you."

She looked at him for the first time since they had boarded. Her eyes were blank, staring, cold. Emotionless, except for a distant, superior sort of rage.

226   "You want," she repeated.

The skyship lurched again. "Ororo!" Nightcrawler said.

"This is no longer my doing," Storm replied. "The storm was supposed to be letting up by now, but it appears to be growing stronger. I will do what I can."

"I don't want this," Jean said. She reached down, her fingers scrabbling at the corset. "I don't like this at all."

"Jean." Cyclops climbed to his feet. "I…"

Don't say it, Wolverine thought. *Don't.*

"…I love you."

She looked up, eyes flaring. Logan let out a growl and lunged—too late. Energy burst forth, searing, ancient, unfathomable. The full, unfettered rage of an elemental force, unleashed at last.

"Hear me, X-Men." Jean rose up above the floor. "No longer am I the woman you knew."

Her hair was a trail of flame; her eyes, blazing orbs of power. The cape and corset of the Black Queen vaporized, reduced to atoms. Jean was once again Phoenix—but her costume, too, was different now. Darker, redder, glowing brighter than the human eye could bear.

"I am fire," she continued, "and life incarnate."

Cyclops moved toward her. Wolverine reached and grabbed hold of his arm. Cyclops whirled, pain and desperation in his eyes.

"Let me go, Logan!"

"No," Wolverine said.

"Now and forever, I am PHOENIX!"

The skyship exploded.

METAL WALLS tore apart like paper. Engines growled, screamed, and choked to silence. For a moment, time froze.

Then Cyclops was falling through sheets of rain.

At first all he could see was Jean. She shone like a star, her arms spread wide, hair blazing bright. Primal energy flared out in all directions, filling the sky. Pieces of the skyship pinwheeled away, looping and arcing through the air.

He twisted and looked down, counting off the X-Men one by one: Nightcrawler, Wolverine, Colossus—all in freefall. Colossus had transformed instinctively to his metallic form. Above them, Storm soared aloft on the raging winds.

"Colossus!" Cyclops yelled. "You won't be harmed by the fall. Try to land first so you can help the others!" He couldn't make out Peter's expression through the driving rain, but the young Russian turned, aimed both fists at the ground, and arrowed downward. The red and yellow trees of New York's Central Park loomed close.

At least we didn't blow ourselves up over Fifth Avenue!

"Nightcrawler, you'll have to teleport down," he called. "Quick, before you build up too much momentum!"

The grimace was visible on Kurt Wagner's face, even through the storm. Clenching his fists, he vanished in a puff of brimstone. He reappeared below, then cried out as he struck the ground and tumbled into a tree.

Cyclops turned his attention to his own predicament. *I could slow my fall with my eye-beams,* he thought, *but the force might snap my neck!*

"Storm! You're our only flier—"

"Already on it."

He turned to look—and saw that she already had Wolverine in her grasp, holding him firmly by his belt. The two of them swooped down behind him.

"Hold still, Cyke."

"Just keep those claws under wraps."

"Don't give me any ideas."

Logan reached out to grab Cyclops under the arms. Firm hands jerked him upward, slowing his momentum. Storm swung the three of them around in a wide arc, avoiding a tree as they approached the ground.

"Logan," he called. "Let me go!"

Wolverine released him. He leapt down onto a patch of muddy grass, kicking up a splash as he landed. The ground was rocky, uneven, with a paved path leading around a pile of boulders. No one else around on this rainswept night.

"Colossus? Nightcrawler?"

Colossus staggered up, his arm around Nightcrawler's shoulders. "We are well, Cyclops."

"We're alive, anyway." Nightcrawler rubbed his head. "What hit us?"

As if in answer, the sky flared bright. Light shone down, slicing through the rain, casting stark shadows between the storm-battered trees. In the center of the light, Jean Grey turned to face downward. Her body, sheathed in the red-and-yellow garb of the Phoenix, glowed with fury.

"Oh," Nightcrawler said. Then his eyes went wide. "*Oh.*"

Without a word, the team sprang into action. Wolverine ran toward Colossus, who clasped his metal hands together. When Logan leaped up to meet him, Colossus grabbed hold of him and hurled him into the air. This was their signature move: the Fastball Special.

Logan hurtled toward Phoenix, his claws bared to strike. She turned, cast the barest of glances in his direction, and gestured. A bolt of telekinetic energy slapped him away, sending him flying out of sight over the trees.

Storm swooped out of the trees, landed atop the pile of boulders, and raised her arms. Gale-force winds erupted around Jean, pushing her away through the air. She waved gloved hands at the wind, momentarily disoriented.

"Peter!" Cyclops yelled. "Now!"

Colossus reached out and grabbed hold of an oak tree—at least ten meters high, its gnarled trunk almost a meter wide. With a grunt, he pulled it free of the ground, its roots shedding soil into the sodden air. He hefted it above his shoulder, taking aim.

Again Phoenix gestured. There was no energy flare, no visible display of power—but suddenly Colossus was flesh and blood again.

She transformed him back—negated the effect of his mutation, Cyclops thought. *How powerful is she?*

Peter Rasputin's now-human muscles strained under the weight of the hundred-year-old tree. He cried out and began to fall, battered by the heavy branches of the tree. Nightcrawler teleported in, grabbed him, and 'ported the two of them away again. The tree crashed to the wet ground.

Light shone down on Cyclops, painting a spotlight around him in the rain. He looked up, raising a hand to shield himself from the blinding glare. Phoenix hovered less than five meters above, staring down at him.

She was smiling.

She's enjoying this, he realized. *Using her power like this—unfettered, without limits—it's like an endorphin rush. It's a physical and emotional stimulant.*

"Jean!" he cried.

A flood of images, of scattered thoughts, washed over him.

Mine is the fire
Foolish man
This life may not be the life I
Don't cry don't cry
You're nothing all of you nothing to me
Foolish man what you offer

He flinched, fell to his knees. He'd experienced her thoughts in this form, like the gushing of a fire hose, back at the Hellfire Club. Yet this was different. The voices within her—they raged beyond human reason now, beyond the capacity of his mind to process.

The circle
The circle unbroken
I am fire and life incarnate
Charged particles
Naked man animal horns
Can't fight him can't fight it
The voice within the voice without

Her bliss, her agony, shot through him like a laser. His mind began to fracture under the assault.

Face on fire
Mind enraged
What you offer
Nothing all of you nothing
What you offer I already possess
Thought you'd enslave me
This isn't it's not it's not freedom
I am fire I am life
I AM PHOENIX I BRING THE STORM

"JEAN!"

Storm's voice wrenched Cyclops out of the mindlink. He looked up, shaking water off his visor. Storm stood atop the pile of rocks, calling up into the driving rain.

"Jean, I would speak with you." Her voice was both commanding and gentle. "Please listen."

Phoenix's lip curled in disgust—but she paused, glowing in the sky. The storm seemed to pause along with her.

"You were like this before," Storm continued. "After the shuttle accident… when you first tapped into the Phoenix power. But that power was tempered, then, by humanity, by mercy. By your connection to your friends."

Nightcrawler teleported in next to Cyclops. "Peter and Logan are down," he said. "We're the only ones left."

Cyclops motioned him to silence.

"Remember," Storm said, keeping her eyes fixed on Jean. "Remember who you are. Remember your friends, the people you love. The ones who love *you*."

Jean hung perfectly still, the flames glowing bright around her. No expression, no trace of emotion crossed her face. Above her, the moon peeked into view through a hole in the clouds. The rain slowed to a trickle.

Did it work? Cyclops wondered. *Did Storm manage to reach her?*

Then a pulse of psychic energy burst forth, filling the air in waves. As it passed through Storm, she staggered and fell from her perch. Nightcrawler, too, sank silently to the ground.

Cyclops braced himself. The sensation was oddly gentle, as if consciousness itself were being plucked from his body. He was briefly aware of the rain, stronger again, pinging and dripping off his visor. Then that, too, faded to ash and memory.

PHOENIX DROPPED to a soft landing among the X-Men's bodies. The storm whipped and surged, lashing against her, but she paid it no heed. Raindrops sizzled on contact with her flame, vanishing into mist.

Her life, now, was power. Coursing through her like an electric charge, growing stronger with each enemy she vanquished. An ancient force made immanent, animating her mortal form—and, at the same time, the ultimate expression of a young woman's rage.

Cells breaking down.

Flesh unraveling.

Fire dancing on skin.

She looked down at the bodies strewn across the muddy grass. The tall dark woman had been her friend. The hairy one... he was dangerous. The large one had been like a child; the blue-furred one had made her laugh.

"Dear ones," she murmured.

Within her the power swelled—and with it, the first stirrings of hunger. A hunger as old as time, as fresh as all the new sensations coursing through her. Nothing here—on this cold, tiny world—could satisfy that hunger. She needed more.

She paused for a moment, her gaze lingering on the last body. The lean, muscled man with the single red eye. He had meant something to her, once. He was special.

No more.

The Dark Phoenix spread her wings, burned bright, and took off for the stars.

INTERLUDE TWO

A GUST of wind blew up, almost wrenching the umbrella out of the young man's hand. His companion yelped as the rain flew into her eyes. She shook her long blond hair and leaned in close, resting her head on his shoulder.

"Peter Parker," she said, "I am *so* glad we finally had a real date."

"Me too," he said. "Some play, huh, Gwen?"

She went rigid, stopping dead along the pathway that led through Central Park. Scattered streetlamps lit the wet grass in a patchwork of shadows.

"What did you call me?"

"I—sorry," Peter said. "I'm sorry, Cissy!"

"*Gwen…*" She started to move away from him, then shrank back from the sheeting rain. "I am so tired of hearing about Gwen Stacy."

Peter Parker swallowed. *She's angry*, he thought. *And she's right.*

"I didn't mean—"

"I get it," she continued. "You lost someone; that's a tragedy. I'm… I'm really sorry."

Peter started to reply, then froze as a loud buzzing flared through his head. *Spider-sense!* He looked around, searching for the cause.

"But you're going to have to move forward sometime," she continued. "You know?"

"What?" he said.

"Peter. Are you even *listening* to me?"

He wasn't. Not anymore. Over Cissy Ironwood's shoulder, a mile or so away, a massive flaming shape had appeared. It loomed over the park: a bird of prey, fiery jaws snapping from side to side.

Peter's mind raced. *Alien invasion? Super villain? Is there a villain that uses bird-fire as a weapon? I'm drawing a blank here!*

But somehow he knew, staring at the flaming shape, that this was no mere super villain. Something much larger, even godlike, was at play here. Something way beyond the scope of a friendly neighborhood Spider-Man. He watched, eyes wide, as the huge bird rose up, wings flapping wildly against the storm. It let out a strange, unearthly shriek, then turned away and headed off into the sky.

He peered upward, scanning the clouds. No trace of the bird-thing remained. It had been hard to make out clearly through the storm, but for just a moment he thought he'd seen a woman's figure at the heart of the flames.

Probably just a trick of the light.

"Peter!"

He turned. Cissy stood soaking wet, her arms crossed—and angrier than ever. In his distracted state, he'd wandered away with the umbrella in his hand, leaving her exposed to the elements.

"Sorry!" He moved toward her, pointing at the sky. "Did you see…?"

"See *what*?"

He realized, from her furious expression, that she hadn't even seen the flame bird. The whole incident had taken less than a minute.

"I don't think this is going to work out," she said.

Peter's spider-sense faded to a dull hum. Whatever that thing had been, the danger it posed was gone… at least for now. He turned back to Cissy with an apologetic shrug.

236   "Probably not," he sighed.

DOCTOR STEPHEN Strange stared at the bookcase. It stretched from floor to ceiling, covering an entire wall of his study. He scanned the shelves, making certain not to focus on any single title. That would defeat the purpose of this exercise.

When he'd come home with his morning coffee, a large garden slug had been crawling up the door. A disquieting omen. After several hours of meditation, he'd been unable to pinpoint the source.

So, with some reluctance, he had turned to an exercise taught to him long ago by his mentor, the Ancient One. The books in this room included ancient Chalcedonian texts, relics from the Library of Alexandria, and even a few 1930s pulp magazines with spells encoded in the patterns of their ragged-edged pages. He had asked his associate Wong to randomize the books, moving them deliberately out of their customary order.

Letting out his breath, he closed his eyes. *Where diligence fails,* he thought, *perhaps synchronicity may serve.*

He reached out and grasped hold of a thick, weathered volume.

Before he could open his eyes, however, a powerful mystic wave struck his mind. Images of passion, anger—and great evil. An avatar from ancient Greek writings: the Phoenix, symbol of fire and rebirth.

Instantly he knew: *This is no threat from without—no incursion from some otherworldly realm. This is happening right here, right now, in this very city.*

I must summon others.

He ran from the study, dropping the book on his desk. Only later would he note its title: *Magick Without Tears,* by Aleister Crowley.

SCOTT LANG, the hero called Ant-Man, stared at the computer monitor. He climbed up the side of the display, pausing to lean over for another look. When he reached the top, he braced himself with his legs and hung down in front of the screen.

"Nope," he said. "Doesn't make any sense upside down, either."

He glanced across the small monitoring room located on the top level of Avengers Tower. Natasha Romanoff paced back and forth, talking intently on a cell phone. She wore her Black Widow uniform, which—Scott realized—probably wasn't a good sign.

Tony Stark leaned against another desk. He wore a two-piece Armani suit and a single Iron Man glove, from which rose a high-res hologram showing heat measurements and spectrometer readings. His lips moved rapidly, silently, his eyes flicking back and forth as he paged through the holographic display.

Scott leaped down onto the desk. "Tony," he called.

Stark twitched, turned his head.

"What's that?" Scott pointed at the screen with his entire, inch-long arm.

Stark walked over, casually deactivating the hologram. "That," he said, "is a thermal reading from a source of enormous power. The blip originated in Central Park, just north of the Great Lawn, and is currently climbing into Earth orbit."

"Yeah, but what *is* it?"

They stared at the image together. The "blip" was roughly oval in shape, with wing-like protuberances on each side. It was solid red at the center, fading to orange and yellow at the edges. An altitude counter on the side of the image showed its progress through the upper layers of the atmosphere.

"I don't know," Tony said.

A clatter came from across the room. Scott whirled to see Natasha staring at them. Her phone lay on the floor.

"Sorry," she said, scooping up the phone in a graceful motion. "I just don't think I've ever heard you say that before."

Tony rolled his eyes. "I say that all the time."

"Is it Thanos?" Scott asked. "Please say it's not Thanos. I'm getting pretty tired of that mitten of his."

"It's not," Stark replied. "Readings don't match. Any luck contacting Thor?"

"Nope." Scott shrugged. "He's… what do you say? Off-planet. Off-realm? Off… someplace."

Tony nodded.

"What about Doctor Strange?" Scott asked.

"He's clueless, too." Tony let out a dry laugh. "First time I've seen that guy's magic wand droop."

He's really worried, Scott realized, watching his teammate closely. *Whatever this is, it's a big deal.*

Natasha strode over, frowning at the screen. "What's our blip doing now?"

"It's accelerating," Tony said, leaning down for a closer look. "Veering… toward the sun, it looks like. Whoa, that's fast… aaaand it's gone." The blip vanished from the screen. A text window appeared.

OBJECT HAS PASSED
BEYOND SENSOR RANGE

"Gone." Scott blinked. "Gone is good, right?"

"Maybe," Natasha said. "Maybe not."

Tony Stark didn't reply. He paced from one side of the room to the other, then back again. Finally, he stopped and touched a stud on his glove.

"Friday," he said. "Open a channel to Starcore."

Scott and Natasha exchanged blank looks. Sometimes, Scott realized, Tony made him feel like a little brother who'd never be allowed to play with the big kids.

"What the hell is a Starcore?" he asked.

"REPLY TO Tony Stark," Dr. Peter Corbeau said. "We are not yet operational. Sensor units are still being installed, and half our staff is en route from Earth. Whatever infra-galactic attack or mole-people invasion he's dealing with, he'll have to handle it himself."

Corbeau looked around the gleaming, freshly built control center. *Good thing it takes seven minutes for radio messages to reach Earth,* he thought. *I really don't feel like arguing with Stark in real time.*

Starcore had been designed, funded, and constructed faster than any satellite installation in history. Corbeau had pulled out all the stops, used his fierce intelligence and charm to ram through multiple levels of financing in record time. But astronauts were still at work outside, hooking up sensor modules and monitoring equipment. Only two of the center's eight command consoles were lit—the bulk of the instrumentation was still dark. The central wall screen hadn't even been activated.

"Peter." A dark-skinned woman rose from the other operational station. "You'll want to see this."

"I don't have time, Shira. We're a solar-monitoring station, not some playboy super hero's personal cell tower."

She held out a tablet to him. "Look."

With an impatient swipe he grabbed the tablet. Turning away, he stared at the display—and froze. Icy panic coursed through him.

"Punch it up," he said.

Shira frowned. "Punch what up?"

"All of it! Everything we've got." He crossed to a terminal, began accessing work logs. "Order all EVA crews to cease operations and get back inside the station. Camera Four is operational, right?"

"I think so." She returned to her station, began working controls. "I take it you've seen that wavelength before?"

"Yes," he said. "In—in a way."

He stared at the screen, at the data sent by Stark. A simple table of figures, a few blurry thermal images—but to Corbeau they recalled things he'd spent the past year trying to forget. Images of dark fury, fueled by a passion beyond human comprehension. Memories of cold fingers probing his brain, tiptoeing through his darkest secrets.

"Camera Four," Shira said.

240 The wall screen flickered to life. It showed stars shining in the

void—and something else. A brightly burning dot, at the extreme left-hand edge of the image.

"Magnify that," he said.

Shira manipulated the controls. As the image zoomed in the dot grew larger, wavering from side to side. The camera stabilized—revealing the fiery shape of a birdlike creature, raging with power. She stared at the screen.

"What the hell is it?"

"Not it," Corbeau said. "She."

"It's coming from the Earth, vectoring sunward," she said. "Radiating energy… levels are off the charts."

"Are our people all inside?"

She nodded. "Last crew just sealed the airlock behind them."

Corbeau stared, mesmerized, as the bird shape drew closer. A year ago, Jean Grey had used the skills taken from Corbeau's mind to pilot a shuttle down to Earth. She'd passed through lethal levels of radiation, but somehow she had survived. Corbeau theorized that the solar rays—the heavy radiation—had altered her at the molecular level, jumpstarting her mutant ability to some unknown degree. In this new form, he believed, Jean had literally forced herself back to life.

It was only a theory, of course. To verify it, he'd have had to examine Jean Grey personally. He'd tried to contact the X-Men, but they hadn't returned his calls. Apparently they only sought him out when they needed his help, in between battles with the Sentinels or Magneto.

Or maybe, he thought, *they just didn't want to face the truth.*

The burning figure—the Phoenix—spread its wings, nearly filling the large screen. At this proximity, Jean's form was clearly visible at its center. Her face was savage, inhuman. The countenance of a wrathful god, sent to rain down judgment on the mortal world.

Panic struck Corbeau again. *Is she coming for me? To kill me, destroy all remnants of her past? Does she blame me, somehow, for what's happened to her?*

He took a deep breath.

No. That's just… more hubris. Whatever Jean Grey has become, she's far beyond caring about one man.

Any man.

"Sensor unit beta just came up," Shira said. "Generating a plot now… the object is veering away from us."

Corbeau turned away from the screen, called up a schematic on his own monitor. A dotted line indicated Jean's path, arcing elliptically away from Earth, passing by the Starcore station to curve around the flaming orb of the sun. A winking dot at the end of the line indicated her current position.

"My god," he said, "she's still accelerating. She's at point eight nine of lightspeed."

"She's diving into the sun!" Shira came up behind him, staring over his shoulder. "Skimming through the corona, moving dangerously close to the photosphere. How can anything survive that?"

"She's *using* it," Corbeau said. "The sun. She's slingshotting around it, using it to boost her velocity." He called up a counter to analyze the object's speed. Point nine of lightspeed. Point nine two. Point nine five.

A shockwave passed through the station. Screens flickered, lights winked off and on again. Corbeau grabbed his armrests, turning to see Shira stumble into a chair at a dormant workstation. Then the wall screen caught his eye. It was frozen on the image of the Phoenix, blazing its way through deep space. Burning deep red, fiery yellow wings bleeding energy, and at its core—like a child trapped in a burning house—a tiny human figure.

The screen went black.

"What the hell was that?" Shira shook her head, toggled the workstation to life.

Corbeau frowned, holding down keys to reboot his own station. "Have you ever seen a hyperspace manifold being formed?"

"No." She stared at him. "No one has."

242   "Then we've just made history. Another Peter Corbeau first…

Remind me to update my personal bio." He turned, and realized she was staring at him. "What?"

"Hang onto that ego, Doc." Shira gave him a wry smile. "It might go down in history, too."

Corbeau stood up and paced across the room. The wall screen flickered back to life as the external camera rebooted. The image blurred, wavered, and refocused automatically on the subject of Starcore's research.

The sun. Source of all life in the solar system, the most powerful fusion generator in twenty-five trillion miles of space. It blazed steady, small flares dancing on the edge of the chromosphere. Nothing disturbed its surface, no anomalous readings showed on the electromagnetic counters.

There was no sign of Jean Grey, of the Phoenix.

She—they—were gone.

The smile faded from Corbeau's face. *I should be relieved*, he thought. *A threat to my life—to all humanity, perhaps—has fled our solar system, possibly forever. Headed for the stars, where she might finally find… well, peace.*

I should be relieved.

Yet somehow, as he returned to the task of rebooting Starcore's systems, all Corbeau felt was a vague, nameless dread.

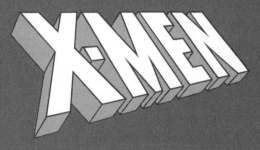

ACT THREE
STORMBRINGER

CHAPTER TWENTY-TWO

HYPERSPACE HIT her like a drug, like needles coursing through her blood. Tachyons redshifted past, quarks tingled on her skin. Stars rushed by, bright stones in the ether-current, no sooner glimpsed than left behind.

The Dark Phoenix threw back her head and laughed.

Her power was no longer a song, but a rich symphony played on the superstrings that held all of time and space together. Here, in this realm beyond lightspeed, she could see them—the forty-two bands of hyperspace. Six points, seven strings emerging from each. They shone through the walls, burned away the thin membranes of existence, laying bare the inner structure of the universe.

She stretched out a talon to pluck a string. It vibrated, sang, sent echoes rippling out among the stars. She was one step closer now. Closer to the primal forces—the last truths. The final knowing.

How? she wondered. *How could I ever have denied myself this?*

This was where she belonged. Among the stars, but apart from them. Within the universe, yet beyond it. Feeding on the fundamental forces, feeling them course into, through, and beyond her. The Phoenix needed no man, no woman, no mortal being. It was pure passion, pure joy. It would live forever.

I will live forever.

As soon as that feeling struck her, another sensation followed. Hunger. Dark, savage, consuming. An instinct from her host's animal past, a need that could not be denied. She doubled over, wrenched with need, desperate for sustenance.

Shivering, she summoned another gateway. It bloomed like a flower before her, a six-dimensional manifold in perfect symmetry. The stars slowed, and the strings of hyperspace gave way to still, frigid vacuum. The Phoenix spread her arms, extending fiery wings to warm herself.

Ahead lay her prize. A main sequence, G-type star. Diameter a little less than one million miles; composition stable. Expected lifespan approximately six billion years.

Eyes blazing, she dove in.

As she entered the heliosphere, the solar wind slammed into her. Rippling through her hair, stinging her face. Whipping around in a spiral pattern, weaving powerful magnetic fields all around. There was something familiar about that.

Spiral patterns. DNA.

Mutation.

Gasping with relief, she drew the energy inside herself. Continued down through the corona, into an area of sharply rising heat, ten million degrees kelvin. Twelve million. Fourteen. She laughed, sang, and drank it all in.

The Phoenix arrowed down, her course straight and true, past the star's dark photosphere, through the turbulent convective zone, into an area of hard radiation. Arms wide, she absorbed it all: heat, plasma, hydrogen and helium, and all the heavy elements.

Voices cried out, faint in her mind. They seemed far away, separated by space and thought and centuries of evolution. She paid them no heed, continuing onward, drawing closer to the center—the source, the beginning, the place where light and heat and life were born.

248   The core of the star.

When she broke through, the heat around her surged again—up to sixteen million kelvin, hotter than any living being in the universe had ever before endured. Pure fusion, wild and uncontrolled, blasting atoms apart, sundering time and space. Here in this floating hell, all matter—all energy—was absorbed and enlisted into a single, unstoppable process: the birth of fire.

The Phoenix spread her wings and fed.

Protons fused together and split violently apart, filling the void within her. Fueling her rage, her passion, her joy. The endless hunger of the Phoenix.

Minutes later she soared through space, blazing with newfound power. The pain was gone; her vitality, her drive, had returned. Again, she laughed.

This is my life, she thought. *This is the life I was meant to lead.*

An object caught her eye. A tiny metal box, powered by controlled-tachyon engines, closing rapidly on her position. The Phoenix's eyes widened; a predatory smile spread across her face.

Changing course, she welcomed this new challenge. Not stopping, not even slowing her pace. Never pausing to look back at the smoldering cinder that—a mere six minutes ago—had been a healthy, shining star.

"FIRST OFFICER. What am I looking at?"

"Transmission from the D'Bari system, Milord Captain. Sent... twelve minutes ago."

Aboard the Shi'ar Imperial dreadnought, First Officer Eluke stared at the horrific image on the main viewscreen. Captain Juber strode forward to join him, past the hovering communications and security stations, through the open space at the base of the three-story bridge.

The screen showed a city street, tall buildings flanking a busy intersection filled with stalled vehicles. Dozens, hundreds of people thronged the street—citizens of D'Bari, with their distinctive olive-green skin and elongated faces. They stared upward as a blinding light washed over them, filling the sky from one horizon to the other.

"The light of Armageddon," Juber whispered.

The people looked up, shielding their eyes. Their large mouths hung open in horror, confusion, fear. One of them turned to the camera, gesturing frantically as he made sharp guttural sounds.

Eluke frowned. "I can run that through the translator—"

"Don't bother," Juber said.

The transmission ended abruptly. The image shifted to a view of D'Bari's sun, throbbing and pulsing wildly.

Juber turned to the navigation station at floor level. "Give me tactical."

He leaned forward, steadying himself against the front railing. As a series of horrific images unfolded on the meters-high screen, Juber ran a hand through the dark feathers framing his head and neck. The feathers betrayed his people's avian nature—the Shi'ar had evolved not from apes, but from birds.

A massive flare billowed out from the sun. The display followed the path of the flare as it passed by three inner planets, each identified by a computer overlay. A fourth world, blue and cloud-covered, lay directly ahead.

"The planet is D'Bari-d," Eluke said. "Source of the transmission. That's the heat flare, following the light they saw a few moments before."

The flare struck the fourth planet. The blue world almost vanished in a flash of blinding light. A spray of atmosphere and elementary particles burst forward from it like a halo.

"The instant the flare struck, the atmosphere and oceans on the day side boiled away. The steam and superheated air whirled around the globe, obliterating everything in their path. The few people awake on the night side probably saw a spectacular Aurora Borealis before death claimed them." Eluke's voice faltered. "The rest died in their sleep."

250   "The lucky ones," Juber said. "Pull back the view to a distance of zero point one light-years."

The image zoomed out. D'Bari's star flashed bright, consuming everything in the system. Juber turned toward an elevated station studded with holographic displays.

"Science Officer?"

"Stellar expansion is slowing." Sonneb, the science officer, ran her hands rapid-fire across the holograms. "Visible contraction now evident in the photosphere. It's acting like a proper supernova, Milord, but at a fantastically accelerated rate."

Juber paused, clenching his fists. The images were monstrous, almost beyond comprehension, but he kept his face stoic. He could not show weakness on the bridge of his ship.

"Explanation?" he asked.

"I have none, Milord," Eluke said. "This was an average, G-normal star. A certain amount of flaring is to be expected, but this…"

"I have checked the morning's scans," the science officer said. "We charted no abnormal matrices in the star, on atomic or subatomic levels. This should not—*could not* have occurred."

Juber stared at the star. It filled the screen now, pulsing and throbbing like a dying heart.

"Not by itself," he murmured.

"Milord!"

Juber turned sharply. He'd never before heard such panic in Eluke's voice.

"Sensors now register a field anomaly." Eluke stood at his station, hands flashing over the controls. "Moving out from the core of the star. Registering up and down the spectrum… at levels so extreme, our instruments cannot get a fix on it—"

"It's a life-form," the science officer said.

Juber squinted at the screen. The star was contracting, its fires dying, and at its center he could see… *something*… As Eluke moved to join him, he heard the first officer's sharp intake of breath.

"Full magnification," Juber said. "There!"

On the screen, a young woman with flame-red hair soared toward them, arms spread wide. Her eyes betrayed a cruel, terrible ecstasy. Behind her, the star shrank and died, the last of its energies funneling into the massive energy trail left in her wake.

"It's humanoid," Eluke said, "but what sort of creature is it?"

I know, Juber thought. *I wish I did not, but I do.*

"The Phoenix," he breathed.

Eluke turned to him. "That's a legend."

"A legend our people have dreaded since they first spread their wings and left the trees." Again, Juber ran a hand nervously through his feather crest. "No judgment is more feared than that of the Phoenix."

"Sharra and K'ythri preserve us," Eluke whispered.

Juber turned. The crew were all watching him, from elevated stations and the security posts on ground level.

"Sound battle stations," he ordered. "We will engage."

Eluke placed a hand on his arm. "Is that wise, Milord?"

"It is a moral obligation." Juber turned back to the screen. "D'Bari was an ally of the Empire. Five billion people, *exterminated* by that… thing. They must be avenged!"

"You heard the captain." Eluke released Juber's arm and strode across the bridge. "Battle stations!"

On screen, the entity paused in space. And smiled.

"Science Officer," Juber said, "am I correct in assuming this creature is drawing its life-energy from the star it has consumed?"

"Readings confirm that, sir."

"Then it is even more imperative that we stop it. Now—before it slaughters more worlds." He paused. "Before its power becomes so great that no force in creation can stand against it."

"Coming up on the entity," Eluke announced.

The woman spread her arms, fiery wings mirroring her motion. The Phoenix energy seemed to burn away the space around her, wreathing her in flame.

"Main batteries," Juber said. "Fire!"

A plasma bolt shot forth from the massive dreadnought. The Phoenix dodged the bolt easily, swooping at near-lightspeed in a loop around the red energy trail.

"She's coming around again," Eluke said.

The Phoenix flared bright, arcing wide in open space. As she turned to close in on the warship, the expression on her face turned to fury.

"Shields!" Juber ordered.

The Phoenix shot forward, gaining speed as she approached. She struck one of the ship's propulsion nacelles, slicing through it in a shower of tachyon particles. The nacelle wing creaked, sparked, and snapped off.

The bridge exploded in chaos. Damage reports poured in: casualty counts, repair orders, energy readouts—a welter of overlapping voices. Eluke moved quickly to Juber's side.

"Tachyon power down to forty percent," he said. "Weaponry down by half."

"Shields?"

"Failing," Eluke said tersely. "We are lucky to be alive, Milord. We must flee while we can!"

Juber turned to him. "Do you honestly think we can outrun our foe, Eluke? Or that it will *allow* us to leave?"

They turned, together, to face the screen. The entity burned brighter than ever, blazing against the stars. It reached the farthest point of its arc, then veered again toward the Shi'ar dreadnought.

"Whatever our fate, my friend, we will meet it with honor." Juber whirled to the communications station. "Prepare to dispatch log message to the Empress."

A massive blast shook the bridge. Juber steadied himself against the railing. The screen was now filled with the fiery, terrible energy flare of the Phoenix.

"Heavy casualties," Eluke reported. "Engineering section exposed to vacuum. We've lost hyperspace capability."

"Log-recording at your command, Milord," the communications officer called. Juber pressed a stud on the railing before him, activating the recording.

"Empress Majestrix," he said, gesturing toward the screen in front of him. "I hope you receive this. We are beaten—no weapons, no power. Crew mostly dead. Ship a ruined, gutted hulk."

"Entity closing," Eluke said.

"Beware, my Empress," Juber continued. "*Beware the Phoenix.*"

As if on cue, the bird of prey filled the screen. Its flame stretched for millions of kilometers now, a force capable of snuffing out whole stars—wielded by a single young woman.

"Dispatch log message," Juber said. "Now!"

"Juber, my captain. My friend." Eluke's hand touched Juber's, clasped it tight. "I believe this is the end."

Juber squeezed the hand tight. He stared into the flames and saw, in their depths, the ruin of the proud Shi'ar civilization. A conflagration that could bring down an empire, that might even consume the universe itself.

Empress Lilandra, he thought. *I am your servant, now and forever. K'ythri grant that you receive my warning—*

The Phoenix blazed once, twice. And Juber's thoughts, his prayers, his proud Imperial warship—all vanished in a spray of raw atoms.

CHAPTER TWENTY-THREE

"GENTLY DOES it… gently. Ach, *no!*"

The circuit board clattered to the kitchen floor. Nightcrawler let out a string of German curses, then lowered the soldering iron and turned to Colossus.

"Peter. This thing is hard enough to assemble without your clumsiness."

"I am sorry." Colossus held up his hands—even in his flesh-and-blood form they were huge. "I think perhaps I am not built for delicate work."

Wolverine sat astride a folding chair on the opposite side of the kitchen, shaking his head back and forth. *This is hopeless,* he thought. *No way we're gonna beat Jeannie, ever again. If she's even still on this flamin' planet.*

"Here, little brother." Storm handed a tablet to Colossus. "You read Dr. MacTaggert's instructions off to us. I will hold the circuitry steady." The two of them switched places, both leaning against the kitchen table. Its surface was strewn with tools, clamps, nuts and bolts, and circuitry stripped from prototype versions of the Cerebro mainframe.

"Perhaps Cyclops could help," Colossus offered.

"He knows no more about mnemonic circuitry than you or I," Storm said, "and he may have a concussion. Let him rest."

Logan turned away, tuning out the chatter. Three snapshots kept replaying in his mind—three memories of Jean Grey's face, in succession, like a slide show. The first was when he'd burst into the sanctum of the Hellfire Club. Jean, in her Black Queen regalia, casting a glare of challenge at him. In an instant, he'd recognized the barely contained fury inside her. He'd seen the damage done by Wyngarde's manipulations.

The second memory had come just a few minutes later. He'd heard the clicking of Cyclops's collar opening, understood that Jean had freed him with her telekinesis. Her eyes had locked onto his, letting him in on her plan—to keep sparring to distract the Inner Circle, while Cyclops freed the others.

Her expression then had been… strange. A hint of a smile, a touch of satisfaction at the deception. But a spark of anger, too—a flame that burned bright within her. A hint that all was not well, that the worst was still to come.

The third memory made him shudder. Jean in midair, hovering over Central Park in the driving rain. Her costume dark and savage, her face twisted into a mask of rage, contempt, and utter dismissal. With a wave of her hand, she'd knocked him out of the sky.

That's when he'd known, beyond a hint of a doubt, that Jean was gone. There was nothing human in that expression, nothing left of the woman he'd known. The woman he'd loved.

She swatted us down like flies. Her friends, her teammates—and, not incidentally, one of the most powerful hero teams in the flamin' world. He shook his head, remembering. *You were right, Chuck. Damn you, anyway. Why'd ya have to be right?*

Three days earlier

"I AM not calling to compliment you," Professor Xavier said. "I need the Wolverine for a mission."

Xavier's face glared out of the small television screen. Wolverine drained his beer and slammed the cup down on the bar in Angel's underground den.

"You got him."

"I am about to become the consort to an empress," Xavier said. "In preparation for this honor, I have undergone schooling in the mythology and traditions of the Shi'ar."

"Sounds boring as hell."

"Actually, it's easier than you might think, for a…" Xavier tapped his bald head. "Anyway. One legend of the Shi'ar people particularly struck me. Their earliest records speak of the Phoenix… an unstoppable force known as 'the end of all that is.'"

Logan hissed in a breath. "I don't like where this is goin'."

"Believe me, neither do I." A pained look crossed Xavier's normally stoic face. "I was prepared to dismiss the story as a coincidence, until I received Moira's new data. Her analyses show Jean's power increasing along a geometric curve, with no end in sight."

Wolverine grimaced. More than anything in the world, he wanted another beer. But he felt rooted to the barstool, unable to move.

"As I said," Xavier continued, "I will be returning to Earth at the earliest opportunity. At that time, I believe I can evaluate Jean's situation and, with a bit of luck, assist her in controlling her rapidly evolving power. But I cannot make the journey until after Lilandra's coronation. Moira's readings leave me worried that— well, that I may be too late."

"Chuck." Wolverine's throat was dry. "What are you trying to say?"

"That Jean Grey, my prize student and a young woman I love like a daughter, is dangerous. Very, very dangerous."

"Got it. I'll let Cyke know—"

"Cyclops's love for Jean is deep and uncompromising. This is not a matter he can deal with." Xavier's eyes glared out of the screen. "Logan, you and I have not always seen eye to eye—"

"That's puttin' it mildly."

"—but I trust you."

Xavier paused, letting his words hang in the air.

"I trust you to do what must be done."

Ice ran up Logan's spine. *Charlie*, he thought, *you cold bastard. Damn you.* His claws clicked free, then slid back into their sheaths. *Damn you forever for layin' this on me.*

"I know." Xavier's voice cracked, ever so slightly. "I know what this means to you, and I shudder to imagine what you must think of me at this moment. But this is much bigger than you or me, or even the team." He regained his composure. "'The end of all that is.'"

Logan didn't respond. He sat perfectly still, letting the rage and frustration wash over him. He shivered, recalling the cruel, desperate training that had been forced upon him in times past. As much as his life with the X-Men, that too was a part of him. A part of who he was.

Like it or not, he would always be Weapon X.

When it was done, he rose to his feet. "Chuck," he said, "I sure hope you're wrong."

He left without waiting for Xavier's answer.

FOR THE past three days, he'd clung to a single hope: that he wouldn't have to do the unthinkable. Even when Jean succumbed to the lure of the Hellfire Club, a part of Logan had believed she'd ultimately claw her way back.

Another dream dead and gone, he thought.

"This diagram is gibberish," Colossus protested. "Have we tried bringing in an expert?"

"Hank McCoy is not available," Storm replied.

The door creaked open. Cyclops stepped into the kitchen wearing civilian clothes and his ruby-quartz sunglasses. He held a hand against his bandaged head, staggering as he pulled up a chair.

"You look like hell, boss," Wolverine said.

"Scott?" Nightcrawler moved to his side. "What is it?"

"I can feel her," Cyclops said. "Somehow… a small trace of our psionic rapport is still active."

Wolverine leapt to his feet. "And?"

"She's far out in space. But she's returning to Earth… and she's hungry." Cyclops turned toward him with a blank red stare. "Again."

CHAPTER TWENTY-FOUR

SHE STOOD on the lawn of a large, well-kept house in Annandale-on-Hudson, a sleepy college town fifty miles northwest of the X-Men's Westchester mansion. Drawn here by a need she could not name, a craving wholly different from the hunger that had taken her to the stars.

The house where I—where she—was born.

The Dark Phoenix unclenched her fists, willing the flames around her to subside. The night grew dark again, lit only by a few distant streetlights. She glanced briefly at the garage, then walked up the front steps.

The door was unlocked, as she knew it would be.

As she stepped into the dark living room, a rush of sensory impressions washed over her. Shelves of books, the accumulation of her father's career as a professor at Bard College. Plants all around—crocuses and herbs and cacti, seedlings in pots, and an aged miniature bonsai tree in its own terrarium. All tended and grown by her horticulturist mother.

A faint smell of garlic chicken in the air. That was her sister's favorite.

Sara must be visiting, she thought.

The look, the feel of everything was familiar, unchanged. But the memories seemed distant, as if they belonged to someone else.

Just like on the shuttle. When she… I… accessed Dr. Corbeau's knowledge. The same sense of intrusion, of discomfort. But these memories don't belong to some stranger. They're mine.

Aren't they?

She strode over to a table and picked up a framed photo. Young Jean Grey, wearing a bright green minidress—her second Marvel Girl uniform. Holding her mask off to the side, sticking her tongue out at the camera.

A single snapshot, she thought, *tucked away on a table. They knew of my life with the X-Men, but they never fully accepted it.*

A pile of cardboard boxes lay on the floor next to the sofa. The Greys must have been doing some housecleaning. She knelt down, started digging through the top box. Papers, notepads… a faded inkjet-printed photo of Sara at a party, years ago. Souvenirs, mementoes of two young women and their college lives.

She pulled out a notebook with a handwritten label on the front.

J.G. – SENIOR YEAR (IF I MAKE IT!)

On the very first page, an entry in Jean's handwriting read: *Interview, Pendant Publishing. Saturday 3 PM, Chancellor's Hall. Don't screw it up girl!*

She flipped the pages. Another entry detailed the trial of writing a sample piece for a reporter's job. A third listed an interview with Goldman Sachs; that one had been violently crossed out in ballpoint pen. Yet another described—in hopeful terms—a Skype meeting for an internship at Doctors Without Borders.

I never made that meeting, she remembered. *That was the weekend we first fought Mesmero.*

She closed the notebook.

Jean Grey, the Phoenix thought. *You could have been so many things, lived so many lives—but you were always too busy. Battling*

evil mutants, following Scott Summers around the globe. Living and
training and fighting alongside the X-Men.

Always too busy dying.

"Jean?"

She whirled around, hair trailing flame in the air. Her father, John Grey, stood on the landing in his robe and slippers. When he saw her face, he hurried down to meet her.

"Jean—my god!"

She flinched away. *No*, she thought. *Oh, please, no!*

"We—we haven't heard from you in weeks. Where have you been?"

She backed away, almost stumbling over the coffee table. *His thoughts—my power is too strong now, too sensitive. He's an open book to me!*

The others followed, their thoughts jangling in the air. Her mother Elaine, smaller than she remembered, in a robe and glasses. Sara, a slightly older version of Jean, with the same emerald eyes.

"Wow," Sara said, running her eyes up and down the Phoenix costume. "Mom wasn't kidding. You *have* changed."

"It's good to see you, dear." Her mother's voice was hesitant.

The Phoenix turned away. *It's the same with all of them*, she thought. *I can't help reading their minds. Nothing's secret—nothing's sacred anymore.*

"That… outfit." Sara reached out a hand, touched Jean's sleeve. "It's true, then? You're some kind of super hero?"

"You look thin, dear," her mother said. "Are you eating enough?"

"I'm fine," the Phoenix said, her voice echoing off the walls.

I'm not fine. Get out of my mind, all of you. Get out!

I should never have come here. I can feel Mom's love for me, her concern, but beneath that feeling—buried so deeply, she probably doesn't even know it exists—she's afraid of me.

"It's very late, Jean," her father said, switching on a light. "Are you in some kind of trouble?"

Dad's worried, too. He's as edgy as Mom. And Sara's terrified. She has two kids—now she's wondering if they'll turn out to be mutants like me.

She looked down at the notebook in her hand. A relic of her old life—just like this house, these people. With their petty lives and their fear of the unknown. Of the gods, the *Homo superior* who would replace them.

A flame rose up from her fingertips. The notebook caught fire and burned to ash, falling like snow on the carpet.

"You fear me," she said. "All of you. As you should."

She lifted her arm, projecting the Phoenix energy toward a hanging fern. She paused, savoring the tension in the room. Then, with a telekinetic twitch, she transformed the plant into glass.

John Grey stepped forward, facing her directly. Rage and pride warred with fear in him. She could feel it in the air, see it written on his face.

"Who are you?" he asked. "*What are you?*"

"I am what I am." His anger echoed in her mind, feeding her own. "I was your daughter."

"Not anymore," he replied. "Leave. Leave this place."

"Watch your tone, old man."

"What's going on out there?" Elaine Grey asked.

The Phoenix whirled around. Jean's mother and sister stood at the back window, staring out at the dark sky—

—except it wasn't dark anymore. A thick white fog had gathered, illuminated by a single floodlight in the backyard. Nothing else could be seen.

"That fog," Sara said. "Where did it come from?"

The Phoenix clenched her fists and flared bright.

"I know," she said.

She took one last look at these people, whom she'd once known so well. The selfish young woman, the scared older one, and the primate-ape who saw himself as his family's defender. They were nothing now, to a being who had traveled the cosmos. Nothing.

She rose up into the air. With barely a thought she opened the window and flew outside. Instantly the fog enveloped her, closing in tight.

I was right, she thought. *This is not natural. Time of year, coordinates—all wrong for this type of weather phenomenon. Which leaves only one answer.*

Storm.

The Phoenix soared upward over the yard, the fog bank following her every move. She could feel the X-Men nearby, their thoughts buzzing like gnats in the air. *Cowering in the shadows*, she thought. *Terrified to confront me. Just like—*

"Surprise, *liebchen*." Nightcrawler appeared in a puff of brimstone. Before the Phoenix could react, he landed on her back and clamped a metal band over her forehead. "Sorry about this…"

She twisted in midair and flung him off her back. He tumbled through the fog, vanishing again with a barely audible *BAMF*.

Most likely teleported down to the ground, she thought, but she couldn't see the ground through the dense fog. She dropped low, searching. A few trees came into view… the neat lines of her mother's garden. Metal lawn table, surrounded by chairs…

She remembered the metallic device just a moment too late. A surge of current pierced her skull, stabbing through her brain. She screamed, flailing in the air. She scrabbled at the device, but— impossibly—it remained firmly fixed to her head.

I am Dark Phoenix, she thought. *I've consumed stars. How…* She reeled, losing her train of thought. *Mind on fire—can't focus. Can't use the power!*

Steel fingers clamped around her ankle, wrenching her down toward the ground.

"Do not fight us, Jean," Colossus said. He stood on top of the metal table, reaching up for her.

Once more the current shot through her. She screamed again.

"The mnemonic scrambler." Nightcrawler's voice, from below. "It's hurting her!"

Colossus maintained his grip. "The harder you struggle, the worse the pain will become," he said.

"Pain?" she snarled. "I will teach you pain, little boy."

She surged upward, gritting her teeth. Colossus kept his grip on her leg, and she lifted him up off the table, into the air. She bent her knee with an effort and kicked out into the air, snapping her leg straight. Colossus lost his grip, tumbled free, and vanished.

That damn fog, she thought. It clung to her, limiting her visibility. *The weather witch, still hiding from my wrath.*

The Phoenix reached out, struggling through the pain. Concentrated on one particular thought pattern, a cluster of electrical impulses that no weather disturbance could conceal. She arrowed through the air, relentless, until a tall, regal figure took shape in the mist. Storm hovered in midair, arms spread. Eyes fierce, teeth gritted, the power of the elements at her fingertips.

"You will not yield," Storm said, turning blank white eyes to face her. "No more than I would, were our positions reversed."

"You were closer to me than my own sister, Ororo," the Phoenix said. "Yet I struck you down once. I *will* do it again."

"I don't want this, Jean." Storm lifted her arms, calling forth a gale-force wind. "None of us does."

The Phoenix cried out again. She flinched from the wind, clawing at the scrambler. It held tight to her forehead, fastened by some unknown combination of magnetism and adhesive bonding. Then a single spark rose up from it.

I'm burning it out, she realized. *A few more minutes…*

"In the name of the love we shared," Storm said, "let us help you."

No, the Phoenix thought. *No more. No more of this!*

She fired off a mental blast, sending the weather-wielding mutant spinning in the air. Storm fell, flailing, summoning just enough of a wind to cushion her fall. She touched down, dazed, in a bed of crushed tulips.

The fog began to clear, the yard spotlight piercing the predawn darkness. The Phoenix spun low, hovering a few feet above the ground. Three minds left conscious, hiding like rats in the shadows around the garden. The rest of the X-Men…

…wait. Was there another? Some lurking presence, concealing its thoughts?

The blasted scrambler, she thought. *Have to concentrate—*

pierce the veil. Who are you? Who's out there?

Wolverine slammed into her, knocking her off-balance. He grabbed her by the shoulders and hurled her to the ground. She struck the mud, crying out as his hand clamped down on her throat.

"Everyone else," he growled, "they're all holdin' back." His fingers were like steel cables on her neck. "They think you're still Jean—they're tryin' to catch you. Put you in a cage, so they can help you."

He pulled back his other hand, unleashed deadly claws.

"That won't work," he said. "Not anymore."

She could feel his pain, like a swarm of bees in the air. *He's trying to convince himself,* she realized. *Steeling himself to do what he must.*

"I gotta end this," he said. "Forgive me, darlin'."

My god, she thought, *what have I done to him? On board the shuttle, when I insisted that he let me die. What burden did I lay on this man's shoulders?*

Logan's grip held her firm; her head jackhammered with pain. A terrible weariness washed over her. The power—the Phoenix Force—seemed to slip away, retreating from the shore of her consciousness.

"Do it," she gasped.

He stared at her, eyes wide.

"You're the only one who—who understands," she said. "You always…"

Still he hesitated. Claws suspended in midair, caught between life and death.

Too late, the Phoenix said, screaming inside her. *Too late now. Too late for everything.*

The mnemonic scrambler sparked and caught fire. The Phoenix reached out and blasted Wolverine, projecting a bolt of psionic energy that fried his nerve impulses in an instant. He lost his grip and flew up into the air.

With barely a thought, she crushed the scrambler to dust. She flung the remains away, metallic shards tumbling to land in the ruins of her mother's garden. Rage coursed through her. *Enough. Enough of this!*

She sensed Nightcrawler creeping toward her in the shadows. Before he could teleport closer, she put him to sleep with a single thought.

Only one enemy remained. Standing at the far end of the yard, near a wooden fence. Staring at her through a glowing crimson eyepiece.

"Jean," Cyclops said. "I need you to stop this."

Wait. She paused, cocked her head. Was there someone else? She could still sense another presence... somewhere nearby...

Incredibly, Cyclops stepped toward her. *Is he suicidal?* "You could take me out at any time," he acknowledged. "But hear me out."

"Hear you out? No, Scott. It's time to finish this."

"Then kill me." He gestured at the bodies of Storm and Wolverine, lying still on the ground. "I can't stop you... I won't even try. Kill me, Phoenix. If you can."

She hesitated. His thoughts were an open book, and he meant every word he said. This was his last gambit—and in a very real sense, it was no gambit at all.

"But if you can't..." He took another step toward her. "... then ask yourself why. You've proven that no force in the universe can stand against you. The X-Men have fought you, defied you, caused you pain—yet still we live. *Why?*"

"You're..." She looked away. "You're beneath my notice."

"No. I think there's another answer." He spread his arms. "You are the Dark Phoenix, whatever that means—but whatever you've become, you're also Jean Grey. No matter how hard you try, you cannot exorcise that part of yourself."

"No," she said.

"You can't kill us because you love us. And we love you."

Again, the weariness. *No,* she thought. *Not now. Not now! I'm so close... so close to freeing myself from all this...*

"The Phoenix knows nothing of love," she said.

Cyclops smiled.

"Nothing of love?" He stepped even closer. "For love of the X-Men, you sacrificed yourself on the shuttle. You nearly died again, when you battled Magneto. You've brought yourself back from the brink time and time again—why is that?"

Not for love, she thought. *No, never. Never that!*

"Nothing of love?" He reached out and touched her face. "Jean, you *are* love."

She felt the tears rising. Touched his hand, pressed it to her cheek. "Don't deny it. Don't deny all that you are… the life that you've made for yourself."

She pulled away, unable to bear the emotion.

"I hunger, Scott." Her voice was low, dark. "For a joy, a rapture beyond human comprehension. That need… it's a part of me, too."

"I know," he replied, his voice quavering. "I—I didn't understand that before. And honestly, I'm not sure how to deal with it." He laughed, a quick nervous laugh. "But I want to try."

"It consumes me," she whispered.

"It doesn't have to." He grasped both her hands, turned her to face him. "Let me help."

The rage—the hunger—abated. She felt spent, exhausted. Washed up, like a corpse, on some distant shore.

"I'd like tha—"

Pain blasted through her. There was no warning, no time, no defense against the attack. It was powerful, relentless, an assault on every cell of her body.

No, she thought dimly, *not on my body.*

My mind.

She swooned, felt Scott's arms grab hold of her. Through a haze of agony, she saw a man in a wheelchair rolling toward them at a rapid clip, leaving a trail of crushed flowers in his wake. His thoughts were hidden, shielded from her power. The only emotions that reached her, as she struggled to remain conscious, were Scott Summers's shock and dismay.

"Professor Xavier?" he said.

CHAPTER TWENTY-FIVE

CYCLOPS WAS so stunned, he almost lost his grip on Jean. Professor Xavier rolled closer, relentless and unstoppable, his eyes dark and intense.

"Professor," Cyclops repeated. "What have you done?"

"What I must," Xavier said.

His tone, Scott thought, *it's so cold. What's happened to him? All those months in space… Has something changed him?*

Xavier rolled to a stop less than a meter away from Cyclops. They stared at each other in silence, there in the shadow of the Grey family house. The air was chilly, and only the Greys' backyard floodlight pierced the darkness, casting shadows on the crushed stems beneath his feet.

"Nothing has changed," Xavier said. Cyclops had forgotten how infuriating it could be when the Professor read his thoughts. "Not with me."

Jean hung limp in Cyclops's arms. "Tell me what you've done!" he demanded.

"A simple mind-blast," Xavier replied, "while she was distracted."

"I wasn't distracting her. I was *reaching* her."

"Not possible."

Cyclops's mind was spinning. Moira MacTaggert had implied that she'd been in touch with the Professor, but…

"When did you arrive on Earth?"

"Only moments ago. There was no time to warn you." Xavier studied Jean. "Stand aside."

"No!"

Cyclops looked around, seeking help. Storm lay closest to him, unmoving on the ground. He could just make out Colossus and Wolverine, lying in a tangle of patio furniture. There was no sign of Nightcrawler. He glanced back at the house. In a second-story window, Jean's relatives watched fearfully.

"You have no idea of the forces at work here, Scott." Xavier glared at Jean. "Only another telepath has the slightest chance against her."

"I don't want to be *against* her."

"Scott! We may have only moments." Xavier raised his index fingers to his temples and leaned forward. "I do not wish you to be hurt."

"*Too late.*"

Jean pulled free, raising both arms. The mental blast seared through Cyclops, knocking him off his feet. He tumbled and fell, striking his head. He cried out, felt himself start to lose consciousness.

When his vision cleared, Jean was advancing on Xavier. The older man held his ground, made no attempt to retreat.

"Meddling old fool," Jean said. "You have signed your death warrant." Her mind flash struck Xavier head-on, shattering his wheelchair and sending his body flying. He dropped to the ground, sprawling, helpless.

Slowly, with great effort, Xavier struggled to rise. He propped himself up on his elbows.

"Perhaps, Phoenix…" he growled.

No, Professor, Scott thought. *Don't do it. She's going to kill you!*

"Perhaps I *will* die today." Xavier coughed dirt and blood.

272   "But if it costs me my life, I will put this right."

"Why, Professor. You sound almost guilty."

She began to glow. The Phoenix flame burned all around her, lighting up the yard. Raging, ravenous. Unstoppable.

"As you should be," she continued. "*You* taught me to use my latent telepathic ability, years ago. You set in motion the chain of events that created first Phoenix, then the Black Queen, and now—finally—Dark Phoenix."

Cyclops rose to his knees. A wave of dizziness washed over him, and he fell back again.

"Behold your creation, Charles Xavier." Jean shone blinding white now, the Phoenix avatar shrieking to the heavens above. "I am the Dark Angel, the Chaos-Bringer. I am ancient and new— the fundamental force of the universe funneled through the rage of a single young woman. I am pure power."

"Power without restraint." Xavier raised his hands to his forehead. "Knowledge without wisdom. Age without maturity…"

Jean was barely visible within the blazing form of the Phoenix. Cyclops shielded his eyes with his hand, watching in dread as her power swelled in all directions. The forward edge of the flame crept closer to the Professor, who lay on the ground. He was helpless—

—or so it seemed.

…*passion without love.*

Cyclops glanced at Xavier, startled. The Professor hadn't spoken those words aloud. Scott had heard them in his mind.

No more. No more talk of love!

Jean's "voice," replying in kind.

Their psi-war… Scott realized. *It's taking place everywhere, on a thousand planes of existence at once. They're blasting telepathic energy all around, like speakers turned up to full volume. I can only "hear" a fraction of it.*

Gradually, the thoughts became more cohesive, as the combatants continued their contest of wills.

I must fight you, Jean, Xavier sent. He was glowing now, too. *And I will win.* Tendrils of mental force shot forth from his mind.

Probing, entering the maelstrom, seeking out the woman inside the wall of fire.

The Phoenix raised its head and laughed.

Will you?

Xavier's next barrage of probes passed through the flames surrounding Jean Grey. The creature faltered, flickering slightly. Within the Phoenix construct, the probes flashed around like a swarm of trapped insects.

Seizing the advantage, Xavier dragged himself forward, eyeing his opponent with a fearsome intensity. A dozen more probes shot out from his forehead, piercing the Phoenix glow.

Oh, Jean sent. *Oh no you don't.*

She surged, shining bright. Xavier's probes whipped around wildly, dissipating into the air. He cried out in pain and grabbed his temples.

S-Scott!

Cyclops's eyes went wide. *Professor?*

I require your help.

Cyclops stared at the Phoenix, at the unearthly energy radiating from the woman he loved. It raged wildly, melting patio chairs, setting small fires all across the devastated garden. Jean was a tiny sliver of yellow and crimson within the blinding cascade.

I'm attempting to… rein in her power, Xavier continued. *But she's fighting me. I cannot do this alone.*

"What—" Cyclops rose to his feet. *Professor, you two are the most powerful telepaths on Earth. What can I do?*

What you were doing before my arrival.

You mean—

Talk to her.

Cyclops swallowed, then nodded. He steeled himself, then turned back to face the blinding light.

Jean?

She—the creature, in its full fury—turned to face him. *No,* it said, *not Jean. PHOENIX.*

Phoenix, then.

He thought furiously. Jean had evolved beyond humanity, beyond mortal concerns. She'd traveled through deep space, seen and done things he'd never be able to understand. How could he reach her? What could he possibly say?

I love you.

You don't know me. Her laugh was like stars crashing together. *You can't even see me.*

I can, he responded. *I see you burning, like a star.*

Xavier rose to a sitting position, bracing himself against a rock.

You shine in my mind, Cyclops continued. *Every day, every moment. Even when you're away.* He laughed. *Even when you're dead.*

He could feel her: Jean. Her human self, damaged but intact, beginning to shine through. Asserting her control, her intellect, her ego structure. Clawing her way to freedom, swimming against the relentless tide of star-spawned madness.

And you're beautiful.

She turned to look at him. The flame flickered low, and for a moment he saw her smile, familiar and haunting and warm.

Oh, you, she said.

Then she turned toward the Professor. Locked eyes with him and gave him a tiny nod.

Xavier closed his eyes. His mind-probes gathered again, moving toward Jean. They passed through her face, her skull, converging on her brain—and Scott saw them, *felt* them, through the link. They sought out her memories, synaptic connections, all manner of electrical impulses. The currents and channels, the power centers that made her the most powerful telepath in the world.

Xavier snipped and stitched, constructing microscopic structures of mental force to control Jean's power. Where her mind surged brightest, the probes built dams and walls, knitted protective screens of force. Created a thousand thousand psionic circuit breakers, a network so vast, so redundantly reinforced, that it could never be breached.

Cyclops reeled. This was surgery of a sort—unprecedented, beyond his comprehension. The mental images terrified him, yet he dared not pull away. *Whatever this is*, he thought, *whatever he's doing to you, Jean—I will stay here with you.*

The end came suddenly.

One moment, the Phoenix flare lit up the countryside like a small sun. Then it flickered and died, a few final wisps vanishing up into the sky. As the predawn light began to rise over the horizon, Jean Grey collapsed to the ground like a puppet with its strings cut.

Cyclops was beside her in a second. He ignored the throbbing in his head, the voices all around. The X-Men crawling to their feet, the Greys and their other daughter running out into the yard. All he saw was Jean. He hoisted her up in his arms, moved her face close to his. She was breathing, but just barely.

Is she… is she still her? The Professor's psychic surgery… did it work?

The Phoenix costume was gone. Jean wore a tattered black dress, its hem ripped and singed. It took him a moment to recognize it—the dress she'd worn the day of the shuttle flight, so many months ago.

Is that a good sign? Maybe it means she's reverted to the person she used to be. But she might still be Dark Phoenix, inside. Or—what if the surgery did something terrible to her?

It doesn't matter, he knew. *I'll love her just the same.*

Jean's eyes fluttered open. She stared at him, peering into his visor. "Hey," she said.

He felt tears rising. *She's herself*, he realized. *She's human. She's Jean again.*

"H-hey, yourself," he replied.

One by one, the X-Men climbed to their feet. Storm and Nightcrawler approached cautiously, while Wolverine held back. Colossus stood holding the Professor in his strong arms, near the wreckage of Xavier's wheelchair. Jean's mother and sister approached, carrying a blanket.

"Jean," Sara said. "Are you cold?"

Jean smiled as she accepted the blanket. "Ororo, Kurt," she said. "Sorry about the bruises."

Storm smiled. "I believe we dished out a few, as well."

"Jeannie," Wolverine said. "You back with us?"

She blinked, shifted in Cyclops's arms. Turned toward Logan, an unusually serious look in her eyes.

"Yeah," she said. "Thanks for... well, you know."

"No big."

Cyclops looked at them both. Something big *had* transpired between them, he realized. Something he might never fully understand.

"Oh, sure." Nightcrawler rolled his eyes, breaking the tension. "Nothing big. Just another night in the Danger Room."

"Scott?" Jean leaned in to his shoulder.

He touched her face, smiling. "Do you want me to carry you inside?"

She locked her eyes on his. Nodded slowly, vigorously. "I do," she whispered.

"Xavier! *Summers!*"

They all turned at the sharp voice. Jean's father stood in the doorway, pointing an accusatory finger at them.

"What the hell is going on here?" John Grey strode forward. "What have you been doing with my daughter?"

"Dad, I'm fine," Jean protested. "Everything's fine now."

"I'll be happy to explain, Dr. Grey," Xavier said. "But first, could I trouble you for a cup of tea? It's been a most—"

THERE WAS no warning. White light, total and enveloping, filled the backyard. In an instant, the X-Men were gone.

Dr. Grey stepped back, shocked. He reached out a hand, touching the space where his daughter had been.

Elaine Grey ran up beside him. "Where did they go?" she asked.

"They just... disappeared."

Elaine didn't respond. Slowly, as if in a daze, she took his hand. They walked back to the house, hand in hand.

Jean's sister remained in the yard. She stared at the trees and hedges, the broken lawn furniture and the ruined garden.

"She said…" Sara whispered. "She said everything was fine."

The first rays of sunlight crept over the tree line, shining into her eyes. Heralding a new day, a cycle of renewal for the world. A world, she somehow knew, that no longer held her sister in it.

She stood alone for a long time, thinking of children and mutants and innocence lost. Her fists clenched and unclenched several times, leaving nail-marks on her palms. And then, as humans do, Sara Grey-Bailey simply turned and walked away, leaving the light behind.

CHAPTER TWENTY-SIX

ONE MOMENT they were in the garden, waiting for the dawn. Nightcrawler, Storm, Wolverine, Cyclops clutching Jean in his arms, and Colossus holding Professor Xavier. Then there was only light—absolute, overwhelming. A white glare that seemed to peel away layer after layer of their bodies: skin, muscle, internal organs. A disorienting, unnatural process.

Only Charles Xavier recognized the sensation, because he'd experienced it before. A Shi'ar teleport beam.

An instant later, they stood in the center of a large chamber, atop a raised platform. Bleachers lining the walls, makeshift rails and benches bolted down in rows. The seats, the aisles, the open area at the base of the bleachers—all of it was filled with grim, armed warriors.

Alien warriors, Xavier observed. A dozen or more races gathered together. The avian Shi'ar, resplendent in their many-colored plumage. A platoon of blue-skinned Centaurians, bows and arrows clipped to their belts; a robotic Recorder, circuits clicking as it monitored the proceedings. A warlike Skrull in violet robes, and a single Kree soldier, eyes hidden by his battle helmet.

"What…" Cyclops looked around.

"Professor?" Colossus asked, shifting his grip. "Where are we?"

Xavier looked up. The ceiling was transparent, revealing a stunning spacescape. The stars glowed more sharply, more clearly than in any view from Earth. There could be no doubt: they were on board a spaceship.

The cargo deck of an Imperial dreadnought, he thought, *hastily refitted into… whatever this is. A courtroom? A combat arena?*

And not just any ship, he realized. *This is the flagship of the Shi'ar Empire.*

Cyclops released Jean. She staggered back, her eyes wide as she took in the large room, the alien warriors. She pulled nervously at the torn hem of her dress.

"Scott?" Nightcrawler asked. "Who are these people?"

"We are surrounded by armed and armored warriors," Storm said, "so I doubt their intentions are friendly."

Wolverine said nothing. He just crouched low, scanning the room.

"X-Men." The voice rang out, deep and confident. "Heed the words of Gladiator, praetor of the Imperial Guard."

They all turned. Gladiator—a tall humanoid in a red-and-blue uniform, his hair sculpted into a striking cobalt Mohawk—stood with hands on his hips. Two members of his guard stood flanking him: Hussar, a savage crimson-skinned woman with a whip, and Oracle, a smaller woman with pale skin and a full head of thick, royal blue hair.

Xavier's eyes strayed to the Kree warrior, who stood rigid in his emerald-and-white uniform—right next to the green-skinned Skrull. The Skrulls were masters of shape-shifting, but this one wore its natural form, its wrinkled chin turned down in a scowl.

The Kree and the Skrull despise each other, Xavier thought. *Their races have fought wars that shook galaxies. For them to actually stand together…*

"Gladiator," he said. "What is the meaning of this?"

The praetor smiled grimly. He commanded the Imperial Guard—the elite force pledged to defend the throne—with an unwavering arrogance. Xavier had never liked the man.

"You are to be judged," he replied.

"I am consort to the Empress." Xavier kept his voice cold. "I answer only to her."

In response, an old man wearing violet robes with a long plume of feathers stepped forward. Xavier recognized him as Prime Minister Araki, political leader of the Shi'ar. Araki gestured at the cluster of guards in the back of the room; like a smooth machine, they stepped aside to reveal a regal woman in silver armor. She wore a gleaming helmet over her feather plume, and held in her hand an intricate, multi-pointed ceremonial staff.

"You stand in the presence of Lilandra Neramani," Araki said. "Majestrix Shi'ar, Empress of all she surveys. Your fate is in her hands."

Xavier's breath caught at the sight of her. *She's so beautiful*, he thought, *and she wears the crown with grace and confidence. She has accomplished so much—and yet, the past few months have been difficult. For us, for our life together.*

Somehow he knew: *That's about to get much worse.*

"X-Men." Lilandra stepped forward. "I am relieved to see you unharmed."

"Lilandra." Cyclops moved toward her—only to be stopped by a brace of guards holding up electrified lances. "What's this about?"

The Empress gestured with her staff. The guards retreated, stepping back into formation in front of the bleachers.

"You have always been my friends," she said, "as well as the students of my consort."

She's not looking at me, Xavier noted.

"But as Empress, my first responsibility is to my people."

"Ach!" Nightcrawler smiled. "Is there some uber-cosmic threat looming? A hive full of bug-eyed monsters from the Crab Nebula, perhaps? If you seek our help, Lilandra, you did not have to kidnap us. We would gladly have come."

"I don't think we're here to bat cleanup," Wolverine growled.

"No," Lilandra acknowledged. "To ensure the survival of the Shi'ar… for the sake of the entire universe…" She swept her staff across the group, stopping when the tip pointed to Jean. "...the Phoenix must be destroyed."

A murmur rose up all around. Armed warriors clapped power-staffs on the ground, banged gloved fists against the benches.

"Phoenix?" Jean blinked. "Me?"

"Lilandra," Xavier said, "you followed me to Earth for this?"

At last she turned to face him. Her eyes were cold, but he could feel the hurt radiating from her. "I had no choice," she said. "You were not... honest about your reasons for leaving."

"Because I... I knew..." He gestured around.

Because I knew you'd come. Because I hoped to avoid... this.

"Knew what?" Cyclops asked. "Why are the Shi'ar so concerned with Jean?"

Xavier turned to study Jean. She bore no trace of the Phoenix entity. Even her clothes had reverted to the outfit she'd worn on that fateful day, when she'd piloted the shuttle down to Earth. His psychic surgery had returned her to that earlier, less powerful form.

And yet...

"'The end of all that is,'" Wolverine said in a low voice.

"What?" Cyclops asked.

"I..." Jean raised a hand to her forehead. "I don't understand."

Lilandra turned to stare at her. Jean held her gaze, blinking in confusion. Lilandra shook her head and turned away.

"Gladiator?"

The praetor clapped his massive hands. The X-Men stepped back as a four-meter-high hologram rose up in the center of the room. It showed a glowing yellow sun, shining in open space.

"This is the star D'Bari," Gladiator said, "as it was two days ago."

As they watched, a small dot appeared behind the star. It drew closer, resolving into the form of the Dark Phoenix, blazing bright with power. Jean's figure was a tiny sliver at the heart of the creature.

"And this is the Dark Angel of legend," Gladiator continued. "The Chaos-Bringer, ravager of worlds."

Xavier glanced at Jean. Her eyes were fixed on the image, staring in horror. As they watched, the Phoenix dove deep into the heart of the star. Its surface began to throb, to pulse, sending out wild, flaring prominences.

"Ravenous from her long journey, the creature consumed the star. As the sun died, so did its planets." Gladiator paused, looked at Xavier. "D'Bari was an *inhabited* system."

The image changed again—to a city center, a crowded thoroughfare on some alien world. Olive-green beings stood clustered together, staring up in fear at the searing light that filled their sky.

"The fourth planet was home to five billion people."

The room went quiet. Lilandra stepped forward and cleared her throat.

"These images were received by an Imperial dreadnought, flying under my flag of authority. This was its final transmission."

The image wavered, replaced by a view of the open, multileveled bridge of the vessel. It was a scene of carnage, with instruments in flames, its crew bruised and battered. A body lay in full uniform, eyes blank and staring, slumped over its station.

The dreadnought's captain, an ashen-faced man with a proud plume of feathers, gestured toward the ship's viewscreen. It showed the Phoenix, relentless in its fury, closing in rapidly.

"I hope you receive this," the captain said. "We are beaten — no weapons, no power. Crew mostly dead. Ship a ruined, gutted hulk." A high-ranking officer moved into the frame.

"Entity closing," he said.

"Beware, my Empress," the captain continued. "*Beware the Phoenix—*"

The transmission ended.

The hologram faded back into the platform.

No, Xavier thought, guilt washing over him. *I knew the risks, but I thought I'd reached Jean in time. All those lives. All those souls...* What had the Phoenix said to him, back in the garden? "*You set in motion this chain of events.*"

"Jean." Colossus was staring at her. "Could you? Did you...?"

"She did," Logan growled.

"It wasn't her," Nightcrawler said.

Storm said nothing, but the look on her face made Xavier shiver. He reinforced his psychic screens, taking care not to read her mind.

"No," Jean whispered. "No…" She leaned in close to Cyclops, clutching her head. She seemed disoriented, confused.

She's remembering, Xavier realized. *The Phoenix power—it's like a drug. It overwhelmed her for a while, overrode her better instincts. But it was still her.*

She did this.

Cyclops held her tight, his hands visibly trembling. His mouth was a thin line, his lips white with tension.

Xavier turned to Lilandra. She stared at him, accusing him with her eyes.

"Beloved consort," she said. "You of all people should have known. You should have warned me."

Xavier said nothing.

"Did you not study the Shi'ar traditions? The legends that tell of the Chaos-Bringer? You knew." She shook her head. "You should have trusted me."

She's right. He looked away. *There's nothing further to say.*

"X-Men," Lilandra said, turning to address them. "I respect your pain, but as Empress I see no alternative."

"I do not like the sound of that," Nightcrawler muttered.

"Surrender her," Lilandra continued, "or suffer the consequences."

Jean looked down, shaking her head. The X-Men exchanged alarmed looks. Colossus's arms were shaking; Xavier had to adjust himself to remain in the big man's grip.

Perhaps, he thought, *a direct mindlink with Lilandra. A last-ditch effort to make her see—*

Cyclops stepped forward.

"Empress Lilandra," he said, "you keep speaking of Dark Phoenix, the destroyer of worlds. But that entity no longer exists." He gestured toward Xavier. "The Professor exorcised that part of Jean's consciousness. Her power is greatly reduced, and fully under her control. She poses no further threat to you, your empire, or the universe."

"Let Jean be," Colossus said—prompting Xavier to look up at him in surprise. "Has she not suffered enough?"

"Suffered?" Prime Minister Araki shook his fist. "Tell that to the legions of D'Bari dead. Their spirits cry out for vengeance!"

The crowd of warriors rose to their feet, roaring in agreement. They stamped their boots, thrust staffs down against the metal benches. The Kree warrior let out a battle cry, prompting a glare of distaste from his Skrull companion.

The X-Men moved together, forming a protective circle around Jean. Wolverine raised his claws.

Lilandra held up her staff. In an instant, the room went quiet. She walked up to the X-Men and stood before Jean Grey—who looked away, grimacing. Lilandra reached out and cupped her chin, studying her.

"What was undone once, may be undone again." Lilandra sounded as if she were reciting an ancient prophecy. "So long as the Phoenix exists—in any form, at any level of power—she is a threat to all that lives. I am sorry, Cyclops. I know you are sincere, but the risk is too great."

Cyclops stepped in, positioning himself between Jean and the Shi'ar ruler. Nightcrawler followed, shielding her from Lilandra. Wolverine gathered with them, and then finally—reluctantly, it seemed to Xavier—Storm joined the group. Only Colossus hung back, still holding the Professor in his arms.

"No," Cyclops said.

Lilandra stepped away. Once again, she raised her staff.

"Warriors," she said. "Take her."

"Empress Majestrix!" Xavier cried. "Hear me."

All eyes turned to him. He held out a hand, straight toward Lilandra.

"Jean Grey Arin'nn Haelar," he said.

There were gasps from the bleachers. Lilandra stood, grim, facing Xavier directly. *You see*, he said, projecting the words into her mind. *I have studied your traditions.*

Lilandra nodded. *The Arin'nn Haelar*, she replied mentally. *The challenge that cannot be refused.*

In her mind, he read respect. And something else, too: a terrible sadness. The full weight of his action struck him: *I've burned a bridge. Crossed a line that can never be uncrossed.*

He broke contact and turned to the X-Men. "For Jean's life," he explained, "I have challenged the Shi'ar to a duel of honor."

"Majestrix." The Kree warrior stepped forward. "My people were promised that the Phoenix entity would be expunged. Nothing was said of any 'duel of honor.'"

Lilandra turned to the Kree. The Skrull hovered behind him, watching warily.

"You are free to consult with your governments," she said. "But they have agreed that this matter will be carried out in accordance with Shi'ar Law."

The Kree frowned.

"You may, of course, monitor the battle on behalf of your respective empires."

The Skrull gestured toward the Kree. "I must stand beside this misbegotten son of a mudworm?" He snorted in outrage. "How long will this battle last?"

"As long as it takes!" Lilandra snapped. "In this matter, Shi'ar Law is the *only* law." The Skrull stepped back, glaring at his Kree companion. The Kree just stared straight ahead, his eyes unreadable beneath his green battle mask.

"Gladiator," Lilandra said, turning to face him. "Is the Guard prepared to carry out this challenge?"

Gladiator bowed. "It is our honor to serve, Majestrix."

"Then your gambit is successful, Charles," Lilandra said. "The Shi'ar accept your challenge. As you knew we would."

"A duel? For my life?" Jean shook her head. "No. No, I won't allow it."

"Jean..." Cyclops said.

"There's been too much death already!"

"Challenge has been made, and duly accepted." Lilandra stared at Xavier, her eyes intense. "There is no turning back from this path."

Xavier swallowed, nodded. Then he turned to Jean, forcing a smile onto his face. "My child," he said. "This is the only way."

"Your courage and loyalty do you credit, X-Men," Lilandra said. "You will have a night to rest, to recover your strength. To prepare, as best you might. The duel begins at dawn."

Gladiator raised an odd device to his lips and let out a low tone. The warriors rose to their feet and began to file out.

A pair of servants with bright green plumage approached the X-Men, gesturing for them to follow. Cyclops held out his hand to Jean. She shivered, took hold, and together they walked out of the room. Storm followed, then Nightcrawler and Wolverine. Colossus shifted awkwardly, cast a questioning glance at the man he still held in his arms. Xavier nodded for him to follow the others.

As the young Russian carried him toward the door, Xavier glanced back into the room. Gladiator was striding toward the opposite exit, his square jaw set, eyes fierce. Oracle and Hussar followed him, the latter slapping her whip lightly against her muscular thigh.

Lilandra stood in the center of the cargo bay, speaking in low tones with the Prime Minister. She looked every inch the Empress, the sovereign ruler of her people. The proud Shi'ar princess with whom Xavier had fallen in love, now ascended to her full potential.

A wave of sadness washed over him.

It's over, he thought. *Even if both our peoples survive this, she and I will never trust each other again.*

Despite his best intentions, his mind strayed to hers. Subtly, silently eavesdropping on her conversation. *The X-Men face hopeless odds, Majestrix,* Araki was saying. *But they are exceptional beings. Suppose they win the challenge?*

Sorrow filled Lilandra's mind, an emotion that mirrored Xavier's own. She looked away from Araki and cast a glance upward at the stars, cold and sharp in the sky.

They will not win, she said, the words echoing in Xavier's mind. *You have my word on that.*

CHAPTER TWENTY-SEVEN

JEAN GREY hadn't been aboard a lot of starships in her life, but this one was like nothing she'd ever imagined. Its corridors were wide, the rooms filled with open spaces. The bridge and engineering sectors were off limits to the X-Men, but Lilandra had granted them access to most of the rest of the ship. It seemed as if she'd been walking for miles.

And it's so quiet.

Maybe, she realized, that wasn't the ship. With her reduced power level, the voices in her head had vanished. The constant hum of thoughts, the inescapable flow of other people's secrets.

The voice of the Phoenix. It's gone, too.

Do I miss it?

She shook her head, troubled, and strode down a narrowing corridor to a circular doorway. It irised open; she stepped through and caught her breath at the sight.

She stood in a transparent observation blister, protruding from the main body of the ship. By craning her neck, she could see the vessel's gunmetal-gray exterior hull. It stretched on into the distance, studded with weapons and battle scars—all leading to the blocky, squarish tachyon engines that had carried the ship across intergalactic space.

The real view, however, was dead ahead. Earth hung in all its glory, glowing bright against the stars. A halo of cloud cover bathed it in blue and white, clearing in patches to reveal the deeper blue of the oceans, the tan and green of continents.

She peered at the clouds, as if trying to pierce their silky veil. Unwanted memories returned to her. Terrible, beautiful images, peeking through the fog of Professor Xavier's psychic circuit breakers.

The shuttle striking the runway, snapping her spine.

Flames across her skin.

A bird of prey formed of primal fire.

Magneto's ribs, cracking under her psychic assault.

The Hellfire pawn, helpless in her grip.

Wyngarde. His arms. His musky smell, his wolfish smile. Blood, hatred, lust—all circling down into a whirlpool of rage. Wyngarde in her grip. His mind ripped open, exposed to the universe. Devoured, swallowed by the whirlpool.

Would you like to see?

And then the Phoenix. Unleashed, unbound. Wolverine swatted from the sky, Colossus stripped of his power, forced back to human form. Storm, Nightcrawler, Cyclops—all blasted to their knees before the majesty of the Chaos-Bringer.

Jean frowned, blinked. Somehow she'd traveled an unimaginable distance. She remembered the hunger, the inescapable need. Recalled the dive into a star, the sizzle of quantum reactions, the sweet pain of hydrogen atoms reforming on her skin. Feeding her, fueling her power. Soothing the need.

Part of her had known. Had sensed the cries, the psychic panic from D'Bari-d. The telepathic scream of billions, meeting their end.

Part of her had enjoyed it.

"Milady?"

Jean whirled. A newcomer stood before her, a member of a

race she'd never seen before, with a long, tapered face and a thick-shouldered coat with ruffles down the front. The effect, like many things in the Shi'ar Empire, was oddly formal.

"How did you know where I was?" Jean asked.

The alien shrugged and held up a piece of bright green cloth, neatly folded into a pile.

"Is this the garment you requested?"

Jean felt a tear rise to her eye. She reached out to accept the clothing.

"Thank you," she said. "That's all I need." The servant bowed, turned, and stepped back through the iris.

Jean turned to stare back out through the observation blister. At the Earth, filling the sky beyond. *So beautiful*, she thought. *So filled with life, so bright and messy and glorious. And I... I could have destroyed it.*

I did destroy it. Or a world very much like it.

"Never," she said aloud. "Never again."

She shrugged off her shoes and began to change.

NIGHTCRAWLER SCRAMBLED up the parallel bars, reaching out for a metal ring hanging nearby. "Hanging" wasn't quite the right word. The network of exercise equipment filled the large gymnasium, jutting and intersecting at odd angles. The effect was very... alien.

Gravity shifted, sending him lurching sideways. He missed his mark, began to fall, and felt his teleportation instinct begin to kick in. Then he stretched an arm forward and managed to take hold of the ring, swinging himself up. Or down. Or something.

"Good," Oracle said. "You're getting the hang of it."

"*Danke,*" he grunted, climbing toward the ceiling. "But I just wanted a workout."

Oracle, the pale blue Imperial Guard soldier, climbed the bars with practiced ease. She lacked Nightcrawler's natural agility, but was more familiar with the gymnasium's layout—and with its ever-changing gravity fields, too.

"The trick is not to try and anticipate the shifts," she said, flinging herself off of a hanging swing. "Just go with it." Nightcrawler watched, impressed, as she landed in a crouch on a narrow beam in the exact center of the room.

"I assume you have practiced here before."

"There are four other chambers similar to this one." She smiled, a slightly haughty expression. "This is a large vessel, human. Over six hundred souls of various races call it home."

"Will we be competing in one of these... chambers... tomorrow?" he asked.

"No." She paused, breathing hard, and smiled. "The Majestrix has selected your moon as the combat site."

He nodded. He liked Oracle, and he'd appreciated her offer to show him the exercise equipment. Most of the Shi'ar seemed so grim, humorless. She was much quicker with a smile, even an occasional joke.

Besides, she was blue.

"You realize you're abetting the enemy here," he said. "If we win tomorrow because of the training you're giving me..."

"I'm not worried," she replied.

No, he realized, *you really aren't.*

"Beware, *Fräulein*." He kept his voice light. "I have moves the Shi'ar galaxy has not seen yet." He launched off a beam and grabbed hold of two more hanging rings. Without losing momentum, he swung forward and let go. His feet danced lightly against a row of ladder rungs, then he pointed his arms outward and leapt for the wall.

"Ah," she said. "I forgot to tell you..."

His hands made contact with the wall—and slipped off. As he flailed in midair, he heard Oracle's voice in his head.

...the wall is a frictionless surface.

He fell, eyes wide with panic. Nightcrawler's powers allowed his hands and feet to adhere to almost any surface. On Earth, he could climb the wall of any building, anywhere.

292   *But we're not on Earth*, he remembered.

The telltale itching of his power tickled at his neck. He looked around for a destination, a spot to teleport to. But the room was filled with metal and plasteel, a maze of workout equipment. If he 'ported blind, he could wind up with a parallel bar through his gut.

A pair of strong arms reached up and grabbed him out of the air. Colossus pulled him close in midair and dropped to the ground, bending his knees to absorb the impact.

"*Danke,*" Nightcrawler said, leaping out of the big man's grip. "Peter, do you know you are a showoff? You could at least have turned to steel before saving my life."

"I am a bit overwhelmed by this vessel, *tovarisch.*" Colossus smiled, a shy grin. "I thought I might engage in a workout."

"Well, don't take lessons from…"

Nightcrawler looked around. Oracle was gone.

"From whom?" Colossus asked.

"Never mind." Nightcrawler leaned against a gym structure, scratching his head. "At least I learned she's a telepath. Seems like every group has one, these days." He led Peter across the floor to a pair of benches. At least on this level the gravity seemed constant.

"Kurt," Colossus said, "I find myself wrestling with a dilemma."

Nightcrawler perched atop a bench. He gestured for Colossus to sit opposite him.

"I am the youngest X-Man," Colossus continued. "Yet I know Jean Grey. I have fought with her, many times. I owe her my life. She has proven herself as both a teammate and a person, over and over again."

"And?"

"When we fought Jean, we were not trying to destroy her. We fought to cure her. That determination came from our love for her—a love that has not changed."

Nightcrawler nodded. "But."

"But the Dark Phoenix entity is… evil." Peter's voice sounded pained. "I know this. I have felt its power, heard it raging within my head. If she truly did those things—"

"Yes," Nightcrawler replied. "I have had similar thoughts."

He paused, thinking back. "As a child, in the circus, I knew a very old man. He was kind to me, fed me sweets when food was scarce. He had survived the Holocaust, the death camps of the Nazis. They murdered his parents, performed hideous experiments on his siblings."

His voice was trembling. He paused to compose himself.

"Peter, I still cannot forgive the butchers who committed those atrocities." He looked up. "How then can I forgive Jean?"

They looked into each other's eyes for a long moment. Then Peter stood up, flexed his arms, and transformed his body into solid steel.

"Because she *is* Jean," he said.

Nightcrawler blinked. He nodded, climbed to his feet, and grabbed hold of a hanging ring. He swung himself up to the lowest rung of the exercise lattice, then hung down by his feet and smiled, upside down, at Colossus.

"You are indeed the youngest X-Man, *mein freund*," he said, "but you may also be the wisest."

"ALL RIGHT, *awright*! I'm comin'."

Logan stomped toward the door of his quarters, dripping water. Wherever the drops touched the strange tile floor, they vanished instantly. *Weird crib*, he thought. *Pretty cozy place to spend the night, but I'd go nuts if I had to live here.*

'Course, by this time tomorrow I may not have to worry about livin' anywhere.

Another knock on the door. He grabbed a towel, almost as an afterthought, and whipped it around his waist. Then he yanked open the door.

"Oh." Storm stood there, wearing an elegant African-print robe. She took in his state of undress and turned to leave. "I apologize. I will see you in the—"

"'Roro." He stepped back, ushering her inside. "It's just me." The towel started to fall, and he grabbed it just in time. Storm smiled.

"Very well," she said, closing the door behind her. "But put on some clothes?"

"For you, sure." He stepped around the corner to a small changing area. "But no mask."

"No. No masks."

"I gather we're talkin' in metaphor now."

He stepped back out, wearing his costume. Storm had seated herself on a low armchair. The arms curved slowly inward, conforming to the shape of her body.

Wolverine had found that hard to get used to. The first time he sat down, he'd instinctively slashed the sofa in self-defense. No trace of that incision remained—apparently the healing power of Shi'ar furniture nearly matched his own.

"What's on your mind, lady?"

She sighed, stared out the viewport at the stars. "I was remembering the days when I was simply Ororo, the wind-rider. I was alone… I was free."

"Romanticizing the past?" Logan grunted, planting himself on a chair.

"Perhaps." She looked down. "But now I am neither alone nor free… and rarely happy."

He nodded. "Tough to cage the beast."

"Yet I *chose* to join the X-Men." She looked up, met his eyes. "To leave Africa, my home, of my own free will. The X-Men have become my family, and Jean Grey the sister I never had."

"I should've killed her, 'Roro."

Storm looked up sharply.

"I coulda done it." He held up a hand, let one deadly claw slide free. "One slash, and none of this'd be happening."

"I… I am very glad you didn't—"

"She begged me to do it." He turned away, staring at his claws. *Shut up*, he told himself. *Don't burden her with this.* Yet once the words started coming, they wouldn't stop. "Nobody understands," he said. "Not you, not the elf, definitely not

Summers. Even Xavier… he saw a problem t'be solved, a blasted enemy to be defeated and locked up in a cage. You all think the Phoenix is *some* thing—this bug-eyed alien that's taken her over."

Storm frowned. "Lilandra's people are familiar with this 'thing.'"

"Maybe," he said. "Maybe there is a 'Phoenix Force,' some great bird of the galaxy that's a quazillion years old and takes people over like a body snatcher." He turned away, paced across the room. "But there's also Jean Grey."

She watched him, puzzled. "That is my point."

"No. No no no." He whirled to face her. "The rage, the killer instinct—everything the Phoenix did, to us an' to that poor planet off in some other galaxy. *It's all inside Jean.* It's part of her, an' I…"

He paused, suddenly exhausted.

"And only you can see it." Storm approached, placed her hands on his shoulders. "Because it's part of you, too."

He looked away.

"I cannot accept that," she said. "Even if what you say is true, there is love within Jean, as well. I believe—I *have* to believe in her redemption." She stepped back, rose to her full height. "I will fight for her."

"It don't matter," he muttered.

She frowned. "What?"

"I mean, it don't matter what my head tells me." He looked up at her. "I'm gonna fight for her, too. We are what we are, 'Roro."

"Yes." An echo of lightning in her fierce eyes. "But living with that is more difficult for some than for others."

He turned away again, stepped into the small kitchen. When he returned he held up a bottle of thick green liquid. "Badoon tequila," he explained. "I swiped it from the cargo bay. Join me?" Before she could reply, he'd taken down two shot glasses and started pouring.

"Logan," Storm said, "I am amazed you've lived this long."

"You an' me both, darlin'." He handed her a glass, held the other one up in a toast. "You an' me both."

AS CYCLOPS stepped through the iris, a soft "oh" escaped his lips.

The observation blister showed a massive starfield. A sliver of Earth was visible to one side, moving rapidly away. The ship was turning, beginning its approach to the arena of tomorrow's battle.

Yet Cyclops barely registered the view. All he saw was Jean, smiling tentatively, framed against the beauty of the stars. She wore a large, pointed domino mask with matching yellow gloves, and a striking green dress that he hadn't seen for a long, long time. She executed an embarrassed curtsy.

"Stupid?" she asked.

He smiled. Moved forward, took her in his arms, and kissed her.

"My Marvel Girl," he murmured in her ear.

"Always," she replied.

Pulling back, he gestured at the costume. "A gift from the Shi'ar?"

"I requested it. They seemed to understand." She frowned. "They're very… ceremonial. In some ways, they remind me of the Hellfire Club."

"That's a disturbing thought."

"I needed a uniform for tomorrow, and I thought…" She looked into his eyes. "I started as Marvel Girl, and I'll end this way if I have to."

All at once, the mood changed. He moved away, sat on a small bench, and looked up at her through ruby quartz. "You won't," he said.

"Scott." She sat next to him, took his hand. "I won't have anyone else dying for me."

"It won't come to that." He squeezed her hand. "We've been through so much—we'll get through this, too. *Without* killing anyone."

She held up her other hand, shrugged off her glove. Turned it in the air, letting the starlight play off of it.

"My powers have declined, Scott. I can still feel you in my

mind, through our link. But I can't transmute matter anymore, and I can only hear surface thoughts… images, impressions, or messages intended directly for me.

"The Phoenix, though…" She stood up, started to pace. "This is hard to explain. It's a part of me, something I've always felt. A sort of rage, but more than just rage. Something that's now dammed up, under control."

Scott watched her, frowning. *What's she trying to say?*

"But the Phoenix is something else, too." She paused. "Something very old, older than you or me or, hell, all of humanity. It was growing, evolving—*mutating*—before we were even a spark in the eye of eternity."

"I… I don't think we can worry about that." He spread his arms in a helpless gesture. "We're only human, right?"

"Well." She pointed at the "X" on his belt. "Almost."

He smiled. "You know what I mean."

"I do, and I know you're human. You and Ororo and Kurt and Peter and dear old Charles, who risked his own sanity to save mine. Logan, too."

Scott shrugged. "*Maybe* Logan."

"All of you." She slipped her glove back on and crossed her arms over her chest. "But I'm not sure about me. Not anymore."

"I am."

She stopped pacing and stood before him, looking down.

"I almost killed you."

"But you didn't."

"Scott, what if Lilandra is right?"

He stood up, touched her face. "You can't give up," he said. "That would be like surrendering to the Dark Phoenix. Letting her—it—win. Admitting that you *are* evil. That your humanity means nothing in the face of some ancient power."

She looked at him, tears welling up.

"And I know that's not true," he continued. "I know the love you feel in your heart. And I have faith—that love will see you through this. Will see all of us through."

She let out a single sob. Then she wiped at her eyes and looked embarrassed.

"Softie," she said, poking him in the chest.

He laughed.

"We've got a big day tomorrow." He gestured at the iris. "Better get to bed."

She smiled up at him, tilted her mask playfully. "Took you long enough to ask."

"God," he said. "I do love you."

He started toward the exit. She hesitated just a moment, turning to stare out the observation blister again. At the Earth, just passing out of sight, as the cold gray orb of the moon swung into view.

I'll never know, he realized suddenly. *I'll never know the impulses that drive her. Never understand the fires within her, the rage and hunger and frustration and, yes, the love.*

I'll never know. And that's all right. He reached out a hand. She took it, smiled, and followed him back into the ship.

HUNN-TAR WAS dying. A platoon of enemy Skrulls, clad in purple exosuits with thin-skin helmets, burst through the plasteel window port of the Kree orbital platform. Hunn-Tar felt the pressure drop, heard a roaring in his ears as the air rushed out, escaping all at once into the void. His face turned cold, his eyelids frozen in place as he watched his comrades—the elite Kree invasion force—flail and writhe, their bodies hurtling out into open space.

Hunn-Tar had died many times these past four years, in his dreams. That battle had been an epic disaster; only he had survived. But this time, something was different. As his feet left the deck, as he flew upward toward raw vacuum, a crimson light filled the sky. A raging bird of prey, forged of pure, elemental fire.

He was instantly awake and on his feet. It took him a moment to remember where he was: aboard the accursed Shi'ar vessel, orbiting that tiny world in the Sol System. In his hand he held a proton knife, its blade glowing with microfusion fire.

A human woman stood before his bed. Her dress was bright green, her eyes sharp and glaring. Her hair flowed in long crimson tresses, like the flaming vision he'd seen in his dream.

She stood perfectly still, making no sound. Her words formed in his brain, as clear as an omni-wave slicing through the stars.

Hunn-Tar of the Kree, she said. *I need your help.*

CHAPTER TWENTY-EIGHT

THE CARGO bay was quiet as Cyclops stepped up to the platform. A few technicians bustled around, adjusting the teleport equipment at the edge of the central platform.

As Storm and the others approached, he gestured for them to wait. His visor blazed scarlet, the energies barely contained behind his ruby-quartz lens. "I just want to tell you..." His voice faltered. He looked down at his assembled teammates: Storm, Colossus, Wolverine, and Nightcrawler, all of them suited up and ready for combat. Jean stood apart from them.

Any or all of them could die today, he thought.

"I want you to know that I'm fighting for Jean," he said. "But I'm not asking any of you to join me. I don't have that right, and I won't think any less of you if you decide to sit this one out."

"*Mein Herr.*" Nightcrawler smiled. "Get real, eh?"

"We have already talked it over, Cyclops," Storm said. "We stand with you."

"To the end," Wolverine added.

"Thank you," Jean said, a tentative smile creeping onto her face. "I'll try not to kill you this ti—"

A door in the far wall slid open. The technicians stiffened and came to attention. Lilandra strode inside, gleaming in her silver regalia. Prime Minister Araki and Professor X followed. Xavier's face was grim—he looked as if he hadn't slept. He rode in a sleek hoverchair that made absolutely no sound. *The wonders of Shi'ar technology,* Cyclops thought.

As Lilandra approached, the X-Men filed one by one up onto the transport platform. Jean flashed Cyclops a quick smile, and he reached out a hand to help her up.

"The Empress Majestrix," Araki announced.

Lilandra stopped in front of the platform. She clapped her staff down once on the metal floor.

"Arin'nn Haelar has been offered, and lawfully accepted." She looked up at Cyclops. "Hear my terms, X-Men. You and my Imperial Guard will do battle until one team or the other is defeated. Should the X-Men emerge victorious, the survivors will be set free. Should you lose…"

Lilandra paused, cast a glance at Xavier. He didn't meet her eyes.

"…should you lose, Jean Grey—the Phoenix—belongs to us. To do with as we see fit, for the good of the universe. Will you abide by those terms?"

"We will," Cyclops said.

Lilandra raised a hand and gestured to a technician. The blinding glare of the teleport effect washed over the X-Men. Cyclops felt his skin peeling away, his body reduced to its raw molecular structure. A moment passed, or an eternity.

Then they were somewhere else. A flat rocky surface surrounded by ancient, decayed ruins. Temples, machines; a long shield wall that had once stood meters high, now crumbled and broken in a dozen spots. Carved faces, thirty feet or more in height, stared down from mountainous cliffs—the walls of the crater, a mile or more away.

"The famous Blue Area of the moon," Nightcrawler said. "Seems like more of a slate gray to me."

Cyclops looked up. The sky was dark; Earth and the sun were both out of view. Stars shone down, brighter than any he'd ever seen from home. The air felt thin, cold against his skin.

Jean stared at a ruined temple, a mixture of alien machinery and Doric columns. It lay collapsed, fallen in an enormous heap on the rocks.

"Kirinos," she murmured.

Cyclops frowned. "Mmm?"

"Just… remembering something."

"I consulted the Shi'ar databanks last night," Storm said. "These ruins were left behind from some ancient conflict between the Kree and the Skrulls. Somehow there is an Earth-normal atmosphere extending all through the crater."

"I can hear machines," Wolverine said. "Hummin' away somewhere underneath us."

Cyclops frowned. He couldn't make out the humming, but Wolverine's hearing was more acute than his own. He did notice a luminescence rising from the surface, bathing the area in pale blue hues. Toward the edge of the crater, jagged holes in the rock revealed cave-like passages leading down into darkness.

"I've psi-scanned the area, Scott," Jean said. "My power isn't what it was, but I can't detect any other thoughts. We're alone here."

"That won't last." Cyclops whirled to address the team again. "On your toes, people. We've met some of the Imperial Guard, but there are others we know nothing about. We need to be ready for anything."

"Peter, Ororo. Kurt." Jean paused. "I just want to say—"

"Jeannie," Wolverine said, sniffing the air.

She looked up, nodded. "I sense them. Multiple telepathic impressions—they just popped up."

"Flash of light, off that way." Wolverine pointed toward a ruined temple in the distance. "Prob'ly the teleporter."

"I will take the high ground," Nightcrawler said. "Get a better look."

"Kurt, *no*!" Cyclops reached for him—too late. His hand passed through a puff of brimstone in the exact spot where his teammate had stood. He swore and looked upward.

"Oh!" Colossus said, pointing up.

Nightcrawler sat perched high above, on a half-crumbled spire. He trembled, not moving.

"You're too high!" Cyclops yelled. "Beyond the top of the crater—that's hard vacuum!"

Nightcrawler clutched silently at his throat as he toppled and began to fall. Storm was airborne in an instant, moving toward him.

"Careful!" Cyclops called. "Remember the lighter gravity. You could fly off into space."

She swooped around in an arc, staying low, then reached out her arms to catch Nightcrawler's rigid body.

"He is falling very slowly," Colossus said.

Cyclops nodded. "The gravity."

Storm grabbed hold of Nightcrawler. His weight knocked her off-balance, sending the two of them lurching toward the ground. She grimaced, strained, and summoned an updraft. They touched down together, a bit more roughly than usual.

"The environment of the crater makes it hard for me to use my powers," Storm said. "I have limited atmospheric 'tools' with which to work."

Colossus took hold of Nightcrawler. "He is so cold!"

"I'm all right." Kurt shrugged him away, smiling sheepishly at Storm. "I suppose I should have read the databanks as well."

Cyclops took hold of him by both shoulders, addressed him directly.

"Next time, think before you act," he said. "There's only six of us—with Jean's life at stake, we can't afford any mistakes." Nightcrawler nodded, rubbing his hands together for warmth.

"Cyclops!"

He whirled. Colossus and Wolverine stood atop a piece of the fallen wall at the far end of the clearing. Logan's eyes were fixed on a tall, devastated machine complex on the other side of the crater.

"Wolverine has spotted the Imperial Guard," Colossus continued. "They are heading this way." Cyclops squinted. He couldn't see the Guard, but he trusted Wolverine's enhanced senses.

"Do we make a stand, boss?" Logan asked.

"When we're ready, and on our own terms. We don't know how many of them there are yet." He looked around, assessing the terrain. "We'll start with hit-and-run tactics. Throw the Imperials off-balance, whittle down their forces."

"I like the sound of that."

Cyclops motioned him over. Jean joined the two of them in a huddle.

"I can sense them," she said. "They're drawing closer."

"Any specifics?" Cyclops asked.

"My power... it's not..." She shook her head, as if trying to clear it. "I think Oracle may be blocking my mental probes."

Cyclops turned to Wolverine. "You ready to lead a team?"

Logan looked at him, surprised. "You ready to trust me?"

"*I* am." Jean turned to Logan. "With my life."

Logan started to reply, then turned away and dropped to the ground. He pressed an ear to the cold stone. "Footsteps," he said. "Heavy ones. Some of 'em must be sneaking up on us from underground." He looked up and met Cyclops's gaze.

This is it, Cyclops thought. *The moment of truth.*

"Go," he said.

Logan leapt up and broke from the huddle. "Petey, Elf," he called. "You're with me." He took off for an opening in the rock. Nightcrawler teleported after him, arriving at the mouth of the cavern first.

Colossus cast a quick glance back. Cyclops nodded, and gestured for him to follow. As Peter ran, his body transformed rapidly into steel. His boots pounded on the rock, leaving deep impressions. When he reached the cave opening, he followed Wolverine and Nightcrawler inside.

"Well." Storm soared low through the air and came to rest between Scott and Jean. "Now what?"

Cyclops looked up. He could see motion now, around one of the half-fallen spires on the far side of the crater.

"We're too exposed here," he said. "Let's take cover. Storm, you're on point."

Instantly a wind rose. Storm wafted upward, staying strictly within the crater's bubble of atmosphere. She pointed toward a clutch of ruins, and veered off in that direction.

"Come on," Cyclops said.

Jean hesitated. She looked back at the spires, where the Imperial Guard were located. "Maybe…" She gestured at the spires. "Maybe I should just let them…"

"No," he said, and reached out his hand. She grimaced, nodded, and grabbed hold. Together they ran, following Storm deeper into the ruins of the Blue Area.

WOLVERINE LED his team down a ramp, through a low-ceilinged corridor. Cables and wires hung loose on all sides, covered with a thick layer of dust. Remnants of the alien technology that had helped create this place.

I got a bad feelin' in my gut, Logan thought. *This ain't gonna be one of those fun historic moon landings.*

Nightcrawler teleported ahead and looked around. He motioned for Wolverine and Colossus to follow.

"It is growing darker," Colossus said. "Should we not—"

"Quiet!" Logan hissed. The hairs on his neck stood up. He'd picked up a scent, one that set off every alarm inside him. *Definitely alien. With a hint of… machine oil. A robot, maybe?*

Whatever it is, it ain't human.

Nightcrawler 'ported ahead again—then let out a yelp. Logan peered past him. The corridor widened out in front of them, the ceiling curving upward. A huge, metallic shape filled the passageway.

"Terrestrial beings." The creature's voice was deep, filtered. "We are Warstar. We offer you a choice: honorable surrender, or honorable death."

"Colossus," Logan said, "this *Lost in Space* reject looks like it's up your alley. Back you up?"

"My pleasure, *tovarisch.*"

306   Colossus marched forward, his footsteps shaking the tunnel.

He pulled back and slammed a metallic fist into Warstar's stomach. The guardsman doubled over, began to fall backward—

—and split in two. As the Warstar body wobbled, regaining its footing, a second creature leaped out of its neck, leaving the body headless.

"Take care of the metal man, C'cll," the small creature said. "The hairy one is mine."

"As you say, B'nee." The other voice was muffled, emanating from somewhere within the large metal body.

The smaller Warstar—B'nee—launched itself straight toward Wolverine. "Logan!" Nightcrawler called. "There are two of them!"

Logan smiled, unsheathed his claws, and slashed out. B'nee twisted in midair, but Logan tagged him across the midsection. Claws screeched against metal, sending sparks shooting up.

"Nightcrawler!" Logan called. "Help Pete with that cut-rate Sentinel."

"As you say, *mein*—"

Nightcrawler's words ended in a strangled cry. Wolverine whirled to see him gasping, a brightly sparking whip coiled around his neck. Farther down the corridor, silhouetted in darkness, Hussar—the crimson Guardsman—jerked the whip hard, lifting Nightcrawler up off his feet.

"Stop struggling, Terran," Hussar said. "You're no match for my neuro-whip."

Out of the corner of his eye, Wolverine saw B'nee—the junior half of Warstar—lunging for another attack. He sheathed his claws and jabbed out with his elbow, slamming the small being into the corridor wall.

Hussar flexed her whip. Nightcrawler flailed in its grip, then landed hard on the cavern floor. The whip uncurled from his neck, retracting as if it were alive. The blue-furred X-Man grunted once and went still.

One down already, Logan thought. *They know all about us—an' we're literally fighting in the dark.*

Colossus traded blows with C'cll, the Warstar host body. They seemed almost evenly matched—but C'cll was backing the X-Man slowly, steadily toward the wall. Wolverine sprinted toward them, loosed his claws, and raked them all the way down C'cll's back.

Can't penetrate that armor! What the hell is it made of?

He glanced down the corridor. Hussar was moving toward them, smiling, snapping her whip in the air.

"Pete," Logan called, leaping around in front of C'cll. "One-two."

Colossus reared back his fist, preparing to strike. Logan sheathed his claws and punched the creature's midsection, at the exact moment Colossus struck its chest. C'cll tottered and fell.

Logan's fist hurt like hell. "That thing'll be back on its feet in a minute." He started back up the passageway. "C'mon."

Colossus hesitated. "But Kurt—"

"He's down. If he's alive, they won't hurt him anymore… those are the rules. If not…" Logan saw Hussar approaching, noticed B'nee picking itself up from the floor. "We gotta get back out in the open—they got all the advantages down here. Let's go!"

Turning, he ran upward, toward the surface. Colossus followed reluctantly, his pace heavy but even.

Logan heard the sound first, muffled by layers of rock. He was about to speak when Colossus turned to him. "What is that?" Peter asked.

"Cyke's optic beams. Up topside." Wolverine grimaced. "Hope he's doin' better than we are—"

He stopped dead in the passageway, holding out an arm. Colossus slammed into it with the full weight of his massive steel body. Logan grunted, shook off the pain, and turned to face the new threat.

A red-and-blue figure stood blocking their way, just ahead. Its tall Mohawk was silhouetted against the light leaking down from the surface.

"Sadly," Gladiator said, "you will never know how your comrades are faring."

"*Tovarisch?*" Colossus moved up against Wolverine. "Your orders?"

Logan tensed, crouching down.

"*Snikt*," he said aloud.

CHAPTER TWENTY-NINE

ON THE surface, the battle had gone wrong from the start. Cyclops stood in a clearing, firing pulsed optic beams up into the sky. Starbolt, a fiery red-and-gold member of the Imperial Guard, dodged them easily, dipping and swooping in the air. He let out a stream of flame from his fingertips, scorching the ground less than a yard from his target's darting figure.

Jean braced herself against a half-destroyed temple. Oracle hovered just above, hands raised to her temples. Their struggle was invisible, waged on the mental plane, but Jean was clearly losing the battle.

The Guard, Storm realized. *They can all fly! That gives them a tremendous advantage.* She rose up into the air, spotting a new enemy. A hulking gray being with an enlarged forehead stalked toward her, shaking the ground. Storm reached out, struggling to gather enough air to form a windstorm. The gray figure paused and shook its head against the gale, but continued forward.

No good. The atmosphere is just too thin.

She rose higher, staying out of its reach. The newcomer didn't pursue her into the air, didn't even look up at her. When it reached a point just below her hovering figure, it crouched down and touched the crater's surface. Too late, she remembered the Guardsman's name.

Earthquake.

The ground trembled and collapsed. Layers of moondust, of decayed flooring from some long-destroyed building, crumbled and fell. Storm spread her arms and rose up into the air, instinctively moving away from the newly created pit.

"Good work, 'Quake," Starbolt called. "Now stand aside!"

Storm whirled—and saw Starbolt hovering in midair, holding Cyclops's struggling figure in his hands. As she watched in horror, the Guardsman reached up and hurled Cyclops down into the pit.

For a split second, Storm hesitated. Then she whirled in midair—only to hear Jean's voice in her mind.

Go. Save him!

She dove down into the pit, dodging sparking cables, shards of machinery. The ruins of whatever civilization had lived here, uncounted eons ago.

"Scott," she called out. "Go limp!"

The bottom of the pit was coming up fast. She stretched her hand out, willing the wind to speed her passage. At the last moment she grabbed hold of Cyclops's leg, arresting his fall, and spread her cape to catch the updrafts. Their descent slowed.

"Thanks," Cyclops said.

She drew him close, reaching out with her power to reverse the wind currents. Slowly, the two of them started to rise.

"Jean—" Cyclops coughed. "She's alone up there."

They burst up out of the pit. Storm caught sight of Jean, backed up against the temple. Oracle and Starbolt hovered side by side above her, projecting mental assaults and flame-bolts at her. Jean was barely keeping them at bay with a flickering psi-shield.

"Storm!" Cyclops wrenched himself free of her grip, leaping toward the ground. "Look out—"

Ororo whirled around in midair. A lean woman hovered nearby, her white bodysuit shrouded by a swirling black-and-yellow cloak. Her face seemed almost featureless in the dim alien lighting. The woman—*Manta,* Storm remembered—spread her cloak open wide. A blinding flash of light enveloped Storm, frying her nerve endings. She struggled to remain airborne, to remain conscious.

I can't, she thought. *I cannot fail Jean now. Not after all we've been through!* But she had no choice. Storm reeled, stars pinwheeling before her eyes. Then she tumbled and fell to the ground, unconscious.

WOLVERINE'S LEG muscles pumped, propelling him up through the shadowy passageway. Behind, he could hear the thundering blows being traded by Colossus and Gladiator.

Hope Petey's okay, he thought. He hated to leave Colossus behind—but he'd received another summons, an urgent telepathic call for help. Jean's voice, echoing in his mind.

Logan, it's Scott. They're killing him.

Hang on, Jeannie. I'm comin'!

The corridor began to lighten as he approached the surface. Logan braced himself. He thought of Colossus, facing off against the most experienced member of the Guard, and of Nightcrawler's unmoving body, helpless in the cavern below.

This battle is only goin' one way. An' it ain't ours.

He reached the end of the tunnel and leapt through the jagged opening. He landed in a crouch in the open air, all his senses on high alert. The first thing he saw was Storm's body, laid out on the crater's surface.

Damn, he thought. *'Roro, I'm sorry, but I'll have to check on you later.*

Across the crater, Cyclops stood against the outside wall of an old temple. He was firing at full power, his eye-beams aimed at a trio of flying enemies: Starbolt, Manta, and Oracle. They dodged in the air, their movements almost casual.

Taking their time.

Logan sprinted toward them, drew his claws—and stopped. Behind Cyclops, sprawled behind a jagged outcropping, Jean lay unconscious. Logan glanced at Scott one more time, watched him fire off another pair of deadly blasts.

Hang on, boss. Just a little longer.

He dropped low, creeping around the edge of the crater. The hovering Guard members hadn't noticed him yet. Flattening himself against machines, he ducked under half-fallen walls, using all his training to remain absolutely silent.

At last he reached Jean. She wasn't moving, and her breathing was shallow. He reached a hand down to her, barely remembering to retract his claws in time. When he touched her face, her eyes flew open.

"Uhh!"

Logan sank to his knees. "Jeannie. Thank god."

"Can't kill me." She smiled, struggled to her knees. "You should know that by now."

Logan grabbed a rock to steady himself as the ground shook. He looked over to see Starbolt firing a sustained burst of flame down at the surface. The fire formed a semicircle, penning Cyclops in against the temple.

"Go," Jean said. "Help him. And, Logan?"

He turned, paused.

"Thanks." She smiled. "For… for all of it."

A thousand replies ran through his mind. *Ain't nothing. We're teammates. For you, Red, sure. You paid me back, a thousand times.*

I love you.

In the end, he just nodded. Then he turned and sprinted off to join the fray.

Cyclops turned to watch as Logan leapt into the air, tagging two of the Guardsmen with a single swipe of his claws. Another one—he wasn't sure which—reached down and shook the ground, sending the ancient structure crumbling, forcing both X-Men down to the surface. The battle turned quickly against them as more and more Guardsmen came out of hiding—a rainbow of costumes filling the night sky, energies blasting from alien hands and mouths and eyes.

Logan began to feel the cumulative effect of the assault. His vision blurred, then started to go dark. Yet as he sank to the floor of the crater unconscious, all he remembered was the smile on Jean Grey's face. The look of deep gratitude and yes, love. Not the romantic love he'd yearned for, not the closeness he'd dreamed of in quiet moments of pain. But love nonetheless, a deep and abiding warmth that would stay with him, guiding and guarding his troubled spirit, until the end of his days.

THE HOLOGRAM rose from the platform in the center of the cargo deck. Two figures wavered, dark against shadows, caught by the microcamera of a Shi'ar dust drone. Charles Xavier leaned forward in his hoverchair, struggling to make out the details.

"Enhance resolution," Lilandra said. At a nearby console, a technician hurried to comply.

The image grew clearer. In the caverns beneath the Blue Area, Gladiator launched himself through the air, planting a shattering punch across Colossus's steel jaw. The young X-Man cried out and flew into the wall, cracking its surface. Bits of stone rained down around him.

No, Xavier thought. *No no no no no no.*

In the hologram, Gladiator strode toward his fallen enemy. *"In order to help your friends, you will have to get through me,"* he said. *"And I honestly don't think that's possible."* Before Colossus could regain his footing, Gladiator fell to a crouch and pounded the X-Man's chest against the floor. Again the aged stone cracked and shattered.

"If—" Colossus coughed, scurrying away along the uneven floor. *"If I have learned anything from my time in the X-Men..."*

He reached behind him and grabbed a section of wall. Its outer covering had been ripped away, revealing a thick, aged support beam. He wrenched the beam free and swung it toward his foe.

"*…it is that nothing is impossible.*"

Gladiator stood perfectly still. The beam cracked in half over his head, leaving him unharmed.

Xavier jumped at a touch on his shoulder. Lilandra stood behind him, staring at the image. They watched together as Gladiator lunged forward and dealt Colossus a crippling blow to the stomach.

"I am sorry, my love," Lilandra said.

Xavier whirled, suddenly furious. "You did not have to do this."

"I did." Her expression was pained but firm.

"I had the situation under control."

"Then why did you lie to me? You said you were returning to Earth to visit *family*." She glared at him. "I am the sworn protector of a thousand worlds. You have never understood."

"I understand more than you think." He turned away. "Your people regard me as a lesser life-form—as some sort of *pet* you've adopted. An amusement."

"Have I ever treated you that way?"

He turned back to the hologram. Colossus and Gladiator were trading blows at close quarters, punches that would shatter a normal person's skull. The tunnel quivered and shook around them.

No, Xavier thought, *you would never do that.* But his anger would not let him say it aloud. "Perhaps, in the end," he said, "you and I are just too *alien*."

Colossus slammed Gladiator into the wall. *Good,* Xavier thought. *Stay on him, Peter. Maybe… maybe there's a chance…*

Gladiator grabbed Colossus around the waist, spun him around, and threw him at the ceiling. The tunnel walls rippled and began to collapse. The two fighters grappled again, oblivious to the stone falling all around. The dust drone swung around, struggling to keep them in view as debris filled the passageway.

"However this ends," Xavier said, "I will be returning to Earth. With my *surviving* students."

314   Lilandra withdrew, her face stony. "I expected no less."

In the hologram, layers of rock tumbled down. Gladiator and Colossus vanished in a cloud of dust and stone. For a moment the image was still—and then the rocks began to move, sliding heavily aside. A single figure in red and blue rose from the floor. His uniform was torn, but his eyes still glared with fierce, unwavering purpose.

Gladiator.

Xavier turned away. "I've seen enough."

"Charles…" Lilandra said. He looked up. There was steel in her eyes. "I would give anything for us to have… for this to have gone another way. But I ask you to consider something. Perhaps we are not so different from each other. Not so alien."

"Perhaps you were simply wrong."

He looked down, blinking away a tear.

"I can feel them," he whispered. "As each one of them falls, their pain echoes in my mind."

She turned away. "You and I," she said. "We could have had the stars."

For a moment, the cargo deck was silent. The hologram lingered on Gladiator as he climbed his way free of the debris. Then the image winked off.

Lilandra turned toward the technician. "How many X-Men still standing?"

Xavier knew the answer before it came.

"Only two, Majestrix." The technician toggled his controls, bringing up a new image. "Just two."

CHAPTER THIRTY

JEAN GREY crouched inside the alcove, pressing a hand to the wall. Engines hummed behind it, concealed behind layer upon layer of rock. Hidden machines, designed to run for hundreds of thousands of years, kept going by some unknown power source.

Will they be enough? she wondered.

A familiar tickle in her brain signaled Scott's approach. She held up both hands, manipulating a vertical wall of moondust she'd erected to hide the alcove from view. The gray particles shimmered and parted at her telekinetic command, creating an entranceway.

Leaning forward, she peered through the opening at the crater outside. A comet trail blazed past, arrowing across the starry sky. That would be Starbolt.

Cyclops leaped in through the entrance. Jean sealed it quickly, before the Guard members could take notice.

"Whoa," he said.

She followed his gaze. The battle had blasted open this area, which appeared to have been an armory. Floor-mounted guns, some of them taller than a man, lined the alcove. Most were long decayed, bits of triggers and control units fallen to the ground or lost to the ages.

Cyclops studied the largest relic: a high-tech cannon three yards long and nearly as tall. He ran a hand across its tarnished muzzle.

"This looks Kree."

"Storm said they lived here, long ago," she agreed. *Change the subject!* "How's Logan?"

"Couldn't reach him. I think he's breathing." He turned to look at her wall of dust. "Very clever."

"It buys us a little time." She took his arm, pulled him away from the weapons. "But sooner or later, they'll find us."

"Yeah."

They stood together for a moment. The machinery seemed to hum louder. Power seeping through the walls, coursing down through the centuries.

He let out a laugh.

"Something's funny?"

"I'm sorry. It's just…" He turned to her, took her by both shoulders. "As horrible as all this is, it sort of reminds me of old times. You and me? Against an army of super-powered villains?"

She nodded. "Like the Brotherhood."

"Or Factor Three. What were *those* guys about?"

She grabbed him, hugged him tight. Nuzzled his shoulder.

"It reminds me more of the shuttle," she whispered. "All our options are bad."

"You were right." His voice broke. "Aboard the shuttle. You saved us all. I wish… I'd give anything if there'd been another way, but you were right and I was wrong." He pulled back, looked at her through that haze of ruby quartz.

Don't cry, she told herself. *Do not cry.*

"I love you," she said. "I used to think… sometimes I thought that made me weak. That it held me back, confined me, made it hard to breathe. But that was just…"

"The Phoenix talking?"

"Maybe. I don't know." She grimaced. "All I know is, the love I feel for you isn't a weakness—it's a strength. It *gives* me strength. Whatever happens, please remember that."

"Jean, there's a lot more I want to say. But I… I don't seem to have the words."

"It's the thought that counts. Remember?" She smiled, tapped his forehead. "And your thoughts, like you, are beautiful."

"No more beautiful than the woman I love."

She raised her head and kissed him, a long, deep kiss.

"You wait here," she said, her voice breaking. "I'll go out there."

He took her hand firmly in his. "We'll do it together."

No, she thought. *Let me do this. I don't want you to get hurt!* But she knew Scott Summers, better than she knew anyone in the world. He would never let her face danger alone.

"All right," she agreed. "Together."

WITH A thought, she dropped the dust wall. The crater came into view, strewn with debris and costumed bodies. The Imperial Guard circled above, like a swarm of insects against the stars.

Cyclops squeezed her hand and started forward. Jean followed, her thoughts whirling… casting back…

…to that day under the autumn trees. Walking together, the air crisp on her sandaled feet. Bright sunlight filtered through a crisscross of leaves.

The air was chill in this alien place, too, but thinner and colder. The ground beneath was gritty, coated with ash and sediment. Peering ahead, she could make out Logan's body over by a pillar. Farther off, Storm's cloak lay crumpled on the ground.

Red leaves and gold, auburn and burnt green. Brittle, dying, poised to fall. Yet still clinging to the branches, to the trees that birthed them.

Clinging to life.

Cyclops pointed up at the dark, merciless sky. "They're coming," he said.

She reached for him, took his hand. Pointed up at the leaves.

"I love the fall."

Gladiator swooped down, muscles tensed for battle. But Oracle swung in front of him, holding up a hand. She fixed Jean with a piercing stare and transmitted a telepathic message.

I told your blue friend, Oracle said. *This outcome was never in doubt.*

Jean glared back. *You remind me,* she replied, *of another icy telepath.*

Moving quickly, Cyclops raised his head and shot off a blast into the air. Oracle dodged, but the beam grazed her side, sending her spinning through the sky. Gladiator called out something in a language Jean didn't recognize.

Then the Guard were everywhere. Warstar, clomping along the jagged surface, its metallic armor glowing with power. Starbolt glowing in the sky, backing up Gladiator's attack. Manta, flaring with light. Even as Jean raised a psi-shield, she knew it wouldn't be strong enough. Cyclops was fending off their enemies—shooting eye-beams high and low, rapid-fire—but there were too many.

And I don't have the power. Not anymore.

As she clicked into battle mode, deflecting plasma bolts and psi-daggers with quick bursts of telekinesis, a deep sense of helplessness settled over her. She could feel all the currents that had led her to this moment. The cosmic forces aboard the shuttle, tingling on her skin. The voice within—incomprehensibly alien, yet as familiar as her own name. The legends of the Shi'ar, passed down through the ages.

The rushing river of history.

The end came all at once. Earthquake reached out and touched the ground, throwing Jean and Cyclops off their feet. Hussar's neuro-whip slashed out to grab Scott around the waist. Starbolt glowed with power, gathering energy in his outstretched hands, as Gladiator swooped down and slammed a fist across Cyclops's chin.

Scott Summers cried out once, fell to the ground, and went still.

Jean felt rage. Primal rage born of love, love that—as she'd said, as she now knew—lent her strength. Strength to rouse her, move her, spur her on. Strength that could accomplish…

…*anything*.

Like dominoes, the barriers fell. Psychic scars tore open, circuit breakers dissolved into neuron ash.

Click

Click

Clickclickclickclickclickclick…

She spread her arms and rose up off the ground, feeling the anger wash over her—consuming all doubts, all reason, all mercy. Knowing, with a deep heartfelt sadness, that she'd been right all along.

The Imperial Guard scattered in the air. The creature soared upward, dark and menacing, towering over them. It screeched in the vacuum, high above the protected environment of the crater.

The Phoenix breathed deep of their fear and smiled.

Welcome, it said, *to the last minutes of your lives.*

CHAPTER THIRTY-ONE

AGAIN, XAVIER knew. While the technicians struggled to read their instruments, while Araki made his frantic appeals, while Shi'ar soldiers hurried into the cargo bay, while the Kree and Skrull representatives rushed to join them—he already knew.

"Majestrix," a technician said, "power levels are off the scale."

"Sharra and K'ythri," Araki said, pointing at a hologram just coming into focus. "Look!"

The Phoenix screamed, burned, raged to the heavens. Its radiance seemed to fill the crater; it loomed larger, fiercer than ever before—even than when it had consumed an entire star. Jean's figure was barely visible within its white-hot core.

In the hologram, a tendril of flame struck Gladiator. He screamed and fell from the sky. The creature began to turn, craning its fiery neck upward. Looking past the remaining Guard members, toward the heavens. Its eyes were cold, devoid of mercy—and aimed straight at the flagship.

"Araki." Lilandra's eyes went wide with alarm. "Begin evacuation procedures—"

Too late, Xavier thought.

Twenty thousand miles away, on the surface of the moon, the Phoenix spat fire into the sky. The energy bolt struck the ship in an instant, punching through the defense screens. The cargo bay lurched violently; gravity failed for a moment, then reasserted itself. Xavier tumbled to the floor, falling free of his hoverchair.

He shook his head, overwhelmed by the panic in the thoughts around him. Voices filled the air.

"—damage report—"

"—plasma energy. Enormous levels—"

"—hull rupture! Bridge exposed to vacuum—"

He felt strong arms lifting him off the floor. Looked up to see Lilandra, staring at him with a mixture of pity and anger.

"Sit there," she said, placing him gently back in his chair, "while I try to save our lives."

"—lost contact with the Guard—"

"—gravity down to thirty percent—"

"—casualties in the dozens—"

"Araki!" Lilandra's voice rang out, cutting through the clamor. "Alert the grand fleet. *Plan Omega*."

"Majestrix," Araki said, climbing shakily to his feet. "Do you realize what you're saying?"

Xavier swiveled his chair to face the hologram. The image flickered as the dust-drone camera faltered beneath the massive energy discharge. When it came into focus, Jean Grey stood atop a fallen temple, her arms spread wide. The Phoenix Force raged, rising up all around her. The ground was littered with bodies.

The ship shook again. Lilandra braced herself against a console, spoke urgently to Araki.

"Send the message," she said. "If we fail in our mission, the fleet is to do anything in their power to ensure that the Phoenix is destroyed."

She turned to the hologram.

"Burn this world." Her voice was cold now, grave. "This system, this entire stellar cluster. *Whatever it takes*."

324 Xavier moved up behind her, sending a mild telepathic prod

her way. But Lilandra just stared at the image, at the Chaos-Bringer that threatened to destroy all existence. The Phoenix filled the crater now—Xavier couldn't even make out the bodies of the Imperial Guard. Or the X-Men.

Lilandra's words echoed in his mind:

"Perhaps you were simply wrong."

Perhaps, he thought. *If so, then this is my fault, my responsibility. And only I can set it right.*

Frantic voices filled the cargo bay. The Kree and Skrull warriors raised weapons, pointing them at each other. Araki waved his staff, struggling to maintain order. Xavier forced their thoughts from his mind. He raised both hands to his temples, sending his consciousness radiating outward.

Scott, he thought. *Hear me. You must hear me.*

Heed my voice… my urgent plea…

…WAKE UP!

Cyclops sat up, instantly awake. He coughed moondust, brushed dirt off his visor.

Scott. The Professor's voice, echoing inside his skull. *Can you hear me?*

Yes, Professor.

Listen carefully. You have to attack the Phoenix.

Cyclops looked up, shielding his eyes from his worst nightmare. Jean stood on the ruins of the temple, dressed once again in the deep-red costume of the Dark Phoenix. Her energy blazed madly, blotting out the stars.

Professor, that's the woman I love!

Not anymore. We made—I made that mistake once. A surge of regret came over the telepathic link. *You have to strike now, while she's weak!*

A muscular man in blue and white, wearing dark red glasses, whizzed by overhead. *Smasher,* Cyclops remembered—yet another member of the Imperial Guard. As the Guardsman drew near Jean, the Phoenix's wing reached out and enveloped him in flame. He cried out and dropped to the ground.

Weak? Cyclops asked. *Are you joking?*

Trust me, Professor Xavier said. *There is an opportunity here.*

I… Cyclops stumbled, clutching his head. His uniform was torn, his chest slashed and bruised. *I don't think I can do this alone, Professor.*

Fortunately…

He whirled at the sound of footsteps.

…you are not alone.

Wolverine led the way, supporting Nightcrawler. Colossus trudged along behind, his metal body dented and specked with debris. Storm hovered in the air behind them, an injured arm wrapped in shreds of her cape.

"Well." Wolverine stared up at the temple. "*This* sucks."

I will link your minds together, Xavier said. *For maximum efficiency.*

Cyclops nodded reluctantly. He closed his eyes, sensing the familiar mental presence of his teammates. Storm, bright and flashing. Colossus, earnest and hopeful. Nightcrawler's light heart, covering sorrow and pain.

And Logan. Scott's rival, the greatest thorn in his side… and possibly the most loyal, honorable X-Man of all.

All set, Professor. We'll follow your lead.

No, Scott.

Cyclops looked up, puzzled.

You are *the X-Men's leader.*

A hundred feelings passed through Cyclops's mind. Gratitude, dread, hope. Warmth and love, regret and terror. An oppressive sense of inescapable destiny.

Then he whirled and fired off an eye-beam at full power. It flashed across a hundred yards in an instant, striking the base of a tall building with pinpoint accuracy. The decayed structure tottered, crumbled, and fell. Jean barely had time to look up before a thousand tons of stone and steel came crashing down on her. She raised a hand, deflecting a small part of the debris—but the rest was enough to force her down, to dim her flame.

Slightly.

Cyclops winced at the sight. He shook his head, forced those feelings away. *I can't be that person now—an ordinary man concerned for the one he loves. I have to be a cold, calculating strategist. It's our only hope of getting out of this alive.*

He concentrated, projecting his thoughts outward. *Nightcrawler*, he called. *Storm!*

Before the thought was complete, Nightcrawler appeared in a puff of smoke directly above Jean's fallen body. He looked up, shielding himself from the last few shards of falling debris. Then turned and wrenched a large rock out of the pile of rubble.

"Forgive me," he said, and brought the rock down toward Jean's head. At the last second she whirled, eyes flashing. Her hand whipped out, projecting a blast that hurled Nightcrawler clear across the crater.

Jean struggled to rise. The Phoenix flame flickered, less steady now. As she climbed upright, a cyclone-level wind grabbed hold of her, lifting her off her feet.

Cyclops, Storm said in his mind. *I cannot maintain this for long. There is not enough... atmosphere.*

Just keep her off-balance, he replied. *Colossus, Wolverine—*

We know, comrade, Colossus said. *Fastball Special!* He lifted Wolverine, holding him with both arms, aiming him toward their struggling target. But then Logan slipped free, leapt to the ground, and—astonishingly—lifted up Colossus in *his* arms.

"Logan!" Colossus exclaimed. "What are you doing?"

"Switching it up, Russkie," Wolverine replied. "In this gravity, I can throw *you*."

Colossus eyed the blazing figure in the distance.

"Oh," he said.

"Besides..." Logan grimaced, shifting his teammate's huge body. "I couldn't finish the job before. Don't trust myself to do it now."

"So... so you are saying *I* must—"

"You'll only get one shot. Make it count." Logan reached back, prepared to throw. "And, Pete?"

"Yes?"

"I'm sorry."

Logan lurched forward, letting fly with all his strength. Colossus arrowed through the air, fists outstretched, a gleaming missile of destruction. He struck the Phoenix head-on, a tremendous blow that whipped her jaw sideways. She cried out and dropped to the ground.

Damn! Jean's voice seemed to resonate, both in the air and in Scott's mind. *You pulled that punch, Peter. And even so… I felt it.*

Cyclops frowned. *Jean?*

You… you really knocked some sense into me. She shook her head, staring up at Colossus. *And I…*

She paused.

I can see it. The Phoenix… what it is, what I am. All *of it.*

The flame seemed lower now, barely visible around her dazed form. Cyclops watched, hardly daring to hope. *Is she back?*

Colossus stood over Jean, his fists clenched. Through the telepathic link, Cyclops could feel his doubt and uncertainty. He started toward them, picking his way across the uneven terrain. Edged his way around a woman lying on the ground, twitching: Oracle, of the Imperial Guard. Alive but, from the look of her, severely injured.

The Phoenix is… it's my life force, Jean continued. *And I provide a living focus for its power… its infinite power. That's… one way to look at it…*

She paused and looked up at the stars.

He crept across shallow troughs left behind by the battle, around the gigantic pit leading down to the moon's lower depths. Wolverine and Storm fell in behind him, keeping silent. Behind Jean, he could see the alcove where they'd hidden from the Imperial Guard. Had that been less than an hour ago?

The Phoenix cannot be controlled. Jean walked up to Colossus, stared him in the eyes. *Not while it has a human vessel. It will inevitably take control again, and then…*

328

She gestured at the destruction all around.

"No." Colossus shook his head. "You cannot ask this of me."

Her eyes blazed. *It's the only way.*

"Jean!" She whirled as Cyclops leapt up onto the platform. "It doesn't have to be like this," he continued. "You have an intellect, a will. Use them—fight this thing!"

She stared at him, the fire in her eyes growing in intensity. Then she closed them. As she'd done in Central Park, the Phoenix sent a wave of mental force rippling outward, like an electromagnetic pulse. When it struck Colossus, Storm, and Wolverine, they spasmed and dropped to the ground.

The energy passed through Cyclops, leaving him unharmed. Jean stared at him for a moment, a terrified look in her eyes. Then she turned and ran.

He sprinted after her, calling her name. But his heart sank as he saw the flame rising around her, flaring up to illuminate the temple ruins. She darted into the alcove, the hidden place that held an arsenal of ancient Kree weapons. He rounded the bend to follow—and stopped short, almost colliding with the immense central cannon.

In that instant—while he was off-balance—she reached out and lifted him into the air.

"J-Jean," he gasped. He couldn't move, could barely breathe. The Phoenix flared high, higher than before, its savage beak towering over the top of the open alcove.

"Fight," Jean said. "You want me to fight?"

He squinted, struggling to make out her figure in the heart of the fire. Her face seemed to flicker, her expression strobing from rage to doubt and back again.

"All I've done is fight," she continued. "It's all I *want* to do. And in my hunger, my fury, I killed five billion people."

"Not… you."

"Yes. Yes, me." She stepped forward, staring up at his immobile form. "I hate this, Scott. I don't want any of this. My heart is filled with rage at the forces that have brought me to this point."

Her face seemed to soften.

"But I can't remain in control of myself all my life. If even one more person died at my hands…"

She closed her eyes. Behind her, the tall Kree cannon glowed and hummed to life.

"Jean?"

"It's better this way." She reached up and touched his face. Her voice, her touch—both were cooler now, softer. Utterly, wonderfully human.

"Jean, no. Don't do it."

"Remember me, okay?" She stepped back, smiling sadly. "Remember that crisp fall day. Remember Marvel Gir—"

"*No!*"

The cannon flared, just once. The beam lanced through her, enveloping her in light. The effect was beyond human comprehension—a power from another age, long forgotten. It reached out and grabbed hold of the Phoenix Force, absorbing and channeling its raging fire.

That fire shot upward from the surface, like a bullet from a pistol. The Phoenix flared briefly in the sky, bright and wild against the stars. Then it shot away, vanishing like a comet.

On the moon, Jean Grey fell.

Cyclops dropped to the ground, free of the telekinetic force field. He crawled to her body, knowing what he would find.

No breath. No pulse.

No sign of life.

"You planned this," he whispered. "You knew there might be no alternative. Knew we could drain you of enough energy that you could… that this…" He shook his head, wiped away tears.

"You picked the mind of the Kree observer." He looked up at the cannon; it was dark again, its power spent. "Knew that his people's ancient technology could… would allow you to…"

And then words failed him, along with his strength. He heaved a great sob and collapsed over her body, weeping like a child.

CHAPTER THIRTY-TWO

A FLASH of teleport light at the crater's edge. Professor Xavier appeared, took in the carnage all around. The exposed pits, the fallen buildings, the scorched and scarred walls.

Could all this have been avoided?

He would never know.

Maneuvering his hoverchair across the surface, he mind-scanned each fallen figure as he passed. The Imperial Guard members were injured, but they would recover. His X-Men were already beginning to awaken.

Scott Summers was seated in a corner of the weapons alcove, his back to a stone wall. He held Jean's head in his arms, stroking her hair. Xavier hovered up beside him and placed a hand on his shoulder.

My first students, Xavier said, keeping his mental voice soft. *And my best.*

Scott didn't look up.

One by one, the X-Men joined them. Nightcrawler, his demonic eyes wide with horror. Logan, with his light tread and rough growl. Storm, wafting like a somber angel on the thin air. Colossus, his flesh-and-blood features twisted into a mask of anguish.

"She could have lived as a god." Xavier gestured down at Jean's body. Her expression, in death, seemed peaceful. Her eyes stared upward, as if seeing beyond this plane of existence. "But it was more important that she die as a human."

"There's..." Scott faltered. "There's so much I don't understand." He reached down and, with a gentle touch, slid her eyes closed.

"I just know I love her."

PROLOGUE

AT THAT exact moment, two hundred forty thousand miles away, an SUV with a pink mustache on its bumper slowed as it approached a familiar address on Graymalkin Lane. It signaled and turned onto a well-kept driveway, passing through the outer gates of the Xavier Institute of Higher Learning.

Inside the car, Kitty Pryde frowned at her phone. Her last four texts had gone unanswered, so she sent another.

ORORO? GUYS? I HAVE ARRIVED! ANYONE HOME?

She paused, then added:

EVERYBODY ALIVE?

The grounds seemed deserted. As they approached the front door, Kitty had to stop herself from phasing through the car door before the driver came to a stop. She wrenched open her side, ran up the steps, and pressed the bell three times.

No answer.

The driver approached, rolling her suitcase behind him. "You want me to wait?" he asked.

She frowned, considered for a moment. A fall breeze blew up, ruffling her curly hair. It felt cool, refreshing. "No thanks." She shrugged. "I always liked being early for school."

"Ah! You are a nerd." The driver smiled at her. "It's good."

She laughed. Arranged her bags around her and sat down on the front steps, soaking in the feel of the grounds. The place where she hoped to spend the rest of her teenage years. Where she would learn to use her mutant powers, for the good of humanity.

She waved as the SUV drove away. Then she kicked her feet up in the air, barely able to contain her excitement.

"Yeah," she said, a wide smile crossing her face. "It's good."

ACKNOWLEDGMENTS

THIS IS the third Marvel novel I've written and, in many ways, the most daunting. Updating this classic for the 21st century presented some real challenges. Steve Saffel's sure editorial hand guided me through all the crucial points; Cat Camacho and Hayley Shepherd provided vital last-minute notes and corrections. Thanks also to the incredible people at Marvel for their help and support—particularly Caitlin O'Connell and, of course, Jeff Youngquist.

Thanks, as well, to everyone who listened as I babbled on about female power and the #metoo era. I want to note especially novelist Corinne Duyvis, who helped immensely through a wholly unexpected conversation at the Emerald City Comic Con. The attitudes and story interpretations in this book, of course, are mine alone, and not the fault of anyone else.

Tom Peyer, Hart Seely, and the staff of AHOY Comics provided constant distractions. Without you guys, I might have finished this book *months* earlier.

And a special shout-out—as always—to the smartest person I know, prolific author (and lovely wife) Liz Sonneborn. Without whom, etc.